The

SAVAGES IN
LOVE AND WAR

FORGE BOOKS BY FRED MUSTARD STEWART

The Naked Savages
The Savages in Love and War
The Young Savages

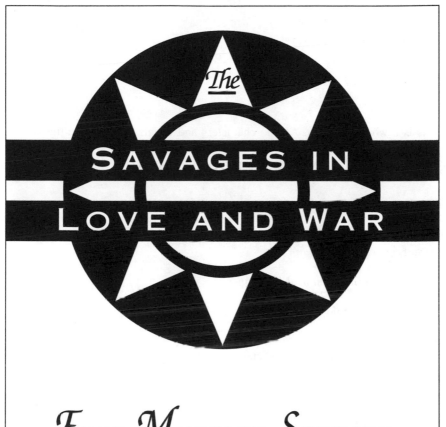

FRED MUSTARD STEWART

A TOM DOHERTY ASSOCIATES BOOK / NEW YORK

THE SAVAGES IN LOVE AND WAR

Copyright © 2001 by Fred Mustard Stewart

This book is printed on acid-free paper.

Edited by Claire Eddy

A Forge Book
Published by Tom Doherty Associates, LLC
175 Fifth Avenue
New York, NY 10010

www.tor.com

Forge® is a registered trademark of Tom Doherty Associates, LLC.

Library of Congress Cataloging-in-Publication Data

Stewart, Fred Mustard
    The Savages in love and war / Fred Mustard Stewart.—1st ed.
        p. cm.
    "A Tom Doherty Associates book."
    ISBN 0-312-87485-5 (alk. paper)
    1. Savage family (Fictitious characters)—Fiction. I. Title.

    PS3569.T464 S28 2001
    813'.54 —dc21

                                                        2001033526

First Edition: September 2001

Printed in the United States of America

0 9 8 7 6 5 4 3 2 1

As always, to my beloved wife, Joan

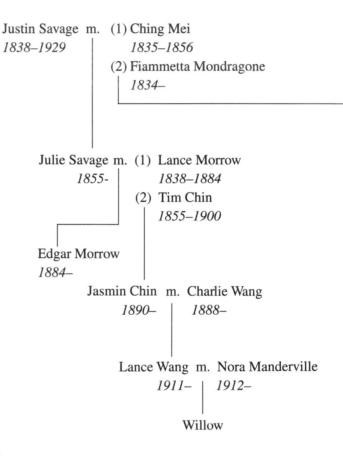

Justin Savage m.   (1) Ching Mei
1838–1929   *1835–1856*
                (2) Fiammetta Mondragone
                    1834–

Julie Savage m. (1) Lance Morrow
    1855-   *1838–1884*
            (2) Tim Chin
                1855–1900

Edgar Morrow
1884–

Jasmin Chin m. Charlie Wang
    1890–   *1888–*

Lance Wang m. Nora Manderville
    1911–   *1912–*

Willow

✺ *The Savage Family* ✺

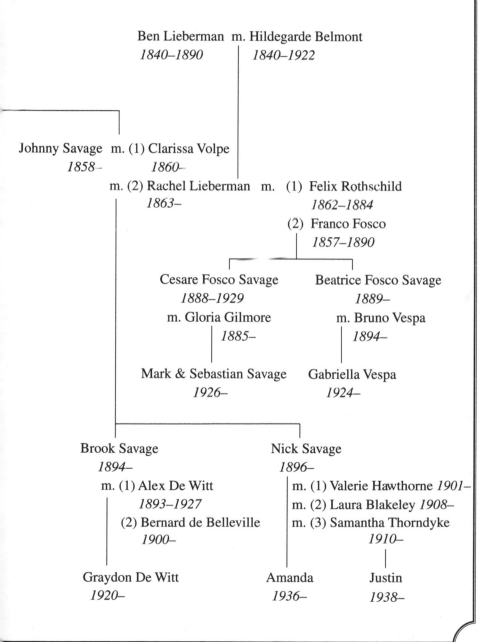

Ben Lieberman m. Hildegarde Belmont
1840–1890   *1840–1922*

Johnny Savage m. (1) Clarissa Volpe
1858–   *1860–*
        m. (2) Rachel Lieberman m. (1) Felix Rothschild
                1863–   *1862–1884*
                              (2) Franco Fosco
                                   1857–1890

Cesare Fosco Savage   Beatrice Fosco Savage
1888–1929   *1889–*
m. Gloria Gilmore   m. Bruno Vespa
    1885–   *1894–*

Mark & Sebastian Savage   Gabriella Vespa
1926–   *1924–*

Brook Savage   Nick Savage
1894–   *1896–*
    m. (1) Alex De Witt   m. (1) Valerie Hawthorne *1901–*
        1893–1927   m. (2) Laura Blakeley *1908–*
    (2) Bernard de Belleville   m. (3) Samantha Thorndyke
        1900–   *1910–*

Graydon De Witt   Amanda   Justin
1920–   *1936–*   *1938–*

Acknowledgments

Again, my thanks to my agent Peter Lampack and my editor Claire Eddy for their help and excellent suggestions.

PART ONE

LOVE IN A DEPRESSION: 1932

1 "NICK, NOW THAT YOU'RE HEAD of your family's bank, I'd like you to be my champion on Wall Street," Franklin Delano Roosevelt said. "As you well know, the economy is a disaster, and there's not much money around. I'll need money to make it to the White House, and there aren't many Wall Streeters who are going to be as generous to my campaign as your mother and father have been. But I have a hunch a young man like you, with your connections in the business world, might dig some gold out of those Republican canyons downtown."

"Franklin, eat your broccoli," said his wife in her high-pitched, patrician voice.

The governor of New York made a face.

"Eleanor, you know I detest broccoli. I always have and, God willing, I always will."

"Nevertheless, it's good for you."

The Roosevelts were entertaining Nick Savage at dinner at their Manhattan townhouse on East Sixty-fifth Street, between Fifth Avenue and Madison. It was a steamy July evening in 1932. Thirty-five-year-old Nick smiled at his host.

"Governor," he said, "I'm eating *my* broccoli."

"Traitor," the governor growled. "At any rate, Nick, can I count on you?"

"Absolutely, sir. You know my family's behind you one hundred percent. We've got to get Hoover out of the White House and you in so we can get this country rolling again."

"Bravo, and well said. I may just use that in one of my speeches. Now Nick, you're going to be on a tight budget. My people are looking for an office downtown, and you won't have the money to hire much of a staff. I'd say ten people at the very top. And as far as your salary is concerned . . ."

"I'm doing this on the house," Nick interrupted. Roosevelt's face burst into the grin for which he was famous.

"I like that line even better." He chuckled. "I was hoping you'd say it. Eleanor, isn't this young man a treasure?"

Eleanor Roosevelt, who was wearing a very unstylish white dress, smiled at their guest.

"Of course he is. And how is your dear father, Nick?"

"Well, he's not in the best of health. He really never has recovered from that car accident a few years ago."

"He's such a wonderful man. And of course, we all adore your mother."

"Happily, she's in great shape. She'll be seventy-two next week, which is hard to believe. She still has the energy of someone half her age."

"A remarkable lady," Franklin said, cutting into his steak. "Eleanor, this steak is as tough as leather. Can't that damned fool cook you hired get a decent piece of beef?"

"This was on sale, Franklin. And eat your broccoli."

The governor of New York made another face.

"Nick," Eleanor went on, "since you're being so kind and generous, I'm going to ask another favor of you."

"Please," Nick said, chewing his steak with some difficulty.

"I have a cousin, a very sweet girl who's twenty-three. Her name is Laura Blakely. I believe you might know her. She used to live in Oyster Bay out on the Island."

"Oh yes, of course," Nick said. "She was married to that great golfer and polo player, Morris Blakely."

"Exactly. Unhappily, Morris lost almost all his money in the crash, as so many people did. And then, four months ago, he committed suicide."

"Good lord, I'm sorry to hear that."

"He became so terribly depressed that he shot himself. It was a terrible tragedy, he was such a nice young man. And Laura was absolutely devoted to him—it was one of the most wonderful romances I've ever known. But now, she's devastated by it. She runs a flower shop near here on Madison Avenue called the Garden of Delights."

"Yes, I know it. My mother uses it."

"Laura has told me she would like to volunteer for Franklin's campaign—at night, you know. It would give her something to do to take her mind off, well, her tragedy. I'd take it as a great favor if you'd talk to her about helping you."

"I'd be delighted to."

Eleanor Roosevelt's wonderful, homely face looked sad.

"I have a terrible feeling she's started drinking," she said. "You know, my dear father had that problem, and it ultimately killed him, so I know the symptoms."

"I know the symptoms all too well myself," Nick said. He was in his third year of being drink-free.

"Yes, I know. That's why I thought you might be able to help her."

"I'll do everything I can, Mrs. Roosevelt."

She smiled at him.

"Thank you, Nick. I had a feeling I could depend on you. Everyone speaks so highly of you, and it's very obvious to me why they do."

"You're very kind, Mrs. Roosevelt."

"Now Franklin, about that broccoli."

Romance was very popular at the bottom of the Great Depression because few people could afford anything else. Nick Savage was hungrily looking for romance.

Not that Nick had any trouble finding available women: tall, trim, with square-jawed Arrow Collar Man good looks, thick curly brown hair and blue eyes, Nick was a target of many young New York women, single, divorced, or married. But he had been so burned by his divorce from his first wife, Valerie, who had blown practically all their money on Wall Street speculation before the big crash of 1929, that he was playing it safe.

The next morning, rather than taking the subway downtown to his office on Pine Street, he took a taxi from his Sutton Place house over to Madison Avenue and Seventy-third Street, getting off and going into the attractive flower shop called Garden of Delights. Inside, a thin woman in a blue dress with blond hair was putting a bow on a box of flowers. She smiled at Nick as he came over to the counter behind which she was standing.

"Good morning," she said. "May I help you?"

"Good morning. Are you Laura Blakely?"

"Yes."

"My name's Nick Savage. We knew each other out on Long Island, I believe."

She smiled, very prettily, he thought. And her blue-green eyes were spectacular.

"Of course. I thought you looked familiar. How are you?"

"I'm fine. I had dinner last night with the Roosevelts, and Mrs. Roosevelt told me you were interested in doing some volunteer work for her husband's presidential campaign. Is that true?"

"Yes, I'd love to be a help. I make good coffee, and I'm a pretty good typist."

"Well, I'm going to be running a campaign to raise money for the governor here in town, and I'd be delighted if you came to work evenings. We should have an office in a couple of days. By the way, I heard about your husband. I'm terribly sorry."

A cloud seemed to float over her face.

"Yes, so am I," she said, simply.

"Would you by any chance be free for dinner tonight?"

"Actually, I am."

"I'll pick you up at seven. We can talk about setting up the office, and . . ." He smiled. ". . . I'd like to get to know you better. Where do you live?"

"I have a card."

She opened her purse and pulled out a card, which she handed him. He glanced at it, then smiled at her.

"See you at seven," he said, and he walked out of the shop.

As president of the Savage Bank and Trust Company of 14 Pine Street with eleven branches throughout the city, Nick earned a salary of thirty thousand dollars a year, which, at a time when 40 percent of Americans made less than one thousand dollars a year, put him in the upper tax brackets, if not making him a Rockefeller. He remembered his extravagant lifestyle in the twenties, in those champagne days before the crash, when everybody was flying high—or so it seemed—in a *Great Gatsby* world of bathtub gin, yacht parties, Charlestons, and living it up. Now, with a seemingly moribund Herbert Hoover in the White House and unemployment in double digits, with former stock brokers selling five cent apples on Wall Street and people just barely scraping by, the heady twenties seemed a sad dream, a burst champagne bubble, as America reeled into the dark thirties. So now Nick watched his money. He kept a car in a garage, but he rarely used it in town, taking subways and, infrequently, taxis.

That night, he would have walked uptown if a fierce thunderstorm hadn't broken on the city, relieving the four-day heat wave. So he caught a taxi at Sutton Place and drove uptown to East Seventy-fifth Street where Laura had a second-floor walk-up apartment in a five-story tenement near the East River. He had phoned Laura before leaving, and she was waiting for him at the curb, wearing a raincoat and holding an umbrella. After she got in the backseat, Nick said, "I made a reservation at Tosca, which is my favorite Italian restaurant. Have you ever been there?"

"No. I don't eat out much. Is it a speakeasy?"

"No. Why?"

He gave the driver an address in the East Eighties, and he made a U-turn at the river and started uptown.

"Why did you ask?" Nick prompted her.

"Oh, I just wondered if one could get a drink there."

"Ah. If Mario knows you—he's the owner—he'll bring you some wine. Actually, the place used to be a speak until two years ago, when the owner was found shot to death. Probably hadn't paid off his bootlegger—the murder was never solved. Mario bought it and made it a legitimate restaurant. I don't drink, so it doesn't matter to me."

"Why don't you drink?" she asked.

"I'm a drunk," he said, simply.

"How long have you not had a drink?"

"Over three years now."

"Do you ever miss it?"

"I try not to think about it."

"Do you think Prohibition has worked?"

"God, no. It's turned the nation into a bunch of drunks. Governor

Roosevelt's for repeal, so if he's elected it will be the end of all this bootlegging nonsense. You can't make people change their personal habits by passing laws."

"I suppose you're right."

The taxi pulled up in front of a brownstone with a bright red canopy marked Tosca Ristorante. Nick got out and paid the driver, tipping him fifty cents, then held the restaurant door for Laura. Inside, Mario, a smiling man whose belly attested to his love of pasta, led the couple through the sparsely inhabited restaurant to a corner table. The large former speakeasy was decorated unoriginally with candlewax-dripping Chianti bottles and, on the walls, large posters of various divas portraying the ill-fated Floria Tosca.

After Mario presented the menus, Nick said, sotto voce, "Mario, my friend would like a glass of wine. Could that be arranged?"

"But of course, Signor Savage." He turned to Laura. "Red or white?"

"White, I believe."

"*Subito*. I have a delicious pinot grigio. This crazy Prohibition! How can anyone live without wine, eh?"

As he waddled off, Laura pulled a pack of Lucky Strikes from her purse.

"Do you mind if I smoke?" she asked.

"Of course not. I'm afraid I don't have a lighter. I don't smoke."

"Good heavens, Mr. Savage, you neither drink nor smoke? What a paragon of virtue you are."

"I gave up smoking when I gave up drinking. They seemed to go together. And please: I'm Nick."

"And I'm Laura."

She lit her own cigarette with a small lighter.

"I can remember a huge party you gave back in twenty-eight, I believe. At your beautiful place on the North Shore. Paul Whiteman's band was playing, and you had a water ballet—oh, it was so gorgeous! And then . . ." She smiled mischievously. "You ran out of the pool house at midnight stark naked and jumped in the pool."

"Oh yes. Of course I was so plastered I didn't remember a thing, but it seems everyone else did. That's one reason I gave up drinking."

She exhaled slowly.

"I thought you were very attractive."

She smiled at him. He looked a bit embarrassed. He opened the menu.

"Well," he said, "I can highly recommend the saltimbocca here."

"We had so much fun back then," Laura said, rather wistfully. "What a blessing we couldn't see what lay ahead."

The skinny young man with thinning sandy hair who was wearing a cheap dark gray suit placed the wooden ladder against the side wall of the white clapboard, phony-colonial house in Syosset, Long Island, and started climbing to the second floor. It was a dark night; the man had left his battered 1925 Model T Ford running on the street near the house. When he reached the window of the second floor, he slowly opened it, then climbed inside. The man knew the house rather well: He had done work on it as an electrician, and he had dated one of the house's maids. A victim of the stock market crash and the Depression, he hated the rich and was desperate for money. The house belonged to Gloria Savage, the widow of Cesare Savage, the ex-bootlegger who had been gunned down by Dutch Schultz back in 'twenty-nine. The intruder assumed that Gloria was rich, even though she actually was barely getting by.

He climbed into the dark bedroom where the identical twins, Mark and Sebastian, were sound asleep in beds on opposite sides of the room. He went to the twin on the right and placed a chloroform-soaked handkerchief over his face. Six-year-old Sebastian Savage quickly passed into oblivion. The intruder picked the child up, put him over his shoulder, and carried him to the window. He climbed out onto the ladder and carried him down to the ground. Leaving the ladder against the house, he carried the child across the lawn of the house to the street, where he put the unconscious boy in the front seat of his Ford, then climbed in the driver's seat, shifted gears, and drove off into the night.

"Is it true your grandfather was a Chinese pirate?" Laura asked as she sipped her third glass of wine at Tosca. "I've always heard that story, which sounds so wonderfully romantic."

"Yes, it's true," Nick said, cutting his veal chop. "He was the illegitimate son of my great-grandfather, who owned a line of clipper ships, and my grandfather wanted to go to sea. But his half-brother, Sylvaner, who was a villain of the worst sort and was jealous of my grandfather, plotted to have him murdered at sea."

"Why?"

"Sylvaner was afraid my great-grandfather would leave everything to my grandfather, because he loved him. At any rate, my grandfather's ship was captured by pirates, and he became the lover of the chief pirate, a Chinese woman named Chang-mei."

"It's wildly romantic!"

"Isn't it? So, my grandfather, after many adventures, became rich and returned to New York to avenge himself against Sylvaner. It's rather like *The Count of Monte Cristo*. And my grandfather succeeded. I'm afraid my family has become a bit stodgy since those romantic days."

Laura sighed.

"The whole world's become a bit stodgy," she said. "Could I have another glass of wine?"

Nick looked at her.

"Do you think you should? That's your fourth."

"I'm not driving anywhere."

Nick shrugged slightly and signaled Mario.

The next morning, Nick was taking a shower in his Sutton Place house when he heard the bedroom phone ring.

"Damn," he muttered, turning off the shower. Wrapping a white towel around his waist, he hurried out of the tiled bathroom into his bedroom to pick up the phone.

"Hello?"

"Nick, something terrible's happened!" It was Rachel Savage, his mother. "Your sister-in-law, Gloria, just called me. Little Sebastian has been kidnapped."

"Oh my God." Stunned, Nick sat on the side of his unmade bed. "When?"

"Early this morning. The kidnapper put a ladder against Gloria's house and climbed into the twins' bedroom—just like the Lindbergh baby kidnapping last spring."

"A copycat crime. There's been a wave of them all over the country. Has she received a ransom note?"

"Not yet."

"But it doesn't make any sense! Gloria doesn't have any money—I mean, big money."

"Nevertheless, Sebastian's gone and she's hysterical. Will you go out to Syosset and be with her? I'm sure she needs help."

"Yes, of course. As soon as I get dressed, I'll get my car. How's Father?"

"He isn't any stronger. And of course this has got him upset. Call me when you get to Syosset."

"Sure. I love you."

Sending her a kiss, he hung up and hurried to the bathroom to dry off.

An hour later as he drove out to Long Island in his Ford Roadster, he thought of his late half-brother, Cesare, the father of the twins. Cesare the glamorous, Cesare the dashing, Cesare the man who at one time Nick admired more than any other person. And of course, Cesare the user.

Cesare, who was as clever as he was ruthless, had seen how to work on Nick's weaknesses. Cesare had actually gotten Nick to embezzle funds from the bank; if it hadn't been for his mother, Nick might have gone to jail. The money was all repaid to the bank, but Cesare had become a bootlegger, made a fortune, and then, in the crash, lost everything, including his life: he had been shot to death by the notorious gangster Dutch Schultz. Now, years later, Cesare's meteoric rise to prominence had taken on the aspects of some sort of cockeyed legend. Nick would never forgive him. But, secretly, he still remembered how dazzling he was.

And now, Cesare's son had become the victim of a crime. Back before the turn of the century, Cesare's father, Franco, had also been gunned down in Central Park. Franco, too, it had been whispered, was a murderer, though it had never been proven. It was as if the Savage family, in so many ways respectable citizens, were haunted by a darker side, a side of crime, intrigue, and violence.

As he neared Syosset, Nick thought of Gloria Gilmore Savage, Cesare's widow, who had, in her way, had a career almost as fascinating as Cesare's. This gorgeous blond, daughter of an upstate New York judge, had been stage-struck and gone to Broadway to become a proverbial star. It hadn't been as easy as she thought: To make ends meet, she had done movie work with D. W. Griffith—movies then being considered trashy by stage actors. Meeting Johnny Savage, Nick's father, at Griffith's studio on Fourteenth Street in Manhattan, she had in short order become Johnny's mistress, inveigling him into helping her career by investing in the movies.

To a certain extent, it had worked: Gloria was liked by the camera, and her career blossomed sufficiently for her to move to Hollywood and become a second-tier silent star. But, after a falling out with Johnny, her career went into a decline, partially due to her involvement with a peculiarly rancid Hollywood scandal as juicy as the Fatty Arbuckle debacle. Returning to New York, Gloria bumped around the city until she bumped into the bed of Cesare, Johnny's stepson and bitter enemy. To the horror of Cesare's mother, Rachel, and the disgust of his stepfather Johnny, Cesare married Gloria, thus bringing the entire Savage clan into the spotlight of public ridicule, since everyone knew Gloria had at one time been her father-in-law's mistress. Add to this Cesare's notoriety as a bootlegger and his violent murder at the hands of Dutch Schultz, and the Savage family was indeed naked to the world.

And now, this, Nick thought as he pulled his Ford into Gloria's driveway. The kidnapping of poor little Sebastian Savage, a beautiful, dark-haired six-year-old innocent. Would this family's troubles never end?

Three police cars were parked beside the house, and several plainclothes cops were conferring as Nick pulled his car up beside them. Getting out, he walked over to introduce himself.

"Good morning," he said to one of them, a man in a brown suit and matching hat who was puffing a cigarette. "I'm Nick Savage, Mrs. Savage's brother-in-law."

"Oh yes," the detective said. "I'm Mark Brohan of the Syosset police. I'm in charge of the case."

They shook hands, Brohan introducing the other, younger detective.

"Any news?" Nick asked.

"Nothing. We've gone over the place with a fine-tooth comb. We found some footprints on the lawn, but no fingerprints anywhere. We have the ladder, which may be useful."

"Any ransom note yet?"

"Not yet. But it's still early. These kidnappers get nervous when it comes time to write the ransom notes because that's usually how they get caught."

"How's Mrs. Savage taking it?"

"As well as can be expected. She's in the kitchen."

"May I go talk to her?"

"Of course."

Nick walked around to the back door of the house which, he knew, had been financed by his mother, since after Cesare's murder, his widow had been left financially destitute. Considering the fact that at one point Rachel had come as close to hating Gloria as she had any person, Nick thought his mother had behaved with considerable magnanimity. But then, Rachel Savage was nothing if not a lady, one of the true grandes dames of New York society.

Going into the kitchen, he saw Gloria sitting at a zinc-topped table drinking coffee and smoking a cigarette. Gloria was in her mid-forties and still an extremely attractive woman; but this morning she looked a mess. Her blond hair needed brushing, she had on no makeup, her eyes were red from crying and she had on a bathrobe that was a bit bedraggled.

"Nick," she exclaimed, immediately going into a cigarette coughing fit. "Thank God you came."

"I came as soon as I heard."

"I look a wreck, but what the hell. Give your old sister-in-law a kiss. This isn't one of my better mornings."

Nick came over to her and kissed her cheek.

"Do you want some coffee?" she asked.

"Sure."

"It's on the stove. Help yourself."

Nick took a cup from a cabinet, filled it from a pot on the stove, then sat down opposite her.

"How's Mark?" he asked.

"Scared. You know how close the twins are. He asked me if I thought Sebastian would be murdered. I lied and told him Sebastian would be home soon, but he didn't believe me. God, Nick, I know I'm not the world's best mother by a long shot, but if something happened to that kid, I'm not sure I could take it—and you know I'm one tough broad. I'm really crazy about the little rascal. I'm crazy about both of them." She sucked on the cigarette, and a tear ran down her cheek. "He looks so much like his father. He's Cesare without all the bad crime stuff. Oh God, Nick, I'm scared silly."

Nick reached across the table and squeezed her hand.

"Everything's going to be fine," he lied.

He was almost as scared as Gloria.

2   "CAN YOU IMAGINE, four years ago we fell in love in this very same place?" Nora Wang said as she danced around the ballroom of the Repulse Bay Hotel in Hong Kong with her dashing husband, Lance. "And now we're practically an old married couple with a darling baby, and we're both in danger of becoming boring respectable citizens?"

"You're never boring, and I'm not all that respectable," Lance said. He was wearing a white dinner jacket, and Nora was in a stunning blue dress she had bought on a shopping trip to Paris three months before. Lance was president of the three highly successful Chin department stores in Hong Kong, Shanghai, and Tokyo; in this capacity, he and Nora made an annual trip to Europe to check out the latest fashions.

"You're extremely respectable," Nora said. "And four years ago when we came here, you got beaten up by those horrid English bullies." In 1928, when Chinese were not allowed in many places in Hong Kong, the handsome, Eton-educated Lance Wang had created a sensation when Nora, the beautiful daughter of the then-governor of the British colony, had invited him to dinner at the Repulse Bay. Later that night, Lance had been attacked by a number of young Englishmen who had been at the hotel. "Now when you come in here," Nora went on, "nobody bats an eye— that is, except all the women who would love for you to make love to them. Of course, I know you never would. Would you?"

Lance, who was captain of one of the local polo teams and an excellent tennis player, grinned.

"You know you won't believe me if I say no. So I'll say yes and make you suffer."

"You horrid man. Well, you'll just remember there are lots of men who'd like to have a fling with me, so don't get any ideas. Your grandmother looks so beautiful tonight, but then she always does. I just hope I'll look as good as she when I'm her age. She's really quite extraordinary."

Nora was referring to an elegant elderly woman seated at a table at one side of the ballroom sipping champagne. Julie Chin was seventy-seven, with snow-white hair. She was wearing a white lace evening gown and a suite of diamonds from her famous jewelry collection: Julie, the owner of the Chin department stores, was one of the richest persons in Hong Kong, as well as one of the greatest benefactresses of local charities. The half-Chinese daughter of Justin Savage, she had grown up in New York; but after the Civil War, she had fled that city and its blistering anti-Asian prejudices, ending up, after many adventures, in Hong Kong the wife of a young Chinese revolutionary who was later murdered by an agent of the Dowager Empress of China. That had happened a long time before. But Julie's mind was still as agile as ever, old age not having dimmed her wits.

And she knew there was trouble at the Tokyo branch of the department store.

It had been Julie's son by her first marriage to a San Francisco wheeler-dealer who had talked her into building the Tokyo store on the Ginza. Edgar Morrow had fallen madly in love with a young Japanese girl he met in Hong Kong, had followed her to Japan and, rather against his mother's wishes, married Suzuki Igitaki, whose brother was a lieutenant in the Japanese Army. Edgar convinced a reluctant Julie to build the Tokyo store, which was designed by Frank Lloyd Wright and which opened its doors in 1922. Within a year, a devastating earthquake wiped out huge sections of Tokyo; although the store withstood the quake, business was sorely crippled by the simple fact that few residents of Tokyo had much money to spend. It took several years for the store to recover, but by that time tensions with the Chinese had mounted because of Japan's invasion of Manchuria on the northern border of China.

The motives of the Japanese seemed simple to those who supported the invasion: Japan was smaller than California with a huge population, and it needed territory to settle and land to exploit. However, to the rest of the world, and in particular to China, the invasion seemed like an act of aggression, neither pure nor simple. And many high-ranking Japanese were either against the invasion or at best lukewarm about it.

To further complicate matters, many young Japanese firebrands, including Edgar's brother-in-law, felt that the Army was being betrayed by corrupt members of the government and the big businessmen who controlled the powerful *zaibatsu* (family businesses like Mitsui and Mitsubishi). These hotheads joined secret societies and, in a time-honored Japanese tradition that made heroes of assassins, pledged to purge corruption and "save the nation" by assassination. The previous May, a number of members of the secret Cherry Society invaded the home of the seventy-five-year-old prime minister, who was against the invasion of Manchuria, and riddled his body with bullets. The assassins, wildly acclaimed by the population, got off with light sentences.

Julie Chin knew that anti-Chinese feelings were running high in Tokyo; a week before, her son Edgar had received a death threat unless he closed the Tokyo store down and left the country.

Julie, who had witnessed the murder of her husband so many years before, had had enough of violence in her lifetime. She ordered Edgar to close the Tokyo store and try to find a buyer for it.

But to her consternation, Edgar had refused.

The eighteen-year-old Chinese girl cried in pain as the doctor delivered her child, holding it up and spanking its bottom until it started to cry.

"Is it a boy?" the mother whispered.

"No, it's a lovely girl," the doctor answered, handing the infant to a nurse. They were in the operating room of the sixty-year-old hospital in Nanking, China.

"Aieee," the young mother wailed, "my husband wanted a son. The gods are cruel."

Standing in a corner watching the operation was a beautiful woman in a yellow silk cheongsam, or long dress with a slit skirt and a mandarin collar. The woman, Jasmin Wang, was the daughter of Julie Chin and the mother of Lance Wang. Many years before when Jasmin was a teenage girl, she had been kidnapped from her Shanghai hotel by a young, self-styled warlord named Charlie Wang who wanted ransom money from Jasmin's rich mother to buy rifles for his ragtag army. The surprising switch was that Jasmin and Charlie fell madly in love with each other and ultimately married, producing their fine son, Lance.

Now, Jasmin left the dirty hospital and got in her Ford to drive through the narrow streets of Nanking to their suburban home in the Purple Mountains. When the Nationalist Government of China, headed by Generalissimo Chiang Kai-shek, had moved from Shanghai inland to the ancient city of Nanking, Chiang had asked Charlie Wang, whose abilities as a military commander had been successfully demonstrated during his days as a warlord, to move with him in the capacity as minister of war. Charlie had accepted, and Jasmin, unlike most of the other government wives who considered Nanking as dreary a provincial town as Shanghai was glitteringly cosmopolitan, had insisted on coming with him. In this, she was joined by Madame Chiang, the beautiful Mayling Soong, Mayling and Jasmin being almost the only women in the dirty town beside the locals.

Nanking was at the time a sad mixture of ancient, crumbling glory and new, raw ugliness. Situated on the southern side of the Yangtze River some hundred miles inland from Shanghai, it had the dubious distinction of having one of the worst climates in China, with raw, icy winters and steaming summers. The Ming tombs and the famous avenues of animal statuary, the walls surrounding lotus-choked pools, a few old houses hidden away, and the purple mountains that guarded the valley were the only compensations for filthy, crowded streets, almost impassable by automobiles, and low-lying huts. The Nationalist Government had, to its credit, begun to tear down the worst slums and tried to beautify the city; but Jasmin knew there was much work to be done.

But watching the operation in the old hospital had given forty-two-year-old Jasmin an idea that was to change her life. Heretofore known in Shanghai society as a beautiful, sophisticated heiress to a huge fortune, now Jasmin mentally rolled up her sleeves and set to work.

"Darling," she said to her husband when she came into the living room of their villa outside the thick walls of the city, "I visited the hospital today and it's disgusting. No wonder there's so much death and disease in this wretched town; but we're going to fix all that."

Her husband, tall, thin Charlie Wang with his hawklike face, looked up from the official papers he was studying.

"Oh?" he said. "And how are we going to fix it?"

"We're going to build a new hospital, and it's going to be the best hospital in all of China."

Charlie considered this a moment as Jasmin came over to kiss him. Then he nodded.

"You know," he said, "it's not a bad idea."

The basis of the simmering conflict in Asia at the time could properly be assigned to the late-colonial assumption on the part of white Europeans and Americans that they were superior, racially and culturally, to the so-called "colored" nations of the world, most of whom had been forced into colonial territories by the western, or white, powers. This despite the fact that the Chinese civilization was infinitely older, and culturally richer, than even the Greek or Roman civilizations. Despite the fact that so much of this "racialism" was based on skin color, paradoxically, white skin had been a mark of feminine beauty in Japan since earliest times, an ancient proverb saying "White skin makes up for seven defects." Japanese writers, early in the Meiji period (the last half of the nineteenth century), had expressed their admiration for the white skin of westerners, and in the 1920s Japan's favorite movie stars were Clara Bow, Gloria Swanson, and Greta Garbo. Although Japan was officially proclaiming itself a champion against the white colonial nations, Japanese did not consider themselves to be "yellow." The women preferred to call the color of their skins *komugi-iro* (wheat color) and the word for lighter shades of their own skin was *shiroi* (white). Traditionally, white was always the color of virtue. The hero in the Kabuki theater always wore white, like the "good" cowboy in American movies.

Which left forty-eight-year-old Edgar Morrow in an odd position.

As a partial Chinese, due to his mother, Julie Chin, he was the target of anti-Chinese prejudice in Tokyo. But as the son of an American and the grandson of Justin Savage, he was also the target of anti-white discrimination—even though the Japanese, in cultural ways, considered white a virtuous color. Racial discrimination seldom makes any sense.

Although Edgar had fallen madly in love with his Japanese wife, Suzuki, when he moved to Japan he retained some of the American habits of his childhood, including an American bed. And one night, a week after his death threat, he was asleep in his western-style bed in his Tokyo home when he was awakened by a loud noise. Bolting upright in his bed, he turned on the light to find that Suzuki was not next to him.

He turned on the bed light just as the shoji to his bedroom slid open, revealing his young brother-in-law, Lieutenant Sokichi Igitaki. Igitaki, dressed in his army uniform, was holding a pistol. Behind him, looking frightened, was Edgar's beautiful wife, Suzuki.

"Edgar," Igitaki said, coming into the room. "Why have you not closed the store?"

"Because I won't be intimidated by a bunch of crazy fanatics," Edgar said.

"Like me? I'm a crazy fanatic. I hate the Chinese, and I hate the whites, and you're both. I never wanted you to marry my sister."

"But I did, and I love her."

"Your mother has told you to close the store. Why haven't you done it?"

"As I said, I won't cave in to fanatics. And why are you aiming that gun at me? Surely you're not going to believe I'd think you'd kill me?"

"I won't kill you if you do what your mother sensibly ordered you to do: Close the store and sell it to a Japanese faction. You are white and Chinese, and you are our enemy. The God-Emperor, Hirohito, has proclaimed a crusade to make Japan the dominant power in Asia and to destroy forever the evil colonial powers of the western white man. You are my brother-in-law, but you are my enemy. You must go. Will you agree?"

Edgar stared at the gun. His brother-in-law, he knew, was a fanatic, a wiry little man who was, oddly, given the circumstances, an adept at the Chinese martial arts. But Edgar couldn't believe he was such a fanatic as to pull the trigger on a member of his family.

"Sokichi," he said, "put the gun down. I'm not going to be bullied."

"Yes," Suzuki said, touching her brother's arm, "you mustn't threaten my husband. After all, we're family."

"No bastard white-Chinese is a member of *my* family," Sokichi said. "Will you close the store?"

Edgar stiffened, unsure of how serious the threat was, but beginning to think it wasn't a bluff.

"No," he said.

Sokichi Igitaki fired. Once. Twice. Three times.

Edgar Morrow collapsed to the side of his bed, blood gushing from the bullet holes in his stomach, his chest, and his brain.

3   SIX-YEAR-OLD SEBASTIAN SAVAGE, tied to a dirty chair in one corner of a wooden garage filled with gasoline cans, bits of motors, a lawn mower, old paint cans, piles of junk, and a small truck that looked too old and beat up to run, was shivering with fear. He had no idea where he was or what had happened to him. All he knew was that he was wearing his pajamas and that it was getting light: Dawn was creeping through the cracks in the walls and the one filthy window above his head. He ached for his mother, Gloria, and his twin, Mark.

But, as terrified as he was, he refused to cry. Sebastian, who knew of his father's extraordinary career only in bits and pieces, was certain that this legendary man he barely remembered, this Cesare who had been gunned down by a legendary gangster, must have had guts. His father would never have cried, and neither would he.

But he was awfully close to tears.

Time dragged by: He had no idea how long before he heard a door slam in the distance. Then, after a few moments, the sagging doors of the garage were opened and a thin young man with sandy hair, wearing a cheap Halloween clown mask, came inside. He stopped a moment, looking at Sebastian. He was wearing dirty corduroy trousers and a zippered leather jacket, and he was carrying a bowl.

"Good morning," he said in a soft voice. "I've brought you some cornflakes for breakfast."

"Who are you?" Sebastian said. "Where am I?"

"You can call me Bobo the Clown. That's all you'll ever know about me. If I showed you my face, I'd have to kill you, and I don't want to kill you. Dead, you're worth nothing to me."

He carried the bowl to Sebastian.

"I'll feed you," he said, taking a spoon from the bowl, filling it with the cereal and then extending it to Sebastian's mouth.

"Open up," he said.

"I don't want your cereal. I hate your cereal, and I hate you, whoever you are. Have you kidnapped me?"

"That's right."

"My mother isn't rich."

"But your grandmother is. She's very rich, like your grandfather. They'll pay for you, and I want money. This damned Depression's killing me. Now please: Open your mouth and eat."

Sebastian looked at the man's pale blue eyes through the slits in the mask.

Slowly, he opened his mouth and swallowed the spoonful of corn-flakes.

In one way, Laura Blakeley was lucky. Unlike the twelve million Americans who were unemployed that summer of 1932, Laura had a job. It only paid thirty dollars a week, but it was a job. As she looked in the mirror in her two-room apartment, adjusting the smart little hat she had paid four dollars for the week before on her natural blond hair, she told herself she had reason to be cheerful. She had her health, her figure, and her looks. Life could be worse.

She straightened the peplum of her black-and-white polka dot suit, checked the seams of her stockings in the full-length mirror, checked her lipstick, then said good-bye to her cat, Cellophane, went to the front door of her second-floor walk-up, let herself out, locked the door, and hurried down the stairs to the street where she began the fifteen-minute walk to the Madison Avenue flower shop she ran.

It was a beautiful, sunshine-filled day after the rain the night before. As she walked west and neared Park Avenue, the tenements of her neighborhood transformed slowly into the beautiful Belle Epoque and Georgian townhouses of the rich, reminding her yet again that not everyone was broke as she was. There were still the rich—not as many as before the crash, true: Laura had read that three years before, there had been over five hundred Americans who paid taxes on incomes of a million dollars or more, but in this year there were only twenty. The long, black limousines on Park Avenue with their uniformed chauffeurs were another reminder of the lifestyle she had enjoyed not so long ago. Laura wasn't a bitter person or even particularly materialistic. But her normal good humor was always tinged with sadness, since her husband's suicide.

When she reached the flower shop at Seventy-third and Madison Avenue, she pulled the keys from her purse and unlocked the front door, checking the floral displays in the window that she had personally arranged. The dahlias were just coming in, and the large, lush blossoms with their stunning colors of pink, magenta, and blazing yellow pleased the eye. One of the nicest features of her job was that she worked with flowers, which she adored and the arrangement of which she had a natural aptitude for. Garden of Delights was a carriage trade shop. Her clients included some of the most social people in New York. One reason she had gotten the job was that she had once belonged to that world. She could speak the lingo.

After checking the flowers in the refrigerated showcases, she called her purveyor in the flower market downtown, placing an order for the next morning. Then, while waiting for her first customer, she opened the *Herald-Tribune* to see what was playing at the movies, films being one escape she could afford. Tallulah Bankhead and Gary Cooper were in a submarine movie, *The Devil and the Deep* at the Paramount; while she liked Gary Cooper, the thought of a submarine movie didn't appeal to her. At the Times Square, Adolphe Menjou was appearing in a mystery called *The Night Club Lady.* Laura liked mysteries, so that was a possibility. Elissa Landi and Paul Lukas were in *A Passport to Hell* at the Winter Garden, and Irene Dunne and John Boles were in *Back Street* at the Mayfair; Laura had read the Fannie Hurst novel and cried at the end, so that was a possibility: Laura liked a good cry.

Her perusal of the movie ads was cut short by the bell tinkling. She looked up to see a tall young man in a well-cut gray suit, sharp blue tie, and gray hat come in the shop from Madison Avenue.

It was Nick Savage.

"Good morning," he said with a smile, coming over to her counter.

"Good morning."

"I've come to bring you some business. Tomorrow's my mother's birthday. I wanted to send her some roses."

"We have some very nice pink ones," Laura said, indicating one of the showcases.

"Yes, they're lovely. Could you send her two dozen by this afternoon? I think you have her address."

"Oh yes, she comes in every once in a while. She's such a beautiful woman."

"Thank you. I think so, too. She's terribly upset, as we all are. Her grandson's been kidnapped."

"Oh, is that the boy out on Long Island?"

"Yes."

"I read about it. The poor thing, and he's only six years old."

"I know. His mother's a wreck, too. I'm going out to Syosset this afternoon to be with her. May I give you a personal check for the flowers?"

"Of course, Nick. The roses are sixteen dollars. And I wanted to thank you for dinner the other night. I had a wonderful time."

"So did I." He smiled at her, pulling a checkbook from his pocket. "I see you're looking at the movies," he went on, writing the check. "Is there anything you'd like to see?"

"Well, I was thinking of seeing *Back Street*."

He finished writing the check, then tore it off and handed it to her with a smile.

"I wish I could take you tonight," he said. "But I'll be out on the Island with my sister-in-law. Maybe some other night?"

"I'd be delighted."

"You know, it's incredible to me that someone as lovely as you isn't being swamped with dates."

She hesitated.

"Well," she finally said, "all my friends know I'm still in mourning for my husband. In fact, you're the first man I've gone out with since he died."

"I take that as a compliment to me."

She smiled.

"It is."

He looked a bit startled, then returned that smile.

Nick picked six-year-old Mark up out of his bed and held him in his arms, hugging and kissing him.

"Uncle Nick," Mark said, "do you think Sebastian's going to be all right?"

"Yes, I think so. I talked to Governor Roosevelt this morning, and he's offered to put extra state troopers on the case as well as his best detectives."

"Really?" Mark sounded impressed. "Boy, Sebastian will really be thrilled when he hears that! State troopers and detectives—wow!"

"And when Sebastian's back home, I'm going to take both of you to a Yankees game."

"Oh boy, that's wonderful!"

"So don't worry about Sebastian. He's going to be home soon, safe and sound."

"I really miss him a lot. You know, we fight sometimes, but I really love him."

"I know you do, and I love you." He gave him another kiss, then lowered him into his bed. "Now you go to sleep and don't worry. Everything's going to be fine."

"Thanks a lot, Uncle Nick. And I love you, too. What was my father like?"

Nick hesitated, thinking of Cesare.

"Well, he was very smart and very handsome—just like you and Sebastian."

"Was he a gangster?"

Oh boy, Nick thought. *How do I answer this one?*

"He was connected to the liquor business," he said, which was one way of saying he was a bootlegger. "But he also was in the stock market, where he made a lot of money."

"Sebastian's awfully worried that he was a gangster, but I guess I don't mind so much. Did you like my father?"

"Oh yes, very much. He was one of the most dazzling men I've ever known."

"What's that mean, 'dazzling'?"

"It means that when he was in the room, nobody else seemed anywhere near as fascinating as he was."

"Gosh, I wish I had known him."

"He was someone I'll never forget. Now, you go to sleep."

He leaned down and kissed him again. Then he left the room, turning out the lights and softly closing the door. He went downstairs in the Syosset house, where Gloria was setting the dining room table for dinner.

"You're so wonderful to come out here and be with us," she said as Nick came into the room. "And you're so good to Mark."

"I love those kids as if they were my own."

"Speaking of which, when are you going to have some of your own?"

"I've been thinking about that lately. Now that I'm thirty-five, I'm beginning to feel Father Time blowing down my neck."

"Wait till you're my age, darling. And don't ask what that is. Is there anyone in particular you're interested in? Or are you still catting around with your usual bunch of aging debutantes?"

"There is someone I just met recently. Actually, I used to know her out on Long Island. It's Morris Blakeley's widow, Laura."

"Oh yes, I've heard about her."

"How did her husband kill himself?"

"Apparently he took one of his hunting rifles, went into a bathroom, stuck it in his mouth and blew his brains out. Laura came in and found him that way."

"Good Lord . . ."

That must be why she drinks, he thought.

Tyler Elwood, wearing nothing but his pajama bottoms, was shaving in the only bathroom in his ramshackle farmhouse outside Hicksville, Long Island, when he saw a figure appear in the mirror behind him. He turned to stare at Sebastian Savage, who was standing in the bathroom door still wearing his pajamas.

"How did you get out of the garage?" Tyler gasped, shaving cream covering most of his face.

"I cut my ropes on the blade of your lawn mower," Sebastian said. His hands were behind his back. "And I know who you are. You came to our house last month to repair my mother's new radio."

Tyler was holding his straight razor in his right hand.

"You stupid brat," he said, softly. "I was trying to save you by wearing the mask. But now I'll have to kill you. You stupid little brat. Damn!"

Holding the razor, he started toward Sebastian. The boy never wavered. He brought his right hand from behind his back and aimed a gun at Tyler, who looked surprised.

"Where'd you get my gun?" he asked, stopping.

"It was on your bed table. And don't try to hurt me, because I'll shoot you. I'm not afraid to do it."

He was lying. He was terrified.

Tyler smiled.

"Come on, kid," he said, holding out his hand. "Give me the gun. I know your father was a gangster . . ."

"No he wasn't!" Sebastian interrupted, angrily.

"Oh come on, everyone knows the story. Your father was a bootlegger who got killed by Dutch Schultz . . ."

"My father was a stockbroker!"

"Yeah, and my father was John D. Rockefeller. Okay, I know you think this is something out of a movie, but you know damned well you're not going to shoot me. You're just a kid."

"Don't come any nearer."

Sebastian was trembling, sweat pouring from his forehead. *He's going to kill me! I have to do something . . . he can see I'm afraid. . . . Wouldn't my father have just killed him right off the bat? But I don't want to be like my father, do I? Oh God, please make this man leave me alone . . . please . . .*

Tyler tried to grab the gun. Sebastian fired it, hitting him in the stomach. Tyler howled with pain, doubling over. Then he tried a second time to grab the gun, but Sebastian fired again, this time hitting him in his arm. Tyler, moaning, blood gushing from both wounds, stumbled back against the toilet and fell on the floor.

"I told you I wasn't afraid," Sebastian said, trembling with terror. *I've almost killed a man,* he thought. *Oh God, maybe I'm beginning to un-derstand my father...* "You should have believed me. But I'm sorry I hurt you." *Look at all that blood... Oh gosh, he's bleeding... I didn't want to hurt him... Oh, all that blood... I think I'm going to be sick to my stomach...*

"Call an ambulance," Tyler gasped, sprawled at the bottom of the toilet. Blood was incarnadining the white tile floor of the bathroom. "I'm going to bleed to death."

"All right," Sebastian said, trembling with fear and disgust at the bloody scene unfolding in front of him. "I'm sorry... I didn't want to hurt you..."

"Well, you did, you little brat..."

"Where's the phone?"

"In the kitchen. Hurry... I'm dying here!"

"Okay."

Sebastian, panicked by the blood and the sight of a man dying, ran into the adjacent bedroom and phoned the police. Then he looked at the gun.

Am I a gangster, just like my father was? he thought. *Oh God, am I going to end up in jail? Or murdered, like he was? But I put holes in that man's skin. And blood is gushing out of it... I didn't want to kill him, but he would have killed me, wouldn't he? It might have been my blood all over the bathroom floor... But I never really believed people died, or at least like this, except in movies...*

Oh gosh, I'm so confused and scared... I want my Momma...

"Gosh, Sebastian, am I glad to see you again!" Mark said as he hugged his brother when the police returned him to the house in Syosset. "Did you really shoot the guy?"

"Yeah, I hit him twice, he was trying to kill me. I told him not to come after me with that razor, but he wouldn't stop," Sebastian said.

"Boy, that's really neat! You're a real hero!"

Sebastian, who was looking troubled, said nothing.

Gloria, who was practically in tears of relief, hugged Sebastian, cov-ering him with kisses.

"Oh darling, I'm so glad you're home safe and sound!" she said. "Were you frightened?" She lovingly smoothed his thick, black hair.

"Yeah, I was." He hugged her and whispered into her ear, "Mom, what really scared me was . . ."

He stopped, tears beginning to run down his cheeks.

Gloria saw the tears.

"What?"

Sebastian started sobbing. Mark stared at him, totally confused. Then, suddenly, Sebastian stopped hugging his mother and ran out of the room. Gloria looked as confused as Mark.

One of the policemen who had brought Sebastian home said, "There'll be reporters here in a few minutes, Mrs. Savage. They'll be wanting to take your son's picture. He may even be in a newsreel."

Mark's face lit up.

"Gee," he said, proudly. "Sebastian's going to be famous!"

Gloria, looking troubled, started out of the room, saying to the cop, "Sebastian's upset, which is only normal, under the circumstances. I'll calm him down before the reporters get here. Would you like some coffee? There's some in the kitchen: Help yourself. Mark, show the gentleman where the kitchen is."

"Okay, Mom. Is it fun being a policeman?"

The cop laughed, following him out of the room.

"Sometimes," he said.

"I'd like to be a policeman when I grow up."

Gloria found Sebastian upstairs in his bedroom. He was lying face-down on his bed, crying his heart out. She came over to him and sat beside him, smoothing the back of his head.

"Darling, what is it?" she said, softly.

He turned over and looked at her with red, tear-stained eyes.

"Oh Momma," he whispered, "am I going to be a gangster, like my father?"

"Of course not. Why would you say that?"

"Because . . ." He burst into tears again, throwing his arms around his mother's waist. "Because I shot the bad man! Oh, I was so scared by all the blood pouring out of that bad man! It was horrible! Momma, I don't want to be a gangster like my father! Tell me I'm not going to be a gangster! And the bad man said my father was a gangster, so it is true, isn't it? He really wasn't a stockbroker?"

Gloria, who had always tried to whitewash Cesare's career to her kids, thought fast.

"Well, he was both, darling . . . I mean, sort of . . ."

"Uncle Nick said he was in the liquor business, like Mr. Kennedy. But Mr. Kennedy isn't a gangster, is he? He's respectable. Oh, I want my father to be respectable!"

"Well, he was, darling. Very respectable."

"Then why was he murdered by a gangster?"

"Well, there were certain stock problems . . ."

"Oh, I don't understand it. But I want to be respectable."

"Of course you do," she soothed, hugging him. "And you're a hero, not a bad person. You did a very brave thing. Most boys your age would have been too afraid to do anything. I'm very proud of you, darling."

Sebastian sniffed, stopping his crying.

"Are you really?" he asked.

"Oh yes, very proud. Now sit up and wipe your eyes. The reporters are coming to talk to you. The whole country's going to know how brave you are."

"You think so? Really?"

"Yes. And I love you very, very much."

Oh God, she thought. *Cesare's been dead three years now, but his ghost still haunts this family.*

"There's terrible news from Julie," Rachel said three mornings later as she and Johnny were eating breakfast in the morning room of their Park Avenue penthouse. The butler had just brought her a cablegram.

"Now what?" Johnny said, drinking his orange juice.

"Edgar's been murdered in Tokyo by his brother-in-law, that young army lieutenant. He came into the bedroom and shot him three times."

"Good lord, why?"

"Apparently, he belongs to some sort of fanatic secret society who hate the Chinese. Julie says they've arrested him, but he's been made into a sort of national hero. And then Edgar's widow, Suzuki, whose brother killed him, was so horrified that she plunged a dagger into her stomach and committed *hara-kiri*. Can you believe with all the madness and trouble in the world, that the Japanese would turn against the Chinese?"

"From what I read in the papers, the Japanese would like to take over China the way they've taken over Manchuria. But poor Julie. I hardly knew Edgar, but I know she loved him. She must be taking this very hard. I'll have to write her."

"Yes, do." Rachel put down the cable and sipped some coffee. "What an odd family we are," she said. "There's been so much trouble in it for years. I sometimes wonder if we're not cursed."

Her husband, whose hair had turned pure white, looked at her with eyes that were beginning to cloud over. Johnny didn't know it, but he was getting cataracts.

"Oh my darling Rachel," he said, softly, "I've thought that for years."

4   THE NEXT SUNDAY, LAURA WAS washing her hair, listening
to *The Jell-O Show* with Jack Benny on the NBC-Red radio network,
when the phone rang. Putting a towel around her head, she went to the
bedroom and picked up the phone.

"Hello?"

"Laura, it's Nick. What are you doing tonight?"

"Nothing."

"Would you like to go to dinner?"

"I'd love to."

"Wonderful. We've got the campaign headquarters—it's not much,
just three rooms in a rather old building near Wall Street. I'm down here
now, getting the place put together, so I won't be able to pick you up.
See you at Tosca at eight?"

"I'll be there."

She hung up, then hurried back into the bathroom to set her hair.

An hour later, she walked uptown to Tosca and went inside where the
owner, Mario, met her.

"Is Mr. Savage here yet?" she asked.

"Oh sure, Signora, over here," Mario said with an accent as thick as
marinara sauce. Picking up two menus, he led her over to a corner table
where Nick was sipping a Coke. Now he stood up and smiled as Mario
seated her. "Good evening. Don't you look nice?"

"Thank you. I'm afraid this dress is a bit out of date, like most of my
wardrobe." She turned to Mario and said, in a soft voice, "I'll have a
glass of that lovely pinot grigio."

Mario shot Nick a nervous glance, then looked back at Laura.

"I'm sorry, Signora, but I can't do that no more. The cops were in
here this afternoon and they give me a bad time so I can't serve no more
the vino." He shrugged helplessly.

"Oh." Laura looked annoyed. Then she opened the menu.

Mario looked at Nick again, then went away. After a moment, Laura put down the menu.

"You know," she said, "I don't feel like Italian food tonight. Would you mind very much if we went somewhere else?"

"Like where?"

"Oh, I don't know. But Italian food without wine is sort of blah."

"There's a French restaurant down the street, but they don't serve wine either."

She drummed her fingers irritably.

"Then why don't we go to my apartment?" she finally said. "I can make us a nice salad."

"Do you have wine at your apartment?"

"Yes. Why do you ask?"

"Because this isn't about Italian food. It's about wine. I told Mario not to serve you any wine—that story about the cops was a lie. The truth is, Laura, you drink too much. Listen: I'm a former souse, I know all about it. But because I care for you, I want you to stop."

She glared at him.

"That's ridiculous," she finally said. "I don't drink during the day at all, but I do like wine with my dinner. And I find it rather insulting that you regard me as some sort of drunk."

"The last time we had dinner here, you drank a whole bottle of wine. And when you went home, you were high as a kite. Or do you remember?"

"Of course I remember!"

"Do you remember that I had to help you up the stairs to your apartment?"

She stood up, picking up her purse.

"When I need psychiatric help," she snapped. "I'll go to a psychiatrist. Good night."

She started toward the door. Nick got out of his chair and hurried after her, taking her arm as Mario watched from the kitchen door, a look of dismay on his face.

"Laura, don't you understand I'm only trying to help you?" Nick said as the other diners stared.

"I don't need help!" she whispered, but the whisper was almost a hiss. "Now let go of me!"

"All right, you can have some wine."

"I don't want any! Let go!"

She kicked his shin so hard he let out a yelp. Then she went to the door and left the restaurant.

Nick stood by himself for a moment as the other diners continued to stare at him, whispering to each other. Then he went back to his table to finish his Coke. Mario came up to him, looking troubled.

"Signor Savage," he whispered, "I'm so sorry but you told me to . . ."

Nick put up his hand to indicate there was no problem.

"It's not your fault. I guess I won't be eating after all. I haven't got much appetite. What do I owe you for the Coke?"

"It's on the house."

"Thanks."

Nick left the restaurant, feeling miserable. He liked Laura enormously and was extremely attracted to her.

But once again, alcohol was invading his life.

He remembered his first marriage with Valerie, the silly shopper. He remembered their extravagant life on the North Shore of Long Island, the so-called Gold Coast. The gorgeous Georgian mansion, the fabulous boozy parties, the madcap zany twenties. He remembered—or perhaps half-remembered, because there had been so much alcohol in his life—the wild life they had led: parties, cocktails, shopping, stock speculation, fancy cars, sex. . . . The Good Life that America in the twenties had bought, lock, stock and barrel, only to have it all turn to dust when Wall Street laid its infamous egg.

And of course, the worst moment of his life, when he realized Cesare had oiled him into embezzling money from the bank to gamble on the hot stock market, the twenties bull market that no one thought would ever stop going up. His blessed mother, Rachel, had saved him from that de-bacle: He could have gone to jail.

But it had taken the crash of 'twenty-nine, and the realization that he and Valerie were practically wiped out financially, to turn his life around, to make him take the pledge against alcohol, a pledge that Valerie wouldn't take—or perhaps couldn't. And Valerie, whose sexy flapper body he had so lusted for when he was younger, had finally revealed herself as a weak, self-indulgent, and more than slightly silly drunk.

For Nick Savage, maturing had been a long and painful process.

But, he thought, *do I want to get involved with another woman who, although enormously attractive, has the same problem I and Valerie had, namely booze?*

And yet . . . there's something about her that's so appealing.

"Who's that man downstairs with Mom?"

The question was asked by six-year-old Mark Savage, who was lying in his bed. The window of the darkened bedroom on the second floor of the Syosset house had been barred by Gloria after Sebastian's kidnapping to prevent any other break-in.

"His name is Chester Wood," Sebastian said. The elder twin by ten minutes was lying in his bed on the other side of the room from Mark. "Mom met him at a cocktail party in New York. She told me he owns a big plumbing company—Wood Plumbing."

"Yeah, I've heard of that."

"He makes bathtubs and stuff. He owns some big factory out in Indiana. I guess he's awful rich. It'd be nice if he fell in love with Mom and married her. I'd like to be rich."

"Our dad was rich and look what happened to him. He got murdered, just like in a gangster movie."

There was a prolonged silence. Then Sebastian said, quietly: "Mark, we're about as close as two people can get, aren't we? I mean, being identical twins and everything."

"Oh sure."

"I love you very much, and I think you love me."

"Of course I do. What are you getting at?"

"I think we have to stop saying that our father was a gangster, because people are going to treat us differently if we do."

"But he *was* a gangster! Everyone knows that."

"Well, maybe they don't know it. They may just think it. Besides, Dad's been dead awhile now and people will start forgetting what he was. So I think we have to start sort of talking about him in a different way."

"Like how?"

"Like saying he was a stockbroker, which he was. I mean, this is for you as well as me. If our father was Al Capone, that would sort of make us dirty for the rest of our lives—don't you see that?"

Now it was Mark's turn to be silent.

"I guess you're right," he finally said. "Except Uncle Nick as much as admitted to me he was a bootlegger."

"It's not a lie, it's a different way of looking at things. You see, I told Mom that when I shot the guy who kidnapped me, I was terrified that I might end up being a gangster like our father. But if I thought of him as a stockbroker instead of a gangster, that would make a big difference in the way I think. Do you understand?"

"Yeah, I guess . . . Okay, so he wasn't a gangster. If that's what you want me to say, I'll do it because I'd do anything for you. Would you do anything for me?"

"Of course."

"I'll remember that."

"Why do you say that?"

"Oh, I don't know. You never know what'll happen. Anyway, I'm sleepy. Good night."

"Good night," Sebastian said in the darkness, thinking how different a twin could really be.

Downstairs in the living room, their mother placed the needle of her phonograph on a record and the lilting strains of the new number-one hit, Cole Porter's "Night and Day," curled out of the machine like smoke.

"Want to dance?" she asked the fifty-year-old man in the rumpled gray business suit sitting on the sofa.

"Gosh, I'm not much of a dancer," Chester Wood said. He was a lanky man with curly brown hair and jug ears.

"I'm not expecting Fred Astaire."

Chester laughed and stood up. He was a bit over six feet tall.

"Well, don't get mad if I step on your toes. You've been warned."

"Chester, I've been stepped on by more men than you'd like to know about."

Chester took her in his arms and they started cheek-to-cheeking around the rather small living room.

"You know," Chester said, "when I was a kid traveling around the country selling my plumbing fixtures, I used to be crazy about the movies. I never dreamed that some day I'd be dancing with a real-live movie star. It's really a thrill for me. Do you miss Hollywood?"

"Not particularly. It was fun at the time, but it's really turning into a jungle. Besides, I couldn't get anything but character parts now. In Hollywood, if you're over twenty-nine, you might as well be dead."

"You don't look a day over twenty-nine to me."

She smiled.

"You're sweet, Chester, but either you've been drinking or you should see an eye doctor."

"Seriously, I think you're the most beautiful woman I've ever met. I know you must think I'm some hick from Indiana . . ."

"Oh, I don't think that!" Gloria interrupted. "I really don't! I like you enormously, Chester, and I mean that."

His brown eyes widened with excitement.

"Do you really?"

"Absolutely."

They continued dancing for a moment. Gloria, like thousands of other American women, had dyed her hair platinum blond to emulate the hottest thing in Hollywood, Jean Harlow, and in her tight-fitting white dress, she looked, in fact, damned glamorous, even for a woman well into her forties. Chester pressed her to him. She didn't resist him.

"I wish you could come out to Indianapolis one day," Chester said. "I'd love to show you my house. It's got eighteen rooms and an indoor swimming pool and tennis courts. It's really beautiful."

"Maybe I will come out one day. I don't think now would be a good time, with your wife just having died. And by the way, I'm sorry for you about that."

"Yes, thanks. Helen was a sweet, wonderful woman who had a painful death. But she's gone now, and I'm very lonely. So maybe some day you can come out. Maybe some day soon."

The record stopped. Chester stopped dancing, still holding Gloria in his arms, looking at her hungrily.

"I'm just crazy about you, Gloria," he said, softly. "You're the most fabulous woman I've ever met, and I know I shouldn't be saying that with my poor wife dead only six months. But it's the truth."

Impulsively, hotly, he put his mouth on her lush lips and kissed her hungrily. Gloria put up no resistance for almost a minute. Then, gently, she pushed him away.

"It's getting late, darling," she said. "You have that train to catch in the morning."

He looked disappointed.

"Yes, I know," he said, checking his watch. "I'm coming back in two weeks for the plumbing convention. I'll be in New York for five nights. Will you save every one of them for me? We can paint the town red and see every Broadway show!"

"Darling, you're not the only man in my life."

"I want to be."

"Well, we'll see. Give me a call before you come back, and we'll make some plans."

"I'll let myself out." He started toward the front door, then stopped and turned. "I'll call you, Gloria. Tomorrow night—no, I'll be on the train. I'll call you when I get back to Indianapolis. I'll call you every night!"

When he left the room, Gloria opened a silver cigarette box on the coffee table, pulled out a Lucky Strike, and lit it with a silver lighter. She exhaled slowly, thinking: *I like that man. Yes, he's a hick, but so what? I like him.*

He's lonely and I'm lonely. He needs me, and I need him. And after all we've been through, "dull" might be just what this family needs.

5 "ROOSEVELT FOR PRESIDENT IN 1932!" screamed the big banner that was stretched across the back wall of the main room of the fundraising headquarters on the third floor of a Broadway office building two blocks from City Hall. The room was filled with a half-dozen desks with telephones and typewriters where volunteers were calling potential donors to the big campaign. Nick was sitting in his much smaller office writing on a pad names of his friends he thought might possibly cough up some serious money even though they were Republicans: these were people he would be calling personally. He had written eight names when the door was opened by Frank Gibson, a kid who was wild for Roosevelt and had volunteered his time.

"Mr. Savage, there's a Laura Blakeley who wants to see you."

Nick looked surprised—and delighted.

"Thanks, Frank. Show her in, please." He had wanted to call her but being with her when she was drinking reminded him of his own demons. It was dangerous.

A few moments later, Laura came in, wearing a light-green dress and a small white hat. She closed the door as Nick stood up.

"I owe you an apology," she said, coming over to his desk. "I behaved dreadfully at the restaurant. I went home and got absolutely plastered all by myself several nights in a row and when I woke up this morning, I realized what you said is true. I'm a drunk. So I've stopped. I know it's going to be hard for a while, and I'd like to ask you for your help. That is, if you ever want to see me again. And if you didn't, I couldn't blame you."

"Of course I'll help you," Nick said. "And I'm thrilled you've stopped."

"I know now that you were trying to help me. Oh Nick, it all began when I opened the bathroom door and saw my husband's blood and brains everywhere . . ." She sank into a chair as Nick came around the desk. "I loved him so much . . . he was such a beautiful man, but he was weak.

He couldn't stand being poor. And I started drinking, a little more each day. . . . It's so easy, so seductive . . . it dulls the pain . . ."

Nick put his hand on her shoulder as she wiped her eyes.

"I know all about it," he said, softly. "I've been there myself."

She took his hand and pressed it to her cheek.

"I'm so sorry I kicked you," she sniffed.

"You should play football. You've got a strong kick."

She looked up at him.

"Well," she said, "since I'm here, you might as well put me to work."

Nick smiled. "If you can type as well as you kick, you're going to be really useful."

Sebastian was tossing a football to Mark on the lawn of their Syosset house. It was a cool afternoon, the week before Labor Day. Sebastian's throwing arm was good, but Mark was the superior athlete and could run like a deer. The football coach at the local high school had his eye on the boy as a possible future star.

Mark caught the ball and threw it back to Sebastian as their mother's car pulled into the driveway. Gloria, wearing a white suit and hat, got out of the car.

"Boys," she called, "come inside. I've something to show you."

Sebastian tossed the football on the lawn.

"Put the ball in the garage," his mother ordered. Sebastian mumbled a grumble, but obeyed.

Inside the kitchen, Gloria pulled off her gloves.

"Mr. Wood's in town for a convention," she said, "and he took me to lunch in New York. Look."

She held out her left hand. On the fourth finger was an enormous, square-cut diamond. The twins stared at it.

"Gosh," Sebastian said. "Is it real?"

"Oh yes."

"Does this mean you're going to marry him?" Mark asked.

"That's right, next month. Your grandmother's very sweetly offered to let us use her apartment for the wedding and reception. Then we're all going to move out to Indianapolis."

"Indianapolis?" Mark said, making a face and pronouncing it like Siberia. "Ugh. I don't want to leave Syosset."

"You're going to love Indianapolis," his mother said. "Chester has a big farm north of the city, and you can have horses if you want. He has tennis courts and an indoor swimming pool. It's going to be like living in a resort."

"Gee," Mark said, "an indoor swimming pool. That sounds nifty. That means we could go swimming all year round, doesn't it?"

Gloria put on the coffeepot.

"Momma," Sebastian asked, "do you love Mr. Wood?"

"Sit down, boys," she said. "I want to have a little talk with you."

"Can I have a Coke?" Mark asked.

"In a minute."

The twins sat down at the kitchen table. Gloria sat between them.

"You see, you're too young to know what love is," she began. "You ask me if I love Chester, and I do. He's really a very fine man, and I'm sure when you get to know him, you'll like him very much. But while I love him, I'm not exactly *in* love with him, the way I was with your father. But I was a lot younger then, and when you're young, physical attraction means a lot more to a woman than it does later on in life."

"Was Father attractive?" Sebastian asked.

"Extremely."

"And Mr. Wood isn't?" Mark asked.

"Oh, he's very nice-looking, but it's not the same as it was with your father. I mean, for me. But Chester has other qualities your father didn't have. He's steady, and he offers me—and you, of course—safety and stability. I'm no longer a young woman, and I have a responsibility to you two. Frankly, my finances are in pretty rotten shape. You know that your grandmother, Rachel, bought this house for us and has helped us out over the years financially, which has been very generous of her. But I'd like very much to be financially independent, and Chester will make that happen."

The twins looked at her for a moment.

"Does that mean," Mark asked, "you're marrying him for his money?"

"That's certainly part of it. And he knows it: I've been totally honest with him, as I am with you. This is something we won't talk about to other people, of course. But I wanted both of you to understand the situation." She reached out and took their hands. "I know this may sound rather cynical," she went on. "Most people like to think love is like Valentine's Day, all roses and cooing doves. But it's a rough world, my darlings, particularly now with this damned Depression, and I have to be practical. I hope you won't hold it against your poor old Momma?"

Both twins got up and came to hug their mother.

"Oh no, Momma," Sebastian said. "We know you're doing what's right for all of us, and we've known that you've been worried about money. Besides, we'd never think twice about what you decide, because you're all we've got and we love you."

"And I love you, my darlings." She kissed both of them.

"But love sounds awfully complicated," Sebastian went on.

"It's simple when you're young, but it gets more complicated later on in life. All I want is for all of us to be happy."

"Oh, I'm happy," Mark said, adding with a mischievous grin, "besides, I think it's going to be fun being rich!"

All three of them laughed.

"Governor Roosevelt has asked me if I'd be interested in an ambassadorship if he wins the election," Nick told Laura as they danced cheek-to-cheek at the Starlight Roof in the newly opened Waldorf-Astoria. The band was playing the new hit song, "You're Getting to be a Habit with Me." It was the first week of September.

"How thrilling!" Laura said. "What did you tell him?" She was wearing one of her three evening dresses while Nick was in white tie and tails.

"I told him I was very honored he thought of me, but that it would be awfully hard for me to leave the bank with business as lousy as it is right now. Of course, I'm sure that if the governor wins, business will pick up. Do you know you dance like Ginger Rogers?"

"Don't I wish. Is the governor pleased with our work?"

"Oh, he's ecstatic. Our little bucket shop has raised over a million for his campaign in six weeks, and that's big money. Do you know you're more beautiful than Ginger Rogers?"

"Really, Nick, be serious."

"You're too modest. You really are beautiful, Laura. And you're a beautiful person, to boot. And I'm so proud of you. How long have you been off the sauce?"

"Almost six weeks, and I really don't miss it. Well, sometimes I do, but then I think of something else I like."

"And what, for instance, might that be?"

"Oh, sometimes you."

She smiled. He held her even closer as the band segued to another hit song, "My Ideal."

"You know," Nick went on, "if I accept an ambassadorship, I'd be awfully handicapped because I don't have a wife. I mean, that's a large part of that game—entertaining and so forth. So you can see that I really do need a wife. And there's another thing: my thirty-sixth birthday is coming up in a few weeks and it's time I settled down and had kids. When I was married to Valerie, we were so busy partying we didn't want kids. But now, I very much want them. So I'm not only looking for a wife, I'm looking for a mother for my kids. And there's something else: I've fallen madly, crazily in love."

"Anyone I know?"

"You."

He twirled her around the dance floor as the romantic music climaxed. Then he led her to their table where the waiter poured them coffee.

"So?" Nick said after they had sat down. "That was a proposal. Maybe not the best one, or the most poetic, but I meant every word. I love you, Laura. I want you to be my wife. I hope with all my heart you'll say yes."

She stirred her coffee thoughtfully a moment. Then she looked up at him.

"Nick, those are the sweetest words any man has ever said to a woman. But . . ." She hesitated, looking troubled.

"You don't love me," he said in a disappointed tone.

"Oh no, I do! Really! I think I've loved you since the first moment I set eyes on you."

His face brightened.

"Then you'll say 'yes'?"

Again, she hesitated.

"Nick, could you take me home? I have to think things over."

"But Laura, what's to think? Is there a problem?"

Her eyes became misty with tears.

"Yes, there is. Oh Nick, please take me home."

"Is there somebody else?"

"No, it's not that. Please."

She opened her purse to take out a handkerchief.

Nick, looking disappointed, signaled for the check.

The next morning, he was seated at his desk in his paneled office in the Savage Bank Building on Pine Street when his secretary, Miss Brook, announced that a Miss Laura Blakely wanted to see him. Surprised, Nick said "Show her in." He got up from his desk as Laura came in. She was wearing a simple black dress with white gloves and a small black hat.

"Good morning," Nick said as she looked around the room, then at him.

"I know you're angry with me," she said, crossing the office to his desk.

"Not angry," he said. "Just disappointed and confused. And a little hurt. I guess I'm not very good at rejection."

"I didn't reject you. May I sit down?"

"Please."

The atmosphere was strained between these two people who, just the night before, had been so happily dancing. Laura sat down in a chair before Nick's desk.

"I didn't sleep last night," she said. "I wanted to call you and I almost did, but I was so uncertain." She sighed. "You see, when I was eight years old I had rheumatic fever. It left me with a slight heart condition. My doctor has told me it could be dangerous for me to have children. I know you want children. When you proposed last night, I so much wanted to say 'yes' because I do love you, Nick. I love you so much that it kills me to tell you the truth about myself. I wanted to not tell you, because I so very much want to be your wife. But I have to be honest with you. And so . . ." She gestured sadly and helplessly. "I'll understand if you retract your proposal, and there certainly will be no hard feelings. Just a great sadness on my part."

Nick stared at her. He could almost hear her heart breaking. Or was it his?

"What do you mean when you say 'dangerous'?" he finally said.

"I might die. Oh Nick, I'm so sorry. I wanted us to be happy more than anything in the world."

A long silence passed as they stared at each other. Then Nick stood up.

"The children don't matter," he said. "Maybe we'll adopt some. Or maybe some day they can fix your heart, who knows? But I love you, Laura. My proposal still holds."

"Are you certain?"

"More certain than anything I've felt in my life."

Her face lit up like a sunrise.

"Then I'll say yes, darling."

Nick came around the desk as Laura stood up. He took her in his arms and kissed her. Then they hugged each other.

"I'm so happy," he whispered. "And last night I thought it was the end of the world."

"So did I. It was the most miserable night of my life . . . well, almost. But now it's a whole new world!"

"How do we celebrate this momentous occasion? Would you like a cup of coffee?"

She glanced at her wristwatch.

"It's almost ten o'clock . . . I have to get uptown and open the flower shop . . ."

"To hell with the flower shop!"

"No, I really must go . . ."

"Tell you what: come to my house tonight and I'll cook us dinner. I want you to see the house anyway, I mean, it'll be your house soon . . . And we can plan the wedding and our honeymoon and the whole works! Oh boy, Laura, I'm so excited I could dance on the ceiling!"

She laughed.

"I wouldn't try it. I'm excited too, darling." She gave him a quick kiss, then hurried to the door, which she opened. "By the way," she said, looking back at him, "what's your address?"

"Fourteen Sutton Place. But I'll pick you up at your place at seven o'clock—and I adore you!"

A mere dozen years before, Sutton Place had been the site of a brewery and tenements. But after the Great War, a few society women, spearheaded by J. P. Morgan's daughter, Anne, and the actress-turned-decorator Elsie de Wolfe, tore down the block between Fifty-seventh and Fifty-eighth Streets on the East River and put up a charming series of townhouses in various architectural styles. Renaming the area Sutton Place, which sounded tonier, they moved in, fleeing the soaring taxes and rising cost of servants in their parents' white elephant Fifth Avenue mansions.

"It's beautiful," Laura exclaimed as she climbed out of the taxi with Nick, looking admiringly at the four-story brick house in the Georgian style. "How long have you lived here?"

"I bought it a year ago," Nick said, paying the cabbie then pulling out a key to unlock his front door. "I like it over here by the river. It's cooler in the summer, and you don't get much traffic noise. And I love to watch the ships and barges go by. It's sort of like being out to sea, without having to worry about getting seasick."

He opened the door and Laura went into a rather narrow hallway with a stair on the right leading to the second floor. Nick turned on the lights.

"Let's go in the drawing room," he said, leading her through a door to the left, turning on more lights.

He took her hat and coat, then turned on the radio. An orchestra was playing "Isn't It Romantic?" which Rudy Vallee began crooning.

"How appropriate," he said, taking her in his arms. They began dancing dreamily around the comfortably furnished room.

"My mother's giving my sister-in-law a wedding next Saturday at her apartment. Gloria's marrying this plumbing manufacturer from the midwest. Anyway, a lot of my family is going to be there. My sister, Brook, and her husband, Bernard, are coming in from Paris with their son, Graydon. But my other sister, Beatrice, and her husband and daughter won't be coming from London. Beatrice never particularly liked Gloria."

"You certainly have an international family."

"I know. Beatrice and her husband left Italy because my brother-in-law hates the Fascists—he was put in jail by them. Anyway, what I'm saying is, it's time for you to meet my family. Are you game?"

"I'm looking forward to it."

He started kissing her. After a moment, they stopped dancing and just stood in the middle of the room, kissing.

"Would you spend the night?" he whispered. "If you don't want to, it won't matter."

She thought a moment.

"I want to," she finally said. "I want to very much."

"Then will you?"

She put her arms around him and kissed him again, hungrily.

"Yes," she whispered.

Seventy-seven-year-old Julie Chin sat on the terrace of her house on the Peak overlooking the Hong Kong harbor and read the letter from Rachel Savage in New York.

"News from our New York relatives," she said to her grandson, Lance Wang. Lance and Nora were sipping gin and tonics. "Mrs. Savage is giving a wedding for Gloria Gilmore."

"Wasn't she the movie star?" Nora said, her blond hair chicly shingled.

"Well, 'star' might be a bit of an overstatement. But she made a lot of movies in the silent days. Anyway, she's marrying a plumbing tycoon from the midwest, and Mrs. Savage is giving the wedding in her penthouse, which is certainly sweet of her. We're all invited, but of course there's not enough time to get to New York."

"I couldn't possibly go for the next few months anyway," Lance said. "Business is too tight."

Julie put down the letter and looked out at the harbor rather dreamily.

"What are you thinking of, Grandmother?" Nora asked.

"I was thinking of the New York I grew up in," Julie said. "Horses and carriages and gaslight . . . how faraway that world seems now. I'd like to see what New York looks like today."

"Then why don't you go?" Lance said.

"I'm too old to go halfway around the world," she said. "Besides, when you get to my age, you're better off leaving the dreams of your youth untouched."

She put the letter on a table, thinking of Edgar. She had sold the Tokyo store at a loss, which didn't matter. Japan was becoming a hotbed of contention, and the Chins were better off out of it.

But she was still furious about Edgar's murderer. Lieutenant Sokichi Igitaki had been given a prison sentence of two years, of which he served two months and was released. He was then promoted to Captain.

"So my kid brother, Nick, is tying the knot again," Brook Savage de Belleville said in a musing tone as she drank a martini in the first-class dining room of the *Île de France*. "God, his first wife, Valerie, was such a silly bitch, but Nicky was just crazy for her. I hope he's picked someone better this time."

"I'm sure he has," her handsome blond husband Bernard said.

"Well, I hope he's done as well as I have," Brook said, smiling at her husband, who was in a dinner jacket. Brook looked glamorous in a silver lamé evening dress designed by her good friend Coco Chanel that showed a good deal of her thirty-eight-year-old cleavage. Her blond hair was cut rather short, in a tailored, mannish look inspired by Chanel. Around her neck was a star-burst diamond necklace also designed by Chanel. Brook, a stunning beauty, had become one of the most fashionable women in Paris, a city not known for warming up to foreigners. "Do you know I'm still absolutely mad for you, and we're an old married couple?" she went on, squeezing Bernard's hand. "I haven't been tempted by another man even once, and with my track record with men, that's saying something."

She fit a cigarette into a black-and-silver holder. Bernard lit it with a silver lighter.

"How do I know you're not lying to me?" Bernard said with a smile. "After all, if you had *cuisses légères*, the first thing you would say to your husband is that you're faithful."

He'd used the French phrase for "loose." Brook laughed.

"You're always way ahead of me, darling. All right: I confess. I have lovers all over Paris. It's such fun. Anyway, I really am looking forward to meeting Nick's bride. He used to be a party-boy, but now Mother tells me he's become a very solid citizen." She inhaled on her cigarette as the big ship took a slow roll to starboard. One day out of New York and the *Île de France* had encountered rough seas.

"I hope Graydon's feeling better," Bernard said of Brook's twelve-year-old son by her first husband. Bernard had adopted the boy.

"I do, too. The poor kid was practically green in the face an hour ago, and the seas don't seem to be calming down."

"Madame la Comtesse de Belleville?"

A uniformed cabin boy came up to the table. He was holding a silver salver with a cablegram on it.

"Yes."

Brook took the cable as Bernard tipped the boy. Brook opened the cable and read it. A look of concern came over her face.

"Dear God," she said. "My father has had a stroke."

6

JOHNNY SAVAGE'S STROKE WAS A relatively mild one, but it had slurred his speech and partially paralyzed his right side, and the doctor told Rachel he wanted to keep him in the hospital for a while to monitor him. This, coming two days before Gloria's wedding to Chester Wood, naturally cast something of a pall on the festivities. But Rachel was determined not to show the strain: being of the Old School, she had been taught that a lady kept her emotions private.

She had the penthouse banked with flowers and hired a caterer to serve food and drinks to the fifty-odd guests.

The bride looked radiant in an aquamarine silk dress by Mainbocher; on her lapel was a diamond, ruby, and emerald peacock brooch that was one of the many expensive presents given her by her besotted husband, Chester, who had found out that Gloria had a passion for jewels.

Nick had wanted to give Laura some money to improve her wardrobe, but she insisted on using her savings to buy a very attractive gray linen dress by Hattie Carnegie. Nick had given her an engagement ring of a ruby surrounded by diamonds. He proudly introduced her to his relatives, all of whom seemed impressed by her, including Gloria, who hugged Nick and said, "I think she's gorgeous! It's as if we've all got marriage fever, isn't it? I'm so happy for you, Nick. You'll keep in touch with us out in Indianapolis, won't you?"

"Absolutely. And congratulations."

"I'll never forget how wonderful you were when Sebastian was kidnapped."

"We're family," he said simply.

After Gloria and Chester were married, bootleg champagne was passed and waiters served hors d'ouevres.

"So Nicky," Brook said as she sipped the bubbly, "I like this Laura. She's very pretty and seems quite nice. When's the wedding?"

"We haven't set a date yet, but it'll be soon. We hope to go to Europe for our honeymoon. Can we stay in Paris with you and Bernard?"

"I'd be furious if you didn't. We'll have lots of parties and we'll introduce you to all our friends, most of whom are slightly outrageous. Laura's a definite improvement over Valerie. Valerie was not one of your better moves, dear brother."

"You don't have to remind me."

"I hope it all turns out well for you and that you'll be very happy. I love you dearly, little brother. If you're as happy as Bernard and I, then you'll be very lucky. And isn't Graydon a knockout of a kid? When our little Maurice died, we were both devastated. And then Bernard adopted Graydon without my even asking him, which I loved him even more for. So Graydon's going to be the next Count de Belleville, though I hope not for a damned long time. This champagne isn't bad, but it isn't very good."

"Mother got it from her bootlegger. It was the best he could find."

"One great advantage of living in France: no prohibition. What a stupid idea. France is falling apart at the seams, politically, but it's still the greatest place in the world to live."

"You don't miss America?"

"Oh yes, but I love my life. I feel almost as French as I do American. And I adore my husband. You know all those silly French farces about French husbands always cheating on their wives? Well, maybe some do, but mine doesn't. We're really crazy about each other. Isn't that wonderful?"

"It certainly is. I'm glad you're so happy."

" 'Happy' doesn't begin to describe it. And I hope the same thing happens to you and Laura."

"It will."

She gave him a kiss, then finished her champagne.

Johnny Savage was dying.

The old man, who had lost a leg in the Spanish-American War—an event that now seemed like ancient history—had never recovered his health after the car accident that put him in a wheelchair for the rest of his life. But two days after Gloria's wedding, he suffered another stroke that was much worse than the first and, the doctor warned Rachel, would probably kill him before long. Rachel, who had adored her husband for so many years, took the news with resignation, outwardly, although inwardly it broke her heart. She called both Nick and Brook, who was still in town. They hurried to the hospital, meeting their mother outside Johnny's room. "It may be your last chance to see him," she said as her children embraced her.

"Is he conscious?" Brook asked.

"He drifts in and out. He can barely talk. It's so sad when I think of how strong he used to be."

She was as usual maintaining her composure, but there were tears in her eyes. Nick squeezed her arm affectionately, then opened the door and went in the room, Brook and Rachel behind him. Johnny was in the bed, looking extremely fragile. Although his eyes were shut, when his children came up to the bed, he opened them and looked at his son. Nick was shocked at how rheumy his eyes looked. He leaned down to kiss his forehead.

"Hi, Dad," he whispered.

A tear appeared in the old man's right eye as he tried to mumble something. Nick leaned down to try and understand what he was saying.

"I'm so proud of the way you turned out," he whispered, slurring his words. "There were times I thought you were going to be a nothing. Or worse, like that bastard, Cesare. But you came through, Nick, and I love you the more for it."

Nick kissed his forehead.

"You're the head of the family now. Take good care of them . . . and your dear, sweet mother."

"I will, Dad. And we all love you. Brook's here."

Brook came up beside her brother, who moved a bit so she could lean down and kiss her father.

"Daddy," she whispered.

The old man looked at her and his thin lips smiled slightly.

"My baby Brook," he said as she squeezed his hand.

"Not so much a baby any longer," she said with a smile.

"You'll always be a baby to me. My beautiful baby Brookie. I'm so . . . ." He hesitated, closing his eyes a moment. Brook wondered if he'd dozed off, but then he opened his eyes again. "I'm so glad you're happy now. You used to be so . . . ."

"Mixed up?" she volunteered.

"Yes . . . But you turned out well. Everything turned out pretty well after all, didn't it?"

"Oh yes, Daddy. Very well."

He closed his eyes again and mumbled something. She leaned closer to try and understand him.

"I'll miss all of you," he whispered.

Then he seemed to fall asleep. Brook kissed him again, then straightened and looked at her mother and brother. Rachel indicated they should leave, which they did, Nick quietly closing the door.

"He's had a good life," Rachel said, in the hallway. "That's about all any of us can ask for."

Johnny died the next day at the age of seventy-four. Many of the city's notables came to Campbell's Funeral Home to pay their respects to a man who had been involved with so many of the major events of the past decades. Rachel, looking beautiful in black, comported herself with dignity.

But when she got home and was alone, she wept for hours.

A week after the funeral, Nick had dinner with his mother in her apartment.

"Laura and I would like to get married next month," he said, "that is, unless you think it's too soon after Father's death."

"No, I don't believe in protracted mourning," Rachel said, sipping her soup. "What's done is done. But a month won't give you much time for planning."

"We don't want a big wedding. We're just going to have a simple ceremony in the house, then I'm taking her to Europe for our honeymoon. Brook and Bernard invited us to stay with them in Paris, which should be fun. Then we're going to London so she can meet Beatrice and Bruno. I told her about how he was persecuted by the Fascists when they were living in Rome, which horrified her. It's too bad, because I'd love to take her to Italy, where she's never been, but with the Fascists running the show over there I'll stay away."

"Would you consider going to Germany?"

"I hadn't thought of it. Why?"

"I'm afraid some of my other relatives may be in danger of persecution. Have you ever read a book called *Mein Kampf*? I believe it's been translated into English, though I read the German version."

"Is that by that German politician, somebody Hitler?"

"Adolf Hitler. The book is absolutely terrifying. He wants to kill all the Jews."

"Don't you think that's just political malarkey?"

"Perhaps. But perhaps not. I have a second cousin, a very talented young man named Fritz Lieber, who lives in Berlin. He has an older brother, Claus, who's studying medicine in Vienna, so Claus is safe."

"Safe from what?"

"From the Nazis."

"But they're not even in power!"

"They may very well soon be. Anyway, Fritz is a pianist who's studied with an acquaintance of mine, the pianist and conductor Edwin Fischer, whose wife, by the way, is a descendant of Felix Mendelssohn. Edwin tells me he thinks Fritz has a brilliant future as a concert pianist. Unfortunately, he has little money and keeps himself going by playing the piano in a rather seedy Berlin nightclub.

"When Edwin told me about him at a cocktail party here in New York, I wrote Fritz a letter urging him to leave Germany. He wrote me back thanking me, but he loves Berlin and says there's absolutely no danger, but I think he's wrong. Would you consider going to Berlin and talking to this Fritz Lieber?"

"Of course, if you want me to. We can go there first, then on to Paris. But what could I say to him?"

"Try to convince him to get out of Germany. I'll even offer him a sum of money if he'll go."

He reached over and took her hand.

"I'd do anything for you, you know that. And I'll do my best to help him. But what if he says no?"

His mother's face, still beautiful despite the wrinkles, looked thoughtful.

"Then there's nothing more we can do. But we must make an effort. We must try. If he doesn't agree, he'll have to face the consequences, if there are any. Who knows? Maybe Hitler's just a rabble-rouser, playing on the Germans' anti-Semitism to get votes. But the anti-Semitism is there. I know. My family knows."

PART TWO

DECADENCE, GERMAN STYLE: 1932–1934

7   A SPOTLIGHT HIT A YOUNG man dressed in drag as Marlene Dietrich in *The Blue Angel*. He was wearing a black silk hat, a black corset, black net stockings attached to the corset with red snaps and silver shoes with stiletto heels. He was straddling a black chair, his long, shaved legs wrapped suggestively around the chair legs, his gloved hands leaning on the back of the chair as he started singing *Falling in Love Again*, accompanied by an upright piano in front of the small stage played by a handsome young man in a tux.

"Falling in love again, never wanted to . . ."

The smoke-filled cabaret was the Eldorado on the Motzstrasse in Berlin, and more than half of the audience was either women dressed as men or men dressed as women, their faces heavily made-up, their eyebrows plucked. Nick and Laura, now on their honeymoon, were at one of the round tables watching the show and drinking tea, much to the disgust of their waiter. But Nick earned his smile by passing him a ten dollar bill American and a scribbled note, asking him to give it to the piano player.

"Men gather to me like moths around the flame,
And if their wings burn I know I'm not to blame."

At the end of the song, the rather shabby red velvet curtain jerked across the small stage and the house lights turned up as the audience applauded, then started talking. Laura looked around the crowded room, then said to Nick: "I wonder if your mother has any idea what kind of a cabaret this is."

"She said it was seedy, which is one way to describe it. There's nothing like this in New York."

"Don't be so sure."

"Well, maybe in Greenwich Village. Here comes Fritz."

The tall, thin young piano player was making his way through the tables. He was very good-looking and had thick, blond hair.

"He looks like a Nazi poster boy," Laura said in admiring tones. "Really smashing."

"Nick Savage," the young man said, extending his hand. "Your mother wrote me you were coming. Welcome to Berlin."

His English was excellent. Nick stood up to shake his hand, then introduced him to Laura. "Can we buy you a drink?"

"I get booze on the house." Fritz joined them, sitting beside Laura. "So, how did you like the show?"

"I don't think it would play very well in Illinois," Nick said.

Fritz laughed.

"You have a point. *Eine fleische vin blanc, bitte,*" he said to the waiter. "You don't drink?" he asked Nick.

"Lost the habit during Prohibition," he replied.

"Ah yes, the noble experiment which didn't quite work out. An insane idea. What's life without alcohol? And how is your mother?"

"She's fine."

"I know she sent you to try and talk me into leaving Germany, but you might as well save your breath. Berlin's my home, and I love it. The Nazis are a bunch of hoodlums, but when Hitler gets in power, which he probably will eventually, the so-called respectable elements will tame him. Cigarette?" He offered Laura a Rothman, but she shook her head. He lit one for himself and sent a cloud of smoke to the tin ceiling. "So, I'm free during the day. I'd love to give you a tour tomorrow, if you'd like. Your mother said you'd be staying at the Adlon?"

"That's right."

"A lovely hotel. The best."

"Why don't you join us there for lunch tomorrow, then perhaps you could give us a tour."

"Excellent. Shall we say one o'clock?" He exhaled. "So you Americans have a new president, this Mr. Roosevelt. Your mother wrote me that you had raised money for him. What's he like?"

"An absolutely charming man," Nick said. "Laura and I are going to his inauguration in March after our honeymoon."

"Do you think Mr. Roosevelt would like our Fuehrer?"

"I don't think so. Mr. Roosevelt's a gentleman."

Fritz stared at him, then burst into laughter.

The waiter delivered Fritz the glass of white wine, then set a telephone on the table and whispered something in his ear.

"Excuse me," Fritz said, picking up the phone. "It's Edmund, my boyfriend." He began speaking in German as Nick and Laura exchanged looks.

The Adlon was Berlin's best hotel, an imposing, neoclassic stone building at number one Unter den Linden, Berlin's Park Avenue, near the Brandenburg Gate and across the street from the British Embassy. The Adlon had been the inspiration for Vicki Baum's famous play, *Grand Hotel*, which was made into a movie starring Garbo, Joan Crawford, and John Barrymore.

The next day, Nick and Laura met Fritz in the lobby shortly after one, and they went to the dining room, which was filled with an elegant crowd of well-dressed people, where the maître d' led them to a table by a window overlooking the rear garden. The dining room was filled with many potted palms, and a trio consisting of a violin, cellist, and pianist were at one end of the room playing Strauss waltzes and operetta hits.

After they had ordered, Nick said, "I know you don't want to leave Germany. But if the Nazis get in power—and they seem to be pretty popular around here—wouldn't you change your mind?"

Fritz shrugged as he lit a cigarette and the waiter served him a glass of wine.

"I doubt it."

"My mother will arrange for you to have ten thousand dollars if you leave Germany and come to America."

Fritz looked surprised.

"Ten thousand dollars?" he said. "That's a lot of money. I'm very flattered that your mother thinks I'm worth that kind of money, and she certainly is a generous woman. But you see, I'm protected."

"How do you mean?"

"My friend, Edmund, is a high-ranking officer in the S.A. The Brownshirts. Nothing can ever happen to me. Don't you understand?"

"You mean, your friend is a Nazi?" Nick said with disbelief.

"Oh yes. And a very important one. He's very close to Ernst Roehm, who's the second most powerful man in the party after Hitler himself. So you see, I'm as safe here as I would be in New York. Perhaps even safer. We have very little crime in Germany, and I hear that New York can be quite dangerous." He finished his wine. "But I'm very touched by your mother's offer. Please tell her I appreciate her concern."

"Yes," Nick said. "I will."

The waiter served the first course, a *celeri rémoulade*.

Nick had arranged with one of the hotel's concierges to hire a car and driver, and after lunch he, Laura, and Fritz climbed in the Mercedes in front of the hotel and commenced a tour of the city. In the eighteenth century, Berlin had been nothing more than a remote, sandy capital of Prussia, itself one of over three hundred sovereign states that jostled for power and influence within the ancient Holy Roman Empire. But by the nineteenth century, Prussia had emerged as the dominant state in Germany. And after Bismarck's defeat of Austria and, later, France in the Franco-Prussian War, Berlin became the capital of modern Germany and entered its richest period, becoming one of the great capitals of Europe. Though it lacked the dazzling beauty of Paris—its architecture tended to be heavy and rather pompous—the city had beautiful parks, in particular the Tiergarten, the Central Park of Berlin, and its wide thoroughfares boasted impressive shops and theaters.

Fritz first showed them the major tourist attractions such as the empty Royal Palace, the Berlin Opera, the Kaiser Wilhelm Memorial Church, and, most notably, the Reichstag.

After touring the fashionable districts in the west side of the city such as Charlottenburg and Spandau, Fritz said, "Now I'll show you where my family came from sixty years ago. It's called the Berlin Scheunenviertel, the district of the poorer, Eastern European Jews." He directed the driver in German, and the Mercedes drove east to the Prenzlauer Strasse. Although Nick was technically a Jew because of his mother, Rachel, he didn't think of himself as "Jewish" and admittedly knew little of Jewish traditions or religion. Through his mother, he had connections to the increasingly powerful New York "Our Crowd" families of rich Jews who themselves, for the most part, while observing the Jewish religion, otherwise had blended with time into the New York melting pot, Park and Fifth Avenues being a long way from the ghettoes of the Lower East Side. It was these Our Crowd Jewish families who had contributed most of the money Nick had raised for Roosevelt's campaign.

But now as Nick saw men in caftans and hats, many of them with *peyes*, walking between Alexanderplatz, Hackescher Markt, and Oranienburger Strasse; when he saw the fruit and vegetable stands, butchers, potato vendors, the small workshops, cobblers and tailor shops hidden away in courtyards and factory lofts; something resonated in his genes, because this was partly his world—as much, in a way, as Sutton Place.

"With all of Hitler's rantings about Jews," he said to Fritz, "no one seems particularly concerned. I mean, it looks like, I don't know, business as usual."

"Oh, it is. Definitely. Business as usual."

"Let's leave Berlin in the morning," Laura said that night as she prepared for bed. "Let's go to Paris. I want to see Brook and Bernard. Besides, I've seen enough here."

"Yes," Nick said, "I agree. I mean, the city's handsome in a rather heavy way, and the people certainly seem content—better off than New Yorkers—but there's something about the place that gives me the creeps, for all that Fritz shrugs the Nazis off."

"Besides," Laura said as she climbed in bed beside him, "I have some rather exciting news, which I didn't want to tell you before because I didn't want to get your hopes up. At Gloria's wedding, I told Brook about my heart problem, and she told me she knows a certain Doctor Alain Kleinwort, who's the leading heart specialist in Europe. She's arranging an appointment for me to see him when we get to Paris. Who knows? Maybe we can have children after all."

"Well, you can see him, which is probably a good idea. But I'm certainly not going to endanger you just to have some kids."

"But Nick, darling, I know you want them. I want them, too. And if Doctor Kleinwort says it's safe, then I want to have them with you. At least one."

Nick looked at her tenderly. Then he took her in his arms and hugged her.

"God, I love you so much," he whispered. "If anything happened to you . . ."

She put her finger on his lips.

"We won't take any chances," she said. "We'll only do it if the doctor says it's safe."

In Paris, Nick and Laura had a glorious time staying with Brook and Bernard in their townhouse on the Avenue Foch and their château in Versailles. The de Belleville marriage was a great success, and Nick was delighted to see that his sister was devoted to her second husband, her first marriage to Graydon's father having been a disaster. The de Belle-villes moved in a fast set, and the visit was climaxed by a fabulous cos-tume party on an island in the Bois de Boulogne given by Prince Jean-Louis de Faucigny-Lucinge and Baron Nicolas de Gunzburg, the son of an extremely rich Jewish banker. Elsa Maxwell came dressed as Em-peror Napoleon III, Coco Chanel dressed as a courtesan of the Second Empire, Brook came as the Empress Eugénie, Nick costumed as Baude-laire and Laura went as a chambermaid. It was all great fun and extremely glamorous.

"Don't be fooled by all the glitter," Bernard said to Nick as he drank champagne by a fountain. "France is riddled with corruption and deca-dence. The France I love is dying, killed by the war."

"But we won," Nick said.

"Did we? I wonder. So many Frenchmen were slaughtered, we've lost our guts. If we're ever challenged again, I think we'd cave in. It's very depressing to me. I mean, look around you. Parties, parties, parties. That's all we're interested in now. Parties and sex. That's why Brook and I find Palestine so invigorating and exciting. Those people are building a home-land over there, and they believe in it. Their enthusiasm is wonderful."

"Do you think the Arabs will ever settle with the Jews?"

"What's to 'settle'? We buy their land at damned good prices, which the landowners are more than eager to do, then the Arabs whose land was bought start screaming that we've stolen their land! If I buy a car from you, have I stolen it? Of course not. No one's stealing the land in Palestine, we're buying it for the settlements. And Brook and I are thrilled to be part of the process: it's given our lives a meaning and serenity that we cherish."

"Well, I certainly can see it. I've never seen Brook so happy."

Nick reflected that his family's involvement with Palestine had begun long before the Balfour Declaration, dating back to his mother's marriage to one of the Rothschilds, a cousin of the Baron Edmund de Rothschild who had begun pouring millions into what was then considered barren desert. If anyone could be said to have founded what would become Israel, it was this fabulously wealthy man. Nick was glad that his sister and brother-in-law were continuing that tradition.

On the third morning of their stay, Laura went to her appointment with Dr. Kleinwort, whose office was on the Avenue Victor Hugo. Nick wanted to go with her, but she insisted on going by herself. "This is a very private thing for me," she told him. "I'm nervous as a cat, because I so hope it goes well. You understand, don't you?"

"Of course," Nick said, giving her a kiss.

When she returned two hours later, she looked radiant.

"The doctor says I'm all right!" she exclaimed, throwing her arms around Nick.

Nick was amazed and delighted.

"You're sure?" he said.

"Absolutely! The doctor says I'm fine! Well . . ." She hesitated. "He says there's some damage to my heart and of course a pregnancy always has risks, but he feels confident I can have a child safely. Isn't it wonderful?"

"Yes, it's wonderful. In fact, it's fabulous."

Nick was so happy, he started to cry.

And as she gazed into Nick's eyes and her happiness reflected in his, so did Laura.

When they returned to America, Nick and Laura went to the inauguration of Franklin Delano Roosevelt, who had won the election by a landslide. It was a windy, rainy Saturday, March 4, 1933, but Roosevelt's inspiring

Inaugural Address, in which he uttered the famous line "We have nothing to fear but fear itself," was a thrilling moment for millions of Americans listening in on radio.

That night, at the Inaugural Ball, Nick, who had raised so much money for the Roosevelt campaign, twirled his beloved Laura around the ballroom and said, "we're broke."

Laura, thinking he was kidding, said, "What?"

"Tomorrow, the new president is going to proclaim a bank holiday."

"What's that mean?"

"It means that all the banks in the country are going to be closed for a while so that panicky investors don't pull out all their money and cause more bank failures. So there's not going to be any money. How much do you have?"

"Oh, I don't know, maybe fifteen dollars."

"And I have thirty-six dollars. That's all the money we have. Isn't it going to be fun?"

Laura looked at him and laughed.

"You're crazy," she said. "How can we live on that?"

"We'll live on love."

And he kissed her.

"Well," she laughed, "movies are only twenty-five cents. And babies are free."

"What do you mean?"

"I was going to save this till midnight, but I can't wait that long. This afternoon, while you were with Mr. Roosevelt, I went to see a doctor and guess what? I'm pregnant."

On a night when much of America was whooping with joy, Nick's whoop was the loudest of all.

8

THE SNAPPY BLACK 1932 PACKARD model KB cabriolet pulled through the imposing whitewashed brick gates and started up a beautifully landscaped drive.

"Gosh," Chester Wood said as he drove, "I'm just so darned thrilled to have you out here, Gloria. I just can't tell you how excited I am."

Gloria Gilmore Savage Wood was sitting next to him, looking stunning in a white fox-trimmed coat and a smart hat with a white feather. "It's exciting for me to be here, Chester," she said.

"And there it is: Whitehall."

An imposing white brick mansion was looming ahead of them. It was two stories high and was a pleasing version of a southern colonial house, fronted by a two-story, four-column portico that was a bit reminiscent of the White House. Chester and Gloria had spent three days of their honeymoon in Chicago, living it up, and then had driven down to Chester's summer home on Lake Wawasee, the lovely lake near Fort Wayne, where they had spent another week thoroughly enjoying themselves. Now they had arrived at his hundred-acre farm north of Indianapolis in the small suburb of Carmel.

"It's beautiful," Gloria said, in an impressed voice.

"Do you like it?" he said, pleased as punch.

"Absolutely."

"My late wife and I built it four years ago. She did all the decorating herself, with the help of a professional. Helen had such great taste. Poor dear: She didn't have much time to enjoy the place. Ah, there's William, the butler. He'll take care of you, give you anything you want. His son's one of the caddies at the country club . . . fine young man. I'm going to help him go to college, one of the Negro colleges like Howard. He's smart as a whip."

Chester parked the car in front of the house. A tall, distinguished-looking man in a white jacket opened the door on Gloria's side.

"Welcome to Whitehall, Mrs. Wood," he said. "And welcome to Indianapolis, ma'am."

"Thank you, William," Gloria said as she got out of the gorgeous car and looked around. It was a lovely spring day in 1933, and the sky was a brilliant blue with an occasional popcorn cloud drifting slowly in the light breeze.

"I'll carry your bags, ma'am," William went on as his employer got out of the car and came around to Gloria. They climbed the three steps to the portico, then crossed to the front door, which was surmounted by a classic stone pointed pediment, with sidelights on either side of the door. Inside, a broad hall with a marble floor bisected the house, going all the way through to a rear door that gave out onto yet another rear portico overlooking a lake. The hall, which was twenty feet wide, was hung on both sides by two life-size portraits, one of Chester, looking properly tycoonish, and across from him a portrait of his late wife, looking lovely in a white satin evening dress. At the front end of the hall, a graceful curving staircase led to the second floor.

"If you'll follow me, ma'am," William said, holding Gloria's two suitcases, "I'll take you to your room."

He started up the stair.

"When you come down," Chester said to Gloria, "we can have cocktails. I have some champagne on ice for you."

"How lovely."

Gloria smiled at him, then started up the curved stair.

When she came downstairs an hour later, having bathed and changed into a dark blue dress that displayed her ample breasts to full advantage, she was surprised to hear organ music.

"Mr. Wood's in there, ma'am," a smiling William said, pointing to a room off the hall. Gloria went through a door to see Chester seated at the console of a pipe organ, which, like the pipe organs in the recently opened Radio City Music Hall, was built into a recess that could be closed off, in this case by wooden doors. Chester was playing "I Love You Truly"— quite well, actually—and the music boomed through the big house. When he finished, he turned and smiled at her.

"Did you like it?" he asked, jumping off the organ bench.

"Chester, you amaze me! You're really good!"

"Well, you know how I love movies. I used to go to the big picture palaces when I was going around the country selling my plumbing fixtures and I'd sit there and listen to those big Wurlitzers and I said to myself, 'Chester, old boy, one day you're going to have a pipe organ and you're going to learn how to play it.' So when we built this house, I had an organ company come out from Boston and install me one. It's got two manuals and over four thousand pipes. They're all in the basement, and the sound comes up through vents in the walls. Good grief, you look gorgeous in that dress. You really are the most beautiful woman in the world."

"Judging from the painting in the hall, Helen was a knockout herself."

He looked slightly sad.

"Yes, she was," he said. "A great beauty and a sweet woman." He brightened. "Now, how about some of that champagne?"

"Sounds lovely."

He lead her into a paneled library that had a built-in bar. She sat on one of the bar stools as he pulled a bottle of champagne from an ice bucket and popped its cork, filling two glasses.

"How are the twins?" he asked.

"They're fine. They're staying with their grandmother in New York until they finish the school term."

"Well." He handed her a glass. "Cheers. And it's just swell to have you in Indiana."

They clicked glasses, and she took a sip.

"Everybody's dying to meet you tomorrow night," he went on. "I've asked thirty for a sit-down dinner."

"Thirty? Can you seat that many?"

"Oh yes. Wait till you see the dining room. Anyway, everyone's real excited. It's not very often we get a movie star in Indianapolis. Finish your drink, then we'll go in for dinner."

The dining room, which was off the great hall opposite the drawing room, was sixty feet long and twenty feet wide, its walls covered with exquisite Chinese wallpaper depicting ladies and gentlemen of the imperial court in an eighteenth-century garden. Down the center of the room was a long mahogany table with silver candlesticks and a huge centerpiece of gorgeous flowers. The windows overlooking the rear lake were hung with rich gold brocade curtains. Chester seated her at one end of the table.

"There's a little surprise for you in your napkin," he said.

"There is?"

She unfolded her napkin. Inside was a magnificent diamond and ruby bracelet.

"Oh, Chester!" she exclaimed, holding it up. "It's gorgeous!"

"Here, I'll put it on for you."

He attached it to her right wrist, then raised her hand to his mouth and kissed it.

"I'm just crazy about you," he whispered.

Gloria looked at this sweet, sincere man and thought, *"some compromises aren't so bad after all."*

Sixteen-year-old Richard Shelby stood at the Whitehall butler's pantry door and stared through the small, diamond-shaped window at the world that was familiar to him, because his father was the butler, but also was as alien to him as Mars. The dining room, with its Chinese wallpaper and crystal chandelier, was a thing of rare beauty, the table extended to its full length to seat the thirty guests, the crème de la crème of Indianapolis society who had been invited to meet Gloria the movie star, the new Mrs. Wood.

"Here, Richard." The voice behind him jolted him out of his reverie. "Pass this tray." It was Rosa Carter, the caterer for the evening, a middle-aged woman who was even whiter than Richard and who had become one of the most prosperous colored persons in Indianapolis because of her cooking and organizing skills ("colored" was the politically correct term for the period. A "colored gentleman" or "colored lady" was the polite way for whites to refer to blacks they liked. Blacks they didn't like was another thing). Rosa handed Richard a silver tray filled with little hot dogs on toothpicks, one of her specialties.

"Yes, ma'am," he said. "When are they going to sit down?"

"In twenty minutes. Any longer than that, and they'll all be drunk."

Richard grinned. Though one of the things the white population of the city complained about most was the black population's penchant for drunkenness, Richard had seen enough of Indianpolis's white society to know that it was in no position to moralize about booze. Taking the tray, he pushed open the door and went through the empty dining room across the great hall to the drawing room, which was packed with women in evening gowns and men in tuxedos—or, as Richard had learned from the late Mrs. Wood, who had taken an interest in the handsome young man, more properly called "dinner jackets." Richard's mind was hungry, and he never missed an opportunity to pick up information about this world so unlike his own.

As was usual at most gatherings above the level of church socials of the period, everyone was smoking. Fortunately, the drawing room's smooth plaster ceiling was eighteen feet high so that the smoke had a chance to dissipate. It was a grand room, a room Richard never failed to admire: sixty feet by thirty, with tall windows overlooking the lake, as in the dining room, it was filled with English and French antiques the late Mrs. Wood had bought in New York and London, along with a number of eighteenth-century English portraits and landscapes, which she had thought were Gainsboroughs, Romneys, and Lawrences (although several of them later turned out to be fakes). At the opposite end of the room, a handsome marble mantel was surmounted by a splendid eighteenth-century gilt mirror, the elaborate frame of which was carved to represent a palm leaf wreathe. In the center of the room was a round, early nineteenth-century English rent table above which hung a glittering crystal chandelier; graceful tables and chairs filled the rest of the room with conversation groupings. The scene was as well-dressed as one of the Hollywood society movies that Richard so loved. Richard had no illusions about the difficult goal he had set for himself. Although Indiana had fought on the Union side in the Civil War, it was still very southern in its racial attitudes, it had the highest Ku Klux Klan membership of any state in the country, and Richard could remember, a mere nine years before, in 1924, when a black man had been lynched in nearby Marion, Indiana, to the enthusiastic applause of the onlooking whites. Although Richard's grandmother had been a slave and his grandfather a Kentucky slaveowner, which made his skin café au lait, he knew that, even if he were as white as a lily, an invisible wall of prejudice would always surround him. But still, with the optimism of the young, he dreamed of somehow breaching that wall.

"Hot dog, ma'am?" he said to a lady in a white evening gown who was on her third martini and looking a bit bleary-eyed.

"Oh. Thanks."

She took one and popped it into her mouth, giving Richard a gin-soaked look of appreciation. Her lover, to whom she was talking, also took one.

"Hello, Richard," he said. "How are you?"

"Good evening, Mr. Lewis. I'm fine."

Mr. Lewis, the younger son of an important local banker, used Richard at the country club as his caddie.

"I've got a foursome at ten in the morning. Can you caddie me?"

"Be glad to, sir. I'll see you then."

Richard moved on through the crowd until he came to Chester and Gloria.

"Ah, Richard," Chester said, patting his shoulder and smiling. "I want you to meet my new wife. You're probably too young to have seen any of her movies, but ten years ago she was right on top in Hollywood. Gloria, this is the fine young man I told you about, Richard Shelby, William's son. I think Richard has a great future."

Gloria, who was wearing a hip-hugging white satin dress that exposed as much of her upper body as decency allowed, as well as four thick diamond bracelets and the diamond and ruby necklace Chester had given her as a wedding present, looked at the young man in the white jacket and gave him her most luscious smile.

"How do you do, Richard?" she said. "You didn't tell me he's an Adonis, darling."

Chester looked a bit bewildered.

"Well, it never occurred to me," he said. "But yes, come to think of it, Richard's a fine-looking young man. And bright as a penny. Great swimmer, too. I let him use the pool in the basement. How's it going in the kitchen, Richard?"

"Rosa says we have to get everybody at the table soon or they'll all be drunk."

Gloria burst into laughter.

"I think Rosa's right!" she exclaimed.

"Darling, I want you to meet a very powerful and very crazy and rather dangerous man," Chester said to his bride as he led her through the crowd at Whitehall. "His name is Bennet Kinkaid, and he's the second richest man in Indianapolis after me. He owns a number of newspapers and radio stations, he's very right-wing and he hates my guts."

"Why?" Gloria asked.

"Oh, business reasons. Plus he thinks I'm too liberal for his tastes. He's with his daughter, Deirdre, who's also rather odd."

He led Gloria up to a tall, very thin man in a dinner jacket whose rather skull-like face was totally devoid of hair, including eyebrows. She judged that Bennet Kinkaid was somewhere in his fifties. Standing beside him was a statuesque, very attractive woman in a beaded evening dress that revealed a terrific figure. She had auburn hair, green eyes, and wore very conservative, but expensive jewelry in great taste.

"Bennet, Deirdre," Chester said, "I wanted you to meet my new wife, Gloria."

Gloria smiled and extended her hand.

"I'm so glad to meet you both," she said.

Bennet Kinkaid shook her hand.

"You're as glamorous as we've heard," he said. "And of course, I was an admirer of your films."

"How very kind."

"My daughter, Deirdre."

Gloria turned to the twenty-nine-year-old woman, whose eyes had a rather strange look to them.

"I've never met a film star," Deirdre said, shaking Gloria's hand. "For that matter, I've never met an actress."

"What a limited life you've led," Gloria said, rather frostily.

"Oh, but I did study drama at Wellesley."

"How fascinating."

"Yes, we put on productions of classic English theater. I enjoyed acting. It's so refreshing."

"And what did you star in, dear? *She Stoops to Conquer*?"

Deirdre's eyes widened slightly. Gloria turned back to Bennet, who said, "Now that you're here in Indianapolis, we hope we can call on you to help in some of our local cultural activities. We're all eager to put Indianapolis on the cultural map."

"Oh, I'm very interested in that," Gloria said, shaking her left arm slightly to move her diamond bracelets. "I'm so vitally interested in the ballet. I assume there's no ballet here?"

Bennet looked a bit baffled.

"Ballet? Uh, no."

"I'd love to get involved with a project to bring ballet to Indianapolis. I can see a beautiful new theater, and then the opening night when Indianapolis puts on the most brilliant new production of *Swan Lake*. Who knows? There may be lurking somewhere in the corn fields of Indiana a young Nijinsky!"

Bennet Kinkaid looked even more baffled.

"Yes, that's exactly what we need in Indiana in Nineteen-thirty-three: ballet and a new Nijinsky."

"I know you think I'm mad, Mr. Kinkaid. But what is life without art and culture? Well, we'll talk about it more later. So delighted to have met both of you."

She smiled and moved off on Chester's arm.

"Well, you certainly baffled them," her husband chuckled. "Ballet in Indianapolis? I love it."

"I wasn't kidding, darling," Gloria said. "I'd love to turn this town into a cultural jewel. I mean it."

Chester looked at his bride with burning intensity.

"My God, I think you do mean it," he said. "What a splendid idea!"

"Would you back me?"

"I'd back you in anything, Gloria. You're the jewel of my life."

She smiled and leaned over to kiss his cheek.

"It's a lovely party, darling," she said. "And I thank you for it. But what's wrong with Bennet Kinkaid? He doesn't seem to have any hair."

"He has a disease called alopecia," Chester whispered. "They say he doesn't even have any pubic hair!"

"It's not the pubic hair that counts, darling. It's what's underneath it that matters."

Chester Wood, the farmboy from Indiana who had made millions, doubled over with laughter, to his guests' surprise.

Shortly after dawn on the morning of June 30, 1934, a long column of cars headed away from the Munich airport and started south toward the lovely resort of Bad Wiesee on the lake called the Tegern See, not far from the Austrian border. In the lead Mercedes was Adolf Hitler and his propaganda minister, Joseph Goebbels. Hitler was in a foul mood, as close to being hysterical as Goebbels had ever seen—and Hitler was well-known for his screaming fits. The German chancellor's near-totalitarian power was experiencing its most serious crisis since his election to the Chancellory of Germany the previous year. For some time, the aristocratic German General Staff had been increasingly critical of the Nazi Brownshirts, the thuggish private army that had been so responsible for bringing Hitler to power in the first place. Now Ernst Roehm, the leader of the Brownshirts, was insisting that the Nazis continue their revolution against the establishment of rich industrialists and landowners. The industrialists and landowners, in turn, were demanding a cessation of the general terror organized by the Nazis, as well as the persecution of the Jews and the churches. Tensions in Berlin had mounted to the point that Hitler had been warned that if he did not curb the Brownshirts, martial law would be declared and control of the country given over to the army. For fourteen years, Roehm had been Hitler's closest confidant. But on this misty morning in the Bavarian Alps, Roehm's fate was sealed.

Despite many warnings, the brawny and brutal head of the Brownshirts apparently had little inkling of what lay in store for him. He and a number of top Brownshirt officials had taken over the Hanslbauer Hotel on the shores of the Tegern See and spent a night of heavy drinking, which ended in a drunken orgy in which many of the Brownshirts stumbled off to bed with their boyfriends, Roehm being a predatory homosexual.

When the column of cars arrived at the Hanslbauer Hotel, a number of Gestapo men jumped out and stormed the hotel, dragging many of the still-drunken men with their lovers out of their beds and taking them outside the hotel where they were summarily shot. Roehm himself, after a screaming scene with Hitler, was taken to a Munich prison where he was given a pistol and fifteen minutes to kill himself. When he failed to do so, two S.S. men entered his cell and shot him point-blank.

One of the Brownshirts who was dragged from his bed and shot was Edmund Heines, the S. A. Obergruppenfuehrer of Silesia, a convicted murderer with a girlish face and a muscular body. Standing by his side as the stormtroopers fired their guns was Heines's long-time lover, a bewildered young piano player named Fritz Lieber.

Fritz died having no idea why.

PART THREE

OF LOVE BEREFT: 1933–1934

9

BY CHRISTMAS 1933, WHAT FEW Americans still thought there could be a quick-fix end to the Depression were becoming disenchanted. Despite the furious activity of the early New Deal, which had managed to stem panic and put many people back to work, the bad times dragged on. Even so, the American love of fun couldn't be completely stifled. Hollywood continued to churn out films of varying quality, musicians like Louis Armstrong and Duke Ellington filled the air with wonderful jazz, Broadway mounted endless cheery musicals, and in a small Peachtree Street apartment in Atlanta, a young reporter named Margaret Mitchell continued to peck away at her typewriter on a seemingly interminable Civil War novel that still had no title and whose vixenish heroine was named Pansy O'Hara.

On Wall Street, business was slow. The Savage Bank limped along, but Nick, an eternal optimist, assumed somewhere along the line things would pick up. And meanwhile, he was wildly in love with his pregnant wife, Laura. She had hired the eminent decorator Elsie de Wolfe to help her redo the Sutton Place house, and a room on the second floor was turned into a nursery, the choice of color awaiting the revealing of the baby's sex.

Then, one snowy night, Nick and Laura were seated in their small dining room eating a candlelit dinner of chicken pot pie as, outside, a snappy breeze swirled the snowflakes in eddies over the dark river. They had been discussing names for the baby for several days, and they had finally decided on Amanda if it were a girl, Laura having a great-aunt Amanda and she had always been partial to the name. The possibility of a boy had caused some disagreement. Nick wanted to name him Justin after his grandfather, but Laura was opting for Walter, after her late father.

"I don't know," Nick said, dubiously. "Walter Savage sounds sort of blah, don't you think? Darling, what's wrong?"

She had dropped her fork on her plate and slumped back in her chair, rolling her head slightly back. Nick leapt up and hurried around the table to come to her. "Are you all right?"

He took her hand. She looked at him. Her face had gone pale.

"I just felt . . . dizzy . . ." she said, in a weak tone.

"Should I call a doctor?"

"Yes, perhaps you'd better."

He squeezed her hand a moment, then hurried into the next room to phone the doctor. When he returned to the dining room a few minutes later, he said, "He'll be here in ten minutes. He only lives a few blocks away. Do you want to go upstairs to bed?"

"I don't think I'm up to climbing the stairs."

"I'll carry you."

"Oh, darling, I'm so big, you'll strain your back."

"Don't be silly. You're light as a feather. Come on: allez oop."

He lifted her out of her chair then carried her to the entrance hall where he took her to their bedroom and laid her on their bed.

"Don't be worried, Nick," she said. "I'll be all right."

"Of course you're going to be all right." He leaned over to kiss her forehead. "You're strong as an ox."

She smiled.

"I love you very much," she whispered. "And we're going to have the most beautiful baby in the world."

After the doctor came, Nick sat in one of the upstairs bedrooms, nervously leafing through magazines. *There's nothing wrong with her,* he kept thinking. *This is just some women's problem.*

When, a half hour later, Dr. Simpson came out of the master bedroom, Nick put down the magazine and hurried out into the upstairs hall. The doctor, a tall, slim man in his forties with slicked-back black hair and a thin mustache, was wearing a well-tailored, double-breasted gray pinstripe suit and carrying his medical bag. He had the sleek manners of a Park Avenue practitioner.

"How is she?" Nick whispered as he came up to him.

"May we talk?"

"Yes, in here."

Nick led him into the empty nursery and turned on a light.

"I've called an ambulance," the doctor said. "And I've got her a private room at Lenox Hill . . ."

"Hospital?" Nick interrupted. "Then there is something wrong with her?"

Dr. Simpson, despite his smooth manner, was a compassionate man. He put his hand on Nick's shoulder. "I just want to take some tests," he said. "She'll probably be out tomorrow. You mustn't be alarmed, but I think to be on the safe side it's better she be around nurses tonight."

"But what is it? Something about the baby—?"

"When Laura first came to me four months ago, I gave her a physical exam, as I do with all my new patients. Took her blood pressure, that sort of thing. Then I checked her heart and found she had a rather irregular heartbeat, which I told her. She got rather upset and told me she was aware of it, that she had had rheumatic fever when she was a child and other doctors had told her she had a problem. But she begged me not to tell you, because she was so anxious to have a child by you. Well, this was unusual, to say the least, but I agreed not to say anything to you. There is, after all, a doctor-patient relationship. But now I think I made a mistake."

"But wait a minute," Nick said, his anxiety rising. "Laura went to a heart specialist in Paris—Dr. Kleinwort, who's supposed to be the best in Europe. He said there was absolutely nothing wrong with her, and she could have children safely."

"I know. She lied to you. Dr. Kleinwort told her not to risk a pregnancy, but she was so desperate to have children with you, she lied so you wouldn't worry."

"Oh my God, the poor darling . . . What can we do?"

"I don't want to say anything until I take some tests. Do you have a maid?"

"Yes, Mathilde, a French-Canadian girl. She's downstairs."

"You might ask her to put some things in a suitcase for Laura. I'll wait till the ambulance gets here."

Nick hesitated, a look of confusion and worry on his face. Then he hurried out of the room.

The next afternoon, a nervous Nick went to Lenox Hill Hospital and sat in one of the waiting rooms, leafing through a copy of *The Saturday*

Evening Post. After a short wait, Dr. Simpson came into the room and lit a cigarette.

"Well?" Nick said, putting aside the magazine. "How is she?"

"You can take her home."

Nick sighed with relief.

"Then there's nothing wrong with her?"

"Well, I didn't mean that."

"Then what did you mean?"

The doctor exhaled.

"I took an X ray of her heart. There is scar tissue in one part of the myocardium . . ."

"What's that?"

"The muscular tissue of the heart. It's in the left ventrical. Also, the mitral valve is somewhat deformed. All of this probably was caused by the rheumatic fever Laura had as a child."

"But she's never had any problems before—at least that I know of."

"I'm aware of that. But the condition of her heart may have gotten worse, possibly because of her pregnancy, although I can't say that for certain."

"But . . ." Nick gestured with frustration. "What should we do?"

The doctor took another drag on his cigarette, then put it out.

"I think we have to consider terminating the pregnancy."

"Why?"

"There is a possibility Laura's heart is too weak to survive childbirth. I'm not saying she'll die if she has the child, but I am saying there is a definite possibility of it. Of course, this is a decision you and she must make. But it has to be done soon, because it's already late. If you decide to abort the child, I can make the arrangements for you. I personally don't approve of abortions in most cases, but in this instance I definitely think it's something we have to consider."

"Oh my God, we've so looked forward to having this baby. . . ." Nick clenched his fists, then unclenched them. "But wouldn't there be a danger in an abortion? I mean, mightn't that damage her heart as much as having the child?"

"The danger is much less."

"Can't something be done to fix her heart?"

"Not with the present technology."

Nick groaned slightly.

"Have you told her?" he asked, after a moment.

"No, I thought I should leave that to you. I'm sorry, Nick."

There were tears in Nick's eyes as he looked at the doctor.

"What would you do?" he asked, quietly. "I mean, if it were your wife?"

"I'd opt for the abortion."

"Oh my God."

Shaking his head sadly, he stood up.

"Do you want me to go with you?" Dr. Simpson asked.

"No. Let me tell her alone."

He left the waiting room and went down the hospital corridor to Laura's room where he knocked on the door, then opened it. Laura was sitting up in bed, looking so healthy and rested he could hardly believe she had a serious medical problem. He smiled at her as he came to her bed and kissed her.

"How are you feeling?" he asked.

"Not bad, actually. And the nurses are so nice here. By the way, thanks for the flowers."

She indicated a big bouquet on the bureau.

"Garden of Delights' finest. Well." He paused rather awkwardly. "You can get dressed now. The doctor says I can take you home."

"What else did he say?"

Another awkward hesitation. *Tell her!* he thought. But he couldn't.

"Let me guess," she said, patting the side of her bed for him to sit on, which he did. "It's my heart."

"Why did you lie to me about Dr. Kleinwort?"

"Oh my darling Nick, I knew you wouldn't let me have the baby, and I want it more than anything else in this world except you, of course. I take full responsibility for lying to you. When I was married to Morris, we were never home, we were always on the road to some polo match or golf tournament. But I'm going to have this baby. Now, what does the doctor want to do? Abort it?"

"Yes, and we have to do it soon."

"I thought that might be the case. Dr. Simpson is very suave, with a good bedside manner, but he's not that suave. The answer is no. We both want the baby, and I won't destroy the life of my child."

"But Laura, you have to think of yourself! There's a definite risk! We can adopt a baby . . ."

She took his hand.

"Save your breath, darling," she said. "I won't change my mind. If I die, well . . ." she shrugged. "I've had a good life, thanks mainly to you. If it's a short one, so be it. But I won't kill our child. It would be like killing part of you and me, which I could never bring myself to do. So kiss me, then take me home. And we won't say anything more about it."

He leaned over, put his arms around her and kissed her mouth. Then he pressed her against him. Again, there were tears in his eyes.

"I love you so much, Laura," he whispered. "I hope you're doing the right thing, but if something happens to you, oh God, it would destroy me, too."

She smiled at him as she ran her hand over his hair.

"No it wouldn't, Nick. You're a strong man and a wonderful man. You'll survive. And anyway, I'm not buried yet. I may surprise all of us and be around for another half century. Now, help me pack, darling. Then, come to think of it, you're going to take me out to lunch. This hospital food is ghastly, and I'm starving."

Laura went into labor five months later. She was rushed to the hospital and, as Nick agonized in the waiting room, she began a four-hour, extremely painful delivery. Finally, almost at midnight, Dr. Simpson came into the waiting room and said to Nick: "Congratulations. You have a lovely, seven pound, two-ounce daughter."

Nick's face lit up.

"And Laura?" he asked.

"She's fine, thank God. I'm very relieved."

"*You're* relieved?" Nick almost laughed. "What about me? Oh, Doc, that's wonderful news! Wonderful! Can I see her?"

"Laura's resting now. She's exhausted. The delivery wasn't easy. But you can see your daughter, if you'd like."

"Amanda! We're calling her Amanda."

"That's a lovely name. You want to come with me?"

Nick followed the doctor down several corridors teeming with nurses, doctors, and orderlies even at this late hour, until they reached a large window. Nick peered through into a big room filled with bassinets. The room was dimly lit to allow the babies to sleep, but there were enough night lights for Nick to see several nurses in attendance. When one of them spotted Dr. Simpson, she came to the door and stepped out into the hall.

"This is Mr. Savage," the doctor said. "He'd like to see his daughter."

"Yes, of course. She's such a beautiful baby."

The nurse went back inside and, after a moment, appeared at the window holding a sleeping baby. Nick stared at his newborn daughter.

"Oh my God," he whispered, "she *is* beautiful! Look, Doc, isn't she beautiful?"

"She is indeed." He looked at his watch. "Well, I'm going home. It's late. At any rate, congratulations again. I think we all have much to be thankful for."

They shook hands, and the doctor started down the corridor as a smiling Nick made funny faces at his daughter.

Dr. Simpson wanted Laura to stay in the hospital for ten days to make sure she was all right. Meanwhile, Nick, as excited by the successful birth as a teenager, enlisted his mother to buy baby clothes and arranged for Elsie de Wolfe to put up a cheery pink and white-striped wallpaper on the walls of the second floor nursery. The vivacious and clever Elsie also installed a pink carpet and put pink organdy curtains on the windows as well as buying a bookshelf for Amanda's future collection of dolls, making the room a sort of little girl's wonderland.

He went to the hospital twice a day to be with Laura and watched with the awe of a first-time father as she breast-fed the baby.

"Aren't babies wonderful?" he said, sitting beside Laura's bed.

"Yes, but wait till we have to change her diaper at three in the morning."

"I'll be the diaper-changer. You won't have to do a thing: You've already done your job, and done it beautifully, I might add. I was so afraid. . . . Well, I won't get into that now. It's over and you're well and Amanda is cuter than Shirley Temple. We're a very fortunate family."

"And a very happy family," Laura said as Amanda let go of her nipple and started crying. "Well, at least we *were*."

Rachel had hired a motherly Irish woman named Mrs. Hogan to be Amanda's nanny, and Mrs. Hogan had already moved into the Sutton Place house by the time Laura and Amanda came home from the hospital. To celebrate the occasion, Nick had cooked Laura's favorite dinner: roast beef and mashed potatoes with peas, a salad and fruit, and cheese for dessert. Nick was no great cook, but he had bought a copy of Fanny Farmer's cookbook and followed the recipes assiduously so that when he brought the roast in from the kitchen, the wonderful smell filled the dining room, prompting Laura to say: "You did this yourself? I'm impressed! It smells wonderful."

"I'm impressed, too," he said, putting the platter on the table. "In fact, I'm amazed. I think this is actually going to be good. Now, you like it rare, right?"

"Mmm. Bloody. And not too many mashed potatoes. I have to lose ten pounds."

"You can diet tomorrow. Tonight we celebrate. My wonderful wife is home, and our beautiful baby is upstairs in her pretty pink bedroom, and the stock market actually went up today, so perhaps this damned Depression is going to start going away . . . What's wrong?"

Laura had started gasping. Nick put down the carving knife and hurried to her end of the table.

"I can't breathe . . ." she whispered.

"Oh my God, Laura . . . Here, take some water . . ."

"Nick, call the doctor . . . I'm having terrible chest pains . . ."

"Oh my God . . . I'll be right back . . ."

He ran to the kitchen, banging through the swinging door and grabbing the phone off the wall, frantically dialing Dr. Simpson's number, which he had memorized.

"Mrs. Simpson?" he said. "This is Nick Savage. Is your husband there? Would you please tell him to come to my house immediately? Something's happening to my wife . . . Yes, please."

He hung up and ran back through the door into the dining room. Laura was lying back in her chair, gasping for breath, one hand on her chest. Nick rushed to her side.

"Nick, there's some medicine in my purse," she whispered. "Get it for me, please. It's in the front hall."

"Yes, of course."

He raced through the drawing room to the front hall, grabbed Laura's leather purse off a table and ran back to the dining room.

"Dr. Simpson gave it to me before I left the hospital, but I forgot about it," she whispered. Her face was turning a faint bluish color. "Give me a spoonful."

Nick was fumbling through the purse. He pulled out a small bottle.

"Is this it?"

"Yes. Hurry . . ."

His hands trembling, he unscrewed the cap and poured the fluid into a spoon, holding it up to her mouth. She ingested the fluid, then leaned back in the chair again.

"It's a little better," she whispered after a moment.

"Thank God. The doctor should be here soon. Oh my poor darling, should I take you up to bed?"

She forced a weak smile.

"No, I'll wait here. My sweet husband, you did everything to make my homecoming special, and here I've ruined it for you. . . ."

"No, no, it's not ruined. . . ."

"Hold me, Nick," she whispered. "I love you so. I love your strong arms."

Awkwardly, he knelt down and took her in his arms. She rested her head on his chest.

"You're going to be all right," he said.

"If not, it doesn't matter," she whispered. "We have Amanda, and I know you'll always be a good father to her, just as you've been a wonderful husband to me. It's odd . . . I'm not afraid . . ."

"I adore you, Laura. You've made my life so happy, and you're going to continue to . . ."

He stopped. She had started gurgling. Her body was trembling.

"Laura . . ."

She was gasping for air now.

"Oh God, Doctor Simpson, please get here. . . . Oh sweet Jesus, Laura, don't leave me . . . please don't leave me . . ."

"Nick . . . Good-bye, my darling. I love you."

Her eyes closed. Suddenly, her body stopped trembling.

"Mrs. Hogan!" he screamed. "Somebody . . ."

The front doorbell rang.

"Oh Christ, I hope he's not too late . . ."

He ran through the house and opened the front door. Dr. Simpson was standing outside, holding a medicine bag.

"Doctor, hurry . . . I don't know what happened . . ."

He ran back to the dining room, Dr. Simpson behind him. Laura was slumped forward in her chair, her head on the dining room table. Dr. Simpson took her wrist and felt it for a moment. Then he looked at Nick and slowly shook his head.

Nick sank to his knees beside the chair and took Laura's hand from the doctor, holding it to his lips and kissing it.

"Laura," he sobbed. "Come back, please. Come back. Don't leave me alone. Please come back." He looked at the doctor, tears streaming down his cheeks.

"What happened?" he sobbed.

"I can't tell yet. Will you allow me to do an autopsy?"

"Oh God, do you have to cut her up?"

"Yes."

"You can't do that . . . her beautiful body . . ."

He was hysterical now.

"Then we'll never know," the doctor said. "But I imagine her heart went into fibrillation."

"I don't know what that means. . . . Oh God, and we were so happy, just a few moments ago, and now . . ." Still holding Laura's hand, Nick stood up and shook his other fist at the ceiling.

"Damn you, God!" he howled. "Damn you!"

Nick was so devastated by the death of his wife that he became dysfunctional, and for the next few days it was his mother who took over the management of the family, making the funeral arrangements.

Rachel also arranged for a small gathering at Nick's house after the funeral, hiring a caterer to serve hors d'oeuvres and a bartender to serve drinks (which now were legal, Prohibition having finally ended on December 6 when Utah became the thirty-sixth state to ratify repeal). But it was by necessity a glum affair; and after a half hour, Nick excused himself and went upstairs to be alone, leaving the party, or what was left of it, to be run by his mother.

When the final guests had left, Rachel came upstairs and went to her son's bedroom. Nick was lying on his back on the bed, staring at the ceiling in the dark. His mother turned on the lights and said, "They're gone."

"Thank God," Nick muttered. "But I appreciate your putting this thing together. I suppose we had to do something."

"Of course we had to." She pulled a chair up to the bed and sat down. "And now what about you?"

"What about me?"

"This has been a terrible shock to you, I realize that. But life goes on. If you want my advice, I'd go back to the bank and get back to work soon. It's the best way to numb your hurt."

"Oh yes, the bank. I suppose you're right. Except I have to take a few days to get Mrs. Hogan settled in and make sure she's going to work out with Amanda. Poor Amanda, poor little thing. She'll never know her mother. Oh God, life can be so damned cruel. God, whoever or whatever He is, must be a real mean son of a bitch."

"Nick, don't talk like that."

"Well, it's true."

"It's only natural for you to be bitter now. And it's true we all live in the shadow of death: That's the way life is, that's the bargain we make when we're born. But we simply have to soldier on." She stood up and leaned over to kiss him. "I love you, my dearest son, and I grieve for you. But you have Amanda."

"Yes," he sighed, "I have Amanda."

She smoothed his hair. Then she left the room, turning out the lights and leaving Nick alone in the dark.

He lay there for almost an hour, thinking of Laura, feeling the lonely emptiness of the house, listening to the silence.

Then he turned on the bed light, got up, went to the bathroom, peed, brushed his hair, and went downstairs. Putting on an overcoat and hat, he left the house, locking the door, and walked west until he came to Third Avenue. There, beneath the rusting Third Avenue El, a number of bars had reopened in the several weeks since repeal. Nick went into one of them, which was crowded with drinkers, and sat at the bar.

"Good evenin', sir," said an Irish bartender. "What can I get you?"

"I'd like," Nick said, "a double Scotch on the rocks."

He looked around him as the bartender made the drink. Booze. Once it had been his best friend, then it became his worst enemy. Did he really want to get drunk? Did he really want to try to forget Laura by becoming like these sad-looking and rather dingy alcoholics? A double Scotch on the rocks might be an anodyne for the terrible ache in his heart, but it wouldn't bring back Laura. Besides, it would desecrate Laura's memory to try and blot his hurt with booze when he had taken her off the stuff.

"Cancel that," he said to the bartender, getting off the bar stool and going back out into the night.

He walked back to Sutton Place, alone and sober and terribly, terribly sad.

GLORIA WOOD TANGOED ACROSS THE dance floor in the arms of a handsome young Cuban as her husband, Chester, watched from a side table in the Zanzibar Night Club in Havana. Chester finished his rum collins, then looked at his wristwatch. It was two in the morning.

"Damn," he muttered to himself. "Damn."

When the tango finally ended, Gloria made her way back to her table on the arm of the young Cuban, who was wearing a white dinner jacket. Gloria had on a black evening dress and was wearing three of the thick diamond bracelets Chester had bought her in the first year of their marriage. "Antonio just told me a dirty joke," she said as he held her chair for her, "but I didn't get it because his accent's so bad. Maybe you can explain it. I'd love another rum collins."

"Gloria, it's late. Let's go back to the ship."

"Oh, don't be such a grump. This is our last night in Havana and I want to have fun. And Antonio wants another drink, don't you?"

The young Cuban with the slicked-back black hair smiled as he pulled a silver cigarette case from his coat.

"Oh yes, please," he said. *"Cigarro?"*

"Thanks."

He lit it for her as a sullen Chester signaled the waiter. *"Dos mas,"* he said, indicating the collins glasses. "And then *la cuenta*, the bill."

"Now tell Chester the joke," Gloria said, exhaling.

Antonio told the joke, but Chester didn't get it either.

"Why did you have to pick up that damned Antonio?" Chester fumed a half hour later after they had returned to their A Deck suite on the *Morro Castle*, the five-year-old Ward Line's luxury liner they had taken to Havana in September of 1934 for a vacation.

"Why?" Gloria said, taking off her diamond bracelets. "Because he's young and good-looking and dances like a dream, that's why."

"Did it ever occur to you I might not enjoy seeing my wife dancing with a damned gigolo?"

"How do you know he's a gigolo?"

"They all are down here."

"Now Chester, that's just plain silly. And I'd think you'd like to see me having a good time. You hate to dance and I love to, so what's the difference?"

"I like you to have fun with me, not with some young whatever-he-is."

"I do have fun with you, and Antonio told me he's a banker."

"As if I believe that one. At any rate, I'll be glad to get back to Indianapolis. This is the last time I'm ever coming to Havana."

"You loved it here last year."

"Well, I don't love it now."

"You're just in a bad mood."

Chester climbed into the big double bed as Gloria put on her nightgown. Then she climbed in bed next to him and snuggled up to him.

"Now, are you going to get in a better mood and give Gloria a kiss?" she purred, rubbing his chest.

Chester's moodiness melted.

"I'll give you more than a kiss," he said, starting to make love to her.

"Chester, wake up! I smell smoke!"

It was two mornings later. Gloria, sitting up in bed, poked her sleeping husband, then turned on the light looking at the clock. It was quarter after four in the morning. The stateroom was filling with a light mist, and the smell was acrid and pungent.

"What is it?" Chester grunted, sitting up beside her.

"There's a fire somewhere! You better call one of the stewards and see what's happening."

"Yes, I can smell it . . ."

Chester sat on the edge of the bed and picked up the phone while Gloria got out of bed and threw a negligé over her satin nightgown.

"There's nobody answering," Chester said, hanging up the phone.

"I think the smoke's coming from below us, up through the vents. What's underneath us?"

"I don't know . . . I think the writing room . . ."

"Put on a bathrobe and let's go see what's going on."

"But there's a bad storm outside."

"So we get wet? So what? Hurry! Oh my God, some vacation!"

The ship was rocking and pitching as it made its way through a severe September storm, with strong winds and lashing rain. Oddly enough, and not known to many of the passengers, the previous evening the ship's captain, Robert Wilmott, had dropped dead of a heart attack at about the same time the luxury cruise ship encountered the storm off the coast of New Jersey, heading north to New York.

Chester and Gloria unlocked the door of their suite just as a fire alarm started ringing shrilly It was dark, and the pelting rain made it difficult to see; but as Gloria peered out, she could see passengers and crew milling about on the after deck, which was illuminated by a spotlight. She saw one of the ship's officers running aft toward her. "Mr. and Mrs. Wood!" he cried, stopping by their door. "The ship's on fire! Put on your life jackets!"

"How bad is it?" Chester yelled.

"Pretty bad!! It's spreading fast . . . midship's turning into an inferno . . . But we can't stop in the water because of the storm . . . we have to keep underway or we'll go broadside to the waves . . . Get on your life jackets . . . hurry! Then come aft."

"Yes, all right . . ." Gloria gulped as the young man took off again toward the after deck. She turned to look at her husband. "Oh God, Chester, do you think we're in danger?"

"Probably not, but he's right. Let's get on the life jackets. You'd better put something warm on."

Three minutes later, they left their stateroom and started aft toward the fantail of the large cruise ship, which was carrying a total of 562 persons, 318 passengers and 244 crew. By now the flames and smoke from midship were licking the sky, the burning sparks shooting into the rainy sky as sirens and alarm bells whined and clanged. Gloria, who had put a raincoat over her negligé and then a life jacket over the raincoat, felt stabs of fear: The scene, with the frightened passengers huddling on the fantail, was pure Dante. A number of officers were mingling among the passengers, and Gloria received even a worse stab of terror as she heard what they were shouting: "We're about a hundred and fifty feet off

Asbury Park, New Jersey . . . most of the lifeboats have been burned in their davots. . . . Jump into the water . . . the alternative is to be burned to death! Jump or burn!"

"Chester," Gloria wailed, "I can't swim . . ."

"You've got your life jacket . . . It looks bad . . . I think they're right, we have to jump or we're goners! Let's get over to the side."

By now, screaming passengers were climbing over the rail and jumping into the choppy black sea, many of them holding hands. Gloria and Chester, the rain plastering their hair to their foreheads, made their way to the rail and looked down. The light from the ship's fire was now so fierce, they could see what was happening in the water below. Some life rafts had managed to be thrown over, and passengers were climbing into them, although the rough sea made it difficult. Others were bobbing up and down in the water, attempting to swim toward shore where lights and some flares could now be seen. Two lifeboats had been lowered into the sea, and people were trying to scramble in, helped by the crewmen manning the oars.

"Look: there are some lifeboats," Chester shouted over the screams. "Let's try to swim to them."

"Chester, I'm scared!"

"So am I, but we'll make it. Come on, take my hand: I'll help you up on the rail, then jump. I'll follow you. And Gloria, I love you. Give me a kiss and be brave."

"I love you, too, darling."

Quickly, they kissed. Then Chester helped her up onto the rail, where she jumped. She hit the water, which, fortunately, was still summer warm, and sank deep into the inky depths, deep enough so that she could hear the not-too-distant churning of the ship's propellers. Then, slowly, it seemed, she surfaced. Gasping for breath, she looked around. The water was filled with screaming people and some silent, floating corpses.

Gloria might have been frightened, certainly understandable under the circumstances, but she had a steely sense of survival. Now, buoyed by her jacket, she started flopping through the water toward the nearest lifeboat, which was only some ten feet away. One of the crewmen held out a hand to her. "Grab my hand!" he cried as, above him, the towering hulk of the flaming ship loomed like some water-born volcano.

Gloria, gasping for breath, managed to do so, and the crewman pulled her over the gunwales where she flopped facedown into the boat's watery bilges, hardly able to believe she was lucky enough to be alive.

Her husband, Chester, was not as lucky. He jumped seconds after Gloria. But he was sucked into the ship's giant screws, which sliced him to death.

By the time an exhausted Gloria was carried onto the beach by local policemen, a crowd of thousands had gathered on the Jersey shore to watch the great ship burn so tantalizingly close while the first light of day competed with the flames to blood the sky. Ambulances from several nearby beach towns had arrived and attendants helped the lucky living into them as the unlucky dead, pulled from the water by young people horrified by the disaster, were piled into hearses.

And everywhere were reporters and radio commentators, describing to a mesmerized nation the greatest maritime disaster since, twenty-two years before, the *Titanic*.

"I'm so sorry about Chester," Nick said the next day as he drove Gloria to New York from Asbury Park. When she called him from the hospital, he had driven down to bring her some money and take her to his house.

"Oh God, Nick, he was such a sweet man," Gloria said. She was still wearing her raincoat over her nightclothes, but had managed to brush her hair. "And now he's dead, and your Laura's dead, and it was just such a short time ago we were all getting married and were so happy. Life can be so damned rotten."

"What will you do? Stay in Indianapolis?"

"I don't know yet. I haven't had time to think. But the twins are in school there, and now with Chester gone, somebody has to watch over the business, and I suppose it has to be me, at least for a while. Of course, I don't know anything about the plumbing business. I don't know anything about business, period."

"If you need any help, feel free to call me. Indianapolis is only a train ride away."

She looked at him and smiled.

"That's so sweet of you," she said. "And I so appreciate your driving down to get me. I must look like something out of a freak show in this outfit."

"You look fine. And you're alive, that's the important thing."

"Yes, I'm alive." She sighed. "I really was so happy with Chester, and now I'm alone again."

"Just like me."

"Have you met anyone you're interested in?"

"No. I don't know if I'll ever marry again. Two times out has made me gun shy. And I don't think I could ever love anyone as much as I loved Laura."

"You mustn't close the door, Nick. You never know when love may come along."

Five days later, Gloria, dressed in a black suit with a black pinwheel hat shrouded in black widow's veil, sat in the downtown Indianapolis office of her late husband's lawyer and listened to Chester's will being read. It was no surprise to her that she inherited everything. What did surprise her was the extent of the estate.

Chester Wood, the hick from Indiana, left an estate of over forty million dollars, an incredible sum at the time.

"Congratulations, Mrs. Wood," the lawyer said after finishing the reading of the will. "I believe you are now one of the richest women in America."

Gloria said nothing, but she was astonished how much money her darling hick had left her.

Seventeen-year-old Richard Shelby came into the paneled library of Whitehall, a room which he had admired many times, and walked across the carpet to the ornate English partner's desk behind which Gloria sat, smoking a cigarette.

"Good morning, Mrs. Wood," Richard said. He was wearing his best blue suit and a new tie, apparel he had bought from his earnings as a caddie at the country club.

"Good morning, Richard," Gloria said.

"I wanted to tell you how sad I am about Mr. Wood," Richard went on. "He was always wonderful to me, and I was really fond of him."

"Thank you, Richard. And my husband was fond of you. I assume you've heard that my husband left a thirty-thousand-dollar trust fund for William."

"Yes, ma'am. My father is mighty pleased, I can tell you that."

"Well, from everything my husband told me, your father earned the money with his many years of loyal service. My husband, as I said, was also very fond of you. He was very eager to help you get a college education. How are your grades, Richard?"

"I don't mean to brag, Mrs. Wood, but I'm third in my class."

"You're not bragging, you're telling the truth. I already checked with the school principal. He tells me you're one of the most outstanding students he's ever taught, a young man of high moral character, and a fine athlete. I mean, Richard, you're a sort of phenomenon. And you're good-looking, too."

The young man looked embarrassed.

"Gosh, Mrs. Wood, I'm not that good."

"Yes you are. Do you have a girlfriend?"

"Well, no one in particular."

"Mmm." She took a drag on the cigarette, then put it out. "What do you want to be in life, Richard?"

"I think I'd like to be a lawyer, if that were possible. I mean, it seems to be one profession a colored boy can get into, and maybe I could do something for my people some day, which would be nice."

"I agree, that would be very nice. Listen, Richard, I'm no saint or crusader, but you have to be blind not to think that this country has to change some day, and I mean change for the better. So, here's the good news: Your principal, Dr. Spaulding, is going to submit an application for you to go to Howard University after you graduate from high school. I'll pay for your tuition, room and board and give you enough pocket money so you won't be strapped. If you work hard and get the grades, I'll pay for you to go to law school, too. Of course, I'm not sure where we could get you in, but I understand that Harvard Law School has been taking colored boys for some time . . ."

"Harvard?" Richard gasped.

"Well, we'll see. The bad news is that I'll expect you to work hard—I started to say 'like a slave,' but that perhaps isn't the most diplomatic way of putting it. But you get the gist. If you let me down, or screw up in some way—and I don't expect you to be a saint—then you'll have disappointed me, which wouldn't please me."

"Gosh, Mrs. Wood . . . I'd never let you down! I mean, this is something I've dreamed of all my life! I'll work . . . Gosh, I'll . . . You'll be proud of me, I swear! I can't thank you enough! I don't know what else to say . . ."

"Then don't say. Just show me. And I'm not being altogether altruistic in this. Some day, you may be able to help me."

"Me? But how?"

"I'm not sure. But some day. We'll see. You're an investment in my future, too. Now, run along and tell your father. I know he'll be pleased, and so am I."

She gave him a smile, which melted his heart.

At the time, most American cities of any importance boasted a country club as the center of social activity. Only Manhattan, which of course wasn't "country," didn't have one, although it had its many city clubs. The country club offered a usually handsome setting for entertainment, golf, tennis, swimming, gambling, boozing, and Getting-in-Trouble: all with the added enticement of exclusivity. In smaller towns that generally had few restaurants of any quality, failure to get into the country club meant social ruin, and very often business failure. Critics could laugh at country clubs' pretensions or scorn their snobbery; but for the locals outside looking in, they were formidable fortresses of the "ins" keeping the "outs" at bay.

In Indianapolis, the most exclusive country club was the Tarkington, named after the turn-of-the-century author, Booth Tarkington, an Indianapolis native. Set in lovely rolling hills in the exclusive northern section of the city, the Tarkington boasted an excellent eighteen-hole golf course, tennis courts, a swimming pool, and an Indiana limestone clubhouse built in the early twenties in an architectural style best described as Midwest French Renaissance, a sprawling two-story folly replete with a porte cochere, turrets, and oriels that had about as much in common with the flat Indiana cornfields as the Château de Versailles. Never mind: the Tarkington was where the action was, it had a surprisingly good wine cellar, and the food wasn't half bad.

When Gloria first came to town as Chester's bride, she set her sights on winning over the local *ton*, convinced that being the wife of one of the richest men in town as well as a fading Hollywood glamour puss would bowl the locals over. It didn't quite work out that way. The members' wives seethed with envy over her flashy jewels, her New York wardrobe, and particularly over the fact that their husbands stopped talking and stared every time Gloria breezed into the dining room or bar. Gloria, a born flirt, of course made things worse by cozying up to the male population of the club and making little pretense over what she thought of the club wives, most of whom were overweight and not exactly intellectually stimulating with their endless discussions of golf scores, current events, bridge, the latest choice of the Book-of-the-Month Club, and recipes.

On the other hand, Gloria made considerable efforts to win over the locals. True to her statement to Bennet Kinkaid, she valiantly tried to organize a fund-raising campaign to finance a local ballet, donating fifteen thousand to get the ball rolling.

She donated a cool half-million dollars to the leading local hospital to build a Chester Wood Wing with facilities to treat advanced diseases, including cancer and heart and kidney problems. For this, even Bennet Kinkaid's newspapers lauded her, despite the fact that Bennet's daughter, Deirdre Kinkaid Slade, disliked Gloria and trashed her at local parties as a cheap Hollywood floozie.

But what turned Bennet into an enemy was when Gloria's factories went on a sit-down strike, demanding unionization, health benefits, and a ten-percent wage increase. Since Wood Plumbing was the leading employer in town, the strike took on great local importance. Bennet, a fierce anti-unionist, wrote thundering editorials against the strike. He also made personal phone calls to Gloria, urging her to hang on and fight the strikers.

To his intense chagrin, Gloria calmly told him she was going to grant the strikers every one of their wishes.

"But you can't!" the hairless Bennet sputtered. "Roosevelt's leading the country down the path to socialism! If we let the unions take over, management will be through, finished, kaput!"

"Darling, all these people want is a little security in their lives and a decent wage. Listen, I was an actress. I know what it's like to be insecure. I know what it's like waiting around for parts, living from hand to mouth. I'm going to give these people what they want and get on with life. I'm making money, why shouldn't they?"

"You'll regret it! When the Communists take over this country . . ."

"Bennet, really. Don't be such a Scrooge. And tell your daughter to stop calling me a floozie."

She hung up.

While her generosity made her a heroine to her hundreds of employees and her charities turned her into one of the most popular persons in the city at a time when rich people were anything but, it had the reverse effect on the city's wildly conservative upper classes. Fueled by Deirdre's dislike and her father's fury, their friends started making Gloria the butt of dirty jokes and rancid gossip. The country club set had her sleeping with every available man in town, and it seemed a foregone conclusion that she and the good-looking young tennis pro were having orgies in either the club's locker room or Whitehall.

The truth was simple and far less interesting: since Chester's death, Gloria hadn't gone to bed with anyone.

Aware of her unpopularity with the town's *ton*, Gloria considered leaving Indianapolis for a place more exciting and less condemningly hostile. She was bored and restless, yet she didn't want to leave Indianapolis, at least for the time being, because the twins were in local schools, and she felt she should stay in town to keep an eye on the factory. Desperate for something to do, she decided to take up golf. Besides, drinking had put more than a few pounds on her, and she thought the exercise would help take them off.

One cool October Saturday morning six weeks after the *Morro Castle* disaster, she drove to the Tarkington Country Club in her new Cadillac convertible and went to the women's locker room where she took her golf bag from her locker. Then she walked to the first tee where she was met by Richard Shelby, whom she had hired to be not only her caddie, but her instructor. She had found out by asking around that the local golf pro, while good, was a bit surly; and she knew from talking to William that Richard was a boy wonder at golf, so she decided to let him earn some extra money and teach her the game.

"Good morning," she said. "How are you this fine day?"

"Feeling fit, Mrs. Wood."

"Now I know the idea of this silly game is to hit the ball somewhere, curse a lot along the way, then try and get it in some hole in the ground. Am I right?"

Richard was laughing.

"Yes, ma'am, particularly in the cursing part. Boy, I've heard some cussing on these links that would embarrass a stevedore."

"So, how do I begin?" she said, handing him her bag.

Richard pulled out a club.

"Well, this is called a driver. You use it to drive the ball from the tee, and the idea is to hit it as far and as straight as you can."

"That sounds simple enough."

"It's a little more complicated than you might think. Here, I've put the ball on the tee—that's that wooden thing it's sitting on. Now, you stand here . . ."

He handed her the driver, then showed her where to stand beside the ball.

"Now you hold the shaft with both hands like this . . ."

As he demonstrated, Deirdre Kinkaid Slade approached the tee with two of her women friends. They had made a threesome tee-off appointment at nine-fifteen.

"It's that damned Hollywood trash, Gloria Wood," Deirdre muttered. "Looks as if she's taking up golf. Too bad for the club."

"Look, ma'am," Richard was saying. "I'll stand behind you and show you how to swing the club."

Positioning himself behind Gloria, he reached around her and gently put his hands on her arms, slowly bringing them up in a backswing.

"You see? Then you bring the club back down like so, and hit the ball. Now, try it once."

He stepped back as Gloria brought her club up, then swung it down, missing the ball entirely.

"Damn!" she growled. "I should stick with tennis."

"No, you'll catch on. Here, let me go through the swing once more."

Standing behind her again, he reached around and put his hands on her arms.

Deirdre, watching with her friends from off the tee, whispered, "The Floozie looks as if she's enjoying being fondled by the colored caddie, who's so good-looking."

Her friends looked shocked.

"Deirdre," one said, "what an awful thing to say!"

"Yes, isn't it. But I'll bet it's true."

11 MARK AND SEBASTIAN WERE SITTING next to each other playing "Chopsticks" on the Whitehall pipe organ, Sebastian playing treble and Mark playing bass. The twins had pulled out all the stops, so the music was blaring throughout the mansion north of Indianapolis, and they were having a ball.

"Mark, keep up!" Sebastian yelled over the music. "I want to go faster!"

"I'm doing the best I can," his twin yelled back, making a glaring false note.

"Boys, stop it!" screamed their mother, appearing behind the console. Gloria had been trying to read the current best-selling historical epic, *Anthony Adverse*, in the nearby library. "I'm going to lock this thing up if you two don't stop driving me nuts playing it!" Gloria went on. "Now turn it off and get out of there. God, I've got a splitting headache."

Sebastian turned off the motor as Mark slid off the wooden bench. In fact, Sebastian was fascinated by the pipe organ, which in some ways was the ultimate toy, a noisemaker par excellence, while his twin was more intrigued by the enormous electric train set his mother had bought them and which was spread out on permanent display in the basement next to the bowling alley. In this fifth year of the Great Depression, Mark and Sebastian led a dreamlike kid's existence which inevitably was spoiling both of them, something Gloria knew in her bones but was too indulgent to prevent. She liked spoiling her children, even though their antics were hard on her nerves.

She had just returned to the peace of the library when William arrived to announce that a Mr. Byron Slade was at the front door, wishing to see her. Gloria put down her book, telling William to show him in. Then she went to a mirror to check her hair and makeup. It was eleven-thirty on a rainy Saturday morning. She had no idea why Byron Slade was coming to call.

"Mrs. Wood?" a voice said behind her.

She turned to see a well-dressed young man standing in the door. She had seen him at the Tarkington Country Club on many occasions and was well aware of his good looks. Tall, trim, with curly blond hair, Byron Slade was a heartthrob who, nevertheless—it was whispered—had yet to cheat on his attractive wife, Deirdre Kinkaid Slade.

"Yes?" Gloria said.

"I'm Byron Slade. I'd like to talk to you for a moment, if I may."

"Please. Come on in. Can I get you something? A drink, or a cup of coffee or tea?"

"No thanks." Putting his hat on a table, he sat on a leather sofa in the paneled library as Gloria took a chair opposite him.

"Mrs. Wood," Byron began, "this is a rather difficult mission for me. You must understand that I am the corporate lawyer for my father-in-law's company."

"Yes, I know. Newspapers, radio stations, that sort of thing."

"Exactly."

"And your father-in-law hates my guts because he thinks I've given in to the unions, in particular, the union that now represents the employees of my company."

"Well, that's your business. I don't want to get into that."

"Then what do you want to get into?"

Gloria took a cigarette from a silver box in front of her and lit it. Byron Slade was staring at her, and she thought the handsome young man was extremely uncomfortable.

"My father-in-law is a member of the Board of Directors of the Tarkington Country Club, of which you are a member. The Tarkington Country Club's by-laws have a morals clause which says that if any member of the club behaves in a manner that is offensive to the other club members, that person should be forced to resign."

"Yes, I know. So?"

Byron squirmed in his chair.

"You, uh, offered me a drink. Maybe I'll change my mind."

"Oh, of course." Gloria stood up. "What would you like?"

"Perhaps a martini?"

"Why not?"

Gloria went to the bar and made him a martini. When she brought it to him, he took a quick sip and seemed to unwind a bit. She sat back down in her chair.

"You were saying?" she prompted.

"Well, there is a lot of feeling in the club that you have broken the morals clause."

"Ah, I see. And with whom am I having wild orgies?"

Byron took another sip of the martini.

"Well, no one is saying that, exactly."

"Then what are they saying?"

"They're saying that your general deportment is not up to the club's standards."

"And what, exactly, does that mean? Does it mean that I'm not fifty pounds overweight, and that I have nothing of interest to say except what my neighbor's bridge score is?"

Byron squirmed.

"Actually, what they're saying is that you're having an affair with Richard Shelby."

Gloria gaped.

"Richard?" she exclaimed. "But he's like my son! Are they insane?"

"Nevertheless, that's what they're saying. And for any club member to have any relationship with a club employee, much less a colored club employee . . . well, that's why the Board of Directors is insisting on your resignation."

Gloria looked at him for a long time.

"This is your wife's doing, isn't it?" she finally said. "Deirdre, who tells everyone in Indianapolis that I'm a Hollywood floozie. That I sleep with every attractive man. Come on, Byron, admit it."

Byron finished his martini.

"You know, this was awfully good. Could I have another?"

Gloria stood up and came over to take his glass.

"I know what people say about me," she said, going to the bar to give him a refill. "Everyone in this town thinks because I was in Hollywood that I sleep with everyone who comes along. You might be surprised to know that since my husband died, I haven't slept with anyone. And to suggest that I would make Richard Shelby my lover is absolutely ridiculous. I adore that young man, but it has nothing to do with sex."

She brought the martini to Byron, who accepted it.

"Well," he said, taking a sip, "you know that you're a terribly glamorous person in this town. I mean, Hollywood and money and . . . well, the whole thing. Indianapolis isn't exactly New York or Paris."

"No kidding."

"So, I guess a lot of people are jealous of you."

"Like your wife."

"Oh, my wife. Deirdre. Well, she's a difficult woman . . ."

He drank more of the martini.

"In what way is she difficult?" Gloria said, sitting down in her chair opposite him.

"I don't want to get into it, except to say that she agrees with a lot of things my father in-law believes, and I don't."

"You mean, right-wing things?"

"Yes, exactly. It's funny, but I wanted to be a reporter when I was young. And then I ended up marrying Deirdre and becoming a lawyer, and now I'm . . ." He shrugged. "Well, anyway. My life didn't turn out the way I wanted."

"Few people's do."

"I guess you're right. But about this country club business . . . will you resign?"

"Of course not. Why should I? I've been a damned vestal virgin."

"Really? That's hard to believe, since you're such an attractive woman."

She smiled.

"How sweet. That's the first nice thing you've said, Byron."

"Well . . ." He finished his martini. "You know, being the son-in-law of Bennet Kinkaid isn't easy."

"I can imagine. Another martini?"

"Sure, why not? You know, this is a really beautiful house. And you're a really beautiful woman."

He held out his empty glass to Gloria, who took it.

"You're not bad-looking yourself, darling."

When Deirdre had married Byron Slade three years before, it had been much against her father's wishes. Bennet Kinkaid expected his daughter to marry someone of her own social standing. Instead, she had fallen in love with the son of a small-town druggist who had gone to college and, later, law school on scholarships, and who also, Bennet was convinced, had left-wing political leanings. After all, hadn't he wanted to be a newspaper reporter, of all things? And weren't all writers leftists?

However, Deirdre was so smitten by Byron, her father grudgingly agreed to the marriage and, as a wedding present, gave the young couple five acres of his forty-acre estate and built them a four-bedroom house. Deirdre was listening to her favorite radio soap opera, *My Gal Sunday*, when Byron came in the house.

"So, how did it go?" she asked. "What did she say?"

Byron took off his coat and hung it in the hall closet.

"She denied everything," he said, coming into the living room.

"Well, of course she would. But is she going to resign from the club?"

"No. And I think you and your father are barking up the wrong tree. She could bring a law suit against the club if you tried to force her out. You'd have to prove she was having an affair with the caddie, and I think that would be damned hard to do in court."

He had gone to the bar and was making himself a martini. His wife looked at him with annoyance. Then she glanced at her watch.

"What took you so long?" she asked. "You've been gone almost two hours."

"Have I? I guess I lost track of the time."

"You've been drinking."

"She offered me a martini. I was a little nervous, so I had one. Anyway, I think you and your father should forget this whole thing. Gloria Wood is an important woman in this town, and she's done a lot for it and will probably do more in the future. Besides . . ." He sat down in a chair before the fireplace and took another sip. ". . . I rather like her."

His wife stared at him.

"You like her?" She almost gasped. "That cheap Hollywood whore?"

"Oh Deirdre, not everyone went to Wellesley like you. Get off your high horse. And forget Gloria Wood. She's never done anything to you, why should you try to hurt her?"

She stalked out of the room.

"Where are you going?" Byron asked.

"To talk to my father!" Deirdre snapped. "Obviously, leaving this in your hands was a big mistake."

She put on her coat and slammed out of the house.

For twenty dollars a month, Richard Shelby had an after-hours job cleaning up the Tarkington Country Club's locker rooms. That night, he finished mopping the toilets of the men's room. Then he wiped the three sinks, put away the cleaning facilities, and left the men's room, turning out the lights and closing the door. He went into the adjacent locker room, which was empty, picked up a few towels, which he took to the steam room towel recepticle and put them in. He checked the steam room to see if it was well secured and all right. Then, satisfied, he put on his jacket and left the Tarkington Country Club.

It was nine P.M. At the other end of the building, he could hear the noise of the dining room and bar: people were drinking, talking, eating, gambling on slot machines, and a local orchestra was playing, filling the night with the latest hit tunes like *Blue Moon*. Indianapolis was having fun.

Richard was used to it. He walked across the asphalt driveway and took his bicycle. Climbing on, he started his trip home to south Indianapolis, where his father and he lived in a small, two-story house that was a step up from a slum. As he drove down the winding drive of the country club, through pleasant woods spiked by handsome houses, his thoughts drifted, as they so often did, to his future and his fierce desire to somehow beat the prejudice against his race. For all of his dreams, he was still a teenage caddie. Yes, he had Mrs. Wood's pledge of paying for his college education, which was a wonderful thing. But still, the mountain of prejudice he was facing was Everest. Well, he was still young. He had a long life ahead of him. Somehow, maybe, he could prevail.

And there was college, where he had just been accepted. With a college education, didn't the future hold all sorts of possibilities?

When, twenty minutes later, he bicycled into the southern part of the city, leaving the handsome Civil War Monument of the Circle and the other buildings that reflected the former prosperity of the midwest metropolis, he started down a deserted business street when a long, black Cadillac limousine pulled out of a side street before him and drove around him, suddenly stopping in front of him. As Richard swerved his bike to avoid hitting the car, a uniformed chauffeur stepped out of the driver's seat and came to him.

"You, boy," the chauffeur said, softly. "There's a gentleman who wants to see you."

"Who?" Richard said in a frightened tone. "What have I done?"

"Why, nothing. You know the gentleman. It's Mr. Kinkaid, from the Country Club. He wants to talk to you. Leave your bike. If someone steals it, Mr. Kinkaid will buy you a new one. Come on."

Totally confused, Richard leaned his bike against a lamppost and followed the chauffeur around the car where the man opened the rear door.

"Climb in."

Richard obeyed. Seated in the back of the long limo was a man smoking a cigar. Although the interior of the car was dark, Richard could see enough to recognize the powerful publisher, who was wearing a dinner jacket. Bennet Kinkaid had piercing gray eyes the intensity of which, even in the darkness of the limousine, Richard could feel. Bennet Kinkaid was a rather frightening person. The chauffeur closed the door and went around to get in the front.

"Good evening, Richard," Bennet Kinkaid said in a pleasant tone. "How are you this evening?"

"Oh, fine, Mr. Kinkaid. Just fine."

"Good."

The chauffeur started the car, driving down the avenue to the first corner, where he turned to the right.

"You're friendly with Mrs. Wood, I believe?" Bennet said in a soft voice. "I've even been told that she is paying your way through college, and that you've been accepted at Howard University. Is that correct?"

"Yes sir. I was accepted last week. I begin there next fall."

"Excellent. I believe there's nothing finer in this country than an education. I'm sure you'll do well, Richard."

"Thank you, sir." Richard had no idea what was going on. The limo reached another corner and again turned to the right.

"Richard, do you know my son-in-law, Mr. Slade?"

"Oh yes sir. I've caddied for him several times. He's a nice man and a very good golfer, too."

"Yes, he is."

Another puff on the cigar. The cigar end glowed in the dark of the limousine.

"Now, Richard, you spend a lot of time at Mrs. Wood's house, don't you? Whitehall? Where your father is the butler?"

"Well, sir, not a lot of time, but I'm there often enough. I do odd jobs for Mrs. Wood."

"Like what?"

"Well, I help out at some of her parties. You know, pass canapés, stuff like that."

The cigar end glowed again.

"Is one of the odd jobs you do for Mrs. Wood going to bed with her?"

Richard was struck dumb for a moment.

"I . . . I beg your pardon, sir?"

"I said, are you her lover? Her boyfriend?"

"Oh no, sir. Mrs. Wood's a lady!"

Bennet chuckled.

"That's your opinion, boy, not mine. How often do you go to bed with her?"

"But sir, I don't! I never have! I wouldn't do it!"

"Then why is she paying your way through college?"

"Well, she . . . she likes me."

"Come now, Richard. I'm not naive. Why would Gloria Wood put a colored boy through college if she weren't getting something out of it? You're a nice-looking young man, and she's a nymphomaniac and a whore."

"Mr. Kinkaid, I swear this isn't true!"

"Whether it's true or not, boy, doesn't matter because everyone thinks it's true. Do you know there are miscegenation laws still on the books in this state? Do you know you could go to prison, boy? That is, if you lived long enough to go to trial. Did you ever hear of the Ku Klux Klan, Richard? They're very strong around here, and they don't like darkies making love to white women. Do you know what they did to a colored boy over in Marion just a few years ago? They lynched him. Do you want to be lynched, Richard?"

Richard was so panicked he was almost in tears.

"Why are you saying these things, Mr. Kinkaid? What have I ever done against you? Or anyone? I've been a good boy all my life."

"That's true, Richard. And none of these things will happen if you just do what I ask you. And there'll be some nice cash in it for you, too."

"What? What do you want me to do?"

Ten minutes later, the car which had been slowly going around the same block, stopped next to Richard's bike, which was still leaning against the lamppost. Richard got out of the car and got on his bike. He started peddling down the empty street, peddling faster and faster as if trying to exorcise his anger and fear with sheer physical exertion.

Fifteen minutes later, he pulled into the short driveway of his father's house, which was a small two-story bungalow on a tight plot of land, much like the other bungalows on the rundown street with the exception that this one was freshly painted and the yard immaculate: William was extremely house-proud. Richard parked his bike in the single garage next to his father's 1928 Chevrolet, then closed the garage doors and went to the front door.

His father was sitting in the living room smoking a pipe and listening to his favorite radio program, *Fibber McGee and Molly*, when Richard came in the room.

"Poppa, I gotta talk to you," he said. "Something terrible has happened."

William turned off the radio, on top of which was a framed photograph of his late wife.

"What's wrong, Richard?"

"Just a while ago, Mr. Kinkaid stopped me with his Cadillac and his chauffeur told me to get in the backseat," Richard said, plopping morosely onto a stool in front of his father. "They're trying to force Mrs. Wood out of the country club, and they want me to say I'm her lover."

"Her lover?" his father exclaimed in disbelief. "You? Are they crazy?"

"I don't know why they even think it," Richard said, on the verge of tears. "I'd never do that, and she wouldn't want me to. Oh Poppa, I'm just sick about it! And I'm scared silly because Mr. Kinkaid said if I don't do what he wants, they'll sick the Klan on me."

He buried his face in his hands and tried not to weep. His father thought a moment. Then he said:

"You've got to get out of town. I'll give you a thousand dollars cash— Mrs. Wood made me put most of the money I got from her husband in the bank, but I don't trust banks, especially after that bank holiday business, so I kept a thousand dollars here in the house. It's in the icebox, in a coffee can. You take that money and get a bus ticket to New York. You stay in New York till next fall—get yourself a job and hide, cause nobody gets lynched in New York. You may get held up or murdered, but you don't get lynched. Then in September you go to college. You'll be safe there."

"But Poppa, I got to graduate from high school in June!"

"We'll work that out, and you've already been accepted to the university. You got to get out of this town. That Mr. Kinkaid's powerful, no telling what tricks he got up his sleeve. When you get to New York, call me and let me know where you are. . . ."

"But I've never been to New York! I've never been anywhere!"

"Time you started seeing the world. Now go on upstairs and pack. Then first thing in the morning get yourself to the bus station and get out. I'll explain things to Mrs. Wood."

"I don't know, Poppa . . . it all seems so crazy . . ."

"Getting lynched isn't crazy. Getting lynched is the end. I've seen a lynching, I've seen the looks in white folks' eyes: to them, a lynching is entertainment, better than a movie. I'm not going to let that happen to my son. Now go on upstairs and pack. Then get a little sleep. Tomorrow, you go. No use talking about it anymore: I've made up my mind."

Richard looked at him a moment, indecision in his eyes. Then he stood up. "You're right, as usual, Poppa. I'll do it."

He came to his father and leaned over to embrace him.

"I love you, Poppa," he said, softly. "I'll miss you. When I get to college, will you come down and see me?"

"Of course. I'll come Thanksgiving, we'll have that together. Everything's going to be fine, Richard. And you're going to make me real proud of you, just as I am now, and always have been. You're the best thing that's ever happened to my life, my beloved son." He kissed his forehead. "Now get upstairs."

"Of all the rotten, stinking tricks!" Gloria snapped the next morning at the breakfast table in Whitehall. William had just told her what happened. "That Bennet Kinkaid's a real snake, and trying to scare Richard into saying he's my lover? My God, they'll do anything to get me out of their damned country club, and I don't even like the damned place! But I won't resign! Oh no, not now! Never! You say you sent Richard to New York?"

"Yes, ma'am. He got on the eight o'clock bus this morning. He should be in Ohio by now."

"That was smart. Where's he going to stay?"

"We don't know yet."

"When you find out, tell him to look up Mr. Nick Savage—I'll give you his phone number. Nick's a nice man— he's my brother-in-law—and he'll help Richard find work. But threatening to lynch Richard—! Well, of course, he just might have. Kinkaid's no friend of colored people, all you have to do is read his editorials to know that, and all the bigots do read them. God, what a world we live in! America the Beautiful, my foot."

"America is beautiful, Mrs. Wood. It's just some Americans who aren't so pretty."

The Kinkaid Communications Building at fifteen stories was one of the tallest buildings in Indianapolis, an Indiana limestone-clad structure on Market Street a few blocks from the towering Soldiers' and Sailors' Monument and not far from the gold-domed State capitol. On the top floor were the executive suites, the largest belonging, naturally, to Bennet Kinkaid. Two weeks after Richard Shelby fled the city for New York, Deirdre was pacing nervously back and forth in front of her father's desk.

"Byron's cheating on me," she was saying, wringing her hands nervously. "I just know it! He comes home late from the office, and I smell perfume on him, and half the time he's half smashed . . . Oh Daddy, I'm just miserable!"

She started crying, sinking into a chair. Her father, his skull-like face cold, looked at her.

"Do you have any idea who the woman is?" he asked.

"Yes! I think it's that damned Gloria Wood! Oh, it's so degrading . . . I could kill her! And I could kill Byron! To betray me with that woman!"

She broke down completely.

"I told you not to marry that bum!" her father said. "He's a pinkie, and always has been!"

"But I love him!" she sobbed.

Her father rolled his eyes.

"Love!" he snorted. "It's time you realized marriages don't have anything to do with love."

"But you loved Mother!"

"That was different. Your Mother wasn't a damned left-wing pinkie. Well, let's get to the bottom of this." He switched on his intercom. "Miss Leslie, tell Mr. Slade to come to my office immediately."

"Yes, sir."

He switched it off. Five minutes later, Byron came in the room, closing the door. He looked at Deirdre, who was wiping her eyes. Then he looked at his father-in-law.

"You wanted to see me?" he asked.

"Yes. Deirdre tells me she thinks you're cheating on her. Is this true?"

Byron said nothing, looking at his wife.

"Is it true?" Bennet roared. "I want an answer, dammit!"

Byron glared at the man he so thoroughly disliked.

"Yes," he said. "It's true."

"Oh Byron," Deirdre sobbed. "How could you have done this to me? And with her, that awful woman, that Hollywood tramp!"

"Is she the one?" Bennet snapped. "Gloria Wood?"

"Yes."

"God damn you! You know how we feel about her! Now you'll make us the laughingstock of Indianapolis!"

"No one knows."

"They'll guess! I demand you stop seeing this woman, and by God, if you don't, you'll be out of a job! And I can make sure you'll never get another job in this state!"

"Oh, stop bullying me," Byron said, sharply. "You always bully me, and I'm sick of it."

"Byron, don't you love me anymore?" Deirdre asked, plaintively.

"I never have loved you," he said. "I only married you for your money, but Gloria's right: she said I made a mistake. She said I should have married for love . . ."

"You talk to that woman about me?" Deirdre gasped.

"You're damned right, and she listens to me, unlike you or your father. Furthermore, she says I should do what I want, not be a lawyer, which I hate, and kissing your father's ass, which I detest! Gloria says I should be a man, not an ass-kisser!"

"Gloria this, Gloria that . . . I can't believe you tell her these things!"

"If you don't like kissing my ass," Bennet said, "you don't have to anymore. You're fired!"

"Good," Byron said, with a smile. "This way, I don't have to feel guilty about leaving town."

"Leaving—? Where are you going?" Deirdre cried out, getting up from her chair.

"New York. Gloria says I should go to journalism school and be a writer, which is what I always wanted to be."

"A writer? You'll starve to death!"

"No I won't. Gloria's going to finance me until I can get a job on a newspaper. So, Deirdre, my dearest wife, and Bennet, my not so dearest father-in-law: I'll call you from New York about the divorce. Good-bye."

Giving them a cheery salute with his hand, he walked out of the office, slamming the door behind him.

Deirdre, her face ashen, whimpered: "He's gone!"

"Good riddance," her father said.

"She did this on purpose! She told him all these things so he'd leave me! Oh, I . . . I loathe that woman!"

"Leave Gloria Wood to me," her father said.

"Mommy, there are ghosts on our front lawn," seven-year-old Sebastian said two nights later as he shook Gloria's arm. His mother sat up in bed and rubbed her eyes.

"Darling, what's wrong?" she asked, yawning and looking at her radium-dial bed clock. It was shortly after midnight.

"There are ghosts in front of the house. About six of them. It's really spooky. Mark's so scared he's hiding under his bed."

Totally confused, Gloria got out of bed, put on her slippers and a negligé, and went to one of the windows of her bedroom. It was a moonlit night with a few clouds scudding across the sky. Below her, on the broad front lawn of Whitehall, there were, in fact, what looked like six ghosts: figures in white robes with white pointed hoods. They were finishing putting up a tall wooden cross.

"My God, it's the Klan!" she muttered. Then she turned on the lights. "Don't worry, darling: they're not ghosts. I'll take care of these idiots."

Taking her son's hand, she hurried across the bedroom, opened the door, and went out to the upstairs hall. She hurried down the circular staircase, turning on more lights. When she reached the ground floor, she started toward the front door. Passing a handsome wooden bombé Italian chest, she hesitated a moment, then opened the drawer and pulled out a pistol that had belonged to her late husband. Holding the gun in her hand, she unbolted the front door and opened it. She stepped out into the cool night and shouted, "Get out of here before I call the police!" To show she meant business, she fired the gun into the air.

Instantly, the wooden cross, which was ten feet high, burst into flames, ignited by a cigarette lighter. As Gloria turned away to protect her eyes from the glare, the Klansmen started shouting:

"Nigger-lover! Nigger-lover! Get out of town, nigger-lover!"

Gloria, enraged, fired her gun again, this time just over their heads.

Then one of the Klansmen picked up a rock and threw it at her, hitting her on the left side of her head.

Gloria slumped to the ground, unconscious, as the Klansmen vanished into the night. Sebastian, who had been watching, terrified, from the staircase, now ran up to his mother and knelt beside her.

"Momma, are you all right?" he said.

Gloria groaned, then sat up, holding her head where the rock had hit her. A large lump was forming.

"I'll live," she growled.

"Should I call the police?"

"No, darling, it wouldn't do any good. The police are in Mr. Kinkaid's pocket."

"Did Mr. Kinkaid send the ghosts?"

"Yes, and I'll pay him back for this one day. Somehow."

Rather shakily, she got to her feet, holding on to the front door for support.

"Why is Mr. Kinkaid such a mean man?" Sebastian asked.

"Because his mother was a dog."

"You mean he's a son of a bitch?"

"Sebastian, don't cuss. Now run get Momma some aspirin from the kitchen and a glass of milk."

Sebastian hurried down the center hall as Gloria closed and locked the door, replacing the gun in the chest.

"And put some Scotch in it!" she yelled.

"Gee, Mr. Savage, this is really some sight!" Richard Shelby said. He was standing next to Nick in the crown of the Statue of Liberty, looking out at New York harbor. "This has got to be the biggest statue in the world, isn't it?"

"I'm not sure," Nick said, "but I think it might be. It was given to the people of America by France some sixty years ago."

"I like that poem by Emma Lazarus."

"Yes, it's a lovely thing."

"I bet Bennet Kinkaid hates it."

"Yes, I imagine he probably does. Shall we go back to Manhattan and get some lunch?"

"Sure."

They walked back down to the base of the statue, then took the ferry back to New York. Gloria had called Nick from Indianapolis and told him the whole story of Richard; when Richard arrived in New York two weeks before, he called Nick who gave him a room in his Sutton Place house and arranged a job for him in a Greenwich Village bookstore, which Richard loved, as he loved New York. In Greenwich Village, for the first time in his life, he didn't feel "colored." He simply felt like a human being.

"Mr. Savage," he said to Nick as they ferried across the bay to Battery

Park, "I can't thank you enough for what you've done for me these past two weeks. You've really been swell, and I love working in the bookstore. This is turning out to be the best summer of my life."

"It's been my pleasure, Richard. And you have a real champion in my sister-in-law."

"Oh, I love Mrs. Wood. But you know, it's a funny thing. The Emma Lazarus poem says that Europe should send all its poor people to America, which is a fine-sounding thing. But it doesn't say anything about my people, who were already here."

Nick looked at him with admiration.

"Richard, I never thought about it that way."

PART FOUR

AN AMERICAN IN PARIS IN LOVE. THE RISING SUN ALSO RISES: 1934–1936

12 FRANKLIN DELANO ROOSEVELT, THE thirty-second president of the United States, lit a cigarette in his long, black holder and leaned back in his chair in the Oval Office of the White House.

"Well, Nick," he said to Nick Savage, "you're looking fine. And how's your lovely mother?"

"She's quite well, Mr. President, I'm happy to say."

"A remarkable lady. And I understand your daughter is almost one year old now?"

"Yes, sir, and she's finally stopped sucking her thumb."

The president chuckled.

"Yes, I remember that problem with my own brood. Ah, the joys of family life. Not to pry, Nick, but as an old family friend I feel I can inquire to a certain extent into your private life. It's been a year now since the unhappy death of your lovely wife, Laura. Have you found any new love interest?"

"Well, I'm afraid not, Mr. President. I've had some dates—a rather odd word for someone my age . . ."

"You're a mere puppy, Nick!" the president interrupted. "If you want to see someone as old as the Sphynx, look at me."

"You're looking good, sir."

"I smoke too much, and the doctors want me to cut down to one martini a night. Who could drink only one martini? But you were saying?"

"Just that I'm looking for love, as they say in the movies, but haven't found it yet."

"Ah well, it will come soon enough. Now Nick, the reason I've dragged you to the White House is, I want to ask you a favor—not for me, of course, but for the government of the United States."

"Anything I can do would be an honor, Mr. President. Except I don't think I can stop the Depression."

Roosevelt laughed.

"My dear Nick, even *I* can't seem to do that! But we're trying. No, what I'm doing is putting together a panel of a half-dozen financial people, like yourself, and economists. The government of France has asked us for a rather large loan to help them through their financial problems, and I'd like to have this panel go over to Paris and check out their books, to put it on an informal level. It wouldn't take more than a month, I should think, and of course it would all be at government expense. However, when it comes to paying you a salary, I'm afraid I'll have to be rather tight-fisted."

"Mr. President, let's forget a salary. Whatever I can do to help you out is my pleasure, and I'll do it for free."

The president beamed.

"I was hoping you'd say that. Excellent! I'll fill you in on all the details later. Now, Eleanor and I are hoping you can dine with us this evening. And speaking of martinis," he checked his watch, "I think it's that happy hour. Will you join me for a cocktail?"

"No thanks, Mr. President. I don't drink."

"Ah yes, I forgot. I wish I had your will power."

The Great Depression had brought misery to millions, but for those lucky ones with money, like Joe Kennedy, the time was one of great style and glamour, a fact Hollywood profited from with its many slick, glamorous movies starring immortal film goddesses like Garbo, Dietrich, Crawford, and Harlow. But perhaps the most glamorous thing of the period was a sleekly enormous French ocean liner called the *Normandie*. At eighty thousand tons, it was the biggest ship built to date; but it was also the swiftest (it could make thirty-one knots), most sophisticated, and most magnificent ship afloat. At a cost of a staggering sixty million dollars, it was also the most expensive ship ever built, and many Frenchmen, knowing that it had been financed by the government, called it the "floating national debt." But the majority of the French looked on it with pride, a thrilling affirmation of the French nation's faith in its future. While the Nazis were building a war machine, the French built a floating Versailles. And, in fact, the first-class dining room, *la grande salle à manger*, was sixty feet longer than the Hall of Mirrors at Versailles.

The liner contained the first seagoing movie theater, seating 380, which could also mount stage productions. There was a Protestant chapel which, by sliding a wall panel, could convert to Catholic. There was a seventy-five-foot long swimming pool, a children's playroom, a grand salon with twenty-two-foot-high windows and shimmering crystal fountains, a kennel with its own doggie sun deck, a shooting gallery, a winter garden filled with exotic plants and caged birds, a boat-deck grill that ran a buffet all day long and far into the night, libraries and, it goes without saying, the most chic boutiques. The ship had the most powerful marine engines in the world and had the world's first rudimentary radar as a precaution against icebergs.

At the zenith of the age of the great ocean liners, the *Normandie* was the talk of the world; and it was no wonder that Nick decided to take the great ship to France because he, like everyone else, wanted to see what it was like. He booked a first-class suite, paying for the added expense out of his own pocket because he wanted to take Amanda and Mrs. Hogan with him.

But there was another reason he chose the *Normandie*: He knew that traveling on the ship would be his cousins from Hong Kong, Lance and Nora Wang, and their daughter, Willow, on a buying trip to Paris for their department store. He had met them at a dinner party his mother gave for them the evening before the sailing and found them delightful and eight-year-old Willow a girl of great beauty. Moreover, their hair-raising stories of Japanese brutalities in China indicated that Nazi Germany was not the only menace in an increasingly dangerous world.

He set eyes on her the first morning out of New York as he swam in the first-class swimming pool, its walls made with tiles of enameled sandstone with bright mosaic friezes. She was a tall woman with a smashing figure, shown to advantage in a white bathing suit, who dived into the water and swam several laps, after which she perched herself on the side of the pool and took off her bathing cap to reveal a glorious head of red hair. Nick swam over to her and jumped out of the pool to sit beside her.

"Good morning," he said. "I wanted to congratulate you. You're a terrific swimmer."

"Why, thank you."

"Is this your first time on this ship?"

"Yes."

"It's quite beautiful, isn't it?"

"Yes, I suppose. But it seems a rather disgusting display of money when the world's in such a terrible financial mess."

"I hadn't thought of it quite that way. I take it you're English?"

"That's right. My name's Samantha Thorndyke."

"And I'm Nick Savage."

"So nice to meet you, Mr. Savage." She looked at the clock on the wall. "Well, I have to go," she said, standing up. "It's time for Lady Chatfield's pills."

"Who's Lady Chatfield?"

"My employer. I'm what's known as a paid companion. You surely don't think I had the money to go first class on this preposterous ship? And if I did have the money, I wouldn't throw it away so foolishly. Good-bye."

Giving him a cool look, she walked away.

Well, Nick thought, *I didn't make much of an impression on her, the ice queen. But she's rather interesting. And stunning.*

Leaving the pool room, he went to the ship's gym, which was next to the pool on D deck, to change, then returned to his suite on the Boat Deck, feeling rather guilty about his luxurious, mahogany and cherry-paneled suite and more than a little annoyed at Samantha Thorndyke for making him feel guilty. Mrs. Hogan was combing Amanda's blond hair in their bedroom—the suite had two bedrooms and baths as well as a comfortable living room. After kissing his daughter and commenting on the weather to Mrs. Hogan—the sea was getting choppy—he walked aft to the Grill Room with its varnished pigskin walls for lunch. He was seated by a window overlooking the first-class promenade deck, which in turn overlooked the tourist-class promenade, which overlooked the tourist-class open promenade, which overlooked the tourist- and third-class pool, which overlooked the third-class open promenade and the stern of the ship. Nick studied the menu, reflecting that the French might have staged a bloody revolution for equality a century and a half before, but their ships were still as class-conscious as the *Titanic.*

After ordering lamb chops, he saw an elderly lady in a long black velvet dress enter the Grill Room accompanied by Samantha Thorndyke. The old woman, who wore four strands of pearls around her neck and a number of diamond rings, walked with difficulty, using a cane. The maître d' led them through the room, which was filling up with hungry passengers, to the table next to Nick's where the old lady ensconced herself by the window, Samantha opposite her. Nick gave the redhead a friendly nod, but Samantha coolly ignored him, opening her menu and starting to read its contents to her employer, who Nick assumed was Lady Chatfield.

She really doesn't like me, he thought, with annoyance. *What did I ever do to her?*

He sulked as, below him on the D deck in the ship's great kitchen, seventy-six chefs and one hundred assistants toiled at a fifty-six-foot-long electric range to prepare 4,100 exquisite meals a day. But by the time Nick's lamb chops arrived, he was in such an irritable mood he had lost his appetite. He picked at his food, ate half his salad as a small orchestra began playing dance music. Then he put down his napkin and stood up. Going to the next table, he said to Samantha, "You know, we Yanks bailed you Brits out of that war twenty years ago. You'd think you could at least be polite."

"Who," Lady Chatfield said in a high-pitched voice as she stared at him through a lorgnette, "is this person? And why is he being so rude?"

"This is a Mr. Savage," Samantha said, giving Nick a lethal look, "whom I met in the swimming pool this morning."

"Well, tell him to go away. I don't pay you to flirt with every good-looking man that comes along."

"I wasn't flirting, milady. Do you mind, Mr. Savage? You're bothering Lady Chatfield."

"Yes, thank you, I will join you," Nick said, pulling out a chair between them and sitting down as he signaled to a waiter to bring over his plate. Then he smiled at Lady Chatfield, who was staring at him. "I think it's so nice to meet people, don't you, Lady Chatfield? It sort of broadens one's views on world affairs. For instance, what do you think of Adolf Hitler?"

"I think of him as little as possible," she said in haughty tones. "Horrid little man with that Charlie Chaplin mustache, always screaming in

German, which I find a dreadfully unattractive language. But who asked you to sit down?"

"I did," Nick said as the waiter placed his plate before him. "I thought we could all become friends."

"Extraordinary," Lady Chatfield said, staring at him. Then she laughed. "What terrible cheek! You Americans always amaze me. Well, young man, since you're here, let's all get to be friends. How were your lamb chops?"

"Excellent. I highly recommend them."

"Good. Samantha, order the lamb for me. And waiter, bring a wine list. I feel like a good, strong claret. Probably be overpriced, but everything is these days. The French are all thieves at heart. What do you do, Mr. Savage?"

"I'm a banker, but right now I'm sort of working for the government."

"I trust you're not a spy?"

"No, ma'am." He turned to Samantha. "Would you like to dance?"

Samantha gave him another look that could kill.

"You don't seem to understand," she said, "I am doing my job."

"Oh Samantha, go dance with him," Lady Chatfield said. "I like to watch young people dance. I'm too decrepit to dance now, but in my day I was considered to be quite good. Show me some of the latest dance steps. Go on now."

She waved her hand dismissively as Nick, a smile on his face, stood up. After hesitating a moment, Samantha also got up. He led her onto the dance floor.

"Are you doing your best to get me fired?" she said as he took her in his arms. "Don't you realize Lady Chatfield hates to be intruded on? And she positively loathes Americans."

"She seems to like me. Why don't you?"

"I don't dislike you, I hardly know you. But I have a job to do, and believe me, I need the money. Lady Chatfield is very fussy and not easy to get along with."

"I think she's charming. Much more charming than you."

"I'm not paid to be charming to pushy Americans."

"Tell me about yourself. I assume you're not married?"

"No I'm not and it's none of your business."

"Are you a Socialist? You were talking like one this morning."

"Yes, I'm a Fabian Socialist and I admire George Bernard Shaw and the Webbs. I suppose, since you're a banker, you're a Republican?"

"Actually, I voted for President Roosevelt. I raised money for him, too."

She looked surprised.

"Really? Well, that's one thing in your favor. You're also a good dancer, but the sommelier is pouring the wine and Lady Chatfield hates to drink by herself."

"When are you off duty?"

"Never, at least on the ship."

"Oh, come now, you can take some time for yourself. I'd like you to meet my baby daughter. She's the most beautiful baby in the world."

"I'm sure, but I really can't."

"Oh, come on. After you put Lady Chatfield to bed tonight. I'm in Suite C on the Boat Deck."

"You really are pushy, aren't you?"

"A veritable Fuller Brush salesman. How about it?"

She sighed.

"All right—on the condition you take me back to Lady Chatfield before she fires me."

"She won't fire you because of me. She likes men, I can tell. Come on: back to the table."

He led her back to the table, where Lady Chatfield was tasting the wine.

"Not bad," she said offhandedly as Nick held Samantha's chair. "I mean the wine. You two dance very well. It was a pleasure to watch you. Mr. Savage, I take it you're traveling alone?"

"Not exactly. I have my young daughter with me and her nanny."

"I see. Then you'll be free to join us this evening for dinner?"

"I'd be delighted to."

"Excellent. I can't talk to Samantha about anything interesting because she's so frightfully left wing: she thinks all rich people are villains, but of course that doesn't stop her from taking my money. She's a sweet thing, though, and I'm fond of her. So: What do *you* think of Adolf Hitler, young man?"

"Frankly, he scares me."

"He does? Then you think he's really a menace to world peace?"

"I do."

"Hmm. Well, then I'm not so unhappy about getting old. I've lived through two wars, and I'm not eager to live through another. Some wine, young man?"

"No thank you. I don't drink."

"An American who doesn't drink? Extraordinary. You are a rare bird, Mr. Savage."

"Nope, just your average alcoholic." He signaled to the waiter. "Is the captain expecting a storm?" he asked. "The sea seems to be getting quite rough."

"Yes, sir, there is a storm ahead. But you will find that the *Normandie* will remain amazingly smooth."

13

THE FIRST-CLASS DINING ROOM on the *Normandie* was three hundred feet long and three decks high, making it the biggest room afloat in the world. It was also the most spectacular, with its handsomely coffered ceiling and its walls of hammered glass and cast-glass panels shimmering with illumination from behind with the brightness of 135,000 candles. That night, the second night out, when Nick arrived in his white tie and tails, as was de rigeur, the first seating of the 864 first-class passengers had begun, and it was as well-dressed a crowd as could be encountered on the heavily traveled Atlantic sea lanes, jewels flashing and women buzzing, drinking, and flirting in some of the most gorgeous evening dresses to be found anywhere in the world. Nick, who was expected, was led across the blue carpeting to a table near a large bronze statue representing Peace where Lady Chatfield, wearing a sapphire and diamond necklace and matching earrings, was seated by herself drinking champagne.

"Ah, here's my American Prince Charming," she said as Nick was seated opposite her. "Samantha, poor child, is, alas, a wretched sailor. All this bobbing about has given her a first-class case of *mal de mer*, so I put her to bed with a cup of soup. I hope you won't be disappointed to have to eat your dinner with an old hag like me."

"Not at all, Lady Chatfield. It's my pleasure. But I hope Samantha's not seriously ill?"

"She'll survive. When we came to New York two weeks ago on the *Queen Mary*, we ran into a frightful storm much worse than this and she was in bed two days, which was a nuisance for me, but there you have it: Samantha's a treasure despite all her left-wing foolishness, and I don't wish to replace her just because she gets seasick. Her father was a vicar in a small church in Northumberland, a sweet man from a very old family, but when he died last year he left poor Samantha without a penny. He was a distant cousin of my late husband, so I felt a responsibility to her and hired her. Would you like some champagne? Ah, I forgot: You don't drink. I do hope you don't harbor any murky intentions about Samantha? As I said, I feel a sense of responsibility to her, and the poor child knows very little about the ways of the world, if you see what I mean. She is quite attractive, isn't she?"

"Very. And while my intentions aren't exactly murky, I'd very much like to get to know her better."

"Mmm. You say you have a daughter traveling with you. Where's the mother?"

"Unfortunately, she died a year ago."

"I see. Well, a handsome bachelor like you is a potential menace to the female sex, so I'll keep my eye on you, young man. But you can be sure of one thing: Samantha won't chase you for your money. She really is a rabid Socialist, which can be quite tiresome. She's never said it, but I know she thinks my poor late husband, Sir Bertrand Chatfield, was the devil incarnate merely because he made an immense fortune in department stores."

"Ah, so you're the Chatfield's Chatfield?"

"Exactly. Twenty-four stores all over Europe, and we just opened one in New York, which is why I came over. I keep a sharp eye on the business, which is certainly tricky with this wretched economy."

"Some cousins of mine, Lance and Nora Wang, are on board. Lance's family owns the Chin department stores in Hong Kong and Shanghai. Perhaps you've heard of them?"

"I have indeed. I'd like to meet them. Why don't you bring them to my cabin for lunch tomorrow? With any luck, Samantha will be feeling better. At least she won't be running to the loo every ten minutes. Will you read me the menu? I have very poor eyesight, such a nuisance. Growing old is really tiresome, but then, as they say, the alternative is worse."

Lady Chatfield had booked one of the four grand luxe suites on the Sun Deck of the *Normandie*, which gave her the exclusivity of a private promenade deck overlooking all the other decks below. When Nick and Lance and Nora Wang appeared at noon the next day, they were ushered into the capacious sitting room, which was big enough to hold its own grand piano with room enough to spare to host at least thirty people for cocktails. A white-jacketed steward was in attendance.

"This place makes our stateroom look like steerage," Nora Wang said as she looked around at the smartly decorated room that was banked with two huge bouquets from the ship's florist shop, which was aft the forward of the ship's three stacks next to the children's playroom. Nora was wearing a well-cut blue suit.

"Yes, Lady Chatfield does things in a big way," Nick said, wondering where Samantha was. "Where's Willow?"

"She's in the children's playroom," Lance said. "They'll feed her lunch."

Just then, Lady Chatfield and Samantha came into the room, Samantha still looking a bit pale. After introductions were made, the party sat down at a white-clothed table and the steward proceeded to serve lunch. The conversation began with talk about the department store business, but Nick barely listened, keeping his eyes glued on Samantha, who was sitting opposite him next to her employer. To his immense satisfaction, Samantha's chilliness of the day before seemed to have melted somewhat, and he noticed that she was sneaking glances at him when Lady Chatfield wasn't looking. The latter was entranced by the Wangs and peppered them with questions about Hong Kong and Shanghai.

"We're very nervous about Shanghai," Lance said as he cut into his Dover sole. "The talk is that the Japanese are itching to invade it."

"The Japanese," Lady Chatfield snorted. "Dreadful people, always wanting to invade something. First Manchuria, then Mongolia, or was it the other way around? What's the world coming to?"

"Something fairly unpleasant, I'm afraid. My parents are in Nanking, where my father is the minister of war on Chiang Kai-shek's staff and my mother runs a children's hospital. My father tells me he's trying to get the Generalissimo to unite with the Communists against the Japanese, but Chiang won't do it. He's more interested in fighting Mao Tse-tung. It's a bit of a mess in China, and I fear it's going to get worse."

"It's all too, too dreadful," Lady Chatfield said, shaking her head. "Barbarians are taking over the world."

"Not everyone's a barbarian," Nora said. "Lance's mother, Jasmin, is a real saint. She could live in the lap of luxury in Hong Kong or Shanghai, but instead she built a lovely hospital in Nanking, which isn't the nicest city in the world by a long shot. And Lance's father, Charlie . . . Well, he's the most romantic man in the world. He was a warlord with his own private army, and he kidnapped Lance's mother then fell in love with her and married her. Isn't that a wonderfully romantic story?"

"It is indeed," said Lady Chatfield, "though kidnapping doesn't seem a proper way to conduct a courtship."

"Oh, Lance's family isn't at all proper, which is why they're so wonderful. Like Lance."

She took her husband's arm and looked at him adoringly.

"You're feeling better?" Nick asked Samantha later, as they were served coffee.

"Yes, thank you."

"They say the best thing for seasickness is to go outside on deck."

"I've heard that."

"I'd be glad to take you for a walk. Now that the storm's over, it's rather nice out. Bit of a wind, though."

"Well . . ."

"Yes, go on, Samantha," Lady Chatfield said. "I want to talk with these charming people about business, which may bore your socialist proclivities. Put on a coat and use our private deck. You know where the door is."

A few minutes later, Nick and Samantha leaned on the rail watching the sea, which was much calmer, as the great ship sliced through the water at thirty knots.

"Are you going to be in Paris?" Nick asked.

"Yes, for a few days. She wants to check out her store there."

"Do you know Paris?"

"I've been there, but I can't say I know it."

"I have a sister who lives there. I generally stay with her, but she's out of town. Where will you be staying?"

"At the Ritz. Lady Chatfield always stays there."

"That's a nice coincidence. I'll be staying there, too."

"Yes, I supposed you would."

"What do you mean by that?"

"Well, you're a millionaire, aren't you? You'd hardly be staying in someplace seedy."

"Do you really resent the fact that I have money?"

"Why shouldn't I? There are so many poor people in this world, it just doesn't seem fair . . ." She shrugged. "Well, I won't bore you with my left-wing drivel, as Lady Chatfield calls it. I couldn't possibly convert you to what I believe, and you'd just resent me for saying what I think." She looked at her watch. "It's time for Lady Chatfield's pills."

"Pills for what?"

"For her heart. She had a mild heart attack two years ago. Of course, she's eighty-six years old, but otherwise she's in fairly good shape. Thank you so much, Mr. Savage. You were right: The fresh air has made me feel better."

"I'm very glad. And my name's Nick. I really would like you to meet my little girl."

"Mr. Savage . . ."

"Nick."

"Mr. Savage, I infer that you are, in your rather clumsy way, trying to become my friend, or perhaps even something more. I'm sure you're a very nice person, but you don't seem to understand the depth of my socialist beliefs. I really dislike your class of people, so there seems to be no point at all for my meeting your daughter or having anything else to do with you."

"But that's so damned unfair!" Nick said, angrily.

"Life is unfair, as the millions of poor, wretched people on this planet could tell you if you'd only listen. So please leave me alone for the rest of the voyage."

She opened the door and went back inside Lady Chatfield's suite.

That night, he invited Lance and Nora to dinner at his table in the first-class dining room.

"You know, I hate the English," he began, as the sommelier poured the elegant Chinese-Anglo couple a glass of Corton-Charlemagne.

"Why would you say that?" Nora said. "After all, I'm English. You're being terribly rude."

"I'm sorry, It's just that . . . well, Lady Chatfield's companion, Samantha, she's so terribly snippy with me. It makes me furious."

Lance laughed.

"Oh well, dear fellow, it just means she's terribly attracted to you."

Nick looked surprised.

"Do you think so?"

"Absolutely. It's the oldest ploy in the book. When you want someone you think you shouldn't want, you insult them. It's fundamental."

Nick sipped his glass of water.

"Lance, you're much more sophisticated than I am."

Lance reached over and squeezed Nora's hand.

"Nick, Nora and I have learned sophistication from the masters: the English Imperialists. And we beat them at their own game."

"Good for you," Nick said, thinking about Samantha.

After the first course was served, beluga caviar with toast, Nick said: "I was so sorry hearing about your grandmother."

"Well, Julie died of old age, and she had a great life," Lance said. "I loved her dearly."

"She was quite a lady. Not to change the subject, but what are your thoughts about the Japanese? They seem to be terribly aggressive."

"They are," Lance said, sipping his wine. "I think they want to take over all of Asia."

"And what if they attack Hong Kong and Shanghai? What will you two do?"

"We'll cope," Nora said, in a crisp English accent.

A week later, Nick came into the Ritz Hotel, returning from a day-long meeting with officials of the Banque de France, when he spotted Samantha waiting for the elevator. After getting his room key at the concierge desk he came over to her.

"Miss Thorndyke," he said. "How's Lady Chatfield?"

She looked surprised to see him.

"Oh yes, Mr. Savage. I'd forgotten you were staying here. Lady Chatfield's fine, thank you."

"I'm glad to hear it."

He watched the elevator door, determined to ignore her. After a moment, she said, "Mr. Savage, I think I owe you an apology."

"Oh? For what?"

"I was rude to you on the ship, and I feel rather upset about it. I suppose it is rather unfair to judge someone for something they can't help. I mean, the fact that you have money. It's as unfair, I suppose, as disliking someone for not having money. So I do want to apologize."

Nick smiled at her.

"Now that's really nice to hear," he said. "And I accept your apology."

"I would like to meet your daughter some time."

"How about now?"

"Well . . ."

The elevator door opened. She smiled at him.

"All right. Where's your room?"

"On the second floor."

"So is Lady Chatfield's." She got in the elevator, as did Nick. "I'll just bring her the marron glacé she sent me for—they're her favorites."

"Wonderful."

When they got off the elevator, they walked down the corridor to a pair of doors.

"I'll just be a moment," Samantha said, putting her room key in the lock.

"I'll wait here for you."

She smiled at him and went inside, closing the door. A moment later, he heard a cry. The door opened and Samantha reappeared. Her face was ashen.

"She's dead!" she exclaimed, softly. "Oh my God . . ."

"Where is she?"

"On her bed. I thought she was asleep, but . . ."

"Let me see."

They hurried inside the living room of the suite overlooking the Place Vendôme. She led him to the bedroom door. He looked in. Lady Chatfield was lying on the bed, seemingly asleep. Nick hurried over and felt her wrist.

Nothing.

"She must have had another heart attack," Samantha said, sinking down into a chair. "And I wasn't here to help her. Oh, I feel so terrible . . ."

"I doubt if there'd been much you could have done for her," Nick said. "Shall I call the hotel management?"

"I suppose." She started weeping.

"You really did care for her, didn't you?" Nick said.

"Oh yes. She really was a sweet woman, even with all her money." She wiped her eyes, thinking. "No, don't call the management until I talk to her solicitor in London."

"Does she have any relatives you should contact?"

"No. The Chatfields had only one son, and he was killed in an automobile accident four years ago. He was a bit of a playboy." She stood up, looking at the body. "Poor, dear creature," she said.

Then she went to the telephone.

Nick looked at Lady Chatfield and thought of Laura, who had gone almost as quickly.

How fleeting life is, he thought. *And how unfair. The only fair thing is death, because it takes us all.*

And how I still miss Laura.

14   TEN DAYS LATER, NICK was studying some papers presented to him by the Banque de France when his phone rang.

"Yes?"

"Mr. Savage, it's Samantha Thorndyke. I don't mean to bother you, but I wondered if I could see you when it's convenient for you."

"Of course. Any time. Where are you?"

"I'm staying at a small hotel on the Left Bank. I had to come back to Paris for some business dealing with Lady Chatfield's estate. I've been in London, taking care of so many things, handling the funeral and so forth."

"Perhaps we could have lunch. I mean, would you be my guest?"

"Well, I'm not very hungry, and I wouldn't want you to spend any thing on me. What I mean is, I want your advice."

"My advice is free, and we'll go to a cheap café the Socialists love. Meet me at noon at La Coupole on the Boulevard du Montparnasse."

"Yes, all right. Thank you."

She hung up.

Three hours later, she joined Nick, who had taken a table on the sidewalk. It was a lovely day and Paris had never looked more vibrant. Nick remembered his brother-in-law's remark about France being full of corruption and decadence; that might have been true, but it was still a wonderful place to be alive in.

"Now," he said after they had ordered, "what's the problem? Have you found a new job?"

She looked startled.

"Oh no. I mean, I have a job."

"Excellent. What is it?"

"Lady Chatfield left most of her estate to a charitable foundation she had set up. The amount of her estate was over fifty million pounds ster-ling."

Nick let out a soft whistle.

"Wow, the old girl was really loaded, wasn't she?"

"She was indeed. I really had no idea . . . I mean, I knew she was rich, but . . . Anyway, she appointed me as one of three directors of the foundation. She said that all of my socialist, left-wing ideas would be helpful in making the Chatfield Foundation spend its money to help the poor. I was really touched by that, particularly after all the kidding I took from her. Her heart really was in the right place after all."

"That's wonderful!" Nick said. "I'm very happy for you, and I think she was right: You'll be perfect for the job."

Samantha looked a little embarrassed. She rubbed her hands rather nervously. Then she blurted out: "She also left me a trust fund of five million pounds! Not to mention her townhouse on Eaton Square and her country estate, Hadley Hall. And I'm legally enjoined from giving any of it away!"

Nick looked truly stunned.

"Good Lord," he said in wonderment, "you're rich!"

"Yes, and it's making me miserable! What in the world am I going to do with all that money? I hate rich people, and now I'm one of them, and I know it's going to corrupt me and turn me into a useless, awful parasite, everything I dislike . . ." She burst into tears. "Oh, I know she meant well, but I also know this was some kind of cruel joke on her part. I'm sure she's laughing at me from heaven or wherever . . ." She pulled a handkerchief from her purse and wiped her eyes. Nick was trying not to laugh. "You're laughing at me, too!" she exclaimed. "And it's not funny! Oh, what am I to do?"

The waiter brought them two café au laits.

"Tonight you're going to let me take you to dinner at a decadently capitalist restaurant so we can commiserate about your terrible luck."

"You *do* think it's funny!" She sniffed. "You're a terrible person and as rude as I thought on the ship."

"I'm awful, a veritable monster. But you will let me take you to dinner?"

She thought a moment, then smiled at him.

"Brook, I'm crazy about her, and she's nutty as a fruitcake!"

It was a week later. Nick was on the phone, talking to his older sister, Brook, who had just gotten back to Paris from Palestine, where she and her husband, Bernard de Belleville, had been working on an archeological dig and furthering their work on the Jewish settlements there. It was through Bernard's interest in archeological digs in Palestine that he had become involved in buying land there for Jewish settlements; Brook had become interested not only because of her husband's interest, but because of her mother's involvement in the Dreyfus Affair in Paris many years before.

"Nutty?" Brook asked. "How so?"

"Oh, she's a Socialist who's hit the jackpot, and she's worried sick that all her money is going to ruin her . . . I mean, it's really sort of funny, except it's also sort of touching. Anyway, I'm nuts about her and I'm going to ask her to marry me."

"Nick, don't go flying off the handle. You have plenty of time. Bring her here tomorrow night and let me meet her. I'm pretty good at sizing up people—and I know, I had rotten judgement with my first husband, so don't remind me. Anyway, be here at eight tomorrow night."

"Isn't tomorrow your birthday?"

"Yes, little brother, it's my forty-first, but you don't have to remind me. I'm depressed beyond belief. God! Forty-one years old. I've got one foot in the grave. Oh well. See you tomorrow. By the way, have you made love to her yet?"

"No."

"That's not your style."

"Brook, I tell you, she's a bit nutty! Her father was a clergyman, and she was very strictly brought up. She tells me she wants to remain 'pure' till she's a bride, and if that's what she wants, I say more power to her. It's sort of charming."

"You're right, it is. I'm dying to meet her. See you tomorrow."

She hung up and thought a moment. She was sitting in her bedroom on the second floor of their house on the Avenue Foch. Then she turned to look at her husband, who was brushing his teeth in the bathroom, a towel around his waist. She got up and went to the door.

"Nick's in love," she said. "With some crazy Socialist Englishwoman. He's bringing her to dinner tomorrow night."

"Nick fell in love with a Socialist? How bizarre."

"Well, apparently she's now a rich Socialist."

She looked at Bernard's smooth back and his still trim figure. She went into the bathroom, came up behind him and put her arms around his waist, giving him a hug. Bernard, whose mouth was full of toothpaste, said, slurringly, "Hey, what are you up to?"

"I just had a mad impulse to give you a hug. Anything wrong with that?"

"Not a bit. Wait a minute."

He took a glass off the sink, filled it with water, then gargled, spitting into the sink. Then he turned and took her in his arms, giving her a kiss.

"How many wives attack their husbands when they're brushing their teeth?" he said with a grin.

"How many wives are as crazy about their husbands as I am? Oh Bernard, how very happy I am with you. And you still make me feel like a lovesick teenager." She sighed. "I think I would have made a very successful whore. I'm really nuts about making love, but only with you."

She kissed him. He ran his hand lovingly through her blond hair.

"And I adore you," he said, softly, kissing her again.

"I had a dream last night," Brook went on. "I dreamed some terrible man took you away from me, and I tried to stop him but I couldn't. You know how it is in dreams, when you try to move but your hands and feet feel weighted down?"

"Yes, I've had those dreams often. It's frightening."

"Oh, I was terribly afraid. And the man took you through a door and closed the door behind him. I ran to the door and tried to open it, but I couldn't. And then I heard a gunshot. And the door swung open, and I was in a strange room that was filled with red smoke. And you were lying on the floor with blood all over your chest."

"Good Lord, this wasn't a dream, it was a nightmare. So, who shot me?"

"I don't know. There was no one else in the room. Then I woke up and looked at you, asleep beside me. And I realized that if you were ever taken from me, my life would be over." She kissed him again. "And then Nick called."

A handsome teenager appeared outside the bathroom door.

"Mom, breakfast is ready."

"We'll be right down, darling."

"Dad, can I have my allowance a day early?" their son, Graydon, went on. "I'm broke."

"You're always broke," Bernard said, as Brook disentangled herself. "We'll discuss your finances at breakfast. Now you two scram so I can take my shower."

The limestone Belle Epoque mansion on the fashionable Avenue Foch that Brook had rented when she moved to Paris in the 'twenties she had bought when its owner died in 1931, including all of its furnishings. When Nick and Samantha arrived in a taxi the next night, they were admitted to the house by a white-jacketed butler who led them into the drawing room where Brook gave him a hug and a kiss. She was dressed fashionably in a light-blue Chanel.

"Nick, darling," she said, looking him over. "God, you look great, young as ever."

"So do you."

She laughed.

"Come on, Nickie, let's not kid ourselves. And this is Samantha?" She came over to shake her hand. "I'm so glad to meet you," she said. "Nick's said so many wonderful things about you."

"Uncle Nick!"

A handsome fourteen-year-old boy ran into the room and came to hug Nick.

"Graydon! My goodness, you've shot up like a rocket!" Nick said. "Samantha, this is my nephew, Graydon. Graydon, Miss Thorndyke."

"How do you do?" he said, turning to shake her hand. *"Maman, puis-je diner avec toi ce soir?"*

"No, darling, it's grown-up time tonight. And speak English. Samantha, I was just making a cocktail. Would you like a drink? Of course, I know Nicky doesn't imbibe."

"Just a glass of sherry, please."

"Brook liked you a lot," Nick said two hours later as he drove Samantha to her hotel in a taxi. "But then I knew she would."

"She's so very nice. And so's her husband. I liked him terribly. He told me at dinner that he and your sister buy land in Palestine to resettle European Jews, which I found fascinating. Is Bernard Jewish?"

"Half. So am I, and so is Brook. Our mother is, you see."

"Well, I rather like that."

"Why so?"

"Oh, I don't know. It makes you more interesting. I like, you know, mixtures."

"Too bad you can't talk to Herr Hitler."

"I only wish I had the chance, the horrible man. The one thing I have against George Bernard Shaw is that he admires Hitler. It makes my skin crawl."

"Here we are at your socialist hotel. How's your room?"

"Tiny and rather ghastly. And the loo is down the hall. And there's an old man next door who snores like crazy. Keeps me up half the night."

"I have plenty of room at the Ritz. I know it would be against your principles to spend the night there, but it's available."

She looked at him as the taxi driver watched them in his rearview mirror.

"But I couldn't possibly do that," she said. "I mean, we're not married. You know my views on that subject."

"But what if we were engaged?"

She looked at him.

"Is that a proposal?" she finally asked.

"Sounds like one to me."

"You wicked man. You pushy American with far too much money for your own good . . ."

"Ah, ah: You're one of us now. Filthy Capitalists."

She sighed.

"I know. It's so hard getting used to. Yes."

"Yes what?"

"Yes I'll marry you and yes I'll spend the night with you."

Nick stared at her a moment. Then he let out a whoop of pure joy.

"Take us to the Ritz!" he cried out to the driver.

Then he took her in his arms and kissed her. For the first time since he had lost Laura, he felt happiness again.

15

ON A SNOWY NIGHT in February, 1936, Captain Sokichi Igitaki of the Japanese Imperial Army led a group of twelve soldiers to the house of the Japanese Finance Minister, Korekiyo Takahashi. Ordered by Igitaki, who had a number of years before murdered his brother-in-law, Edgar Morrow, the soldiers broke down the door of the sprawling, half-western house in a Tokyo suburb. Entering the house, they seized half a dozen police guards and servants and held them under arms. Igitaki took the remaining soldiers and started through the house, kicking down the doors of rooms as they searched for their victim, Takahashi.

The aged Finance minister was alone in a large bedroom in the Japanese side of the house. He was a remarkable man who had started out as a footman, then rose to become president of the Bank of Japan and a member of the House of Peers. The army officers loathed him because the previous year he had fought the huge military budget.

Finally, Igitaki found him. Brandishing a pistol, he kicked Takahashi's quilt off him, shouting, *"Tenchu!"* (Punishment of Heaven). He aimed his gun at the old man, who looked at him and shouted "Idiot!"

Igitaki fired, emptying his gun. Another officer leaped forward and swung his sword, hitting the old man so hard he cut off his right arm. He then stabbed him in the stomach, slashing him viciously right to left, disembowelling him.

Having heard the commotion, Takahashi's wife came into the room from the western side of the house and screamed in horror.

Captain Igitaki, putting away his gun, bowed politely and said, "Excuse me for the annoyance I have caused."

Then the soldiers left the house as the guards and servants stared at the blood-gushing mutilated corpse of their master.

Jasmin Wang had named the two-story hospital she and her husband had built in Nanking after her late mother. The Julie Chin Memorial Hospital was a two-story brick building set in a small, pleasant park in the middle of the old city, the land having been donated by Generalissimo Chiang Kai-shek as part of the National Government's effort to modernize Nanking and clear away much of its ancient slums. The handsome building had a Chinese-style red tile roof, but otherwise its clean lines were relatively modern. It had two hundred beds, and its equipment, paid for by Jasmin out of her own inheritance, was state of the art. There was a staff of twenty doctors, most of them trained in the west, and fifty nurses. Madame Chiang, who had officiated at the opening of the hospital two years before, had proudly announced that it was "the best hospital in China," a remark that brought tears of joy to Jasmin's eyes. She felt the hospital, which had been her idea, was the high point of her life to date.

The morning after the assassination of Finance Minister Takahashi, Jasmin was eating breakfast with her tall husband, Charlie Wang, in the dining room of their pleasant villa in the Purple Mountains northeast of the Nanking city walls when a servant came in with a telephone, which he plugged in the wall.

"Sir, it is the Generalissimo," the servant said, handing Charlie the phone.

"Good morning, sir," Charlie said as Jasmin indicated she wanted more tea. The servant refilled her cup as Charlie, the Minister of War of the National Government, listened to his boss.

"It sounds very bad," he said. "I'll be there as soon as I can."

He hung up.

"What's wrong?" Jasmin said as Charlie gulped down his coffee.

"There's been an attempted coup in Tokyo," Charlie said. "A bunch of hotheaded young officers have tried to murder the Prime Minister, the Finance Minister, the Lord Keeper of the Privy Seal and the Grand Chamberlain. Word is just coming over the radio. The Generalissimo is very nervous. He thinks if the fanatics get control of the government, they'll attack Shanghai next." He finished his coffee and stood up.

"And then?" Jasmin asked as he hurried to her to give her a kiss.

"And then us."

And he ran out of the room, leaving Jasmin in stunned silence.

PART FIVE

AN AMERICAN NAZI. TWINS. 1936

16

GLORIA GILMORE SAVAGE WOOD was racing her brand-new Chris-Craft speedboat across the waters of Lake Wawasee in northern Indiana when she spotted one of her twin sons waving at her from the white dock of their summer home.

"Isn't that one of your kids?" asked her houseguest and current lover, Dr. Ross Treadwell, an Indianapolis surgeon.

"Yes. Must be some trouble," Gloria said, slowing the powerful boat and turning it toward the dock.

"Which one, Mark or Sebastian?"

"I'm not sure. I think it's Sebastian."

It was the fiercely hot August of 1936, when the attention of the world was on the Berlin Olympics where Hitler and his henchmen were impressing the thousands of tourists by putting a smiling face on the brutal Nazi regime. But here, in rural Indiana, with the beautiful lake with its peaceful cottages lining the arbored shores, Nazis seemed far, far away. Gloria, who was wearing a tight white bathing suit and dark glasses, slowed the engine further as the sleek speedboat with its chrome-trimmed wooden hull neared the dock.

"What's wrong?" Gloria called.

"Mark's sick," Sebastian yelled. "He says he can't move his legs."

"Oh my God," Gloria muttered, backing the engine to stop the boat as it bumped up against the two dock fenders. Polio had been rampaging through the Midwest, forcing many cities and towns to impose strict quarantines. Forty-two-year-old Ross, who was also in a bathing suit, hopped out and quickly tied the boat's lines to the dock, then helped Gloria out.

"Where is Mark?" she asked.

"In his room. He went to bed about an hour ago. Do you think he has polio?"

"We mustn't think that," his mother said, although it was exactly what she was thinking. "Come on, Ross. Thank God you're here, you can take a look at him."

She hurried down the dock past the boathouse to start climbing the stairs that led up a rather steep hill to her fourteen-room cottage overlooking the lake. She was followed by Ross, but Sebastian stayed on the dock. He was scared for his brother, and he was scared for himself.

Gloria's cottage, which had been built in 1915, was a two-story white clapboard building with green shutters on its windows and a big screened porch on its front. The house was shaded by a number of ancient trees which, along with the proximity of the lake, kept it cool on even the hottest days, like this one. Gloria and Ross hurried through the screened porch into the capacious living room, which was casually strewn with unpretentious summer furniture, then up the staircase to the second floor, which held six bedrooms and three baths.

"Let me look at him," Ross whispered when they reached the end of the hall. "You stay out here. If he has it, there's no use exposing you."

"But I want to see him! And I want him to see me."

"Then stay at the door."

Ross knocked on the door, then opened it.

"Mark," he said. "How are you feeling?"

The handsome ten-year-old was sitting up in his bed, with one hand on his right leg. He looked terrified.

"I can't move my legs!" he said, on the verge of tears. "I can't even feel anything in them. Mom, I'm scared! I'm really scared!"

Gloria, who was also scared, smiled and said, "Everything's going to be fine, darling. Ross will take care of you."

Then she went back into the hall. A few minutes later, Ross left the bedroom and quietly closed the door.

"It's polio," he whispered. "We have to get him to a hospital, fast."

An ambulance rushed him to a hospital in nearby Fort Wayne. But by midnight, the insidious disease had paralyzed his entire body, preventing him even from breathing.

Mark Savage was put in an iron lung, an ugly steel box that mechanically forced his body to breathe. Only Mark's head was free of the machine. The boy was crying with fear as his mother, Ross, and a nurse stood by.

"Momma, I hate this box," he sobbed. "Please let me out of it. I can't move! It's horrible!"

Gloria, whose heart was breaking, smoothed his hair with her hand.

"Darling, you'll be out soon," she said.

"How soon?"

"Maybe a few days, even a week."

"A week? I can't stand being in here a week! Let me out! Please let me out!"

"Mark," Ross said, "we have to keep you in the box until your body is strong enough to breathe for you. You must understand that. If we take you out of the box now, you'll suffocate to death."

The boy stared at him a moment, terror in his eyes. Then he burst into tears again.

"I'd rather die," he sobbed. "I hate this box! I'd rather die."

The nurse whispered to Gloria that they should leave so she could give Mark a sedative and get him to sleep. Gloria nodded, then said to Mark, "We have to leave now, darling, but we'll be back in the morning . . ."

"Don't leave me, Momma! Please!"

"We have to. You be a brave little boy."

"I'm not brave, I'm scared!"

She leaned down and kissed his forehead.

"You'll be out soon."

As she and Ross left the hospital to get in their station wagon and return to Lake Wawasee, Gloria started to cry herself.

"The poor kid," she sobbed. "The poor darling boy. What a rotten, stinking bit of luck—particularly him, who's such a great athlete. Will he ever get out of that horrible box?"

Ross started the station wagon, a grim look on his face.

"Do you want to hear the truth?" he said.

"No, but tell me anyway."

"The doctor told me confidentially he thinks Mark will be in the iron lung for the rest of his life, and from what I saw, I think he's probably right."

Gloria stared at him as he drove out of the hospital driveway.

"The rest of his life?" she said. "You mean, there's no hope?"

"There's always hope, I suppose. But not much."

Gloria doubled over in the front seat, buried her face in her hands and keened like a woman gone mad with grief.

Article published on the front page of the Indianapolis *Times-Gazette*, written by the newspaper's publisher, Mr. Bennet Kinkaid.

BERLIN. August 6, 1936. My daughter, Deirdre, and I arrived in this vibrant city yesterday, having flown from London to Temple-hof, a splendid, newly enlarged airfield, on the outskirts of the city, and we taxied to our hotel. Berlin is bursting with tourists come to see the Olympic Games and, much like myself, curious to see what the Nazis have accomplished in their three and a half years in power. The Hitler regime has received mounting criticism in America, but I must report that at first glance, a foreigner like myself can only be impressed: Berlin looks prosperous, its streets are beflagged, there is excitement in the air, the people are well-dressed and nowhere have I seen, at least so far, any signs of the anti-Jewish propaganda that has been increasingly reported in the foreign press. It has been said that at Hitler's orders, anti-Jewish signs were taken down for the Games, and this may well be true. But if Jews are being persecuted in Germany, it is certainly not evident to me.

My daughter and I ensconced ourselves in the Eden Hotel, a most impressive place, and I was surprised to find a bouquet of flowers and a bowl of fresh fruit in our suite with a welcome note from none other than Dr. Goebbels, the Minister of Propaganda. Also an envelope containing free tickets to the games, and invitations to various social functions being given by the Nazi big-wigs, including a party being given in a few nights by Dr. Goebbels and his wife. Apparently, Dr. Goebbels has decided to try to improve Germany's American press, which is to the good. The millions of Americans of German descent deserve a more balanced press coverage of this great nation than they have been getting.

This morning, my daughter and I were driven to the Olympic

Stadium, which is really a collection of stadia, all quite handsome. We watched polo for a while, then walked to the biggest stadium, which seats 100,000 and, I am told, is always full. We watched hurdling and running; whenever there is a win, the whole stadium stands up and attempts to sing the National Anthem of the victorius team. When a German team wins, the Germans sing not only *Deutschland über Alles* but the *Horst Wessel* song, the Nazi anthem, which is rather catchy.

After a while, there was a surging and the crowd bellowed "Heil!" A large, rotund man in a white uniform appeared in the Government box and the crowd went wild as the loudspeakers bellowed "We want our Hermann!" It was Hermann Goering, the second most powerful man in Germany and, judging from the enthusiasm of the crowd, one of the most beloved. Goering bowed to the crowd several times, almost like an actor—which, after all, good politicians usually are—then he sat down and the games proceeded. A short while later, the crowd again became electrified: Hitler himself was arriving! When he came into the box to join Goering, the crowd went crazy. He was wearing a brown uniform, and looks like the caricatures we see so often in the press. He may have a Charlie Chaplin mustache, but the spell this man has cast over the German public cannot be denied. I confess I was more excited than when I met Mussolini three years ago in Rome, and much more excited than when I was blessed by the Pope in 1927. This man Hitler is awesome. He makes most American politicians look like bumbling amateurs.

My daughter and I returned to our hotel and dressed for a State Banquet Dr. Goebbels had invited us to. It was a warm evening, but the invitation said evening dress, so I put on my white tie and tails, and Deirdre looked lovely in a light blue chiffon gown. We were surprised to find that a Government car had been sent to convey us to the Opera House: if it was meant to impress me, I'll admit it worked. At the Opera House, at least a hundred footmen wearing pink livery and carrying torches in glass holders lined the entrance. A reception took place in the foyer where Frau Goering, a tall, handsome, and seemingly almost naked woman, was the principal figure moving about among a crowd of bejeweled Royalties and ambassadors. Berlin has not known anything like this since the 1914 war and I was quite conscious that the Germans were making every effort to show the world the grandeur, the permanence, and respectability of the new regime.

Finally, dinner was announced and we went into the Opera House itself where a floor had been laid over the seats. An excellent dinner was served to two thousand guests, and the wines flowed—especially Henkel champagne, for the wife of Herr von Ribbentrop, the new German ambassador to London, is the Henkel heiress. During dinner, entertainment was provided by a corps de ballet. On the right side of the stage sat Dr. Goebbels with his wife and the Crown Prince of Italy. On the left were the Goerings, with the Crown Prince of Sweden and the King of Bulgaria. Rather oddly, in my opinion, Herr Hitler was nowhere in evidence, though I suspect that he is too shrewd and conscious of his image as a National Socialist to mingle with all this glitter: He stays home and works for the nation—or at least that's what he wants to convey. Or maybe he just doesn't like parties, who knows?

At the conclusion of dinner, a distinguished-looking gentleman came to our table and introduced himself as Prince Philip of Hesse. He said that Dr. Goebbels would like us to join him for a glass of champagne, to which we of course agreed. We were led to the stage where we were introduced. Dr. Goebbels, a former playwright who took his Ph.D. from Heidelberg at the age of twenty-four, is a wiry little man who, it is rumored, is a voracious womanizer and, since he controls the German film industry, has access, one would assume, to his choice of starlets. Whether this is true or not, his wife, Magda, seems quite devoted. I thanked both Goebbelses for their kind hospitality, using Prince Philip as interpreter—his English is perfect—and, after a glass of excellent champagne, Deidre and I returned to our hotel exhausted but impressed.

All Americans who love our country, as I do, and who have watched America struggle through a miserable Depression with an inept Government that seems to be able to come up with nothing better than wildly expensive porkbarrel projects of dubious value, should perhaps learn something from the Nazis who, after all, are relentlessly anti-Bolshevik and who have made Germany an economic success. More from Berlin, this fascinating city, later.

"Have you read this crap Bennet Kinkaid's writing from Berlin?" Gloria asked Ross Treadwell. They were having dinner at Whitehall. "He's making the Nazis look like geniuses! It makes me sick."

"Yes," Ross said. "I've been reading the pieces, and I understand the liberals in town are really up in arms about them, as well they might be. But it's hard for me to think anybody would believe what he's saying about the Nazis. Everybody knows Bennet's about as far to the right as the law allows—or even further."

"Don't be so sure. A lot of people admire Hitler, and Bennet is just fueling their prejudices. They'll eat up what he's writing. He's an American Nazi, sending his damned Ku Klux Klan goons out here to burn a cross."

"Are you sure he sent them?"

"Of course. Who else? If I could have proven it, I would have sued him. Well, maybe darling Deirdre will be raped by a storm Trooper, although she'd probably love it."

"Did I tell you she asked me to take her to the fund-raising ball for the hospital?"

"My God, she has nerve. She must have known you were taking me."

"She said she didn't, but who knows? I think she's got her eyes on me."

"If she touches you, I'll tear her hair out by the roots, which need a new dye job anyway. You know she hates my guts for making Byron Slade act like a man and walk out on her. He's happy as a clam at journalism school at Columbia University. But the amusing thing is, now that Deirdre's head of the Hospital Fund, she has to be nice to me because I'm her biggest benefactor. I keep writing checks to her just to force her to smile at me. It's a real giggle."

William came into the dining room to pass the white wine, which they were serving with the *vitello tonnato*, a dish Gloria had introduced to Indianapolis, a city which, during the Depression, knew nothing about the delights of Italian cooking except spaghetti and meatballs.

After William left the room, Ross said, "Mark asked me again today to kill him."

Gloria closed her eyes a moment.

"Oh my God," she said, opening her eyes. "The poor kid. I know he's miserable. Is there nothing you can do for him?"

"No. I've communicated with the top polio specialists in the country, and we've had the best look at him. It's hopeless, and he knows it."

"How do you know?"

"He told me. Mark's very bright. He sees what's in our faces. He told me he'd rather be dead than be in the iron lung the rest of his life. In a way, I suppose . . . well, I might think that way in his position. But of course we have to keep him alive and pray for a miracle."

"My architects are working on the plans for the polio clinic, but I'm afraid it may be too late for Mark. It's so sad. That strong, young body with all the potential of a useful life, and now he can't even breathe for himself. And Sebastian's devastated, of course. Oh, I know they fought from time to time, but they were so very, very close, almost like two parts of the same person. They say that's true about identical twins." She sighed. "And now his life's ruined by this damned disease. Well, I'll go up and see him after dinner."

"I'll go with you."

Mark's bedroom was on the second floor of Whitehall, looking out over the front lawn. On the walls were tacked up Mark's sports heroes, including Johnny Weissmuller, the swimming champion who had become the movies' second, and most popular, Tarzan. It was a bright, cheerful room with a plaid bedspread and matching curtains. A radio was on, broadcasting a baseball game. It was a typical boy's room.

Almost typical. In the middle stood the steel cylinder that wheezed softly as it mechanically forced Mark's body to breathe. The boy's head stuck out of one end of the machine, facing the ceiling. The machine stood on steel supports four feet off the floor.

When Gloria and Ross came in the room, Mark turned his head to look at them.

"How's the game?" Gloria asked, forcing a cheerful smile.

"The Yankees are losing," Mark said. "You can turn it off."

She did as Ross came over and smoothed Mark's hair.

"How are you feeling, Skipper?" he asked.

"Oh, great. Just great. Did you think about what I asked you?"

"You know I can't do that, Mark. We're going to beat this thing . . ."

"No we're not!" he interrupted, angrily. "Don't treat me like some moron! I know there's no cure and I'm going to die in this thing sooner or later and believe me, I'd rather it would be sooner! It's like a prison! I'm in a prison, and I'll never get out. Please help me escape from this prison."

There were tears in his eyes. Gloria, watching and listening, was shocked at the intensity in his voice. She came over and leaned down to kiss him.

"Darling," she said, "you must never give up hope."

"There is no hope. Momma, will you make him kill me? Please? Please do that for me. If you love me, please do it."

"Mark, you must get these thoughts out of your head."

"How? I lie here day and night with nothing to do but think, think, think how to get out of here, but there is no way except death. If I could kill myself, I would, but I can't move . . . I can't move . . ."

He started sobbing.

"Go away," he sobbed. "Leave me alone. Don't come back until you'll do what I ask. Go away."

Gloria, devastated, motioned to Ross, and he started toward the door.

"Good night, darling," Gloria said. "We all love you."

"Go away. Don't come back till you'll do what I want."

They left the room, softly closing the door, the boy's sobbing ringing in their ears and haunting their brains.

Article on the front page of the Indianapolis *Times-Gazette* written by the publisher, Bennet Kinkaid.

BERLIN, August 13, 1936. Deirdre and I continue to be impressed by what we see in Germany. The love of the German people for their Fuehrer is in evidence everywhere. While the rest of Europe and America are still struggling to come out of the worst Depression in decades, Germany is bustling with activity, the German economy is booming, and the German people are united. While America is beset with labor unrest and strikes, such a thing is unheard of here. Unemployment is practically nonexistant, and German workers are given free vacations abroad and provided with job security and health benefits. There is much to be learned from the German success story.

Meanwhile, the Olympic Games continue and I have had the opportunity of getting to know some of the leading personalities of the regime better. It seems that I have been rather taken up by the leading Nazis, a strange situation for a middle-aged newspaper publisher from Indiana, but one that affords me a somewhat unique insight into the leaders of this surprising nation. Of course, I realize they sense that I am not entirely against them, and they know how to pour on the honey. Still, the more I see, the more I feel there is much to be learned from these men who so many on our side of the ocean dismiss as "thugs" and "gangsters." It is true they have used strong-arm methods in the past, but we must never forget that Herr Hitler was legally elected to his position by the German people.

The other night we were invited by the newly appointed Ambassador to London, Herr von Ribbentrop, to a party given by him and his champagne-heiress wife at their villa in the fashionable Berlin suburb of Dalheim. Von Ribbentrop, a former champagne salesman, is good-looking in a rather flashy way, well-dressed, charming and suave, though he gives the impression of being steel under all that charm, as do all the Nazi leaders. His wife is more Germanic and controls the purse-strings. We were presented with a thick pamphlet cataloguing all 600 guests, and indicating where we were to sit at dinner, which was served in an enormous marquee. I found myself seated next to Lady Camrose, an Englishwoman married to an M.P. who is a friend and supporter of the out-of-fashion Winston Churchill. She seemed as impressed by all this splendor as I was, which rather surprised me, the Churchill party in England being not favorable to the Hitler regime.

After the excellent dinner, there was some quite good singing. Then a dance band played, a bar was set up, and there was much drinking. Goering, his merry eyes twinkling, came up to Deirdre and me and shook our hands asking, through an interpreter, if we were enjoying ourselves. I, being a little tipsy and most taken by this disarming man, gushed about how much we were impressed by all we saw, which seemed to please him. Deirdre and I stayed at the party till three. I was somewhat surprised by the large number of English people there, which suggests that, despite what we read in the press, Perfidious Albion is far from united in its opposition to the Nazis.

Tonight, we went to the party given by the Goerings, and I am hard put to describe this dazzling event. Our Government car picked us up at the hotel and drove us to the Ministerium in the center of Berlin, the huge palace the Goerings inhabit. Its great gardens were lit up and 700 or 800 guests were gaping at the display and the splendor—it seems that no one cares how much the Nazis spend to impress us foreigners. Goering, wreathed in smiles and decorations, received us genially, his charming wife at his side. After another excellent, wine-flowing dinner, a corps de ballet danced in the moonlight; it was lovely beyond belief, and it was whispered that von Ribbentrop was green with envy that Goering's show was better than his (it is said the two men dislike each other and vie for the Fuehrer's favor: It is all rather like the court of a Roman Emperor). The end of the garden, which had been in darkness, was suddenly flood-lit and a procession of white horses, donkeys, and peasants appeared from nowhere. They led the guests into a fantastic sort of amusement park, especially built for the evening, where there were carousels, cafés with beer and champagne, peasants dancing and *"schuhplattling,"* women carrying baskets of pretzels, a ship and a beerhouse—Ziegfeld couldn't have done it better.

After a while, Deirdre and I returned to the gardens where we had dined. A dance floor had been laid and orchestras were playing. Frau Goering asked if we would like to see the house, and we followed her inside to the vast Ministerium where the Goerings live in theatrical splendor. The rooms are all large and nearly empty, unimpressive except for their size. Goering's private study has many telephones and outsize photographs of German and foreign celebritites; from this room, I suppose, he directs the destinies of millions of Germans. There were two portraits of his wives, and there were flowers before the painting of his first wife, the Swedish Baroness he adored. He has built her a fantastic tomb on his country estate. There is something rather pagan about Goering, a touch of the gladiatorial arena. People say that he can be ruthless, but outwardly he seems all vanity and childish love of display. All a bit overwhelming to a plain-speaking American like myself, but nevertheless quite fascinating.

More from Berlin later.

17　Sᴇʙᴀsᴛɪᴀɴ Sᴀᴠᴀɢᴇ ᴋɴᴏᴄᴋᴇᴅ ᴏɴ the door of his twin brother's room, then opened the door and came into the room.

"How ya doing?" Sebastian said, like his mother forcing cheerfulness as he came over to stand beside the iron lung. Also like his mother, Sebastian was devasted by what had happened to his beloved twin. His mind was twisted by a combination of guilt—by the fact that Mark had been the victim, and not he—as well as fear: but for a twist of fate or luck or whatever, he could be in that horrible box rather than Mark. Mark had long, sleepless nights; but so did Sebastian.

"Oh, I'm swell," Mark said. "Shall we go for a swim, like Tarzan? Or maybe play some baseball?"

Sebastian put his hand on Mark's forehead and smoothed it.

"Well, maybe some day we can," he said, softly. "Can I get you anything?"

"You can do something for me," Mark said.

"Sure, Mark. Anything."

"Kill me."

"Come on, guy, that's crazy . . ."

"Kill me, Sebastian! Let me out of this prison! It's the only way I'll ever get out! I can't stand being in here! Please, kill me! Pull the plug on this thing and let me suffocate to death! Oh my God, let me escape from this horror! Kill me, please."

Sebastian backed away, a look of amazement and fear on his face.

"I couldn't do that, Mark," he said. "I never could do that to you! You've got to get these thoughts out of your head. You're going to be all right: you have to keep fighting, keep hoping . . ."

"There's no hope," Mark said, bitterly. "No hope. Please kill me. I'm asking you, if you love me, kill me. No one will ever know. No one will ever blame you. Just pull the plug and let me die. Please."

"Stop talking like this!" Sebastian cried, backing to the door. "I don't want to hear this!"

"I've asked Momma, I've asked the doctor, but no one will do it for me. You've got to do it for me, Sebastian. You're my only hope. Please. Remember once when I asked you if you'd do anything for me, and you swore you would?"

"I can't remember . . ."

"Yes you do! It was after you were kidnapped. We swore to each other we'd always do what the other wanted! If you were in this box instead of me, I'd do it for you if you asked. Please, Sebastian: You're part of me. Please say yes."

A look of terror on his face, Sebastian blurted out: "No!" Then he turned, opened the door, and ran out of the room.

Article on the front page of the Indianapolis *Times-Gazette* written by its publisher, Bennet Kinkaid.

BERLIN, August 16, 1936. The Berlin Olympics are over. There were long processions at the main stadium, Hitler stood up, the Olympic torch faded, and the crowd on this final day 140,000 strong sang "Deutschland über Alles." It was a sight I shall never forget.

Last night, the final of the fantastic entertainments here in Berlin was given by Dr. Goebbels and after it I had an interesting conversation with this talented, if somewhat sinister, little man who wields so much power in the Nazi state. Our government car picked Deirdre and me up at our hotel and drove us out near the Wannsee where, on an island called the Pfaueninsel that had once belonged to the Kaiser's family, Dr. and Mrs. Goebbels hosted an "Italian Night." Bridges and pontoons had been thrown across the water to the island. Deirdre and I walked across one of them (neither of us had dressed formally; the invitation read *"Sommerfest"*) and were greeted by girls in theatrical uniforms who indicated to us a chart containing the seating arrangements for the two thousand guests. After being greeted by the host and hostess, we walked around a while, enjoying the lovely island and the balmy evening. Then, as directed, we went to a broad terrace overlooking the lake beneath a canopy of five thousand Chinese lanterns and sat down to eat yet another marvelous meal, washed down by the finest German and French wines as the Berlin Philharmonic played, stars from the State Opera sang, and dancers from the Opera ballet performed. Why it was billed an "Italian Night" is rather confusing; it was more like something out of the Arabian Nights. At the conclusion of the dinner, cannons began roaring (I wasn't sure where they were, but the noise was deafening) and the sky blazed with a half-hour fireworks display that was one of the most spectacular I've ever seen. When it was all over, Deirdre and I prepared to leave. When we reached our automobile, our chauffeur told me Dr. Goebbels had invited me to meet him the next morning at ten at his office in the Propaganda Ministry on the Wilhelmstrasse.

The next morning, I was picked up at the hotel and driven to the Propaganda Ministry where I went to Dr. Goebbels's impressive office. He shook my hand and asked, through his interpreter, how I had enjoyed his party the previous night, to which I honestly responded that I had loved it. Then he sat behind his desk and said, "I know how hostile the American press is to us, and that you have been much more friendly than most American newspapers. I have only one complaint, dear Mr. Kinkaid. You wrote in one of your dispatches that we had taken down all anti-Jewish signs for the Olympic Games. This is certainly not true, and I would ask you to correct that at the first opportunity."

I hedged as best I could, because I knew from many sources that it was true. At any rate, he went on to say that "America is controlled by Jewish interests as Germany was before we came to power."

"Dr. Goebbels," I said, "I don't think it's fair to say that my country is 'controlled' by Jewish interests."

"Ah, but isn't Hollywood dominated by Jews?"

"Perhaps. But Hollywood is hardly America."

"And Wall Street? You won't deny that the Jews have power in the financial community?"

"Yes, they have power, but they don't dominate it."

"But don't you see, dear Mr. Kinkaid, that in time they will? Your press doesn't understand this, but I hoped that you, having a more open mind and having seen what we have accomplished here, might begin to understand why we are taking certain measures against these people and inform Americans that we are not monsters, but only patriotic Germans trying to protect our nation." He glanced at his watch, then said, "Now, if you will excuse me, I have an appointment." He stood up and came around his desk to shake my hand. I noticed that he had a definite limp and have found out since that at the age of seven he had been operated on for an attack of osteomyelitis, or inflammation of the bone marrow, which had left his left leg slightly shorter than his right, and rather withered. He took my right hand in both of his and gave me a hearty shake, saying, "It was an honor to meet you, Mr. Kinkaid, and I wish you a successful voyage back to the States. And try to remember us as people who love our country just as you love yours."

I thanked him for all his kindnesses and returned to my hotel, where Deirdre had packed. And so, this afternoon, we left Berlin.

While I certainly don't agree with Dr. Goebbels's remarks about the Jews, I do believe that the Nazis are not, as he said, "monsters" and that they have accomplished much in a few short years. Whether they will continue to succeed, of course, no one knows. Whatever the future of the Nazis may be, it certainly should continue to be interesting.

And now—home!

18   Like Johnny Weissmuller, Ross Treadwell had been a champion swimmer at college and an all-around good athlete. In fact, it was his love of water sports that had brought him and Gloria together at Lake Wawasee: Ross loved the exciting new sport of water skiing, which had developed earlier on from aquaplaning, and since Gloria's speedboat was the fastest on the lake and she enjoyed driving it, they had a common interest that quickly developed into hot sex. Ross, who still had a youthful swimmer's body like Weissmuller, had never married, telling Gloria he had so far no interest in becoming a family man and had plenty of time yet to acquire it. She was fascinated by Ross's hungry desire to explore all the far shores of sex. Early in their relationship, Ross had told Gloria he wanted to spank her in the nude; rather to Gloria's surprise, they both found the fetish arousing. Then, to her greater surprise, Ross told her he wanted her to spank him. This was not as successful for Gloria—she found it somehow ridiculous—but Ross had groaned with ecstasy (his father had been a Methodist preacher of the old school which she figured, with amateur psychology, might have had something to do with his pleasure).

Then one night Ross had appeared at Whitehall with a suitcase. When Gloria had asked him what he was up to, he told her he had a surprise for her.

"It's a new look," he said. "You know how we've tried so many sex games. I think you'll get a kick out of this. I certainly get a kick out of it."

"What is it?"

"Well . . . I want to surprise you. I've done it before. It somehow makes sex slightly different."

"I hope it's not *too* different. I like sex pretty much as it is."

He kissed her.

"You'll see. It'll be sexy and fun. Give me fifteen minutes, then come on up. You might make us a drink."

He went upstairs. Gloria mixed a batch of martinis and waited until she heard him yell, "Okay!" She carried the drinks up the curved stair and walked down the hall to her bedroom. When she opened her bedroom door, to her utter amazement Ross was standing in the middle of the room in a tight-fitting corset with black lace stockings, high heels, a white wig and his face fully made-up. Her first reaction—or rather, her second after the initial shock—was to dissolve into howls of laughter, which annoyed Ross.

"What's so funny?" he snapped.

"You!" She giggled. "You're a great-looking man, darling, but you're a lousy-looking woman."

"I don't think so. I think I look pretty sexy."

"Have it your way. In Hollywood, this wouldn't be so crazy. But Indianapolis? Oh boy. Well, I learn something everyday. Let's drink to your new look, then we can talk about the latest fashions."

"To hell with you," he snarled, taking off his corset.

"There's no need getting angry . . ."

"Says you! This is the way I express something within me, and I enjoy it! I don't do it very often, but when I do it I don't want to be laughed at!"

"Really, Ross, you're making a mountain out of a molehill. I'm sorry I laughed at you . . ."

"No you're not." He pulled off his wig and took off his high heel shoes. Gloria started to get mad herself.

"If you're going to take it this way, then maybe you'd better leave," she said.

"Don't worry, I'm going."

He slammed into the bathroom to change back into his regular clothes. When he emerged five minutes later, he said to Gloria: "By the way, you can forget the hospital ball. I'm going to ask Deirdre. She's dying for me to take her."

"You go to hell!" Gloria yelled as he picked up his costume and left the room.

Sebastian Savage quietly opened the door of his brother's bedroom and stepped inside. It was just getting dark. The radio was on, playing a baseball game.

"Who's winning?" Sebastian asked, closing the door behind him.

"The Red Sox," Mark said. "It's a boring game. You can turn it off."

Sebastian went over to the radio and turned it off. The soft wheezing of the iron lung replaced the noise.

"How are you?" Sebastian asked, coming over to his brother and smoothing his hair.

"I've just entered a dance marathon. They say I have a chance to win."

"I'll bet you could have. You were always better than I at, you know, things. You could always throw better than I, do everything better. I used to be so jealous."

"Well, you don't have to be anymore."

Silence except for the soft wheeze of the machine.

"I've been thinking about what you asked me to do," Sebastian finally said.

"And?"

"Were you serious?"

Mark hesitated.

"Yes."

"Are you still serious? I mean, you haven't changed your mind?"

Wheeze. Wheeze. Wheeze.

"I haven't changed my mind. This is like being buried alive. Have you changed yours?"

"Yes. I'll do it for you, Mark, if you want. Just tell me when and I'll pull the plug. I'll come in every day after school to see you, and when you're ready, say 'go.' "

"Oh, Sebastian," his twin whispered, tears appearing in his eyes. "I love you, brother. This is the surest sign of your love. And we'll always be together anyway, because we're the same person. I'll be in Heaven with Jesus, and you'll be here with Momma. We'll talk to each other, and be just as close as we've always been. You know there's always been a special thing between us, because we're identical twins. I mean, I sometimes dream your dreams."

"Yes, and I dream yours. I always know what you're thinking, Mark. And I know you know what I'm thinking. Am I right?"

"Oh yes, dear brother. We're very special people. That's why we must have this perfect trust between us. If you kill me, it won't be murder. It will be a gift, from one part of you to me. Do you understand that?"

"Yes, I think I do."

"And when I die, we'll still be together. We'll talk and play and fight just the same as before. But after I'm dead, put the plug back in the wall. That way, no one will ever suspect you of murdering me."

Sebastian looked agonized.

"But isn't it murder?" he whispered.

"No! Not when I ask you to do it! It's a gift. Always remember that: It will be your greatest gift to me. And never tell anyone, not even Momma. You must swear to me to keep it a secret. Our secret. Do you swear?"

Sebastian, who was pale with fright, gulped and said: "Yes, I swear."

"Good. Now kiss me and say good-bye."

Sebastian leaned down and kissed his forehead.

The twins looked into each other's eyes for a while. Then Mark whispered: "Go."

"Now?"

"Yes. Do it. Go. Let's get it over with. Let me be free. And someday we'll meet in Heaven again and it will be like the good old days. We can throw footballs."

Sebastian hesitated. Then he straightened and went over to the wall and reached down to take hold of the cord. Again, he looked at Mark, who was watching him, a smile on his face.

"Go on," Mark said. "Pull it. Set me free."

"Good-bye. I love you."

Sebastian pulled the plug.

The wheezing stopped. Sebastian watched his brother, a look of horror on his face. Mark started to gag. His face became contorted.

And then, peace.

When Mark was dead, Sebastian plugged in the machine again and left the room.

Gloria was so devastated by the death of Mark that the day after his burial in Crown Heights Cemetery she took Sebastian on the train to New York where they boarded the *Normandie* for Europe. Gloria wasn't only fleeing

Indianapolis, with all its sorry memories; she also was trying to protect Sebastian from the disease she thought had killed his brother, for the polio epidemic was persisting into the fall.

As the luxurious liner slipped down the Hudson River into the open sea, the cool air revived her spirits. So much so that the first night out, when she took Sebastian to the first-class *salle à manger* for dinner she began to think that life was worth living after all. The custom of the sea was that the first night no one dressed formally, so there was a relaxed feeling in the air. But Gloria was aware that her ten-year-old son was anything but relaxed.

"What's wrong?" she asked as Sebastian sluggishly stirred his onion soup.

"Nothing."

"Oh, come on. You look absolutely grim."

"I'm telling you, it's nothing."

"Well, of course you're missing Mark. So am I—dreadfully. But . . ."

To her surprise, her son threw down his napkin, got up and almost ran down the length of the enormous dining room, past the statue representing Peace, and vanished. When a waiter came up to her, Gloria stood up and said, "I think my son is sick. I'll be back in a bit."

"Yes, madame."

She hurried out of the dining room and went to her suite, letting herself in. She found that Sebastian had gotten undressed and put himself into bed. She turned on the light, coming into his room.

"Darling, what is the matter?" she asked, coming over to his bed. He was lying on his side.

After a moment, he said, in a soft voice, "I killed Mark."

His mother slowly lowered herself onto the edge of his bed.

"You're not serious," she finally said.

He sat upright, a look of pain on his face.

"He begged me to kill him!" he said. "He said he couldn't stand being in the iron lung, it was like being buried alive! I didn't want to—I told him I wouldn't do it, that he should get those thoughts out of his mind, but he kept at it! He said if I really loved him, I would kill him! And so . . . finally I did. I did what he told me to do: I pulled the plug on the machine and watched him die. Oh ..." He burst into tears and threw himself into his mother's arms. "It was horrible! I loved Mark! It was horrible watching him die! I mean, he was my brother! I feel like I've killed part of myself. But I did it. And then ..." He straightened, sniffing. "And then I put the plug back in the wall to start the machine again like he told me to so no one would think he had been murdered. But that's what it was: I murdered my own brother. Oh God, Momma, I feel so horrible about it ... but he begged me to do it! Was I wrong? Am I a murderer? Are they going to put me in the electric chair? Am I like my father after all?"

Gloria squeezed him, smoothing his hair.

"Of course not, darling," she said. "I can't say you did the right thing, but I can understand why you did it. He begged me to do it, and Ross. And maybe, in the long run, it was for the best. I know how miserable Mark was, and the doctors told me there was really very little hope for him ever getting better. . . ."

"Oh Momma, he was such a good athlete and it was so cruel to see him there in that horrible machine, unable to move or do anything ... I felt so sorry for him! I mean, he was like ... like myself! He even looked like me! Tell me I didn't do the wrong thing! Tell me I'm not a murderer!"

Gloria rocked slowly back and forth for a moment, holding him in her arms. Then she kissed him on the temple.

"You're not a murderer, darling," she said. "Now, this must be our secret: We'll never let anyone else know about this. All right? Do you swear?"

"Oh yes, Momma. I swear. It's our secret forever."

"And you mustn't feel guilty about what you did. I know you did it out of love for Mark, but Mark is gone now, and I know he's happier wherever he is . . ."

"Do you think he's in Heaven with Jesus?"

"Yes, I'm sure he is. And I know he's forgiven you . . ."

"He begged me to do it!"

"Yes, I know. And I love you very much, just as I loved Mark. Now, you go to sleep, my darling. And don't feel bad about anything. All right?"

"All right. Momma, I love you very much."

"And I love you."

She kissed him, then lowered him back down to the bed again, pulling the blanket up to his chin. Then she got up and went to the door of the room, turning out the light and closing the door. She returned to the first-class dining room and went back to her table, ordering a martini from the waiter.

She sat by herself, stunned by what her son had told her. She understood why he had done it: She had seen the anguish on Mark's face.

But still, Cain had killed Abel. And the image of their father swam before Gloria's eyes.

"Mark, please forgive me for killing you."

Sebastian was lying in his bed in the suite of the Savoy Hotel in London that his mother had taken. Outside his windows, the lights of the Thames Embankment glowed in a light fog.

"And there's something else you have to forgive me," Sebastian continued, whispering. He was looking at one of the windows. "I broke our pledge of secrecy. I told Momma about what I'd done to you. I had to. I was feeling so guilty about what I did to you. Oh, I know you wanted me to, but still and all . . . the only thing that makes me feel better about the whole thing is the way you smiled at me just before I pulled the plug. You know how we always knew what each other was thinking? Well, I knew you were thinking that I was freeing you from prison, and that made me feel better. But still, I had to tell Momma. Do you forgive me?"

The door to the room opened and Gloria appeared, wearing a bathrobe.

"Sebastian," she said, "who are you talking to?"

The boy sat up and looked at his mother.

"Mark," he said.

Gloria stared at him.

"Sebastian killed Mark?" Nick said three weeks later as he and Gloria had lunch in Peacock Alley at the Waldorf.

"Yes, but you must swear to keep it a secret," Gloria said. "I told him it would be our secret. Mark was so miserable in the iron lung, he begged us all to kill him and finally Sebastian did it. But since then, he's started talking to Mark, which really has me worried."

"What do you mean?"

"He talks to him when no one's in the room. Actually, he's talked to him when I'm in the room. I ask him why he's doing it, and he tells me Mark's in front of the window, or by the fireplace, or wherever. It's extremely weird. So while I was in London, I took him to be examined by a Doctor van Osgold, a Viennese who's supposed to be the best child psychiatrist in the world. Dr. van Osgold had three hour-long sessions with Sebastian, and he told me that he's basically all right, but that talking to Mark is a little game he made up to assuage his guilt about killing his brother."

"So you told the doctor he'd killed Mark?"

"Yes, I felt I had to. But he's bound by the doctor-patient relationship to keep it confidential."

"Where's Sebastian now?"

"I sent him to a double feature. He adores the movies."

"Did he resent going to the psychiatrist?"

"A little, at first. But then he seemed to enjoy it. Dr. van Osgold said he's very, very clever and very narcissistic, or self-centered. But he said he'll grow out of all this in time. Have I done the right thing, Nick? You know I adore that child, even more so now that Mark's gone, and I know I spoil him. Since he doesn't have a proper father, I have to turn to you. I hope you don't mind."

"Of course I don't. Are you going to continue sending him to a doctor?"

"There's a young psychiatrist who's just opened an office in Indianapolis. I'm going to talk to him when we get home. In a way, I hate to do it. I mean, I suppose it's bound to make him feel different, and if his friends found out about it, they might start treating him like some sort of freak. But we'll see."

"You know, part of the problem may be as simple as the fact that he doesn't have a father."

She sighed and ordered another martini.

"Well, I suppose you're right," she said. "But I don't seem to have much luck with men. In fact, you could say I'm the kiss of death for husbands. First, Cesare got murdered. Then poor Chester got killed on the *Morro Castle*. And I've just learned that my last boyfriend, Ross Tread-well, has married Deirdre Kinkaid, of all people. I suppose she was paying me back for losing her previous husband. I talked him into leaving her and going to journalism school. So I'm not having much luck with men."

"Listen, Gloria, you're an attractive woman and a good person. Love will come to you, just as it came to me."

She smiled.

"So you and Samantha are happy?"

"Blissful. And I do think you've done the right thing with Sebastian."

She sighed and looked at Nick sadly.

"I certainly hope you're right."

PART SIX

BEHIND THE CHRYSANTHEMUM CURTAIN: 1937

19   HE WAS FIVE-FOOT-SIX, RATHER TALL for a Japanese of his generation, with a slightly receding chin, a thin black mustache, and thick black hair. He was not allowed to be touched by anyone outside his immediate family; even his doctor had to put on silk gloves when he examined him, and his tailor was not allowed to measure him, forcing him to estimate his measurements, which was the main reason his clothes always looked slightly misfitting. His vision was terrible, but he had not been allowed to wear glasses until he was fifteen because gods could not be seen to have any physical defects. But then, since he didn't believe he was a god, he insisted on putting on glasses so he could see where he was going. His personal fortune was estimated at one hundred million dollars, an immense sum for 1937, but he didn't even have a family name. He was known simply as the Emperor Hirohito, although his millions of adoring subjects, who believed absolutely that he was the one hundred and twenty fourth descendant in a straight line from his legendary ancestor, Jimmu, who was a direct descendant of the sun goddess Amaterasu, were not allowed to speak his name or even look at him on the rare occasions when he emerged from the 123 moated acres of the Imperial Palace in Tokyo.

Theoretically, he was all-powerful; but the reality was that his power was somewhat limited by tradition. He was a bird in a gilded cage, the reality of the Chrysanthemum Throne hidden behind a Chrysanthemum Curtain of myth and a complicity of silence among those who came into contact with his world.

On a hot August night in 1937, General Matsui Iwane was summoned to the Imperial Palace by the emperor. He approached the mortarless, sixty-foot-high granite walls of the moated palace, walls erected in the sixteenth century, from the southwest in an official car. Matsui was sixty and not a well man, suffering from tuberculosis, among other things. Only five-feet high, his weight was down to a hundred pounds. Matsui had been informed the day before that the Emperor was going to offer him the command of the Japanese troops in China, which was somewhat odd in light of the fact that Matsui had for long been a proponent of peace with China.

The car crossed the moat that surrounded the Imperial Palace grounds, the granite battlements topped by pine trees, and entered the Imperial Gardens, perhaps the most carefully tended gardens in the world. In the distance rose the giant hardwoods in the Emperor's private park, the Fukiage Gardens. Matsui had never penetrated farther into the Inner Palace grounds than the courtyard of white pebbles and the ghostly white wood Shrine of the Sacred Mirror where Hirothito worshipped his ancestors. Few but servants and members of the imperial family went farther.

But tonight was different. Matsui's car went between the office buildings of the government ministries on the right and the southwest wall of the palace on his left. Then through Cherry Field Gate into the imperial public gardens. Thence across another moat through Foot-of-the-Slope Gate, arriving at a cluster of office buildings where clerks of the Imperial Household Ministry tended Hirohito's vast fortune. Here the car stopped. General Matsui got out to be greeted by an aide who would lead him into the Imperial Presence. His samurai sword banging his ankle, he was led through raked pebble courtyards and gardens of dwarf trees, past the sprawling banquet hall and Privy Council chamber to the eastern entrance of the Outer Palace. Matsui realized, with some disappointment, that he would not be meeting the Emperor in his private, western-style study, where it was whispered that he relaxed and spoke man-to-man rather than god-to-man, but rather in the official audience chamber, the magnificent Phoenix Hall, where Hirohito spoke in his high-pitched official voice used as his position of high priest of the national Shinto religion.

This was indeed the case. Matsui was led through a reception area of gold screens and down a corridor to the entrance to the Phoenix Hall, where he was greeted by the Emperor's chief aide-de-camp. In accordance with ancient custom, Matsui untied his samurai sword and handed it to the junior aide who had led him through the palace, to be kept while he was meeting with the Emperor. Then he was led into the Phoenix Hall, so named for the fiery mythological birds that were carved in silver everywhere on the floor, walls, and ceiling of the enormous room.

Matsui was left alone, bowing double and remaining so while he waited for the Emperor. It was hot and sticky, and he felt uncomfortable and sweaty. But he, like every other Japanese, had taken vows as children to die for the Emperor. The least he could do was sweat for him.

"We greet you and urge you to stand at ease," a voice said. Matsui looked up to see Hirohito in a uniform, which was also slightly sweaty. Hirohito might be a god, but he seemed to have no control over the weather. The general straightened.

"Good evening, Your Majesty," he said.

"I believe you know why I sent for you," the thirty-seven-year-old Emperor went on, dropping the royal "we" in a further welcome sign of relaxation. "For a number of years, it has been the government's policy to drive the white man out of Asia and replace the Imperialist colonial powers, the British, French, German, and Russians, with Japanese ascendancy. To achieve this, we have made military incursions over the past in several areas in China, notably Taiwan, Manchuria, and Mongolia. As you are aware, we occupied Korea some forty years ago. We are now prepared to assimilate all of China. I believe you personally know General Chiang Kai-shek?"

"Yes, Your Majesty. I met him several times when he was the director of the Whampoa Military Academy."

"Chiang has spent the past few years fighting the Chinese Communists under Mao Tse-tung, but recently he has turned against us. China is weak and its leaders fight each other. China would be much better if it submitted to Japanese authority: We could make China strong. It has been the government's aim to march from Shanghai, where we are already established militarily, up the Yangtze River to Nanking, Chiang's capital, and force him to flee. However, lately Chiang's men have been fighting much better than we expected. Consequently, I have decided to send two new divisions to Shanghai under your command. You will solidify our military position there, and then march to Nanking and take it. Are you comfortable with this decision? I know you have had some medical problems."

"I am in full agreement, Your Majesty. My health is not a problem."

"Excellent. Then we will have a further briefing in the morning, as it is late and disagreeably hot. You must be tired."

"You are very kind to even consider my comfort, Your Majesty. *Banzai!* Ten thousand years!"

Hirohito smiled slightly.

"We will settle for one thousand," he said, "as long as they are years of Japanese control over Asia. The years of the white man are over. The years of the "yellow man" as those in the West call us, are beginning."

Forty-six-year-old Jasmin Chin Wang wiped her handkerchief over her forehead. It was extremely hot in Nanking, and even the whirring fans in her ground-floor office in the hospital that she had built and then ran couldn't stir the damp, heavy air. Jasmin was still a delicate beauty. As her daughter-in-law, Nora Wang, had told Lady Chatfield on the *Normandie*, Jasmin could have lived a luxurious life in either Hong Kong or Shanghai. When her mother, Julie Savage Chin, died three years before, Jasmin had inherited her fortune based on the successful Chin department stores in Hong Kong and Shanghai, as well as the considerable real estate holdings Julie had acquired over the years—Julie having been the half-Chinese daughter of the patriarch of the Savage family, the formidable Justin Savage.

But Jasmin had opted for a life of service instead. When her husband, the former warlord Charlie Wang, had joined Generalissimo Chiang Kai-shek in China's new capital, Nanking, as a general in his nationalist army, Jasmine had gone with him and singlehandedly, with fierce determination that surprised people who assumed this beauty was a social butterfly, wheedled the Generalissimo into donating the land for the hospital. Jasmin, who had gone to Wellesley, knew how to get things done. She was further aided by her close friendship with Madame Chiang, the American-educated beauty who was one of the three famous Soong sisters.

After Jasmin had finished going through her correspondence, she left her office to make an inspection tour of the two-story hospital she had built. It was considered one of the finest hospitals in China, if not all Asia, and Jasmin was fiercely proud of it. Her staff of doctors and nurses adored her, although they were careful never to cross her: Jasmin had a strong temper. One of the young doctors, who had been educated in America and was a passionate fan of Hollywood movies, borrowed the epithet a wit had bestowed on Jeannette MacDonald and called Jasmin the Iron Butterfly, a nickname that stuck.

The Iron Butterfly was joined by her assistant, Smith-educated Nancy Chan, the daughter of a Shanghai businessman, and the two toured the wards of the busy hospital. The heat had caused an outbreak of cholera, and the cholera ward was filled. Jasmin, as well as her staff, was well aware that the best protection against cholera was clean water and food, and Nanking had a modern water processing plant, purifying the water of the muddily septic Yangtze River. But while Chiang Kai-shek had built many modern government buildings in the ancient walled city of Nanking and plumbing was available to the better-off citizens, in the southern slums of the city of one million inhabitants sanitation was medieval. And every summer without fail, cholera broke out. Jasmin was proud that the survival rate of the cholera patients in her hospital was 99 percent—almost unheard of in China—and that most of the children brought to her hospital were treated and released in less than three weeks.

When Jasmin's tour was completed, she talked for a while with Nancy Chan, a pretty thirty-year-old whose husband was one of the staff doctors, then went outside and climbed in her white Buick two-seater to go have lunch with her husband. Much of Nanking had been destroyed eighty years before during the bloody Taiping Rebellion that had convulsed China for so many years, so that the modern buildings had been able to avoid the narrow, twisting alleys of ancient China and it was possible to drive cars without difficulty. The new Nanking was a monumental government park, filled with new public buildings and open vistas in which pheasants nested. Only in the southern slums, where cholera bred, was there any indication of old China.

Jasmin's Buick reached the Great Peace Gate in the northeast part of the city and she drove through the ancient, notched brick city walls that were an astonishing twenty feet thick and fifty feet high. Outside the city, she drove to the Purple Mountains, a suburb where the city's rich and influential families lived and where the huge tomb of China's "George Washington," Sun Yat-Sen, was located. She drove through a gate and parked in front of the eight-room, airy villa she and her husband had bought when they moved to Nanking. Getting out of her car, she walked up to the covered front porch of the house, then into the entrance hall. The house had thick brick walls and high ceilings with fans that kept it pleasant even during the hottest weather. Furthermore, large double doors on three sides of the house opened to the surrounding porch and the lovely, treed gardens, admitting cooling breezes. Jasmin, who was wearing a simple white dress, gave her wide-brimmed white hat to her butler, Ho, and asked, "Is my husband home yet?"

"Yes, Tai-Tai." Ho said, bowing as he used the Chinese word for madame. "He is in the study. He seems very upset."

Jasmin walked through the western-style house to the study, where her husband, Charlie Wang, was listening to the radio.

"It's happened," he said to Jasmin. "General Matsui has landed in Shanghai with thirty-five thousand fresh troops. What we've suspected all along is happening: The Japanese are going to come here and try to take Nanking."

"Do you think they can?"

"I think they have a fifty-fifty chance. I think we have to make plans to get you out of the city, back to Hong Kong."

She stared at her still-handsome husband, whose tall body was still as slim as when she first met him.

"I'll never leave you or the hospital," she said, quietly.

"You may have no choice. Nor may I. The Generalissimo is making plans to move the capital to Hankow if the Japanese are too strong for us. We'd have to go with him."

She considered this a moment. Then she said: "Well, we'll see what happens. But I can't believe the Japanese would do anything to the hospital. If worse comes to worst, I'll make some sort of arrangement with them. But I won't abandon what I've devoted ten years of my life to."

Her husband was well aware that the Iron Butterfly had a will that matched—or exceeded—his own.

"Nevertheless," Charlie said, "in an emergency you know our plan of escape."

"Of course, darling. But you mustn't be an alarmist. I'm sure things will work out."

20 SHANGHAI WAS THE WORLD'S most cosmopolitan city. Great Britain, the United States, France, Japan, and China all had military missions there. American hotels, English clubs, French cafés, Russian bakeries, German rathskellers, and Japanese geisha houses all were there, as well as branch offices of most of the major corporations of the world. There were opium dens and brothels—and the worst slums in China. The foreigners were there to protect their nationals in the International Settlement and the French Concession, extraterritorial areas that had been wrung out of the Imperial Chinese in the previous century, as a result of the Opium Wars. With a large fleet of Japanese destroyers, cruisers, and battleships at anchor in the mouth of the Yangtze River, Shanghai was a tinderbox ready to explode.

"I fear I have made a mistake appointing General Matsui in charge of our China operation," Emperor Hirohito said to his good friend and Prime Minister, Prince Konoye. The two men were sitting in the Emperor's western-style study in the Imperial Palace in Tokyo. There was a carpet on the tatami and a leather sofa on which the Emperor occasionally took naps. On the walls were mementos from the six-month European tour he had taken in 1921, including photos of himself with the Prince of Wales and King George V of England, Marshal Pétain of France, and Crown Prince Leopold of Belgium. Busts of his western heroes stood on tables. At one end of the room, a shoji opened onto the private golf course he had had built, golf being a sport he had taken up with fervor when he was in Scotland, a covered riding ring, and a bombproof underground shelter, which housed the Imperial Library. Other western habits Hiroshito had brought back were his love of English-style breakfasts and Scotch whiskey.

"How so, Your Majesty?" Prince Konoye asked. Prince Konoye, a slender, rather effete aristocrat whose son was an undergraduate at Princeton, was a member of the Fujiwara clan, the second most powerful family in Japan whose members had been close advisors to the Emperors for over a thousand years.

"I knew he was sick with tuberculosis," the Emperor said, "but he assured me his health was not a problem. But he is having such little effect in Shanghai, I can't help but think he must be ill. For almost two months, our troops have been fighting in the streets of Shanghai and making no progress toward the real target, Nanking. The casualties are mounting, the numbers appalling, and Chiang Kai-shek—instead of being humiliated, which was our intention—has become more popular, a sort of national hero. I am very displeased with the way things are going, and I'm thinking of replacing General Matsui."

"With whom, Your Majesty?"

"My uncle, Prince Asaka. He's a tough, professional soldier. And even though he sided with my brother, Prince Chichibu, in the army fight last year, for which I censured him, I think he could do a better job than General Matsui."

"If I might make a suggestion, Your Majesty?"

"Yes, of course."

"I would give General Matsui a little more time. To replace him so quickly, after only a few months, might hurt the morale of the troops."

Hirohito considered this a moment.

"Yes, perhaps you're right," he finally said. "I'll give him more time. But I want results! I want victory! I want China."

"Your Majesty is no doubt aware of the story of the fourteenth-century Mongol conqueror, Tamerlane. It is said that when he besieged a city, he spent the first day outside the walls in a white tent as a sign of mercy to the besieged population. On the second day, he stayed in a red tent as a sign of mercy to the women and children inside the walls. And on the third day, he stayed in a black tent as a sign of mercy to no one. When our troops ultimately reach the walls of Nanking, which tent would you want your commander to be in?"

The Emperor of Japan looked at his prime minister and said, in cool tones, "The black tent."

Despite his initial setbacks in the streets of Shanghai, by late November General Matsui had broken his army out of Shanghai and, joined by two other Japanese armies, had managed to rout Chiang Kai-shek's troops, marching west along the Yangtze River, over one hundred miles, until the three victorious armies were drawn up before the ancient fifty-foot-high brick walls of Nanking. Within the city, panic was setting in. Already, many of the government officials had fled the city, and over eight hundred thousand civilians, eighty percent of the total population, had left, traveling farther upstream along the mighty Yangtze River. Rumors were rife that the Japanese planned a bloodbath.

Jasmin had become increasingly frantic. Around noon on December 5, 1937, her husband's staff car pulled up in front of her hospital and Charlie got out to hurry inside, going directly to Jasmin's office.

"Charlie, what's happening?" Jasmine asked as he came in the room.

"The Generalissimo has just learned that the Japanese are now demanding unconditional surrender. We're going to have to leave the city."

"But you said the other day Chiang was going to accept their terms!"

"The Japanese changed their minds. Now we have no choice but to leave. The Generalissimo has ordered me to Hankow. We have to get home and pack what we can take. I've already called Ho."

Charlie, who had been a general in the Republican army, had been promoted to minister of war.

"But I can't leave until I've made arrangements for the hospital," Jasmin said.

Charlie came around her desk and put his hands on her arms.

"Jasmin, we've argued this a dozen times," he said. "And a dozen times I've told you you have to close the hospital."

"How can I close it? I have forty-three children sick with the flu, I have twenty-seven tuberculosis cases . . ."

"You'll have to send them home," he interrupted. "When the Japanese come, believe me, if they find them in the hospital they'll butcher them."

"They couldn't be so cruel!" she exclaimed, on the verge of tears. "They're children! You've just been listening to all these rumors going around . . ."

"We've intercepted radio messages. General Nakajima, who's in command of the 16th Division, intends to butcher everyone he can get his hands on. The man's a sadist, and he's not a liar: He does what he says he's going to do. And today, Hirohito put his uncle, Prince Asaka, in charge of the entire operation in China, and Asaka is as much a Sadist as Nakajima. We have to leave!"

"But General Matsui has been friendly to China before! Surely I could turn over the hospital to him . . ."

"General Matsui is incapacitated with his tuberculosis, and Hirohito has sacked him. I'm telling you, Jasmin, we have no choice. We're flying out of here this afternoon to Hankow, and the Generalissimo will be coming as soon as he can. Nanking is finished. I'm going to the house now. You do what you have to here then come home as soon as you can. And hurry! We don't have much time."

He kissed her, then hurried out of the office. Jasmin, telling herself he was right and she had no options but to close the hospital, called her assistant, Nancy Chan.

An hour later, as the children were being evacuated from the hospital, Jasmin closed and locked her office, bid a tearful farewell to her staff, then got in her white Buick and drove through the city to the Great Peace Gate, which she drove through on her way home. Events were happening so fast she could barely keep up with them. Her heart was heavy at the thought of closing the hospital, but she knew Charlie had been right: There was no alternative, and the children would be safer with their parents. She had distributed all the medical supplies to the children, as well as all the food on the premises, which otherwise would have been confiscated by the Japanese. It was a cold, depressingly gray day. Jasmin felt as depressed as the skies looked.

Passing Sun Yat-sen's huge mausoleum, she came into the suburbs and arrived at her villa's gate where, to her amazement, she was stopped by two Japanese soldiers. One came up to her and rapped on the window. She rolled it down.

"Where are you going?" the soldier asked in surprisingly good Mandarin.

"I live here," she said.

The soldier looked at her suspiciously, then stepped back and looked at her car.

"What is this car?" he asked.

"It's a Buick."

"What's a Buick? I never heard of it."

"It's an American car."

"But you're Chinese."

"Yes, I'm well aware of that. Are you going to let me pass?"

"You are the wife of General Wang?"

"Yes."

"This villa has been taken over by General Nakajima. Park your car and go inside where you will receive instructions."

"Is my husband—?"

"He's inside. Go!"

He aimed his rifle at her face. Jasmin had no idea the Japanese had gotten this close to the city, but she didn't ask any more questions. Driving through the gate, she parked her car beside a Japanese truck. Getting out, she went to the front door, which was guarded by another Japanese soldier. He opened the door and gave her a shove, pushing her inside. She went to the living room, where Charlie was seated in his favorite chair, smoking a cigarette as four Japanese soldiers stood around, holding their guns. The soldiers stared at Jasmin as she came in.

"How did these soldiers get through our lines?" she asked Charlie.

"It seems our army has fled," Charlie said, standing up to kiss her. "Along with most of our brave generals. I knew this might happen, but I didn't think it would happen so fast. These men don't speak English. They're waiting for General Nakajima to arrive. We have to get to the plane."

"But how?"

"You know. The basement. I'm going to try out my Japanese on them. It's pretty basic, but wish me luck. And don't look scared."

"I'm afraid I am."

"We'll just play it very calmly."

He pulled a pack of cigarettes from the pocket of his coat and turned to one of the soldiers, offering him one. The soldier, hesitated, then accepted it. Charlie spoke to him in Japanese. The soldier looked surprised, then shook his head, lighting the cigarette. The other soldiers started arguing with the first one.

"What's happening?" Jasmin asked.

"I've offered them some of our wine downstairs. He's afraid to take anything that will belong to General Nakajima, but the others are trying to talk him into it. I think they'll win."

In fact, after a few minutes the first soldier grunted at Charlie and shook his head in the affirmative. Charlie turned to his wife.

"Come on," he said.

The soldier had pulled his service revolver from his waist holster. Now, pointing it at Charlie, he followed him and Jasmin out of the room into the kitchen, where Ho was sitting at the table, looking nervous. Charlie opened the basement door and started down the steps, turning on the electric light. Jasmin followed him, the Japanese soldier behind her. When they got to the bottom of the stairs, Charlie pulled a keyring from his pocket and went over to a large wooden door. He unlocked the door, swung it open, then reached in and turned on a ceiling light. He went inside the large wine cellar where his and Jasmin's collection of over five hundred bottles of European and Chinese wines and champagne were held in wooden bins. Charlie pulled out a bottle of Veuve Clicquot '23 and showed it to the soldier, saying something in Japanese. The soldier, looking awed, took the bottle, staring at the label.

"I told him this bottle was worth more than thirty dollars, which is more than he makes a month," Charlie said, smiling at the soldier. "Give him another."

Jasmin obeyed, pulling out a second bottle of champagne and handing it to the soldier.

"And a third and fourth," Charlie said.

Jasmin did so. The soldier, looking as if he had just won a lottery, grunted in Japanese, holding the four bottles and his service revolver with difficulty.

Charlie, who had backed up against the opposite wall, now swung a bottle of Chinese wine around from his back and crashed it down on the soldier's head, smashing the bottle. The soldier grunted as he collapsed to the floor, dropping the champagne bottles, one of which smashed.

"Too bad," Charlie said, leaning down to take the soldier's gun. "That's one of my favorite years. Let's go to the tunnel."

He closed the wine cellar door, then hurried to the rear and pulled open a section of the wooden bins, which swung inward, revealing a tunnel.

"Hurry!" he whispered.

Jasmine ran into the tunnel, which was dimly lit by ceiling bulbs, as Charlie reclosed the bin and followed her.

"How smart of you to put this tunnel in last year," she whispered.

"I knew the Japanese were thinking of taking Nanking, so I decided it would be better safe than sorry. You have your car keys?"

"Oh yes."

"Good."

They reached the end of the tunnel. Charlie opened a steel door in the ceiling and scrambled up a wooden ladder, coming out near the rear wall of the garden. He helped Jasmin out, then closed the trap door.

"Your car," he whispered. "Fast, before we're spotted."

They ran back to the side of the house then to the front, where Charlie stopped, peering around the corner, the gun in his hand. He signaled to Jasmin, and ran to the driveway, where Jasmin had parked her Buick in front of the Japanese truck. Charlie opened the door and climbed in the driver's seat while Jasmin hurried around and got in beside him. Charlie started the car.

The Japanese soldier at the front door, who had been leaning against the wall, half dozing, now sprang to attention and yelled at them. Charlie gunned the engine and roared down the driveway to the gate, where the two soldiers who had stopped Jasmin were standing, smoking.

"Duck down!" Charlie yelled as he sped toward the soldiers, going seventy miles an hour. The soldiers jumped out of the way as the Buick roared out the gate. Then the soldiers started firing at the car, but Charlie was driving so fast they were soon out of range.

"Well done, darling!" Jasmin exclaimed as she sat up.

"Let's just hope we can get to the city gates before they catch us," Charlie said, roaring around a farmer and two cows. Jasmin looked back.

"I don't see them yet," she said.

"They'll be chasing us in the truck. Fortunately, Japanese trucks aren't as fast as your Buick."

"So our army has finally gone. What a shame."

"Yes, it is a shame, but the morale was disastrous. Our men just ran.

They're afraid of the Japanese. Something tells me it's going to be a long time before we'll be able to come back to Nanking again. And here's the gate."

"And there's the truck!" Jasmin cried, looking back. In the far distance, the Japanese truck had just appeared.

"Hang on!" Charlie yelled as he sped toward the ancient brick walls of the city, honking his horn to warn the pedestrians to get out of the way. They scattered as the white Buick roared through the gate.

Twenty minutes later, after having lost the truck, Charlie drove out of the city, this time through the River Gate where, at a small wooden dock, his two-engine Fokker seaplane was tied up on the Yangtze. Charlie and Jasmin jumped out and started toward the plane, which Charlie had bought two years before and taken lessons to learn how to fly. It had been partly a hobby and partly an escape device.

"What's that?" Jasmin asked, pointing to a distant boat on the river. Charlie squinted at the distant object as he untied the mooring ropes of the plane.

"That, my beautiful wife, is a Japanese gunboat. Let's go!"

They climbed in the plane, Jasmin attaching her seatbelt as Charlie started the engines.

"What's the boat doing?" he yelled over the engine noise as he moved the plane into the river.

"It's coming toward us."

"Damn. And the wind's coming from the east, so I'll have to take off toward them. Well, hang on. I'm going to try to get over them before they get a bead on us."

The river was choppy and the plane rocked as Charlie turned it to the east. Then he opened the throttle. The little plane sent up a sheet of muddy spray as it roared down the huge river toward the gunboat.

"Lift!" Charlie yelled in frustration. "Take off! Lift!"

Boom! The gunboat fired a cannon on its bow.

"Take off!"

The cannon shell exploded in the water slightly to the port of the plane which now, finally, lifted off the water and started into the air.

Boom!

The boat fired again. The shell exploded near the plane, its shock waves jolting the plane.

"Take my gun!" Charlie yelled. "I'm going to fly right over them. Take a potshot at the bastards. Maybe we'll get lucky and they'll keep their heads down."

Jasmin took his gun as he headed the plane directly at the gunboat. Jasmin could see the Japanese sailors scrambling to try to aim their bow gun at them. She leaned out the side window and aimed her gun down, firing as Charlie roared the plane over their heads.

"I think I got one!" she cried with delight.

"Damned good shooting," Charlie said as he banked the plane in a 180-degree turn west and started toward Hankow. "I wish I'd had you in my army."

Jasmin leaned over and kissed his cheek.

"You're fabulous," she said. And she meant it.

Prince Konoye, the prime minister of Japan, was a man of many contradictions. He had considerable charm, so much so that he often struck others as being shallow, if not actually weak. While coming from one of the most distinguished families in Japan, he disliked millionaires and considered himself a Socialist. He didn't particularly like Americans, whom he considered brash, and yet he sent his son, Fumitaka, to Lawrenceville and Princeton. He loved his wife, but was also in love with his mistress. He preferred wearing kimonos, but was at ease in western clothes. He treated Hirohito rather intimately. While others in the presence of the Emperor sat ramrod-straight on the edge of their chairs, Prince Konoye sprawled informally, not as an insult but because he felt, with considerable justification, that he came from just as good a family.

He was sprawling in a chair in the Emperor's study while Hirohito was on the phone. When he hung up, the Emperor said: "That was General Nakajima," the Emperor said. "Our armies have taken Nanking."

Prince Konoye sat upright.

"Congratulations, Your Majesty!" he exclaimed. "What a great victory."

"Yes, I'm pleased. Chiang Kai-shek has escaped with what's left of his government, and perhaps now the Chinese will see what a weakling he is and come to their senses. General Nakajima has asked permission to make an example to the city population for their resistance, weak as it was. Many of Chiang's soldiers have thrown away their uniforms and are trying to hide, but Nakajima is rounding them up."

"And what will he do?"

Hirohito smiled slightly.

"Black tent," was all he said.

Prince Konoye looked rather nervous.

"If I may suggest, Your Majesty," he said, "it would be useful to instruct General Nakajima to spare any and all Americans and Europeans. We would not want public opinion in America to turn against us more than it already is."

"The United States treats us Japanese with hatred and contempt, and the government of President Roosevelt is distinctly anti-Japanese, as you well know. All Americans are racists, just like the British. I couldn't care less about American public opinion." He hesitated, adding, "But of course, General Nakajima will be careful with the foreigners. He is, after all, a gentleman, as are all my officers."

The Rape of Nanking, which went on during December of 1937 and January of 1938, shocked the civilized world and was perhaps the most horrible of all the atrocities committed by the Japanese. The Japanese entered the city on Sunday, December 12, with orders from Prince Asaka, the Emperor's uncle, to kill all captives. The executions and looting began almost immediately. General Nakajima, that great gentleman, ordered the Chinese soldiers remaining in the city to be rounded up and killed with bayonets to save bullets. Samurai swords were used for random decapitations and often, to test their strength, they were swung down from above, cleaving the skull in two. Women were repeatedly raped, then killed, their bodies mutilated. Many women were tied to beds to be used to satisfy any passerby's lust. Men were bound hand and foot and planted neck deep in earth, their exposed heads trampled by horses or doused with boiling water or crushed under tank tracks. Afterward, it was tallied that over twenty thousand women of all ages, from eight to eighty, had been raped, and over two hundred thousand men, at least a quarter of them civilians, murdered. A third of the city was destroyed by fire, and everything of value looted. Many were sent north in cattle cars to Harbin, in Manchuria, to something called, mysteriously, Unit 731. This was set up as early as 1930 by General Shiro Ishii and was a bacterial warfare experimental program. Prisoners were fed food laced with anthrax, typhoid, and other pathogens. When they became infected, they were strapped to operating tables and literally vivisected: Their bodies were cut open for examination while they were still alive.

All of these horrible events Jasmin and Charlie were informed of in Hankow, where they had been joined by the Generalissimo and what was left of his government. But what broke Jasmin's heart was the news that the Japanese had not only sacked her hospital, but burned it to the ground.

PART SEVEN

NAZIS: 1938–1939

"MR. SAVAGE, IT'S THE PRESIDENT of the United States."

The speaker was Ellen Terry, Nick's young new secretary, and she sounded rather awestruck as she stood in the door of Nick's spacious office overlooking Pine Street. Ellen had never spoken to anyone in the White House, much less the president. But it had been President Roosevelt himself on the phone: there was no mistaking his patrician drawl that had become, in the past six years, so well-known to all Americans from his many radio addresses and newsreel appearances. Love him or hate him, Franklin Delano Roosevelt was the best-known American in the world, with the possible exception of Shirley Temple, and perhaps the most famous person in the world after Adolf Hitler.

Nick picked up his phone with alacrity.

"Mr. President," he said. "Nick Savage here."

"Ah, Nick, how are you?"

"I'm just fine, sir. And you?"

"As well as can be expected. Nick, I have a favor to ask of you, and I hope you're in an agreeable mood."

"He wants me to be the new American ambassador to Germany," Nick said that night as he dined with Samantha and Rachel in his mother's Park Avenue apartment.

"Well, it's a great honor," Rachel said, "but why you? You have no experience in foreign service."

"That's what I said, but he brushed that off. He said most of the ambassadors don't have any experience—certainly Joe Kennedy doesn't, and he's ambassador to England. But he wants me because I've been to Germany and he knows what I think of the Nazis."

"He told Nick that Hitler is really getting out of hand the way he's treating the Jews in Germany," Samantha said. "There's not much the president can do, but by sending Nick, who's partially Jewish, he hopes that might send some sort of message to the top Nazis. I'm tremendously excited about it."

"So am I," Nick said. "Maybe this will give me a chance to make up for the dumb things I've done in my life."

With Nick's decision to accept the president's job offer, he took a crash course in foreign affairs as well as trying to learn the rudiments of German at Berlitz. Hitler's real intentions had become evident two years before when, in March of 1936, he sent his troops into the Rhineland. The French Army, which at the time heavily outmanned the Germans, instead of attacking the Germans had done nothing.

Then, in the spring of the next year, 1937, Hitler had taken over Austria without firing a shot. Again, neither the French nor the British did anything.

Next, Hitler had turned his attention to Czechoslovakia. Using the excuse that a number of Germans in western Czechoslovakia were being mistreated by the Czech government, Hitler threatened to invade Czechoslovakia unless his demands were met. His demands were met, infamously, at Munich. By the fall of 1938, Hitler had taken over the entire country.

Hitler incessantly talked peace but used the threat of war to gobble up more and more of Europe and got away with it. Nick realized that by going to Berlin, he was entering a nightmare world.

Letter from Nick Savage to his mother.

Berlin. October 15, 1938.

Dear Mother:

We have moved in to the embassy, which is a big old house on the Unter den Linden, rather drafty and not particularly comfortable: neither Samantha nor I like it very much, but we shan't complain. The embassy staff seem nice and, so far, are competent:

I am told by Bob Lister, who's the number-two man under me, that he thinks our phones are tapped by the Gestapo. All the embassies think that so I believe it's probably true. The Gestapo are paranoid about knowing everything that goes on in this country: I guess privacy is a luxury for democracies only.

Yesterday I put on my white tie and tails and was driven to the Foreign Office to deliver my ambassadorial credentials. I met Hitler, who shook my hand and said he hoped I would enjoy Berlin, then he left the room. I'm told he doesn't think much of America or Americans—he considers us a "mongrel" nation, as he puts it, and apparently was amazed that we were represented by colored athletes like Jesse Owens at the Olympics here two years ago. At any rate, I'm now official. Perhaps in time I'll be able to improve what Herr Hitler thinks of us Americans, but I'm not counting on it.

Samantha is well, as is the baby, and we all send you our love.

Nick.

Berlin. October 27, 1938.

Dear Mother:

We're pretty well settled in now, and Amanda runs around the embassy as if she owns the place. We're right next to the Tiergarten, which is really a lovely park, and whenever the weather permits, Samantha and I take long walks in it. We've gotten to know the diplomatic community here—or at least most of them. They are a wildly entertaining lot. There seem to be parties and receptions practically every night: I imagine if the money these governments spend on partying could be channeled into more useful events, this damned Depression might go away. Incidentally, and rather ironically, the biggest spenders are the Russians, who also have the biggest embassy, a huge palace dating from Tsarist days. The champagne and vodka flow at the Russkies, and the caviar never runs out. So much for Communism. Samantha and I are giving our first reception next week, something I would gladly skip if I could, but it's expected of us, so we'll do it. Samantha is fabulous at dealing with the caterers.

So far, the Nazi bigwigs have been chilly to me, I think because they know I am half-Jewish. The one exception is Herr Goering, the immensely fat chief of the Luftwaffe. For some reason, he couldn't be more friendly to us. Von Ribbentrop, the former champagne salesman who is now Foreign Minister, on the other hand practically cuts me dead at receptions. He's a vain, frivolous, rather, in my opinion, stupid man who loves to talk to everyone except me. It's all very curious. Perhaps I'll find out more in time.

We are all in good health.

Much love,
Nick.

Berlin. November 11, 1938.

Dear Mother:

An absolute catastrophe happened here the other night—I'm sure you've read about it in the New York papers. The Nazis launched a terrible pogrom against the Berlin Jews, burning and looting their shops, breaking windows—they're calling it *Kristallnacht*, the night of the broken windows—and murdering many. I don't have any figures, but the rumors going around town are that hundreds may have been killed. Of course, the Nazi press is blaming it all on the Jews, saying that the murder, pillage, and arson were caused by "spontaneous demonstrations" of patriotic Germans enraged by the murder in Paris of a third secretary of the German embassy by a young German Jew. But I don't believe this for an instant, and neither do most of the other diplomats here. The police did nothing to stop the looting and burning, and many say they were doing much of it themselves.

Yesterday, I went to the Chancellery to make a formal protest—I did this on my own, by the way, and may get hell for it from Washington—but was told curtly that it was an internal

German matter and no business of foreigners. The Nazis must be fools if they think that they can totally ignore world opinion, and from what I read in the foreign press and hear on the BBC, this pogrom has caused a real uproar abroad, as well it should. I don't understand the Nazis' murderous hatred of the Jews here when they have historically contributed so much to Germany. It's as if the Nazis are crazed on the subject!

On a totally frivolous and inconsequential level, our first reception last week was an enormous success, but it burns me to realize I was paying to entertain the few Nazi bigwigs that showed up. I wish I'd put rat poison in their champagne!

Much love,
Nick.

Berlin. December 4, 1938,

Dear Mother:

After less than two months in Berlin, I have come to hate this government of thugs so much I don't know how much longer I can take it. Besides, I have made an enemy of the number-two man in the country which perhaps has cancelled my usefulness here as ambassador—we shall see. It happened this way.

Despite the uproar over *Kristallnacht*, the round of diplomatic parties continues as if nothing had happened, which is foolish, if not immoral, on the part of the European powers because Hitler thinks he can get away with anything with them—which apparently he can! Last week, Samantha and I were invited to a reception at the French Embassy here, which is near our embassy, cattycornered to the Adlon Hotel. The embassy is a gorgeous palace, hung with Gobelins tapestries, beautiful furniture, portraits of Louis XIV and XV and—to tweek the Germans' noses—a magnificent rug with a large gold N in the middle of it—N for Napoleon to remind the Germans every time they walk over it that Napoleon creamed the Prussians on many occasions in the past. The reception was very glittery and glamorous, with all the wives dripping jewels—Samantha was the most beautiful, in my biased opinion. We were sipping water when up comes fat Hermann Goering in an outlandish white uniform covered with medals and sashes. He was in a beamish mood—as I think I told you, he's the only Nazi bigwig that seems to like us, though now I know why. He kissed Samantha's hand and then asked us if we would like to be his guests the next weekend at his country estate, Karinhall. I was a bit taken aback and hardly eager to accept the hospitality of the man everyone is saying was behind last month's horrible pogrom. Yet on the other hand, it's my duty as ambassador to try to get along with the leaders of the country, so, reluctantly, I accepted. And, to be honest, I was curious to see Karinhall, which everyone says is filled with fantastic treasures, most of them looted from rich Jews.

The following Saturday morning, we were driven out to Karinhall in my embassy car. It was snowing rather heavily, but we could see that the place is a great estate of many wooded hectares. The house itself is huge and rather ugly in a heavy German style. It is said that Goering has made himself one of the richest men in Germany, and he and his second wife certainly live in princely style (Karinhall was named after his first Swedish wife who died). Servants were everywhere, and we were taken with our luggage to a grand suite on the second floor where a private maid unpacked for us. We changed, then went downstairs for lunch. The French ambassador, André François-Poncet, and his wife were also guests, along with the Hungarian ambassador and several powerful German businessmen and their wives. The walls of Karinhall are hung with Old Master paintings, some excellent, some second rate, hung in vast profusion three and four tiers high. There are also suits of armor and some statuary, and in the great hall of the house there are at least five hundred stag horns on the walls: Goering is, among many other things, Reichsminister of the Hunt.

After we were greeted by our host and his attractive wife, we were led into a vast dining room where we sat down to a lavish lunch where the most expensive wines flowed (I of course drank nothing but water). Afterward, Goering took us downstairs where,

in his cellars, he has stored more of his treasures, which he displayed to us with almost childish glee and which included sacks
full of diamonds and other precious stones, a wine cellar with at
least several thousand bottles of the finest French and German
vintages, and, strangely enough, a huge electric train set. (Is it
possible this fat man who has murdered God knows how many
people is really a monstrous child who never grew up?)

I was quickly growing tired of Karinhall and its host, but we
had to get through the evening, a formal dinner. Afterward, many
of the guests sat down to play bridge or watch a movie in his
private theater, but Goering asked me to join him in his private
study, which I did.

Now, you'll probably think I'm making this up, because it
seems incredible that the second most powerful man in a civilized
country like Germany (maybe it's not so civilized, come to think
of it) could behave the way Goering did. First, speaking through
his interpreter, a rather gnomish man named Kruger, I think, he
offered me a brandy, which I declined, so he poured himself one,
motioning me to take a seat in a leather sofa, which I did. I'll do
my best to remember exactly what was said. He began by saying,
"I believe you had a distant cousin named Fritz Lieber who was
killed during the Roehm-attempted putsch four years ago?"

"Yes, though from what I read he was murdered."

"Ernst Roehm was plotting to overthrow the Fuehrer. He and
all his associates—most of whom were degenerates, like your
cousin—were traitors and deserved to die. Fritz had an older
brother named Claus. Did you know that?"

"Yes. After graduating from medical school in Vienna, he
moved to Mannheim, where he's now a doctor."

Goering pulled a wallet from his tail coat and extracted a
snapshot, which he handed me. It was a photograph of a young
man with dark hair and a thin, quite handsome face that reminded
me of Fritz, whom I met in Berlin five or six years ago when you
asked me to try to get him to leave Germany. The young man,
who looked very sad, was wearing a rumpled striped prisoner's
uniform, standing in front of a barbed-wire fence.

"That's Claus Lieber," Goering said.

"Is he in a prison?"

"He's in a concentration camp outside Munich called Dachau."

"Why? What did he do?"

Goering shrugged as he lit a cigar.

"He broke some of our racial laws. Unfortunately, Dachau is not a very pleasant place. Prisoners get killed there, attempting to escape. When I learned that he was a relative of yours, I of course wanted you to know, being, as I am, so very fond of you and your lovely wife. This Claus Lieber is a very bright young man. He has much to live for. That is, if he could get out of Dachau."

He took a sip of brandy, keeping his beady eyes on me. I realized he was playing some sort of game with me.

"Could he get out of Dachau?" I asked, quietly, playing it as carefully as I could.

"In Germany, anything is possible if you know the right people. And I am the right person to know."

"Herr Reich Marshal," I said, using his formal title, "anything you could do to help this young man I would consider a great personal favor."

Goering, who had perched himself on the edge of his desk, his enormous hammy legs bulging under his formal tails, took a puff of the cigar.

"Then perhaps I can do something for you, and you can do something for me. Our German economy is booming, but we are rather short of liquid funds, by which I mean that we have to buy so many of our natural resources, like oil, abroad that it puts a drain on our financial system. You are an influential banker on Wall Street. If you could put together a consortium of bankers to raise for us a loan of, say, one hundred million dollars, I can get Claus Lieber out of Dachau—and, for that matter, out of Germany. Of course there would be a nice personal profit for you for arranging the loan. And for me." He smiled.

I was so stunned by what he said—which was, let's face it, nothing but crude blackmail—that I couldn't think of anything to say for a few seconds. Finally, I said, "You must understand, Herr Reich Marshal, that in my capacity as ambassador I could never get involved in a financial deal with your government."

"Come now, Savage," he said, "we're both men of the world. Life is run by a handful of people at the top, like you and me. We write the rules. Anything can be arranged. You wish your ambassadorship to be successful, I'm sure. You're not much liked in Berlin. There's a feeling that you are secretly against the regime. But I could make you liked. I can open every door, even the Fuehrer's. There are strains between our two countries, which there shouldn't be. Germany has no quarrel with America—in fact, we want to be America's friend. If you want your cousin's release from Dachau, the loan is part of the deal. Otherwise, life for your cousin could become much less pleasant—and rather more brief."

Again, he sipped his brandy, his eyes on me. I'm afraid I was sweating, something I rarely do, particularly on a cold December night. I got up and told him I would have to think it over, which was a lie. Except he had me in a corner. Did I want to send Claus Lieber—that sad young man in the snapshot—to his death? I had to have time. Perhaps there was some other way to buy Goering off.

But the man is a pig, totally drunk with his almost absolute power. I have a much bleaker view of the future now than I had before. And I know that if I don't make a deal with him, he will become my enemy. And Hermann Goering would be an extremely dangerous enemy. I'm even thinking of sending Amanda and Mrs. Hogan back to the States for their own safety, as painful as that would be for me and Samantha.

All my love,
Nick.

22 "MY GOD, RICHARD," GLORIA Wood said, looking at the tall young man in the dark blue suit, "you're getting to be a real heartthrob! If I were half my age, I'd be making googoo eyes at you."

Richard Shelby, who was now twenty-one, looked embarrassed. He was home from college for the Christmas holidays, and he had come to Whitehall to pay Gloria a visit. It was an icy day with heavy snow outside; but inside the pillared mansion, everything was warm and beautiful, and an eighteen-foot-high Christmas tree was in front of the windows, its boughs gaily lit and decorated.

Gloria laughed and squeezed his arm.

"I've embarrassed you," she said. "I'm an aging flirt, and I can't help it. But don't worry: you're safe with me. Would you like a drink?"

"I wouldn't mind a beer, ma'am."

"Well, run into the kitchen and get one. You know where everything is. And tell your father I'd love a dry martini. Then come back and tell me all about college. William tells me you're getting terrific grades, which I'm so pleased about."

"Yes, I think I'm doing pretty well."

"You're too modest. And you're on the swimming team I hear? And playing football? You're a star! It's so wonderful. By the way, if you want to use the pool in the basement to work out, you're free to do so, as always. Now run along. It's almost cocktail hour, and I'm thirsty."

"Be right back, ma'am. And I might take you up on using the pool."

"Any time."

Richard hurried out of the drawing room and went back to the enormous kitchen, where his father was polishing silver.

"Mrs. Wood wants a martini," he said, going to the refrigerator. "And I'm having a beer."

"Where?" William asked, putting down the silver bowl he was working on.

"In the drawing room. With her. She wants to hear about college. And Poppa, I want to ask her about Harvard Law."

"Now Richard, don't you get pushy with her. For all Mrs. Wood has done for you, I'm not going to have her think you want more."

Richard pulled a Budweiser from the fridge.

"Poppa, she was the one who mentioned law school in the first place! I'm not being pushy."

"See that you don't. And I'm not sure I like the idea of you having drinks with her in the drawing room."

"Poppa, she asked me! Times are changing! This isn't *Gone with the Wind*. This is Nineteen-thirty-eight!"

"Maybe so. But don't be too sure. Well, go on, then. Tell her I'll bring her martini in a minute."

Richard poured his beer into a tall glass, then went through the butler's pantry into the hallway leading to the drawing room. Whitehall brought back so many memories to him, memories of watching the white guests through the diamond-shaped peep-window in the pantry door and marveling at that beautiful world, so much like in the movies. And now, he was closer to that world. He was a star at Howard, just like Mrs. Wood said. And he could be a star in America someday.

When he came into the drawing room, Gloria was sitting by the fireplace where logs were cheerfully burning. She was wearing a smart black cocktail dress with a string of pearls and several thick diamond bracelets. Time was marching on with Gloria, as with everyone else, leaving its footprints on her face. But she was still a beautiful woman.

"Poppa will be right in with your drink," he said.

"Thanks. Sit down, Richard, and tell me how things are going with you. Do you have a girlfriend?"

He took a seat on one of the sofas.

"I don't have too much time for girls, what with studies and sports."

"Well, take some time. Listen: Youth is a wonderful thing, and it goes like the wind. Have some fun, Richard. 'Gather ye rosebuds while ye may,' as Shakespeare said."

"Excuse me, ma'am, but it wasn't Shakespeare. It was Robert Herrick in a poem called *To the Virgins, to Make Much of Time*."

Gloria laughed.

"Good Lord, Richard, you're becoming *too* educated! You'll be the class know-it-all."

"I'm sorry, ma'am, but it's one of my favorite poems."

"So you like poetry?"

"Very much. I even tried to write some once, but it was pretty lousy. I guess I'd better stick to the law."

"Speaking of which, we have to talk about law school. Ah, here's my drink." William had just come into the drawing room, carrying a martini on a silver salver. "William, this son of yours is too bright by half. He's showing me up for the uneducated idiot I am. You know, Richard, I never went to college, I went into show business when I was your age. So I'm living my college days vicariously through you."

The doorbell rang.

"Are you expecting someone, Mrs. Wood?" William asked.

"I expect it's some Christmas presents I bought for Sebastian. He probably doesn't know where the service entrance is." She took the martini.

"Shall I tell him to go round back?"

"No, just have him bring it in here. It's snowing heavily. I think it may be Sebastian's new bicycle. Have him put it here, by the tree."

"Yes, ma'am."

As William went to the entrance hall, Gloria turned to Richard, who was halfway through his beer.

"Now," she said. "Law school. I recently made a small donation to Harvard, to get my foot in the door, so to speak. Not only for you, but for Sebastian—I have to think of him, too, of course. Anyway, I made some discreet inquiries about Harvard Law, and I was told they are admitting properly qualified colored men, like yourself. So I think, if you keep on doing the splendid work you are, you probably could sail right in."

"Harvard Law," Richard said, in awestruck tones. "It doesn't seem possible."

"As Cole Porter says, today anything goes."

William appeared in the doorway.

"Mrs. Wood, it's Mrs. Treadwell."

Gloria looked confused.

"Deirdre? What in the world is she doing here?"

"She has brought some Christmas gifts."

"Well, show her in."

William returned a moment later, leading in Deirdre Treadwell, who was looking spectacular in a snow-dusted sable coat with matching hat. She was carrying several gift-wrapped packages. She looked first at Gloria, then Richard, then back at Gloria, who stood up.

"Deirdre," she said. "I must say I'm surprised to see you here."

"Ross says Indianapolis is too small a town for feuds. He wants us to bury the hatchet. I do so hope we can make that happen."

"How sweet of Ross, who's such a dear man," Gloria said. "And he's absolutely right: Feuds are a bore. Can you stay for a drink?"

Deirdre glanced again at Richard, who had also stood up, holding his beer glass. Then she looked back at Gloria.

"No thanks, I have to get home. But these presents are for you and Sebastian. And Ross and I do wish you both a most merry Christmas. And of course, we all appreciate so much your donations to the hospital."

She handed the packages to William, then turned and left the room.

"Isn't that Mr. Kinkaid's daughter?" Richard asked, softly.

"Yes," Gloria said. "She married my ex-boyfriend, Dr. Treadwell. She really detests me, but she has to be nice because of the hospital. She stole away my boyfriend and married him, which made me furious at the time, but I guess she was just getting me back because I caused her husband to leave her. It's a merry world here in Indianapolis. I still can't stand her father."

Richard finished his beer.

"I'll never forget when he threatened to have me lynched," he said. "I was never so scared in my life."

"Thank God the lynching days are over," Gloria said. "Maybe Indiana is becoming civilized, at last. Would you like another beer?"

"No thanks, Mrs. Wood. I'd better get going. I have to do some Christmas shopping myself. And what you said about Harvard Law . . . Well, that's my life's dream. You sure have made my Christmas."

"We're all very proud of you, Richard. You're going to make a great lawyer."

"It's all thanks to you, ma'am."

"Listen, I just put up the money. You did the hard work. That's the important part. And merry Christmas, Richard. And a most happy New Year."

She held out her hands and took his, kissing his cheek.

"Nineteen thirty-nine," he said, thoughtfully. "Yes, let's hope it will be a happy year."

"Well, I delivered the presents to Gloria Wood," Deirdre said to her husband, who was putting logs on the fire in the living room of their house, "and guess what I saw?"

"Gloria, I suppose. How is she?"

"Getting a little long in the tooth, if you ask me."

Ross laughed, as he kissed her.

"Let's face it, you were never her biggest fan," he said.

"She's a cheap slut. I never saw what you saw in her, though I suppose the attraction was obvious. But anyway, I came into the house and she was having drinks with that former caddie at the country club, I can't think of his name—the butler's son."

"Oh yes, Richard Shelby."

"That's it. I always thought there was something going on between those two, and now I'm sure of it."

"Deirdre, you're not going to stir up that old canard again."

She lit a cigarette.

"My father thought it, too. Why would she pay his college tuition?"

"I think it's rather admirable of her. The kid's bright, and I hear he's a great athlete."

"Yes, I'm sure—in bed."

Her husband laughed as he sprawled on a sofa.

"For a well-bred young lady, my love, you have the most wonderfully dirty mind. What fun you must have had at Wellesley."

"Really, Ross, I find that a rather offensive remark, especially since you're the last person to talk about dirty minds. And I find it offensive that you take all this so . . . so fliply. It's disgusting what she's doing with that young man, and I think someone should put a stop to it."

"But why?"

"You know damned well why. My father has always said if the races start mixing, there won't be any white people left."

"In the first place, you have no proof they're 'mixing,' if that's the word you want to use."

"I'll get proof," she said, firmly. "And I'll run that woman out of this town. And the only reason you defend her is that I think you still have an itch for that slut. Am I right?"

"No, but you can think what you want. I still say you're making a mountain out of a mole hill."

"We'll see."

She stubbed her cigarette out in an ashtray. Then she went into the front hall and put on her fur coat and hat.

"I'll grant you that if Gloria Wood is drinking with the Shelby boy in her living room," Bennet Kinkaid said twenty minutes later, "then she probably is sleeping with him."

"I'm sure of it, Daddy," Deirdre said. They were in the library of Bennet's Tudor-style, twenty-room mansion. "And he's no boy anymore. He's a full-grown man and extremely handsome. If this sort of thing is allowed to go on, you know what's going to happen to this town."

"Not to mention this country. I should have taken care of Shelby before, but he slipped out on me and ran off to New York."

"You know what kind of a woman Gloria Wood is? Hollywood trash who'd sleep with any man she could get her hands on. But this time, she's gone too far."

"You're right, Deirdre. And you were right to tell me about this. I'll take care of it."

"What are you going to do?"

"You'll see."

Gloria was about to leave her suite at the Waldorf-Astoria to take Sebastian to Rockefeller Center to see the Christmas lights and go ice skating when her phone rang.

"Yes?"

"Mrs. Wood, it's William. Something terrible has happened! Oh my God!"

The poor man was sobbing.

"William, what's wrong?"

"They come in the middle of the night and kidnapped my boy, my beautiful son! Oh my God, they gonna kill him!"

"Who? William, please, try and calm down. Who kidnapped him?"

"Three men from the Klan! They broke into our house last night and grabbed Richard, took him away in a truck."

"Did you get the license?"

"No ma'am, they tied me up in the kitchen. It took me two hours to get loose, then I called the police but by the time they got to the house, there wasn't nothing they could do. I don't think they was much interested in doing anything anyway. Oh, Mrs. Wood, I'm so heartsick! They got my Richard! They gonna kill him!"

"William, I'm going to call my lawyer, Mr. Whitlock. He's very influential in Indianapolis, and he'll force the police to track these men down. Meanwhile, Sebastian and I will get back to Indianapolis as soon as we can. Don't despair, William. We're going to save Richard."

"God bless you, Mrs. Wood. I knew you'd help me. God bless you."

And he hung up.

"Sebastian," Gloria said, hanging up. "Get packed. We have to go home."

"But we haven't finished our Christmas shopping."

"We'll finish it in Indianapolis. This is an emergency."

"What happened to Richard?"

"The Klan kidnapped him, and I know who's behind this. That bastard, Bennet Kinkaid."

The setting was quintessential American Gothic: pure Grant Wood, or a Walker Evans Depression-era photograph: a lonely, two-story, paint-peeling farmhouse set beside a sagging red barn with a big MAIL POUCH TOBACCO sign painted on one side, the whole set in the middle of fifty acres of flat Indiana farmland halfway between Indianapolis and Muncie, the town where the Ball family had made a fortune manufacturing glass Mason Ball jars for home canning. The farmhouse was dark except for one window on the ground floor. Above it, a gibbous moon hung in a misty sky.

It was shortly after two in the morning. After a few minutes, a rather rattletrap pickup truck drove down the country road and turned into the dirt driveway leading to the farmhouse. The truck parked beneath a big, leafless tree. Three men in white robes and white pointed hoods climbed out of the rear of the truck, while another robed and hooded man climbed out of the driver's seat. He held a coil of thick rope.

Expertly, the driver tied a hangman's noose at one end of the rope. Then he walked around the truck and threw the other end of the rope up into the tree, arching it over a thick lateral branch. He looped the rope one more time over the branch, then pulled it taut, leaving the noose dangling in the rear of the open truck.

"Let's go get the nigger," the driver said to the other hooded men. They walked to the back door of the farmhouse and let themselves in. They walked through the dark kitchen into the dining room, where one ceiling light bulb cast a pale illumination over the peeling, rosebud wallpaper and the cheap, circa-1905 wooden furniture. Seated in one chair, his hands tied behind his back and a piece of tape over his mouth, was Richard Shelby.

"Hello, boy," the truck driver said, coming into the room. "It's time you paid your debt to society."

Richard, his eyes wide with fear, twisted in his chair, trying hopelessly to free himself from his tight bonds. He grunted through the gag. The dim light from the ceiling bulb made his pale skin seem even paler, as if he were staring death in the face. He was wearing the blue pajamas he had been kidnapped in; despite the cold, they were soaked with sweat under the armpits and over his chest. Richard's strong, young heart was pounding with terror.

The Klansmen walked over to him.

"You know what your crime is, boy?" he addressed Richard.

Richard, sweat pouring off his forehead, shook his head negatively.

"You made love to a white woman, boy. You made love to Mrs. Wood."

Richard again shook his head negatively, even more violently than before.

"Don't try to deny it, boy. That was a big mistake, and you're gonna pay for that mistake. We can't allow niggers making love to white ladies. Who knows what would happen if that was allowed to go on? Hmm? Why, the whole country might end up creamed coffee. That would be bad, boy. America is a white country. Always has been and always will be. You gotta understand that. 'Course, in a few minutes, it won't matter whether you do or not. Know what I mean?"

He grinned and winked. Richard stared at him, trembling violently.

"Untie him," the driver said. "Then we'll take him out to the truck."

"Watch him," another Klansman said. "He's strong. When he gets untied . . ."

The driver pulled a gun from under his sheet.

"If he tries anything, we'll save the tree a lot of trouble."

Richard grunted in absolute terror.

Three of the Klansmen grabbed Richard by the arms and around the waist as he kicked and thrashed with all his considerable strength. Then they dragged him into the farmhouse kitchen, out the back door into the icy night. The truck squatted in the moonlight beneath the large oak tree, the hangman's noose dangling from the branch above it. The Klansmen dragged Richard to the truck, then hoisted him up into the rear where they swiftly retied his wrists behind him. Then one of them slipped the hangman's noose over his head and tightened it around his neck. The driver got into the front seat and started the engine. Then he climbed back out and walked around to the rear of the truck.

"Richard Shelby," he announced as Richard stared down at him. "You have been condemned to death by lynchin' because you made love to a white woman, thereby breaking the miscegenation laws of this state."

Again, Richard grunted, shaking his head negatively.

"May God rest your nigger soul."

The driver went back to the front of the truck and climbed in the seat. Revving the engine a moment, he shifted into first and pressed the accelerator. The truck lurched forward. Richard fell off the rear of the truck, the noose around his neck.

Instantly, the rope just above the hangman's knot broke, and Richard fell on the ground, amazed that he was still alive.

The Klansmen, howling with laughter, grabbed him and picked him off the ground as one of them removed the rope around his neck.

"Did we scare you, boy?" one of them jeered. "I bet you about pissed in your pants!"

"Get him in the truck," another said. "We'll take him back to his Pa's house. Bet he never fools around with no white woman again . . ."

Richard, tears of terror in his eyes, was pushed back into the rear of the truck, sprawling on his stomach as the robed Klansmen climbed in beside him.

The truck took off toward Indianapolis.

"My boy, he just sits in that hospital bed and he don't say a word," William said, tears running down his cheeks as he sat at the zinc-topped table in the middle of the kitchen at Whitehall. "It's like he's a zombie or something. It's like he's dead!"

"The doctor said he's been traumatized," Gloria said. She was sitting at the table opposite her long-time butler.

"Yes, ma'am, I heard that, but I don't understand what that word means."

"It means that something happened to Richard that so frightened him it put his brain into shock. And from the marks on Richard's neck, the doctors think perhaps the Klansmen tried to lynch him, as horrible as that may be."

"But what did my boy do?" William cried. "Why would they want to harm him? He's a good boy. He's a college boy! It don't make any sense!"

"I've hired the Pinkerton detective agency out of Chicago to investigate this mess, and if they can prove that Kinkaid's responsible, then by God, I'll sue him. But . . ." She sighed. ". . . We shouldn't get our hopes up. Kinkaid's powerful in this town, and the police won't lift a finger against him, so who knows, he may get away with it." She forced a smile. "But the doctors say Richard will probably be all right. It will just take some time for his brain to recover from the shock."

"But what if it don't? My son, with all his hope and promise—what if his brain don't recover? What if he's a zombie the rest of his life? Oh, ma'am, there ought to be a law against this sort of thing. There ought to be a law."

"There will be someday. It just takes time."

"But how long? How long?"

Four days later, William sat beside his son's bed in the Holy Cross Hospital on Indianapolis's south side and looked at Richard, who was sitting up in his bed, staring at the window with dead eyes. Around his neck, the marks from the hangman's noose were scabbing, marks that were a reminder of how near death he had come. He was wearing a white hospital smock.

After a few minutes, a white Dominican nun, a Sister of Mercy, with a white wimple and black robes, came into the room. William looked at her, fear in his eyes.

"Sister, he don't seem to be no different," he whispered. "He just sits there and stares."

"We must have faith," the portly nurse said, coming around the table and shaking down a thermometer, which she gently inserted into Richard's mouth. "Plus everything modern medicine can do. Modern medicine is wonderful, but without God, it's just a tool."

"Yes, ma'am, I know what you mean."

"Get it under your tongue, Richard," she said, adjusting the thermometer. Then, as William looked on anxiously, she checked his pulse, then removed the thermometer and read it.

"He's normal," she said. "Excellent."

She smoothed his bedcover and smiled at William as she walked to the door. "We'll bring him lunch in a while," she said. "Meat loaf today."

"That's good. Richard likes meat loaf. With lots of gravy. He loves gravy."

"We'll pour it on." She glanced at her watch. "You'll have to be leaving in a few minutes. Visiting hours are almost over."

"Yes, ma'am. I know."

She smiled and left the room.

William turned back to look at Richard, who was still staring at the window. Outside, the sun was shining. William reached over and took his son's hand.

"Come back to us, Richard," he whispered. "Please come back. You got a heap of living in front of you. You got a great life. You gotta come back, son. You work on it, you hear?"

Richard continued to stare at the window.

After a moment, William released his hand, got off his chair and kneeled by the side of the bed. He folded his hands and closed his eyes.

"Dear Lord," he whispered, "I've had a good life, so I ain't complaining. You gave me a loving wife, even though you took her away. You gave me good work and I've got money in the bank, more money than I ever dreamed of having—though I don't exactly trust that bank, but anyhow. So I ain't complaining, Lord. Don't get me wrong.

"But Lord, you gotta bring me back my boy. He's such a fine young man with so much promise. He could do so much for this world, and it's just not fair what they done to him, that Mr. Kinkaid and his Klansmen. To hang a noose around his young neck and pretend to lynch him? It's just not right! That's a terrible thing to do. Course, it woulda been worse if they'd actually done it and killed him. But here he is, neither dead or alive, and you've gotta do something about that, Lord. Please. If you need a price, then take me, for what I'm worth, which ain't much, I know. But bring back my son. Please. Thank you, Lord."

There were tears rolling down his cheeks as he opened his eyes. Then, with some difficulty, because William had the beginnings of arthritis, he stood back up. He looked at Richard a moment. Then he leaned over and kissed his forehead.

"I'll be back tomorrow, Richard," he whispered. "And you work on it, you hear?"

Richard continued to stare at the window.

William shook his head sadly, then turned and walked to the door. He was just opening it when he heard a familiar voice behind him.

"Poppa, what am I doing here?"

William, a look of infinite joy and amazement in his eyes, turned to see Richard looking at him, a puzzled expression on his face.

"Richard," he exclaimed. "You've come back! Thank you, God! Thank you!"

23

Berlin. December 18, 1938.

Dear Mother:

Hermann Goering is so totally amoral, unscrupulous, greedy, and murderous I can't imagine he's not the spawn of Satan. For all I know, he may also be a vampire. God help the world if these Nazis ever achieve their ambitions, which, according to the consensus in the diplomatic community here, is to control Europe and perhaps bring down the British Empire.

At any rate, after the disastrous weekend at Karinhall, Samantha and I returned to Berlin. Samantha confirmed what I already believed, that it was out of the question for me to do what Goering wanted—namely, arrange a hundred-million-dollar loan for Germany. But he had us in this awful corner: if we didn't do something, Claus Lieber's life was in jeopardy. When I showed Samantha the snapshot of him in Dachau—for Goering had told me to keep it—she was moved to tears, and as exasperated as I was. But Samantha, God love her, has a good head on her shoulders—as you know, she's been extremely successful running the Chatfield Foundation—and she said I had to bargain with Goering for Claus's life.

So I called the Ministerium and made an appointment to see Goering in his office. It was a bitterly cold morning when I drove to his office, and believe me, I wasn't looking forward to the meeting: to haggle over a person's life is an awesome responsibility, and I now know enough about the Nazi regime to realize human life means nothing to them.

When I came into his office, Goering was pleasant enough, shaking my hand, asking after Samantha's health—the usual pleasantries of civilized banter, and the man can be charming when he wants, but so can the Devil, I suppose. Anyway, I got straight to the point. I told him it was impossible for me to do what he wanted, but that if the German government wanted to request a loan from the United States, it should be done through the regular channels, i.e. the Ministry of Finance.

"But my dear Savage," he said, annoyance in his voice, "you don't seem to understand: then you and I couldn't skim off our fees. They're worth several million dollars!"

He said it so openly, almost so innocently, that I could see that the idea of enriching himself at the expense of his country didn't bother him at all! It was almost taken for granted that one enriched oneself. Well, I suppose I'm more naif than I realize: after all, American politicians are notorious self-enrichers. At any rate, I told him it was out of the question, which he wasn't happy about hearing. He said: "Then I'll have to tell the authorities at Dachau to make new arrangements for your relative."

So, there it was, out in the open. I began haggling with him, and as embarrassed as I am to use that verb, that's really what we were doing, like buying something in a Moroccan bazaar. When I asked, bluntly, how much did he want to free Claus from Dachau, he brazenly said a million dollars, which floored me. Yes, I know one can't put a price on a human life, but that was absurd, which he knew. But like any good merchant, he put a crazy price up front, knowing it would go down. I finally got him down to $50,000, half upon "signing," the rest when Claus is delivered to the embassy, which should be tomorrow. I signed Goering a check for $25,000, and will pay the rest on delivery—like a suit, except this is a human being. The whole business was immensely distasteful, and I feel dirty having been mixed up in it, but what else could I do? I have no doubt at all that this young man would have been murdered if I hadn't "bought" him.

And the way the Nazis execute people is as brutal and medieval as the other aspects of the regime: they chop off your head with an axe. On that cheery note, I'll end this depressing letter.

Much love,
Nick.

Berlin. December 20, 1938.

Dear Mother:

Claus Lieber was delivered to the embassy yesterday morning. He is a sweet young man who hasn't had a decent meal since he was arrested two months ago, so the first thing we did was to sit him down at the dining room table and feed him some soup, for if we had given him anything heavier, like pork chops and sauerkraut, it would probably have made him sick. As he wolfed down the soup, I asked him the particulars of his arrest—if you recall, I wrote you that Goering had said he had broken the "racial laws." Well, he was arrested because he is a Jew, as simple as that. When he asked me how I had gotten him out and I explained the whole sordid business, he was amazed that I had paid out $50,000—he said "That's almost as much as your president makes!," which is true, Mr. Roosevelt's salary is $75,000 a year. All of his family's personal wealth has been confiscated, but he swore to me he would pay me back. I told him he wasn't obligated to do that, but he was so upset he vowed to do it someday.

The Gestapo had delivered him in his prison uniform, which was filthy, so after he had eaten I took him to my bathroom and gave him clean underclothes and a pair of my slacks, a shirt, tie etc. He showered and shaved and when he came downstairs he told us he felt clean for the first time in months. He can't weigh more than 120 pounds, so of course my clothes were too big for him, but he looks presentable. Then I told him I had made arrangements to get him out of Germany tomorrow—that is, today—for I thought we should lose no time in getting him out of the clutches of the Nazis: Goering is certainly capable of re-arresting him on some trumped-up charge. So this morning he was flown in a small plane I had chartered from Templehof Airfield to Paris. I gave him $1000 cash to get him started in his new life and told him to look up my sister, Brook: He was so grateful he was in tears as he bade us good-bye. I have no doubt he'll succeed now that he's out of this hateful country with its malicious race laws. Samantha and I are happy that we've been able to save at least one Jew, but I fear there are thousands more here who face a dark future.

Much love,
Nick.

24

Berlin. December 23, 1938.

Dear Mother:

More miserable weather in this wretched city. Fog and drizzle that then turns to snow and ice and then goes back to fog and drizzle. The sun hasn't shown for ten days, but it doesn't seem to faze the Germans. The shoppers seem quite cheerful as they go about their Christmas buying. The brightly lit and gaily decorated stores like the huge K.D.W. on the west side of the Wittenberg-platz—everyone calls it Kadewe—are bulging with goodies to buy, and cafés like the Kranzler on the Kurfürstendamm are packed. Samantha and I don't go out much, mainly because on the nights we don't have to go to a diplomatic do we like to stay home with Amanda, who is turning into a beautiful, sweet child who can *sprechen Deutsch* almost as well as English—you know how quickly children pick up languages.

And speaking of children, Samantha is pregnant! We're both absolutely thrilled.

You will be glad to know that Claus Lieber is doing well in Paris, and Brook tells me by phone that she's very fond of him. However, he has caused me a new problem with our fat Herr Goering. Having survived the horrors of Dachau, Claus called a news conference in Paris and announced that he is going to America to give lectures on the truth of the Nazi regime, the lectures to be financed by various Jewish groups in New York and Chicago. Well, this sent Goering into a fury. He called me and demanded I come to his office, where he read me the riot act. He said that I had not lived up to my side of the bargain, that he would never have released Claus if he had thought he was going to turn the whole thing into a publicity stunt . . . he said, and I quote: "Why can't you handle this Jew scum?"

I said, "Herr Reich Marshal, you don't seem to understand that America is a democracy that guarantees freedom of speech. There's nothing I could do to shut Claus Lieber up even if I wanted to. Which I don't. And you know, if you wouldn't stick people in concentration camps, there wouldn't be any bad publicity about Germany."

Well. Goering, who invented the concentration camps (this isn't exactly true: They were invented by the English during the Boer War), didn't like to hear this at all. His piggish little eyes flashed fire as he said to me: "You'll be sorry for this, Mr. Savage."

So who knows what bad times lie ahead of me?

You won't get this until after the holidays, but dear Mother, all of us send you our love and best wishes and season's greetings.

Your devoted son,

Nick.

P.S. Hitler has been quiet lately—thank God for small favors—but André François-Poncet, the French Ambassador here, tells me he predicts war within a year. Since André is one of the best-informed men in Berlin, this doesn't bode well for the future. Let's pray he's wrong.

N.

Berlin. December 24, 1938.

Dear Mother:

It certainly didn't take long for Goering to revenge himself against me for the Claus Lieber affair.

As I've told you, we've long suspected that our phones are tapped. Well, we now know for sure: all the embassy staff is complaining about the clicks we hear on the phones. I've called the Foreign Office to complain, but they of course deny everything and merely stonewall me.

But even worse, the German press, controlled by Dr. Goebbels, has launched a vicious criticism of America, which it calls a "mongrel" nation of blacks, immigrants, and Jews. They've even picked out Mayor LaGuardia of New York, of all people! The *Völkischer Beobachter* and the *Angriff*, two official newspapers, have denounced Fiorello as being a Communist, whoremonger, and head of the Jewish cabal that allegedly rules America (I am told that LaGuardia is half-Jewish, like me). Well, it's fantastic. These people are maniacs.

Again, Happy New Year to you, dearest Mother.

Love,
Nick.

Berlin. December 27, 1938.

Dear Mother:

The Christmas spirit has obviously not had any effect on the Nazis.

This morning, the embassy received an anonymous phone call threatening an attack on me and Samantha. I'm sure it's nothing but a most insidious form of psychological warfare, inspired once again by Goering's wrath against me. But psychological warfare works. Samantha is almost hysterical, and she's begging me to quit this post, which I'm considering doing. After all, with the top Nazis so poisoned against me, there's not much I can do for my country. And I suppose it could be argued I'm more a liability than an asset. It's all very depressing.

More later.

Much love,
Nick.

Berlin. December 28, 1938.

Dear Mother:

A strange occurrence today in this strangest of all cities. Samantha has a slight cold, so I took my daily walk in the Tiergarten by myself. It was an icy day, but at least the sun was out for the first time in ages and I was in a cheery mood—or as cheery as one can get in Germany—when I noticed an attractive and well-dressed woman coming toward me. When she reached me, she asked if she could talk to me, speaking excellent English. She seemed nervous, and was looking around, as if afraid someone might be watching her. "Mr. Savage," she said, "can you walk with me for a while?" I said of course, and we walked on through the beautiful, snowy park while she told me this remarkable story. "My name is Magda Hirsch," she said, "and my husband, Leo, is an American-born Jew who spent the first five years of his life in Newark, New Jersey. Then in nineteen-twenty, his parents, who were German, moved back to Germany for business reasons and Leo's been here ever since. Three days ago, he was arrested by the Gestapo." "Why?" I asked. "They claim he was part of a plot to assassinate the Fuehrer, which is complete nonsense, a total lie!" She went on to tell me that a friend of her husband had asked him to deliver a box to an address in Berlin, which he did, having no idea what was in the box. But the Gestapo claims the box held explosives . . . "Which is a lie!" she blurted out, on the verge of tears. "But of course the Gestapo doesn't care, and he won't get a fair trial—how could he, being a Jew? But since he was born in America, I thought perhaps you could help him. I was afraid to go to the American Embassy, because the Gestapo may be watching me—they may be watching me now, I don't know . . . But please, Mr. Savage, I know you're a kind man . . . please do something to help my poor husband!"

I told her I'd do everything in my power, but when I asked her if her husband had any proof of being an American citizen, she said no, that in the eighteen years since he was brought to Germany he lost his passport and both his parents are dead so she can't prove anything at all. This didn't help, needless to say, but the poor woman was so wretched I told her I'd try to arrange an interview with her husband, since the Gestapo has refused to let her see him. All she knows is that he's in the Gestapo prison on Prinz Albrechtstrasse. Then she gave me her card with her address, telling me not to phone her because she was certain her phone was tapped. Then she hurried away.

When I got back to the embassy, I phoned the Gestapo head-quarters, told them who I am and demanded to be permitted to talk to this Leo Hirsch. Rather to my surprise—for the Gestapo are usually anything but cooperative—they said yes, so I am to see him at the prison at ten o'clock the day after New Year's. I don't know if I'll be able to do any good, but I'll try. Otherwise, I fear that Leo Hirsch's future may not be bright. What a New Year's Eve present!

All my love,

Nick.

Berlin. January 2, 1939.

Dear Mother:

I fear I am in serious trouble. Let me get the facts down, while they are still fresh in my mind.

This morning I was driven in the embassy car to the Gestapo prison on Prinz Albrechtstrasse, a building about as gloomy and threatening as you would expect and which brought to mind those fantastic eighteenth-century Piranesi drawings of imaginary prisons. I was taken to the office of a certain Captain Gerhard Frisch, a young man with a surprisingly baby face and unsurprisingly blond Aryan hair. Frisch greeted me with Teutonic formality, shaking my hand and offering me a chair in his tidy office over-looking what I assume was the exercise yard of the prison. He informed me bluntly enough that there was no proof that Leo Hirsch was an American citizen, but that as a favor to me, I would be allowed to speak with him for five minutes. I asked if Hirsch had a lawyer, and Captain Frisch said, rather curtly, "of course," but offered no further illumination. He buzzed a button, and a brutish-looking Gestapo lieutenant came in to lead me down to Hirsch's cell. The lieutenant, who looked as if he came off one of the FBI's most-wanted posters, led me to a stone stair, then down to a dank and freezing cold stone corridor lined with steel cell doors and illuminated by ceiling lights protected by iron bars. It was 22 degrees Fahrenheit outside, but the Gestapo obviously doesn't consider it necessary to heat its cells and it couldn't have been more than 35 degrees inside this basement—if that: You could see your breath! Fortunately for me, I was wearing the camel's hair overcoat you gave me two Christmases ago as well as a pair of gloves, or I undoubtedly would have caught pneumonia. You can imagine my surprise when the Gestapo brute opened one of the cell doors and I saw Leo Hirsch curled up on his bunk wearing nothing but a thin prison striped uniform. "You have five minutes," I was told. I went inside the cell and introduced myself to Hirsch, who is a fine-looking young man who was shivering from the cold and, probably, from fear as well. I took off my overcoat and started to put it around him, but the Gestapo lieutenant told me that was not allowed. I asked Hirsch if he was being properly represented legally and he shrugged sadly and said, "My lawyer was assigned by the Gestapo, Mr. Ambassador, so what do you think?" I told him that I had sent a cable to the Mayor of Newark seeking confirmation of his birth there and that I was at his service to do anything he wanted. The young man thanked me and asked about his wife. I told him she seemed to be well but was naturally worried about him. "Tell her I love her," he said, at which point I was told that my time was up. We shook hands and I left the dismal cell, my spirits not exactly soaring for Leo's prospects.

When I was back in my car, I pulled out the card Magda Hirsch had given me and gave my driver an address on the Budapesterstrasse. We drove to a middle-class neighborhood and stopped before a five-story stone building that looked as if it dated from the turn of the century. Going to the front door, I saw that the Hirsches lived on the third floor. I rang their bell, then went inside and started climbing the stairs. When I got to the third floor, Magda Hirsch was waiting for me in the open door of her apartment. I shook her hand, and she led me inside, closing the door. "I've just seen your husband," I said. "And he seems to be all right, considering the circumstances." "Well," she says, "I'm glad to hear that, and I certainly appreciate it, Mr. Savage. Would you like a drink?"

I was rather surprised at her offer, since the last thing I considered was that this was a social visit, and I declined, returning to the subject of her husband. All of a sudden, to my amazement, Mrs. Hirsch started ripping her dress and screaming "Rape! Help me! Rape!" The door burst open and four Gestapo men ran in the room, guns drawn. "This man tried to rape me!" Magda cried, pointing to me, and I realized—too late, I fear—that this whole thing had been a setup. When the Gestapo men tried to arrest me, I angrily told them I was the American Ambassador, pulling out my wallet to show them my identity papers, at which point the bastards started snickering at me. I turned to Magda Hirsch, who was smiling slightly, and told her, "This is a fine way to thank me for helping your husband."

"My husband?" she said. "Why Mr. Savage, I'm not married. I don't know what you're talking about."

I was furious, but common sense told me to get out of there as fast as I could, which I did, but the damage has been done. All the evening papers have headlined the story "American Ambassador Caught in Love-Nest," that sort of thing: I'm sure the whole thing was orchestrated by Goebbels, who totally controls the press, and instigated by Goering, who has never forgiven me for refusing to go along with his loan scheme, not to mention the Claus Lieber affair. The radio tonight is trumpeting the story, and outraged Foreign Ministry officials are demanding my recall to Washington.

I was duped in a first-class fashion, and I'm furious at these criminals who pass themselves off as statesmen, but my naiveté has cost me my good name. Samantha has been wonderful, standing by me and never for a moment believing that I had tried to rape this Hirsch woman—who, by the way, I have since found out is a minor film actress and it is rumored that Dr. Goebbels beds her . . . what a cesspool this city is!—and Samantha says that I probably should resign, as whatever good I can do in Berlin is totally canceled by this rancid little affair. Since she is as sick of this city as I am, I probably will resign, possibly tomorrow. But I go to bed tonight with a heavy heart. I don't know how anyone could succeed at this job, but I have to face the uncomfortable truth that I have failed. It's not a nice feeling.

All my love,

Nick.

25

"DADDY, I'M HAVING SOME RATHER strange problems with Ross," Deirdre Treadwell said to her father. She was in his big, paneled office overlooking downtown Indianapolis.

"Now what?" Bennet Kinkaid said.

"Well, it's terribly personal."

"Is he playing around? I warned you before you married him that he was a womanizer."

"No, it's not that. At least, I don't think it is."

"Well then, what is it?"

"He keeps dressing up as a woman."

Bennet's hairless, skull-like face stared at her.

"Is he a pansy?" he whispered.

"No. At least, I don't think he is. And he's certainly a wonderful lover. But every once in a while, he comes in our bedroom dressed as a woman. He says it expresses something inside him, and he thinks it makes him sexier."

"Does it?"

"Well . . . I mean, it's all so weird. I've tried to get him to go see a psychiatrist, but he refuses. He says there's absolutely nothing wrong with him. But he seems to be doing it more and more often. It's really upsetting me. I don't know how to deal with it. I mean, it may be some new fashion, you know what I mean? Men dressing up as women?"

Her father snorted.

" 'Fashion' is one word for 'perversion.' I think Ross is sick."

"Well, perhaps. I don't know. It seems to make him happy. I just don't know how to deal with it. And, in a way, it's sort of, well, exciting."

"Good Lord, Deirdre, are you getting as sick as Ross?"

"I don't know, daddy. Oh, life is so confusing."

She shrugged helplessly. Her father's phone rang.

"Excuse me." Bennet picked up the phone. "Yes? Oh hello, Martin.

How are you?" He listened a moment, frowning, as Deirdre lit a cigarette. "How many shares? Fifty thousand? What do you think it means?"

Deirdre picked up a copy of *Life* magazine and flipped through its pages.

"So this New York brokerage house has bought in the past week three-hundred-thousand shares?" her father went on. "What's the stock at now? Eight? Well, it's going up, that's good. And you have no idea who's buying the shares? Huh. Well, keep me informed."

He hung up.

"Who was that?"

Bennet looked worried.

"My stockbroker. Somebody's buying big chunks of our stock. We don't know who it is, or why he's buying."

"So anyway, Daddy, what should I do about Ross?"

"What do I know? Buy him a purse."

"Daddy, Ross wants to divorce me."

It was two weeks later. She was back in her father's office.

"Divorce? Why?"

She pulled a handkerchief from her purse and dabbed her eyes.

"It's over this dressing up as a woman thing," she sniffed. "I finally put my foot down and told him that if he didn't stop doing it, I'd leave him. I'm terribly afraid the children will see him. He got furious with me and said he had been faithful to me and there were no grounds for divorce. After a terrible scene, we finally worked out an amicable settlement, which is going to cost me a lot of money, I'm afraid. Ross wants a hundred thousand dollars, and I agreed to it."

"A hundred thousand?" exclaimed her father. "Why in the world did you agree to that much? It's a fortune!"

"I know, but it seemed the easiest way out. And the stock's gone so high, I thought it was a good time to sell . . ."

Her father tensed.

"You sold some of your stock?" he asked.

"Yes."

"How much?"

"Twelve thousand shares. They were offering ten dollars a share, so now I can pay off Ross and build that addition to the house I've been wanting."

"You fool!" Bennet screamed. "You damned fool! Oh my God . . . whom did you sell it to?"

"The buyer was a brokerage firm in New York. I forget their name. One of those long ones, Tutweiler, Whitlock . . . something like that."

"Damn, damn, damn!" He picked up his phone. "Get me Martin O'Brien, quick!"

"Daddy, what in the world are you so upset about?"

"Someone's trying to raid our stock! Thanks to you, whoever it is now has more stock than I do!"

The next morning, Gloria Wood came into Bennet's office, accompanied by her lawyer, Albert Whitlock. Gloria wore a smart black suit under her sable coat and a simple string of pearls. Her lawyer was a heavy-set man in a blue pinstripe suit who was carrying a leather briefcase.

"So it was you," Bennet said, sitting at his desk. "What do you want?"

"I want you out," Gloria said, taking a seat. "Albert, explain to him."

"According to the bylaws of your company," Albert said, sitting next to Gloria, "the majority stockholder has the power to name the publisher. My client, Mrs. Wood, now owns eight-hundred-and-forty-thousand shares, which makes her the majority shareholder of the Kinkaid Communications Corporation. Mrs. Wood wants you to resign as president of the corporation and as publisher of this newspaper. Effective immediately."

"Now Bennet," Gloria said, "in case you haven't guessed why I'm doing this, I'll tell you. I'm doing this because a) you are a Nazi bastard. And b) you terrified Richard Shelby, who is my protégé and with whom, by the way, I have never gone to bed. My love for Richard is not a sexual one, which your gutter mentality—as well as that stupid daughter of yours—could never appreciate. Fortunately, Richard is all right now, otherwise I would sue you to kingdom come. So. Are we all understood?"

Bennet stood up, his face a study in fury.

"You bitch," he said, softly.

"Hollywood floozie," she said with a smile. "Tramp. Whore. You're so unoriginal."

"I'll buy more stock!"

"You can't. There isn't any more to buy. Ask your broker, if you don't believe me. I bought up every share of Kinkaid stock. It cost me a damned fortune, but it was worth every penny just to throw you out on your ear. Now get out of here. I'll have your papers packed up and delivered to you."

Bennet slowly walked to the door.

"Oh, by the way," Gloria said, "you might like to know whom I'm hiring to replace you. It's your former son-in-law, Byron Slade, who's graduated from Columbia Journalism and is a whiz of a reporter on the *New York Times.* And . . ." She smiled. "He's a liberal."

Bennet Kinkaid howled with rage.

PART EIGHT

HEROES: 1942–1945

26

"DO YOU THINK HITLER will win the war?"

It was a cold, clear London night in October 1942, and the speaker was Lady Edwina Ashley, who Colonel Nick Savage thought was one of the most beautiful women he'd ever seen. Edwina was sitting next to him in the dining room of Chatfield House, the four-story townhouse on Eaton Square that Samantha had inherited from her former employer, Lady Chatfield. The occasion was a dinner party Nick and Samantha were giving for several of their London friends, including Sir Andrew Ashley, the current head of Chatfield Department Stores, Ltd., and his wife, Edwina.

"Definitely not," Nick said.

"But it seems that everything's going his way," Edwina said. She was twenty-eight with blond hair Nick was sure was dyed. She had a peaches-and-cream complexion, luscious blue eyes, and her shimmering white satin evening dress revealed a good deal of her voluptuous breasts. "I mean, there's not much left of Europe that's not in his pocket, is there? And now that he's attacked Russia, I suppose he'll conquer that, too. It's all rather depressing."

"But there's a bright side. In my opinion, he's bitten off more than he can chew."

"Well, I certainly hope you're right." She had a rather smoky voice with an upper-class English accent, and her lips, like her nails, were painted a very intense red. She had a thick diamond and sapphire bracelet on her right wrist, and a diamond brooch on her dress just where her cleavage dived into the satin. She smelled faintly of an alluring perfume. She had a seductive way of making a man feel he was the most important person in the room; Nick thought that if it were an act, it was a very attractive and flattering one. "My husband tells me," she went on, "that you're stationed here in London to do some intelligence work. Are you a spy?"

Nick smiled.

"I'm afraid it's nothing that glamorous," he said. "But it's glamorous enough that I can't talk about it."

"Hush hush? How very intriguing. Now I'm really curious. I understand your daughter is in the country?"

"Yes, Amanda. And our four-year-old son, Justin. We keep them and the nanny at Hadley Hall in Devonshire because of the air raids. We see them on weekends."

An aged waiter poured some wine. Though London had been heavily bombed for months and vast sections of the East End had been reduced to rubble, and though there was serious rationing, still life went on, money was being spent as if it were the end of the world—which many people thought it was—and Londoners figuratively thumbed their noses at the Germans by refusing to give in or give up. Along with the house, Samantha had inherited Lady Chatfield's extensive wine cellar, so she had been able to continue her entertaining that was so important to the Chatfield Fund, although her staff had been reduced to her cook-housecleaner and Algernon, her seventy-four-year-old butler-waiter, everyone else having been drafted. The dining room, which Lady Chatfield had had redecorated in the twenties by Monsieur Boudin, at the time the most celebrated decorator in the world, was a gorgeous, shimmering masterpiece of blue and silver, elaborately faux-Baroque in style with huge mirrors soaring to the ceiling. With Samantha's fine food and wine, it was possible to forget here, at least for a few hours, the terrible devastation that was occurring in the world. However, Algernon, the aged butler-sommelier, had the presence of mind to announce to the guests: "Owing to the recent bombardments, we felt it prudent to decant the entire cave."

Among the guests were the glamorous Anglo-Chinese couple, Lance and Nora Wang, who had fled Hong Kong when the Japanese invaded the British colony in 1942. Lance was seated on the other side of Lady Ashley. She turned to the black-tied Chinese department store executive who was Nick's cousin.

"And you, Lance," she said. "Now that you've left Hong Kong, are you still playing polo?"

"I'm afraid not, Lady Ashley. I've joined the RAF."

"How amusing. A Chinese flying for the English?"

"But you're equally amusing, Lady Ashley. A German having dinner in London during the Blitz?"

Lady Ashley gave him a daggered look.

Also among the guests was Nick's other sister, Beatrice Vespa, who had married an Italian doctor who had been tortured by the Fascists. Beatrice and her husband, Bruno, had left Italy before the war and settled in London, where they were raising their daughter, sixteen-year-old Gabriella. Gabriella, a smoldering, dark-haired beauty who was attending a boarding school for girls in Sussex, was sitting next to her mother, eying with interest her far-flung family relatives. Her father, Bruno, was working with M.I.6, the British Intelligence, using his inside information about the Fascist regime in Italy to help bring down his hated opponent, Mussolini. Beatrice was doing volunteer work for the Red Cross.

This elegant paradise on Eaton Square was suddenly shattered. As Algernon was passing the Krug '20 champagne, the distant air-raid sirens started wailing and the entire company, including Algernon and the cook, put on their coats and hurried out into the cold night to repair to the nearest air-raid shelter, as above them searchlights pierced the black sky and antiaircraft guns fired at Hermann Goering's not-as-successful-as-expected Luftwaffe.

"What were you and Edwina talking about?" Samantha asked three hours later as she and Nick were undressing in their bedroom. The air raid had lasted only twenty-five minutes—a bomb had gone off in nearby Belgrave Square—and then everyone had returned to Chatfield House for dessert, coffee, and brandy. Londoners had grown used to dinner parties interrupted by bombs: some even called it "air-raid chic," though there wasn't much chic about being blown up.

"Oh, she was rambling on about the war," Nick said, undoing his black bow tie. "She seems to think Hitler's winning."

"That's because her father's German," Samantha said, putting away her pearl necklace. "When von Ribbentrop was ambassador here, her father was high up in the embassy, so even though her mother's English and she's spent most of her life here, she's pretty pro-German. I don't trust her. I hope you didn't tell her anything about your job?"

"Of course not."

"I like Andrew, but he's an old fool when it comes to women. He's sixty-eight, old enough to be her grandfather. She's his third wife, you know."

"I didn't know, but I guessed she wasn't his first." He removed his cufflinks, then said, casually, "I'll be going to France tomorrow."

Samantha had put on a white negligé. Now she looked at her husband. "France?" she said, incredulously. "What do you mean?"

"Well, I guess it's time I tell you what's been going on. Up till now, I've been under orders not to tell anyone, including you. But now that the operation is getting under way, General Dumont has told me I can bring you in on everything. You know there's a resistance movement in France that's working against the Germans. My brother-in-law, Bernard de Belle-ville, is one of the leaders of the movement—though so far, the Germans haven't figured that out. Bernard and Brook are still in Paris, which I think is terribly risky, but Brook told me she refuses to leave her husband." He shrugged. "That's sort of admirable, I guess, but dangerous. They could have gotten out when the Nazis occupied Paris, but they didn't."

"But Nick, what does all this have to do with you? I thought you were intelligence liaison with the Pentagon?"

"Yes, I am. But I volunteered to make contact with Bernard. You see, the Resistance needs money to buy equipment—guns, dynamite to blow up bridges and train tunnels . . . they're starting a massive sabotage cam-paign against the Germans which we all hope will cripple them badly. Of course, Brook and Bernard have money in the bank, but if they started taking out the kind of money they need, the Nazis would start asking questions. So I'm going to take them the money. A million dollars in bearer bonds, which can be converted to cash in banks in unoccupied France. The reason I got the job is that I know my brother-in-law, obvi-ously. A courier could be fooled by someone acting as Bernard and they can't afford that risk."

He had put on his pajamas. Now he climbed into their double bed as she continued to stare at him.

"But darling," she finally said, "that's incredibly dangerous!"

"Yes, I know."

"I mean, my God, if you're caught, they'll kill you!"

"That's probably right. Hitler has put out something called *Nacht und Nebel* or Night and Fog, which in effect says to hell with the Geneva convention, if anyone is caught they go into the night and fog—in other words, they're dead. The Nazis have such a poetic gift for words."

"But how will you get into France?"

"I'm going to parachute tomorrow night. They'll drop me near Paris, then I'll walk to Bernard's château near Versailles."

"You've never parachuted!"

"I've been training for the past month. You'd be surprised how an old guy like me can learn to roll on the ground. I've also been taking an immersion course in French, so I'll be able to get by. If everything works right, I'm to be picked up by a submarine off the north coast of Brittany in three nights."

"But if everything doesn't work right . . . ? Oh Nick, you can't do this! There're the children to consider . . ."

"Millions of people in this war have children to consider."

"I don't care about millions of people, I care about you! Surely there's someone else who can do this!"

"But I'm the only one who knows Bernard and how to get to him. Please, Samantha, don't make this any more difficult for me than it is already. I've volunteered and everything is planned and ready. Now come be with me."

He pointed to the bed. Samantha came over and got in bed beside him. He took her in his arms and kissed her.

"You know," he said, "my grandfather, Justin, was a sort of hero. My father lost a leg in the Spanish-American War, and he was a hero to me. This is my chance to do something a little heroic. I hate the Nazis so much, this is my chance to pay them back, big. I hope to come out of this a live hero. But if I end up a dead one, it will be worth it if I can help in some way. A lot of people are giving their lives to rid the world of these gangsters . . . So, we'll see. I've made sure everything is right for you and the children if I don't come back. And I want you to know that I've been very, very happy being married to you. I was a lucky man to meet you, my darling Samantha. And I love you very much."

He kissed her.

"Oh Nick," she said, hugging him. "Every minute with you—even our fights—has been wonderful. And I adore you. But please, please come back."

He smiled and kissed her again.

"I'll do my damndest. Now, since this is our last night together for a while, I suggest we make good use of it."

27   THE NEXT NIGHT, SHORTLY before midnight, Nick was tapped on the shoulder, then he jumped out of the B-17 bomber and hurtled down through the dark night sky toward the French countryside below. After counting to ten slowly, he pulled the rip cord and saw his chute billow open above him. He was dressed in a cheap tweed suit with a black overcoat to protect him against the chilly night; around his waist was a money belt containing ten hundred-thousand-dollar bearer bonds, it having been decided that American currency would be the most welcome on the black market where the weapons and explosives would be bought by the resistance fighters.

France was dark, not only because of regulations forbidding lighted windows to aid the Allied bombers but because electricity was in increasingly short supply. But Nick's eyes quickly acquired their night vision, and he was able to guide his chute to drop him into an open field. Quickly, he folded the chute, then carried it into a nearby wood and buried it under some dead leaves and underbrush.

Then he started walking, hoping to find a road with signs that would guide him to Versailles, which, according to the plane's navigator, should be less than five kilometers away.

It was eerily quiet, except for a distant barking dog. After five minutes or so, he came onto a country road, which he started walking down. In a while, he saw headlights approaching him, and he hurried into a roadside ditch, ducking down so as not to be seen. The headlights were wartime narrow horizontal slits, so as to minimize the light exposure to aircraft. As the vehicle passed him, Nick saw that it was a German military truck, with German troops sitting in the back.

When the truck had gone, he went back on the road and, after a while, saw a sign ahead which, when he came up to it and squinted in the dark, he saw read VERSAILLES, 2 K. Delighted with this, he hurried on and within twenty minutes he was on the outskirts of the town, which was dark and empty. Nick knew there was a midnight curfew, so he kept in the shadows as much as possible and took side streets until he reached the gates of his sister and brother-in-law's château. Opening the wrought iron gate, he slipped inside then hurried down the gravel drive until he reached the small but charming building, which was entirely dark.

Going to the front door, he knocked.

Silence.

He knocked again.

Nothing.

Confused, he tried the door, which was unlocked. He pushed it open and went inside the entrance hall. Darkness.

"Hello?" he called out.

Nothing.

He closed the front door and turned on a lamp on a small table, having seen that all the windows of the building were closed over by shutters. He walked into the adjacent salon, then returned to the entrance hall and went into the dining room and through that to the kitchen, turning on another light. He started to turn off the light when a phone rang.

Startled, he went to the phone and picked it up, saying nothing.

"Nick?" It was his sister, Brook.

"Yes. What's happened? Where are you?"

"Bernard's been arrested by the Gestapo. I don't know what it's all about yet, but the moment I do I'll call you. Stay there. There's food in the kitchen, and you can sleep in one of the rooms upstairs. Don't try to call me. You're all right?"

"Yes, so far."

"Good. I'll call you in the morning. And welcome to France."

She hung up, as did Nick. He thought a moment, then went to the refrigerator and looked inside. There was a cold chicken, some eggs and salad, and several bottles of wine.

He took out the chicken, sat down at the kitchen table, and tore off a thigh, which he devoured hungrily.

Welcome to France, he thought. *Wonderful. Everything's screwed up already.*

I wonder if I'll ever get out of here alive?

A gentle, melancholy rain was falling on occupied Paris the next morning when, at ten o'clock, an official Mercedes-Benz staff car pulled up in front of Brook's Belle Epoque limestone mansion on the Avenue Foch and a German captain climbed out of the backseat. Looking at the house a moment, he went to the front door and rang the bell. After a moment, a white-jacketed butler answered the door. Seeing the Nazi uniform, the old man looked rather nervous.

"Captain Otto Preizing to see Countess de Belleville," the Nazi snapped.

"Madame is still in bed," the old butler said, trembling slightly at the captain's harsh tone.

"At ten in the morning? No wonder France lost the war. Tell her to get dressed immediately. Reich Marshal Goering wants to see her at the Ritz Hotel. I'll wait for her downstairs. Show me where to go."

"Yes, of course. This way, please."

The butler led him through the entrance hall to the salon overlooking Avenue Foch.

"I'll tell Madame immediately," the butler said, almost scurrying out of the room. Captain Preizing pulled a gold cigarette case from the pocket of his jacket, extracted a cigarette, and lit it with a malachite lighter from a table. As he exhaled, he looked around the richly decorated room. The captain, one of Goering's many aides, was the son of a Berlin doctor— Goering, who was something of a snob, preferred his close associates to come from what he considered "cultivated" backgrounds—and he recognized the value of the furnishings in the room. He was about to put the malachite lighter back on the table when he changed his mind and slipped it in his overcoat pocket instead.

Fifteen minutes later, Brook came into the room wearing a mink coat and a smart black hat that tilted slightly over her forehead.

"Why does Herr Goering want to see me?" she asked.

The captain, who had been sitting in a chair leafing through a French fashion magazine, got to his feet and clicked his heels.

"The Reich Marshal will tell you himself," he said. "We will go now. My car is in front."

"Do you know where my husband is?"

"The Reich Marshal will tell you, if he so desires."

"Am I under arrest?"

"Not yet. And no more questions!"

As they drove through the streets of Paris—which were mostly empty because of strict gas rationing and the fact that there were only seven thousand cars with driving permits in the city, Parisians doing their shopping and other chores on bicycles or vélo-taxis, which were essentially bicycle rickshaws carrying two passengers in little carts connected to the rear of the bicycle— Brook sat in the backseat next to the captain, trying to remain calm. But in fact, she was scared almost out of her wits. When the Gestapo had arrested Bernard the previous day, they had said nothing about the reason of his arrest: They had just appeared at the doorstep and taken him. Brook was certain that the arrest had something to do with Bernard's clandestine activities with the Resistance, in which case it meant almost certain death. And, to make her agony even worse, if they knew about Nick, it meant almost certain death for him, too. To lose her husband would be a tragedy, but to lose her husband and her brother would be almost more than she could bear. Her only consolation was that she had gotten her twenty-two-year-old son, Graydon, back to the States before the Nazis took Paris; Graydon was now an Ensign in the American Navy.

When they arrived at the Place Vendôme, the driver, a corporal, drove around the column of Napoleon and parked in front of the Ritz, above which was flying the Nazi flag, with a big swastika. Brook knew that the elegant hotel had been commandeered by the Germans, with the exception of Coco Chanel's suite: the couturier had been protected by her high-ranking German lover, Hans Gunther von Dincklage, which did not endear the famed designer to the Parisians. Brook got out of the staff car and followed Captain Preizing into the lobby of the hotel, where several armed guards snapped to attention as he gave a halfhearted Hitler salute. Getting in the elevator, they were taken to the third floor where they walked to a door guarded by yet another armed guard, this one in a Gestapo uniform. Preizing knocked on the door, then opened it, gesturing to Brook to enter, which she did.

The suite, one of the grandest in the hotel, overlooked the Place Vendôme and was richly decorated. Seated at a round table spooning a chocolate soufflé was an enormously fat man in a richly embroidered silk bathrobe. He looked at Brook, then, without stopping eating or getting up, he gestured to a chair on the other side of the table.

"Good morning, Madame," he said, speaking through a young female translator who was sitting on a chair slightly behind him. "Would you like something to eat or drink?"

"No thank you," Brook said, taking the proffered chair. "It's a little early for lunch."

"This isn't lunch," Goering said. "I always have a snack at eleven in the morning. That way, I don't overeat at lunch. I may be winning the war but, alas, I'm losing the battle of my waistline. That's a very handsome mink coat. Why don't you take it off? You'll be too warm in here. The Ritz tends to be overheated."

"I'll leave it on, thank you."

Brook, like everyone else in Paris, was well aware that Goering was enriching himself as fast as his greedy hands could clutch, including making a fortune off the French and Italian black market. Goering looked at her rather darkly.

"Where is my husband?" she asked.

Goering went back to his soufflé.

"He's at Drancy," he said. "In a nice, warm cell."

Drancy, a suburb of Paris near Le Bourget Airport (where Lindbergh had landed fifteen years before, ending his famous flight), was the site of a German-French concentration camp.

"Herr Reich Marshal, could you tell me why he's been arrested? You know we've always supported the occupation. You know that practically all of our friends support it also." Which was only partially a lie. Brook and Bernard maintained a collaborationist front to disguise their activities with the Resistance.

Goering wiped his mouth, then pulled a bottle of Puligny-Montrachet from an ice bucket and refilled his wine glass.

"Well, as to that," he said, "there are a number of things. But for the moment, we are investigating his tax returns."

"Is there some problem with them?"

"Perhaps. The accountants will tell me. Meanwhile, we'll keep him with us, just to be sure he does nothing foolish. How is your brother, the former ambassador? Mr. Nick Savage."

Keep cool, she thought. *Keep cool.*

"He's fine, as far as I know," she said. "It's rather difficult to communicate."

"I understand President Roosevelt gave him a commission in the American army."

"I believe that's correct."

Goering sipped the wine.

"When your brother was in Berlin, I met him on a number of occasions. I even tried to interest him in organizing an American loan for Germany. Unfortunately, that little deal fell through. And then, of course, your naughty brother got caught with that prostitute. Very embarrassing for him. He has such an attractive wife, you'd think he'd be faithful to her, as I am faithful to my adored Emmy. But, then, some men can't keep their pants on. By the way, your brother is in England, doing intelligence work."

"I'm surprised that someone with your vast responsibilities would know that, Herr Reich Marshal."

"The secret to success, dear lady, is knowing the details. I have many sources of information in London."

At least he doesn't think Nick's in France, she thought, *which is a blessing. Unless he's toying with me. Oh God, I wish he'd get to the point!*

"I came to dislike your brother," Goering went on. "I felt he was against our regime, against what we're trying to do in Europe. The old Europe of many countries fighting each other is out of date, you know. Europe must be united, one mighty power that will control the world, which is what we're doing. But your brother was against us. One feels these things. Is your husband against us?"

"If he were, wouldn't he have left Paris before you took over?"

"Mmm. Perhaps."

"My husband has never been interested in politics. In fact, he was glad when the Third Republic collapsed."

"Really? That's interesting. Most encouraging. Then perhaps I've misjudged your husband, Madame. Perhaps we can work something out—an arrangement, if you see what I mean. Since your brother cost me so much money back in Berlin, perhaps you can make that up to me."

He finished his soufflé, wiped his mouth, and smiled at her. Brook looked at him, confused. It was like looking at a cobra.

"I'm not quite following you, Herr Reich Marshal," she finally said.

"Money," he said. "Your brother paid me fifty thousand American dollars to obtain the release of one of your Jewish cousins. How much more money would you pay me for the release of your husband? Who, after all, I assume means more to you than your cousin did."

So that's it! she thought. *He doesn't know about the Resistance plot or Nick, he's simply blackmailing me! The fat, rotten, murdering bastard!*

"How much, Herr Reich Marshal?" she said, quietly.

"You have a beautiful mansion on the Avenue Foch. Of course, real estate prices are depressed at the moment, but after the war I'm sure they'll go up again. And, as fond of the Ritz as I am, it would be nice for my wife to have a Paris residence. And it would be a wonderful thing on your part—a show of solidarity with the German occupiers of your beautiful city—if you donated your house to me." She stared at him. He smiled. "Come now, Countess, you're a rich woman. You've got a château at Versailles, your husband's one of the leading landlords of Paris." He spread his hands. "It's time you shared some of your wealth."

"You mean, if I give you my house, you'll free my husband?"

"Of course. It's so simple. You think about it and give me a call when you're ready. My lawyers can process the transaction quickly. You're sure you wouldn't like to stay for lunch? The food here is so wonderful. As decadent as the French are, their food and wine are unbeatable. When the war is over, I intend to spend a lot of time in Paris. Perhaps even . . ." Again, he smiled. ". . . New York."

Brook stood up.

"No thanks. I mean, about lunch. About your suggestion, I can give you an answer right now. I'll bring you the deed in the morning. I trust you'll give me a few days to move out?"

"Of course. Take all the time you want. Take a month. I'm in no hurry."

"And you'll free my husband tomorrow?"

"Exactly. Perhaps the three of us can have lunch together soon. Now, if you'll excuse me, my barber is waiting to shave me."

He lumbered out of his chair. Brook went to the door of the suite, thinking, *you may have my house, but you don't have my husband or my brother.*

The next afternoon, Nick was starting to take a nap in his second-floor bedroom in the Versailles château when he heard a car come up the gravel drive. Getting off his bed, he went to one of the shuttered windows and looked down through the slats to see a black Citroën park before the front door and Brook and Bernard get out. Relieved, he hurried downstairs just as they came inside.

"How did you get away from the Gestapo?" he asked Bernard as he hugged and kissed his sister.

"We'll tell you during lunch," Brook said, turning to her husband who still had the youthful good looks that had thrilled her so many years before when they had fallen in love in the very same château. "We've brought some food. Let's go to the kitchen. I'm starving."

"So Goering blackmailed you, just as he blackmailed me in Berlin to free Claus Lieber," Nick said ten minutes later as they devoured an omelet.

"I'm sure it gave him the idea," Brook said, drinking some white wine. "But who cares? The important thing is, he doesn't suspect that we're financing the Resistance. By the way, a minor detail, but do you have the bearer bonds?"

"They're here." He pulled up his shirt and handed the money belt to Bernard. "It's a relief to get rid of it."

Bernard put the belt around his waist and said: "I have a courier waiting for this in Paris."

"Where will it go?"

"What you don't know you can't tell. I have forged papers for you," Bernard went on, "and a ticket for a train tomorrow for St. Brieuc."

"Where's that?"

"It's a small town on the north coast of Brittany. You'll be met at the train station by a man who'll call himself Jules—he'll be driving a two-

door black Fiat. He'll take you to Perros Guirec, which is a town farther
west on the Brittany coast. He has a house right on the sea, and tomorrow
night he'll take you out in a rowboat to a buoy where the submarine will
surface and take you back to England."

"It sounds like everything's working out," Nick said. "I'm impressed,
not to mention relieved. I've been nervous as a cat here alone."

"I don't blame you, Nicky, but you'll be home soon," Brook said.
"And give our love to Samantha and the kids. Now let's finish lunch and
wash up. We have to get back to Paris. We're giving a cocktail party
tonight . . ."

"It's part of the charade," Bernard said. "We've asked all our collab-
orator friends—and believe me, we have plenty—as a front so no one
will suspect that we're up to something. We'll hide you upstairs in one
of the servant rooms."

"We even have some Nazis coming," Brook said. "Oh, it's going to
be a jolly evening."

"And we have black market caviar," Bernard said. "We'll sneak you
some upstairs."

"I never thought," Nick said, wryly, "being a spy could get you
caviar."

The several dozen cocktail guests in the smoke-filled salon of the house
on the Avenue Foch were chattering and drinking, discussing the latest
rumors that filled the occupied city, flirting and feeling lucky that they
could, at least for a few hours until the curfew began, enjoy some sem-
blance of normality in a world at war. Several well-dressed French women
in the room were accompanied by men in Nazi uniforms. One beautiful
young English woman was talking in flawless German to an older man
also in a German uniform. Although strict clothes rationing had been
imposed, for some peculiar reason there was no rationing on hats, so the
women, except for the hostess, were all wearing flamboyant millenary
concoctions. As a Moroccan servant in a white djellabah passed hors
d'oeuvres on a silver tray, Brook, looking smashing in a prewar black
cocktail dress, mingled with her guests. Bernard excused himself from
one of the women he had been talking to, and surreptitiously took several

caviar-heaped crackers from the Moroccan. He went into the entrance hall where he climbed the stairs to the second floor. Going down the hall, he knocked on a bedroom door, then opened it. Inside, Nick was sitting in a chair reading.

"I brought you some caviar," Bernard said after he closed the door. "Sorry you're missing all the fun."

He brought the crackers to Nick, who put down his book and took them.

"Thanks," he said. "So everyone's having a good time?"

"You'd never know there's a war on. Even the Germans are relaxing. In fact, two of them are getting quite high on the booze."

"I'd love to see that." He popped a cracker into his mouth. "The caviar's delicious. Thanks."

"When everyone's gone, we can eat dinner," Bernard said, going to the door to let himself out. "I'd better get downstairs." Nick swallowed the second caviar cracker, then returned to his reading.

Twenty minutes later, he let himself out of his room and walked down the hall to the nearest bathroom to take a pee. He opened the door to see a beautiful young blond, who was cleaning a spot off her dress with some cleaning fluid. She looked at Nick with surprise.

"What in the world are you doing here?" she asked in English as Nick stared at her.

It was Lady Edwina Ashley.

28 RICHARD SHELBY SAT AT a window in the coach section of
a Pennsylvania Railroad train taking him from New York to Indianapolis,
watched the flat Ohio countryside speed by and thought about death. First,
his father's death; Richard was returning home from Fort Dix to attend his
father's funeral, William having died of cancer a few days earlier. Second,
his own death. Indianapolis was seared in his mind as a city of death, his
horrifying near-death at the hands of the Klan when they staged his fake
lynching at the farm near Muncie. Richard had finally recovered from the
trauma that had kept him silent for so long, but he would never forget the
horror of that night, a horror that still, four years later, haunted his dreams.

But now, a new danger was casting the shadow of death over his
young life. After graduating from college, Richard had volunteered to go
to Officers Training School at Fort Sill in Oklahoma where he became a
second lieutenant. America's fortunes in the global conflict were at low
ebb in 1942; Richard's all-black regiment was slated to be shipping out
sometime soon to an unknown destination, but the possibility of seeing
combat was high, and combat, in this bloodiest of all wars, meant possible
death. Richard was sharing the fate of thousands of his generation: he
hoped to save the world, but he might lose his life doing it.

He had often asked himself why he should fight for a country that
had treated him so miserably, that was still segregated officially in the
south and unofficially in so many ways in the north, not to mention the
armed forces. He had even thought of becoming a conscientious objector.
But then, he told himself that whatever his destiny was, this war was
somehow part of it; and to avoid the fight would somehow diminish him.

Four hours later, when his train pulled into Indianapolis's Union Station, Richard got off, carrying his suitcase, and was met by Gloria Wood,
who had kept him apprised of his father's condition by phone and had
invited him to stay at Whitehall until after the funeral, and sixteen-year-
old Sebastian. After they greeted each other, they drove to the funeral

home to view his father's remains, then went to Whitehall where Gloria cooked the three of them lunch, generously using many of her meat rationing coupons to make hamburgers for the hungry lieutenant. Sebastian sat in silence through the meal as Gloria brought Richard up to date, including the welcome news that Bennet Kinkaid had died of a heart attack. At the end of lunch, Sebastian excused himself and went upstairs.

"What's wrong with Sebastian?" Richard asked in a soft voice. "He didn't say a word."

"He's moody. It started with Mark's death," Gloria said. "In fact, he's gotten terribly moody since I became engaged. He doesn't want me to get married and I'm awfully worried about him. He goes to a psychiatrist once a week, but. . . ." She shrugged. "He tells me he can't tell whether Sebastian is lying to him or not. Sebastian went to a famous child psychiatrist in London, and he's so bright he may have picked up the tricks of the trade. So I don't know."

"Tell me about your fiancé," Richard said. "You told me on the phone he's English?"

Gloria's face lit up.

"Yes, and a pilot for the RAF who shot down fifty-seven German planes and is a real hero! Mr. Churchill sent him to America to go on tour to raise money for England. I'm connected to one of the charities running his tour, and we met several months ago in Chicago. He's very dashing and charming, and we've both fallen quite madly in love, even though I'm, well, a bit older. His name's Lord Dudley Belgrave."

"A lord?" Richard said, impressed. "Does that mean you'll be a lady?"

"Yes, finally," Gloria laughed. "His father's an earl and his family dates back to Henry the something-or-other, the Eighth, I think. I'm so lousy on English history. Dudley's out in San Francisco now finishing up his tour, but he's coming back to Indianapolis next week and we're going to get married here, in Whitehall." She frowned. "The only trouble is Sebastian. He hates him. He tells me he's certain Dudley is marrying me for my money—what's left of it after these wartime taxes. And it's true that Dudley's family is practically broke. But I'm sure Sebastian's wrong! And Dudley would be a wonderful father for him. I've been looking for so long for someone to marry and I know Dudley is right for both of us, but there you have it: Sebastian hates him. I don't know. It's very discouraging. Well," she forced a smile, "I didn't mean to burden you with my little domestic problems. I'm sure you have much more important things on your mind." She stood up. "I'll clean up . . ."

"No, let me do it."

"Please: You must be tired after your trip."

"Well, I didn't get much sleep on the train, thinking about Poppa and all the things that happened to me in this town. If you're sure I can't help, I think I'll go up and take a little nap."

"Please do. And Richard: I'm so sorry about your father. He was a truly wonderful man."

"Yes, he was. And thanks, Mrs. Wood."

As Gloria stacked the dirty dishes, Richard climbed the stairs to his bedroom.

29   IN THE BATHROOM OF the house on Avenue Foch in Paris, Nick stared at Lady Edwina Ashley and wondered what the hell to say or do. Obviously, he couldn't tell her the truth: that he had parachuted into France to deliver a million dollars' worth of bearer bonds to his brother-in-law for the French Resistance. He quickly decided the best defense was to go on the offense.

"Lady Edwina," he said, with a pleasant smile, "might I ask what in the world *you're* doing here?"

She put down the rag she had been using to rub cleaning fluid on the spot on her smart gray dress, opened her bag and removed a cigarette, which she lit, watching him like a cat watching a canary.

"That Moroccan sent me up here to get a spot off my dress."

"I meant, how did you get to Paris?"

"I came over to spend a few weeks with my father," she said, exhaling, "who's stationed here in Paris on the staff of General von Stuelpnagel, the military governor of France. Father's downstairs, drinking some excellent champagne. I flew from London to Sweden, then came over to Germany and took the train to Paris. How did you get here?"

He was mesmerized by the large diamond on one of her fingers and by the fierce red polish on her nails. She was one cool, sexy blond.

"Well, to tell the truth," he lied, "I came over the same way to see my sister, Countess de Belleville, and to have a little vacation from my wife."

She smiled slightly, her lipstick the same fierce red as her nail polish.

"Why Mr. Savage, you naughty man," she said. "I'm shocked that you'd cheat on dear Samantha, who, as far as I know, has never so much as looked at another man. You should be ashamed."

"Well, I am. That's why I'm rather keeping out of sight tonight. I wouldn't want to run into anyone I know."

"But you have: me. Do you have a little *môme* here in Paris that you keep on the side?"

"Yes. She's a model for Chanel."

"Really? How interesting. But she must be rather hard up right now, because Chanel has been closed since the Occupation."

Nick mentally kicked himself. He forced a smile.

"I should have said an ex-model. And you're right, she's terribly hard up. I brought her some money to tide her over until she can find work."

She put out her cigarette in an ashtray.

"Are you staying here with your sister?" she asked. "Or with your girlfriend?"

"I'm here. Because of the curfew, I can't see Garance at night. We have fun in the afternoon."

"How romantic. Well, perhaps we could arrange to have some fun in the evening. I've always thought you're such an attractive man."

She blew him a little kiss and left the bathroom.

Nick heaved a sigh of relief and congratulated himself for quick thinking: Nothing like a little whiff of romantic scandal to take people's minds off the ugly realities of life. He closed the bathroom door, took his pee, then went back to his room to continue reading his book.

After only a few minutes, the door burst open and Bernard hurried in, closing the door.

"What did you say to Edwina Ashley?" he whispered.

"I told her I was in Paris to see my girlfriend."

"She didn't believe a word of it. She's talking to her father, and I understand enough German to catch what she was saying—that there's something odd going on here with an American intelligence officer in the house—you. Her father's on the phone now, calling the Gestapo. You'd better get out now. And Nick, give me your word of honor you'll take Brook with you."

"Brook? Why?"

"When the Gestapo gets here, they're going to arrest both of us. I'll stay and deal with them: there's a chance the Resistance can help me. But it's too dangerous for Brook . . . give me your word of honor."

Nick was on his feet, galvanized by the news.

"The caterer has a vélo-taxi outside the back door. Put Brook in the back and take her to two-twenty-one *bis* rue de l'Université—do you know where it is?"

"On the Left Bank?"

"Exactly. Take the Pont de l'Alma. Ask for Marie Antoinette—that's her code name. Stay there tonight, then take the train to Brittany tomorrow. Now get out: hurry! Go through the kitchen! I'll get Brook."

"But what will happen to you?"

"Don't worry about me. Go! Hurry! The Gestapo will be here any minute!"

Nick threw his arms around his brother-in-law and gave him a quick hug. Then he hurried out of the room and went down the back stairs to the kitchen where the Moroccan was opening more champagne. The ominous screeching honking-geese siren of the Gestapo began to be heard coming from the direction of the Place de l'Etoile.

Bernard hurried in from the butler's pantry with Brook.

"I'm not going to leave you!" she was saying in English.

"Don't argue with me," Bernard whispered as the Moroccan looked on, totally confused.

"No, Bernard, I won't go!"

"You know what will happen!"

"I don't care! I love you . . ."

"And I love you," Bernard said, punching her on the chin so hard that she fell backward into his arms. "Open the back door!" he said to Nick, holding his unconscious wife in his arms. "We'll put her in the vélo."

Nick, stunned by Bernard's action, obeyed, opening the kitchen door. Outside, in an alley, was the vélo-taxi. As Nick climbed on the bicycle seat, Bernard put Brook in the rear buggy, where she slumped almost drunkenly to the side. Bernard gave her a quick kiss, then said to Nick: "Go! Hurry! Two-twenty-one *bis* rue de l'Université. Marie Antoinette. Good luck. And Nick: Take care of Brook and our son."

He hurried back inside the house as the Gestapo siren grew louder. Nick began peddling down the alley.

It was a dank, chilly night, and he knew he had only a few hours before the midnight curfew began—*le dernier métro* left at eleven P.M. Peddling as fast as he could, he took the first side street in the direction of the Avenue Marceau, which would take him to the Pont de l'Alma. The streets of the city were as usual almost deserted, so he made good time.

Reaching the Pont de l'Alma, he crossed the Seine on the bridge and reached the Left Bank of the ancient city where, after passing the Quai d'Orsay, he turned left on the rue de l'Université. A Gestapo squad car passed him, but its occupants seemed uninterested in the lone bicyclist with his drunken passenger in the back.

Although it was difficult to make out address numbers in the dimly lit city, Nick finally spotted two-twenty-one *bis*. Dismounting, he went to the front door and rang the bell of the ancient, four-story building, noticing that the ground floor contained a photographer's shop.

After a moment, the door was opened by a rather fat, middle-aged lady in slippers, her badly dyed hair in curlers.

"Je cherche Marie Antoinette," Nick said in his by now quite good French. *"Je viens de Monsieur de Belleville."*

The fat lady looked at Brook, still slumped in the back of the vélo.

"You have the Countess?"

"Yes."

"Merde. That makes it more difficult. Get her—fast!"

Nick hurried to the bike and picked his sister up in his arms, carrying her back to the door.

"Entrez," Marie Antoinette said. *"Vite."*

Nick hurried inside as Marie Antoinette quickly closed the door and locked it.

"Montons," she said, starting up a narrow staircase that was tilted by the centuries. Nick, puffing as he carried Brook, started up behind her.

The statuesque topless redhead was dancing to the 1938 hit American song "Bei Mir Bist du Schön" at the Schéhérazade night club as a room full of Luftwaffe officers watched with beery smiles. The dancer, whose body was gorgeous, wore spangly gloves, a silk chiffon skirt that opened in front, gold high-heeled shoes with ankle straps, and nothing else, her firm, naked breasts jiggling slightly as she twirled to the sensuous strains of the song—oddly, the Germans, supposedly dedicated to their Fuehrer's desire to rid the world of Jews, didn't seem to be bothered at all by the Yiddish lyrics of the song. Schéhérazade, the favorite night club of the Germans in Paris, had been taken over by Goering for the night to throw a birthday party for one of his top aides, and the fat Reich Marshal,

wearing the gaudy white, jewel-studded uniform he had designed for himself, was sitting at a front table with three of his comrades beaming booz-
ily at the dancer, tapping his pudgy fingers on the tabletop in time with
the music. At the cloakroom in the front of the club a bored hat-check
girl smoked as, above her, racks groaned with Nazi uniform hats. The
French waiters busily passed food and drink, aware that Goering was
known to tip lavishly when he was in the mood—and, to the Germans'
credit, they paid regularly at all the top Paris hotels they had requisitioned,
including the Ritz, the Meurice, the Continental, the Majestic, the Lutétia,
the Scribe, and the Raphaël.

Though strict rationing of food and wine left most Parisians perpet-
ually hungry (a whole generation of the French grew up generally shorter
in height and with bad teeth because of a lack of calcium in their diet
during the Occupation), if you had the money and connections you could
live better than anyone in Europe. One could gorge at the Berkeley, Chez
Laurent, at the Pavillon de l'Elysée, the Pré Catalan, at Claridge's, Ciros',
Chez Carrère, the Café de Paris, Drouant . . . Picasso, who remained in
Paris throughout the entire Occupation, ate juicy steaks at the Catalan in
the rue des Grands-Augustins, often hosting Braque, Sartre, Simone de
Beauvoir, and Albert Camus. Maxim's had been taken over by the Berlin
restaurateur Otto Horcher (who also ran a top restaurant in Madrid), but
the staff remained the same and every night the old headwaiter Albert
showed prominent Germans, including, frequently, Goering, to their tables
with a courtesy that almost cost him his life after the war. Fouquet's,
Lapérouse, the Tour d'Argent, and Le Grand Véfour all remained open
for business, and business boomed. One could still buy caviar at Petros-
sian's, and the luxury shops of the Faubourg Saint-Honoré continued to
sell items like leather goods and jewelry unmatched for quality anywhere
in Europe. Ironically for Hitler, Paris had become the favorite posting of
the Germans, who much preferred its attractions to their own, severely
rationed country.

The topless dancer was still gyrating to "Bei Mir Bist du Schön" when
the headwaiter came to Goering's table carrying a phone and whispered
in his ear, placing the phone in front of him. Annoyed at the intrusion,
the Reich Marshal, who was now tipping the scales at well over three
hundred pounds, picked up the phone and barked into it.

"Reich Marshal, I hate to bother you," said Colonel-General Heinrich von Memel, one of Goering's top aides, "but the Gestapo just called with a matter of some delicacy."

"What is it?"

"The Gestapo has just arrested Count de Belleville and are holding him for the moment at eleven, rue des Saussaies." This was the Gestapo headquarters in Paris. "Being aware that the Countess is a personal acquaintance of yours, they thought they should inquire how you wanted this handled."

Goering looked surprised.

"But why was he arrested?"

"Because the Countess's brother was in the house on Avenue Foch. The brother is a certain Colonel Nick Savage, who is with American Intelligence in London."

"Yes, I know him well. And Lady Edwina Ashley told me some time ago that he was in London. What was he doing in Paris?"

"That's what we would like to know. Colonel Savage escaped from the house, presumably with the countess, but the Gestapo suspects his presence there might have something to do with the Resistance. De Belleville denies this, saying he had come to visit his sister, but this makes no sense since she seems to have gone away with him."

"Exactly."

"Lady Ashley was at the house—the de Bellevilles were giving a cocktail party—when she ran into Savage in a bathroom."

"A bathroom?" Goering said, in a confused tone.

"Lady Ashley was removing a spot from her dress. She immediately told her suspicions to her father, Baron von Brockhoven, who was also at the party, and he called the Gestapo."

"Have they searched the house?"

"Yes, and they found nothing suspicious."

Goering thought for a moment.

"It certainly does sound peculiar," he finally said. "I mean, that Savage was there. You say he escaped? Has he been found yet?"

"No, Reich Marshal. The Gestapo is putting out an all-points bulletin on him. They have photographs of him from the time he was ambassador in Berlin."

"He'll undoubtedly try to get out of Paris. Cover all the train stations."

"Yes, Reich Marshal."

"Question de Belleville. Take him to the Fort de Vincennes."

"How vigorously should we question him?"

"Till he talks."

Goering hung up and refilled his beer glass as his eyes returned to the topless dancer's naked breasts.

30 THE CAPTAIN OF U-BOAT 139 looked through his periscope, the crosshairs of which were centered on the port side of the American troop ship U.S.S. *Jersey City*, en route from New York to Casablanca, Morocco.

"Fire one," the captain ordered.

"Fire one."

A torpedo shot from the submarine, speeding toward the *Jersey City*, a quarter of a mile to the south in the Atlantic.

"Fire two."

"Fire two."

On the fantail of the *Jersey City*, Lieutenant Richard Shelby was leaning on the rail, watching the churning wake of the ship and chatting with Sergeant Joe Washington, a twenty-year-old from Atlanta, Georgia. Richard and Joe were members of the all-black Company D of the U.S. Army. The other passengers on the converted tramp steamer were twenty-five hundred white Americans en route to north Africa to join the Allied buildup under Generals Montgomery and Eisenhower to drive the Germans and Italians out of the continent in preparation for the future invasion of Sicily and Italy. It was 10:35 on a blisteringly hot morning.

"Jesus!" Joe Washington exclaimed, pointing to something in the water. "It's a fucking torpedo!"

Before Richard could react, a tremendous explosion rocked the ship, followed a few seconds later by a second explosion. The *Jersey City* started listing to port as the screams and yells of its passengers and crew filled the air along with flames and billowing smoke. An announcement came over the loud-speaker system: "Now hear this: now hear this: all damage control units report to the engine room!"

"Fuck damage control!" Joe Washington yelled to Richard. "This ship's going down! Let's get to a lifeboat!"

The two young men ran forward on the starboard side, but they were stopped by the flames and smoke. The *Jersey City* was now listing at a forty-five-degree angle and sinking fast. It was too late to launch lifeboats, and men were already jumping overboard off the starboard side.

"Let's jump!" Richard yelled. "Nothing else to do!"

They untied their shoes and threw them off, then climbed over the rail and jumped into the ocean.

"Swim away from the ship!" Richard yelled. "Or we'll be sucked under with it."

"You're right!"

They started swimming. The screams of the passengers were hysterical as the *Jersey City* suddenly turned turtle, instantly drowning over twelve hundred men. The ship sank within five minutes of being torpedoed, one of the forty Allied ships that were sunk by Hitler's U-boats on that one single day.

"A raft!" Richard yelled. "There's a raft!"

The two men started swimming toward a small rubber raft that had fallen off the port side of the ship before it sank. Richard reached it first, hoisting himself onto it as Joe Washington, puffing with exertion, grabbed the side.

"Here," Richard said, grabbing Joe's arm and helping him aboard.

"Shit, man, that boat went down fast!" Joe puffed.

"Yeah, a little late for damage control. Those torpedoes must have blown out half the hull. Look: That guy's going down!"

He pointed at a white officer who was howling with fear, struggling to keep afloat but obviously not able to swim. The water was filled with men trying to save themselves.

"I'm coming!" Richard yelled.

"Are you crazy?" Joe said. "Let him drown. He's white."

"We've got room for one more."

Richard dived into the water again, swimming with powerful strokes to the officer.

"Hang on," he told him.

"I can't swim," the young man gasped. "I've got cramps."

"Yeah. Hang on. Put your arms around my neck."

The officer obeyed, groaning at the stabbing pains in his stomach. Richard started swimming back toward the raft.

The U-boat 139 had surfaced, and German crew members were scrambling out of the hatch onto the forward deck, attaching a machine gun to a portable stand. Now they started raking the water with machine-gun bullets, killing the survivors of the capsized ship, who were screaming in terror.

"Jesus, hurry up!" Joe Washington yelled from the raft. "They're going to kill all of us!"

The officer hanging on to Richard howled with pain as a bullet hit his left arm. He let go of Richard and sank into the water. Richard dived down to grab him, hauling him back up to the surface. They were five feet from the raft. Joe Washington had jumped into the water to avoid being hit by the bullets. The other survivors had been devastated by the gunfire; literally hundreds of bodies were floating in the blue water, which was turning red from the blood. As Richard, Joe, and the officer hid in the water behind the raft, the German crewmen—either thinking they had killed all the survivors, or having sated their bloodlust—dismantled the gun and returned into the submarine, closing the hatch behind them.

U-boat 139 started to submerge.

Silence.

Richard, who was holding the white officer, said to Joe, "Help me get him onto the raft. He's losing a lot of blood."

"Let him die," Joe said. "We've got no food or water, we have to think of ourselves. If we get out of this, it'll be a miracle. We don't need this asshole."

"Hey, Joe, you know? We're all in this together. Help me."

"Shit."

They managed to hoist the officer into the raft, where he lay facedown. Then the two black men hoisted themselves in. Richard leaned down near the officer.

"How you doing?" he asked.

"I'm swell," he whispered. "Feel like the Hit Parade."

"Let me look at your arm."

Gently, he unbuttoned the man's shirt and carefully exposed his left shoulder and arm. The bullet had gone through the arm a few inches above the elbow and blood was gushing from the wound.

"Okay," Richard said, "I'm going to make a tourniquet with your shirt. Just take it easy."

He removed the man's shirt, twisted it into a tourniquet, then tied it around his arm above the wound as Joe Washington watched from the other side of the small raft. The ocean was calm, but the sun was broiling. Now Richard gently helped the wounded man turn over onto his back.

"How you doing?" he said again.

The white man whispered, "I feel great."

"Seriously."

"I feel awful. Weak. A lot of pain. I was sitting in the wardroom having a cup of coffee and a doughnut when the goddam place blew to hell. Was it a torpedo?"

"Yeah. Two. A U-boat. The bastards machine-gunned most of the survivors. I guess we're the lucky ones. What's your name?"

"Graydon. Graydon de Belleville, Lieutenant Junior Grade, U.S. Navy. I was a member of the crew. What's yours?"

"Lieutenant Richard Shelby. And this is Sergeant Joe Washington. We're both in Company D, or what's left of it. Do you have any idea where the hell we are?"

"Yeah. I had the midwatch last night, and then we were about seventy nautical miles northeast of the Madeira Islands."

"How far are we from Casablanca?"

"About two hundred miles."

"Any chance of our drifting to Africa?"

"No. We're in the Canary current. If we're lucky, we might drift south to the Canary Islands."

"And what if we're not lucky?" Joe Washington said.

No one said anything.

In the distance, sharks were beginning to fight over the floating bodies of the crewmen of the U.S.S. *Jersey City*, turning the bloody water into a maelstrom.

"Those damned Germans are swiping everything in Paris," Marie Antoinette said as she sat opposite Nick in the dingy kitchen of her tiny second-floor flat on the rue de l'Université. "And what do we do? Nothing. It's a damned shame."

"Well, maybe things are going to be changing now," Nick said. He was drinking some watery onion soup the woman had heated up for him. "Maybe you people in the Resistance can really start hurting the krauts."

"Let's hope," she said. She was smoking a Gaulois cigarette, and the second and third fingers of her right hand were stained yellow by the tobacco. Her stringy blond hair was in curlers; she was in the process of tying a bandana over it. "There's a café at the corner. I'll run down and get you some ham."

"No, I'm fine."

"I have to get some coffee and cigarettes anyway," she said, standing up and putting on a threadbare coat. "I'll be back in ten minutes. Make yourself at home." She looked at Brook, who was still unconscious, stretched out on a rather shabby sofa. "You say her husband slugged her?"

"Yes. She didn't want to leave him."

"He did the right thing. I'll be back in a bit. Don't answer the phone if it rings." She went to the door and left.

Nick continued sipping the soup. After a few minutes, Brook groaned. She opened her eyes.

"Where am I?"

She sat up, rubbing her jaw where Bernard had hit her.

"We're in the flat of a woman code-named Marie Antoinette," Nick said. "We're staying here tonight."

"But why am I here?"

"Because you're going with me back to England."

"Where's Bernard?"

"Unfortunately, I'm afraid right now he's with the Gestapo. He made me swear to take you with me."

"But . . ."

"Brook, don't argue. What's done is done. There's no point in your becoming a martyr."

She slumped slightly.

"Bernard should have come, too," she said, sadly.

"He said the Resistance would help him."

"That's wishful thinking. Oh God, he's so damned stubborn. I begged him not to get involved with the Resistance, but he hates the Germans and he wants to make France what it used to be when he was a kid. So am I going to end up a widow because he's a damned patriot?"

"Brook, he wouldn't want to hear you talk that way."

She sighed.

"I know. Oh, Nicky, everything's such a bloody mess. I hate this damned war."

"I don't think there are many who like it."

"But if the Gestapo have him, they'll torture him and nobody, not even Bernard who's so brave, can stand up to their torture! Oh Nick, if I lose him, I couldn't go on living!" She started crying.

"Everything's going to be all right," Nick said, hugging his sister.

"Everybody always says that," she sobbed. "But nothing ever turns out all right. Oh Nicky, I can't stand losing Bernard! He's my whole life!"

"Calm down, darling. Don't project. We don't know what's going to happen yet."

The door opened and Marie Antoinette came in, carrying a paper bag.

"I put your vélo inside so it wouldn't get stolen," she said to Nick. "They're worth a fortune these days. Ah, the countess is awake. Feeling a little rocky, my dear?"

Brook nodded weakly.

"I'll make us all some coffee." She put her bag on the counter and filled her kettle with water. "They're putting up posters with your picture on it," she said to Nick. "They'll be all over the city by the morning. When's your train?"

"It leaves from the Gare St. Lazare at eleven in the morning."

"Then we'll have to disguise you. If the Gestapo gets their hands on you, it's not going to be fun." She looked at him a moment. "I'm getting an idea. You may not like it, but it's your best bet."

"What's your idea?"

"Come into my bedroom. You may not believe it from the way I look now, but once I was an actress, and I'm damned good at makeup. We're going to turn you into a woman." She smiled. "I think you'd be a knockout as a blond. You may even get picked up by a German soldier. They're a rutty bunch now that they're away from their fat frauleins and meeting some real French women. Come on."

"Marie Antoinette, I don't think that's such a good idea. Couldn't I be a priest?"

"There have been four fake-Resistance priests shot in the Fort de Vincennes in the past six months. The Gestapo looks for priests. Got a better idea?"

Nick thought a moment, then shook his head.

"I didn't think so. Come on. And we'll give your sister a black wig, just in case. Wait: pull up your pants leg."

Nick stood up and pulled up his right leg.

"Mmm," she said. "Nice legs, but a little hairy. I'll loan you my razor."

"Good God. But what about my ID papers?"

"Did you see the photography studio on the ground floor?"

"Yes."

"It's mine. I'll give you a new photo and I can fake the official seal. I'll do the same for Brook. Who do you think made the one you have now?"

"You?"

"That's right. I only have one pair of silk stockings left, and you're not going to get them. I'll have to paint your legs and paint on seams: that's what all the women in Paris are doing. All the silk stockings end up in Berlin, thanks to the dirty Fritzes. I've got an old dress that I'm too fat to wear but should be just about right for you. Let's go!" She started past Brook. "So he's your brother?" she asked.

"That's right," Brook said. "And I adore him!"

Marie Antoinette chuckled.

"Tomorrow, you're going to be sisters. On the way to Brittany to see your grandmother. Follow me," she said to Nick.

She led him into a small bedroom.

"Take your pants off," she said. "I'll get you a razor."

"I don't know how to shave my legs."

"Then I'll do it for you."

She went into a tiny adjacent bathroom as Nick took down his pants, then sat on the edge of the bed. Marie Antoinette came back into the room with a shaving mug and a straight razor.

"Take off your shoes and socks," she ordered. He obeyed.

She kneeled beside him and started putting the shaving cream on his legs.

"Do you have to go above my knees?" he asked.

"All the way to the crotch."

"Why?"

"If a horny German puts his hand above your knee and feels hair, he may kill you."

"Okay, you win. Shave everything. I'll do it for the war effort. But I don't like it."

Marie Antoinette chuckled.

"I'll shave everything," she said, putting the razor against his soapy thigh and then slowly bringing the razor down. "Except that all-American and very impressive you-know-what."

The next morning at ten, two women emerged from Marie Antoinette's building, one wheeling out the vélo. Nick was wearing a trim, black-brimmed hat with a veil dating from five years before, black pumps on smoothly shaved legs, and a rather bulky black overcoat with big shoulder pads. He carried a big purse. Marie Antoinette had given him her best blond wig left over from her acting days. Nick had been surprised when he looked in the mirror to see that he made a rather attractive woman. It was a very odd feeling.

It was a cool, sunny morning after the dreariness of the previous evening. Nick got on the bicycle seat as Brook, in a black wig, climbed in the rear. Marie Antoinette had loaned her a purse and given them enough francs to handle expenses. Now Nick bicycled through the near-empty streets, spotting his wanted signs several times on buildings, which was also an odd feeling and a rather nerve-wracking one. It took him less than a half hour to reach the train station. Dismounting from the bike, he padlocked it in a bicycle rack (bikes had become almost as expensive as cars; to have not locked the bike would have attracted notice), then walked with Brook into the big nineteenth-century station and read the bulletin boards, looking for their train. The eleven o'clock for St. Brieuc was on track seven, and it was on time.

"I'll go buy my ticket," Brook said quietly.

When she returned with her ticket, they started toward their track. The station wasn't particularly crowded and Nick was relieved to see that he attracted little attention: Apparently, Marie Antoinette's makeup job had been successful. There were a few German soldiers in the station, some as guards, others as passengers, but they seemed uninterested in him. Reaching track seven, they saw that the train was just pulling into the station. Taking his tickets and identification papers from his purse, he waited until the train had stopped before him. Then, as he had a reserved seat, he and Brook climbed aboard his car and made their way to his seat number, which was by a window. He sat down with Brook opposite him and started counting the minutes until the train left the station for Brittany, at which time he figured he would be relatively safe.

The train wasn't crowded, which was not surprising as few people would be going to Brittany at this time of the year. Less than a dozen passengers came aboard his car, and no one paid much attention to them. Nick was beginning to feel relaxed for the first time since fleeing the Avenue Foch the night before.

The conductor blew his whistle and called *"En voiture,"* when a young German soldier came aboard and started down the aisle toward Nick. The soldier was tall and rather gangly with a long nose and a somewhat goofy look in his eyes. He wore corporal's stripes on his green uniform, and on his left hip was the leather holster of his service revolver. To Nick's horror, the soldier stopped by Brook, smiled and said in heavily accented French, "Is this seat free?"

Brook nodded. The soldier sat down next to her. Nick turned to stare out the window as the train pulled out of the station. *Keep cool,* he thought. *Keep cool.*

"Would you care for a cigarette?" the German asked, proferring a pack to Brook.

"No thanks," she said.

"Ah. Do you mind if I do?"

"No, go ahead."

The soldier lit up and exhaled.

"My name's Dietrich," he said. "What's yours?"

"Marie," Brook said, thinking fast.

"Ah, a lovely name. A lovely name for a lovely lady, if I may say so. Is this other lady traveling with you?"

He smiled at Nick.

"Yes," Brook said. "She's my sister. We're going to visit our grandmother in Brittany."

Dietrich was staring at Nick.

"Brittany's so lovely. I used to go there as a child with my parents. By the way, have I seen you before? You look vaguely familiar."

"I don't think so," Nick whispered, hoping Dietrich wasn't subconsciously connecting his face to his wanted poster. "I have a sore throat."

"I'm sorry to hear that," Dietrich said, taking another puff on his smoke. "Well, we have a long train ride ahead of us. I hope I can get to know you lovely sisters better."

He smiled at Nick. Sweat started trickling down Nick's sides. What Marie Antoinette had said jokingly was apparently happening: They were being picked up by a rutty German soldier! Nick was terrified of discovery for Brook and himself.

"Why was your brother-in-law hiding in your house?" The Gestapo captain said.

"I've told you a dozen times: he has a girlfriend in Paris." Bernard de Belleville was sitting in a wooden chair beneath a green-shaded ceiling light in the interrogation room of the German prison at Fort de Vincennes in east Paris. His hands were tied behind his back. Now the Gestapo captain slapped him hard, twice.

"You lie!" he screamed. "I want the truth, you Jew bastard, and I'll get it out of you. Now, one more time: What was your brother-in-law doing in your house?"

"He came to see his girlfriend."

"Do you think I'm a fool? Why would an American intelligence officer sneak into Paris during wartime to see a woman? It defies common sense."

"Nevertheless, that's the truth."

The captain stepped back.

"I'll give you ten minutes to reconsider your position," he said. "Then, if you have not changed your mind and still refuse to cooperate, I will be forced to take extremely harsh measures. Ten minutes."

He turned and left the room, saying something in German to the four other Gestapomen in the room.

Bernard was sweating with terror. Wild rumors had swept Paris of the tortures the Gestapo could inflict. One story that had nauseated him was that they would gouge out the eyes of their victims, insert live cockroaches in the bloody sockets, and then sew the eyelids up. He was also terrified for Brook's safety. He prayed that she and Nick would make it to Brittany: If they were caught, the fact that they were Americans wouldn't mean a damn to the Gestapo. The Germans had long since thrown out the rules of civilized behavior.

But if he told them what they wanted to hear, he would jeopardize the entire fledgling Resistance movement. He knew the name of the man who was organizing it: Jean Moulin, a young former leftish politician who had escaped from France to Portugal and was working from abroad to gear up the entire movement. If he gave the Gestapo Moulin's name, it could mean the destruction of the Resistance before it even began.

The Gestapo captain returned to the room, having smoked a cigarette.

"Well?" he said, coming up to Bernard. "Have you thought about what I said?"

"Yes."

"Why was your brother-in-law in your house?"

"To see his girlfriend."

Silence.

"You will come to regret your foolishness."

He barked an order in German. The other guards came to Bernard and tore off his clothes. Then an electric magneto was brought into the room. Wired clamps were attached to Bernard's nipples and genitals.

The Gestapo captain threw a switch.

Bernard's scream was heard through the thick stone walls of the fortress as far away as the execution room twenty feet down the hall.

31 GLORIA WOOD THREW AN engagement party for herself and Lord Dudley Belgrave, and Indianapolis society, whatever their private opinions of Gloria, flocked to Whitehall to fawn over the dashing RAF hero, who was staying in a guest room next door to Gloria's bedroom. It was a black-tie affair, and the guests, tired of food rationing, gas rationing, and all the other inconveniences of wartime America—not to mention the staggeringly high taxes to finance the defeat of Hitler—put on their finery and trooped to Gloria's mansion to forget it all for a while. Champagne flowed—domestic, since imported was practically impossible to obtain— and Gloria had brought in a dance band from Chicago. As she cheek-to-cheeked with her fiancé, Gloria murmured dreamily, "Darling, are you as wildly, absurdly happy as I am?"

"Happier," Dudley said with a smile. He was a tall, thin man with a trim mustache. In his RAF uniform, he looked dashingly heroic enough to have lured over three million dollars from Americans for the English war effort.

"You couldn't possibly be happier than I. And I can hardly wait till all these boring people leave so we can go upstairs and make wild, passionate love."

"Gloria, darling, I sometimes get the impression you're living entirely for pleasure."

"Is there anything else to live for?" She sighed as the band segued into "There'll Be Bluebirds Over the White Cliffs of Dover."

Upstairs, in his bedroom, Sebastian lay on his bed listening to the music with his bedlight on.

"Mark," he said, softly, "we have to stop Momma from marrying this guy."

He listened for a moment.

"I'm glad you agree with me, brother," he went on. "You know, it's odd: You don't look any older than when you died, but I guess when you're dead, you don't grow older. That's sort of nice, isn't it? So what can we do to stop Momma? She's sending me away to school in the fall, and Dudley will have her all to himself. He doesn't love her, I can tell. He just wants to spend all her money, and we've got to stop him. But I can't quite figure out how."

Again, he listened for a while. Then he said: "Well, that would certainly stop Dudley, but what if it hurt Momma? I wouldn't want that to happen. I mean, I love her."

He listened.

"Oh, of course," he said. "I hadn't thought of that. And that would make me so happy, Mark, because I love you so much and I really didn't want to kill you. But you made me do it. Not a day goes by when I don't remember the look on your face when you died. You looked so happy."

The small rubber raft drifted slowly in the Canary current as the three American servicemen, two black and one white, lay in the broiling sun and thought about death. It had been three days since the U.S.S. *Jersey City* had been sunk by two Nazi torpedos. For three days, they had had neither food nor water, and desperation was swirling around their brains like yellow fog.

"Maybe you should throw me over," Graydon de Belleville whispered. "I'm pretty well gone."

Joe Washington looked at Richard Shelby.

"He's got a point, Richard," he said.

"Joe, shut up. And you, too, Graydon. We're not going to have any phony heroics. We're all going to make it, and if we don't, we'll all die."

Joe Washington sat up with some difficulty.

"But I don't want to die!" he said. "You know what it's like growing up in Atlanta, Georgia? You know what it's like being called 'boy' and 'nigger' and Christ knows what else? This white boy says throw him over, I say let's do him a favor."

Richard hunched himself up on his elbows.

"Yeah, you've got the great big secret, Joe: Colored folks are treated like shit in America. Hey, I never knew that! What a surprise. You know, I was lynched!"

"Lynched? Are you kidding?"

"Yes, lynched! By a very important publisher in Indianapolis, and he got mad at me and he got the Klan to come one morning and grab me out of my bed and they took me to some farm and tied my hands behind my back and stuck me on a truck and put a rope around my neck and they lynched me! Except it was all a joke, because they had frayed the rope. So I wasn't lynched. But it scared the shit out of me, so if anyone has something to bitch about in this raft, it's me. So shut up, okay? Nobody's going to push anybody overboard, and we're all going to make it."

Silence. Graydon, whose pale face was burning badly in the fierce sun, causing blisters to form on his cheeks and forehead, said incredulously, "I can't believe someone lynched you. Who was this crazy publisher in Indianapolis?"

"A man named Bennet Kinkaid."

"Oh yes, my mother mentioned him to me before the war. He was some sort of far-right nut."

"That's him."

They sat in silence for a while as the raft drifted slowly south. Then Richard said, "Where are you from, Graydon?"

"Paris."

"Paris, France? Then what are you doing in the American Navy?"

"My mother's American and she sent me to New York when the Nazis took Paris. I stayed for a while with my grandmother, Rachel Savage."

Richard looked surprised.

"You're a Savage?"

"Yes."

"Are you related to Nick Savage?"

"He's my mother's brother. Do you know him?"

"I met him in New York. He was nice to me, put me up, got me a job in a bookstore for the summer. A very nice guy."

"Yeah, my mother's crazy about him."

"Huh. Small world."

"Real small," Joe Washington said. "Especially in this raft. You know, we can sit here and talk and bitch and argue, but none of that is gonna save us. In about a day or two, we're gonna start dying if we don't get something to eat and drink, and I hear it's not a nice way to go."

"Well, what do you suggest?" Richard said. "That we find a cruise ship and have a three-course lunch?"

"Did you ever hear of the Donner Party?"

"Sure. What about them?"

"When they got caught in the Donner Pass going to California, they were reduced to . . ."

He didn't finish the sentence. But he was looking meaningfully at Graydon de Belleville.

Richard's eyes widened.

"You shut up, Joe Washington," he whispered. "You shut the fuck up."

But Joe Washington continued to look at Graydon, who looked back at him, horror in his eyes.

"He's already," Joe Washington said, staring at the blisters on his white face, "half cooked."

"I love Paris," said Dietrich, the long-nosed, slightly goofy-looking German soldier sitting next to Brook on the train to Brittany, "but sometimes the French make me sick. No offense, Madame. I see you have a wedding ring."

"Yes, I have a husband," Brook said, thinking of Bernard, wondering what was happening to him, terrified that he was in the hands of the Gestapo. *Please don't be killed, my darling*, she thought. *Please. I can't live without you.*

"I see. At any rate, I ride the Métro and I listen to the Parisians talking, particularly the kids. All they're interested in is food and making love. They couldn't care less about the war or politics or the glorious things happening in Europe. Just food and love. It's shocking."

"Maybe they don't think what's happening in Europe is all that glorious," Brook said.

"Then they're wrong. And the Zazous! Do you go to the Latin Quarter or Le Colisée, that café on the Champs Elysée, where all the Zazous meet?"

"Yes, I've seen the Zazous," Brook said. "They're pretty awful."

"They're a disgrace. Rich young kids who make fun of everything, France and Germany alike. They wear their hair long, to their shoulders, and rub oil in it so they look greasy, and they wear big, long jackets and thin trousers. I suppose they think they're chic, but to me they're just disgusting. They believe in nothing at all except mockery and showing themselves off. I've always believed in something, and I'm proud of it."

"You mean, you believe in Hitler?"

"Yes, of course. I don't suppose you do, being French. Do you mind if I have another cigarette?"

"No, of course not."

As Dietrich lit up, the aged conductor came through the car to take the tickets and check the ID papers. Nick held his breath as the old man looked at his photograph, which Marie Antoinette had faked the night before. Then he handed the documents back and passed on down the aisle.

"Is your sister married?" Dietrich asked, exhaling luxuriously.

"No," Nick whispered.

"Do you have a boyfriend?"

"Yes."

Dietrich smiled.

"I'll bet you have several. A woman with good-looking legs like your . . . Are those silk stockings?"

"No," Nick said. "I can't afford them. I just paint my legs."

"Ah, yes. A lot of women are doing that now. It's very seductive." He turned to Brook. "But you have on silk stockings. You should lend your sister some of yours."

"This is my last pair."

"Huh." More exhaling. "Where does your grandmother live in Brittany?"

"Perros Guirec."

"Really? What a coincidence! I'm going to Perros Guirec myself! My parents used to rent a house there in the summer, and when I was a kid I spent a lot of time there. It's such a beautiful place, the coast is so wonderful, and the seafood! Well, the oysters there are the best in the world, in my opinion. How are you getting to Perros? The train stops at St. Brieuc."

"Our friend is meeting us in his car."

"I don't suppose you could give me a lift to Perros? It would save me hiring a taxi."

"You'd have to ask Jules. That's my friend."

"Oh. All right. I'd consider it a great favor. And I'd be glad to take all of you out to dinner as payment for the car ride."

"That's very kind of you," Brook said. "Now, if you don't mind, I'm rather tired. I'd like to take a little nap."

"Oh yes, certainly. I'll be quiet."

Brook turned on her side, presenting her back to Dietrich. In fact, she was exhausted. The anxiety about Bernard and the nervousness of their situation had drained her of energy.

Dietrich continued smoking, eying Nick.

I could swear I've seen her before, he thought. *But where?*

32   THE TRAIN ARRIVED AT the small channel port of St. Brieuc at five that afternoon, and Dietrich followed Nick and Brook out onto the station platform.

"There's Jules," Nick said after a moment, spotting the black Fiat in the near-empty parking lot. "Let us go talk to him about giving you a ride. You wait here."

"Fine."

Dietrich lit a cigarette as Nick and Brook hurried over to a tall, saturnine man in a trenchcoat and rather battered brown hat.

"Jules, I'm Nick Savage. And this is Bernard's wife."

The Frenchman looked confused.

"Why are you dressed like that?"

"They found out about me in Paris so I had to disguise myself. See that German soldier on the platform?"

"Yes . . ."

"He wants a lift to Perros Guirec, and I think it wouldn't be a bad idea to have a German soldier in our car. I think he's got a bit of a crush on Brook, maybe even on me."

"Is he a Gestapette?"

"A what?"

"A German *pédé*. *Tapette* is slang for homosexual, and you put it together with Gestapo and you get Gestappete, a German homosexual."

"No, he thinks I'm a woman."

Jules shrugged.

"Well then, why not? A German in the car couldn't hurt. But no necking in the backseat."

"I'll sit in front."

He turned and beckoned to Dietrich, who put out his cigarette and started toward the car.

"I told him my name's Marie," Brook said. "And he knows nothing about Bernard or Nick."

"I understand."

Dietrich joined them, introductions were made, then Jules and Nick got in the front seat and Dietrich and Brook climbed in back. Jules started the car and began driving through the charming village.

"Would you mind taking the coast road?" Dietrich asked from the backseat. "I remember how beautiful the coast is here. It's called *La Côte de Granit Rose,* isn't it?"

"That's right," Jules said. "but the coast road is longer and takes more gas."

"I'll pay for the extra gas, and I've got gas coupons."

"Very well, we'll take your way."

When they left St. Brieuc, Jules followed the coast road, which actually wound inland much of the way, only to reappear along the wild Breton coast periodically. *La Côte de Granit Rose* was a fascinating series of steep, rose colored cliffs alternating with enchanting bays with beaches of soft white sand. On this clear, rather chilly afternoon, the channel beat against many rocks in the water as well as a number of distant small isles. With fishing boats plying their trade in the water and occasional oystermen and clammers in the shallows, the war seemed far in this idyllic scene, as far away as it did in Paris, which had become a Mecca for pleasure-seekers from all over occupied Europe. They passed through many villages and ports with the strange-sounding Breton names stemming from ancient Celtic: Kerbors, Plougescant, Pellinec, Crechavel . . .

"This brings back so many memories," Dietrich said from the backseat. "You know, it was on one of these beaches that I lost my virginity. I was only fourteen years old and so afraid of girls. But one summer when my parents took me to Perros, I met this older girl in the market who took a liking to me. I kept meeting her at the market, and one day she asked me if I wanted to go on a picnic with her. So I said yes, scared to death, of course, and she made up a picnic lunch and we went to a beach—actually very near here. And she seduced me! Oh, what a wonderful memory! She was the sweetest, sexiest girl, and she knew all about lovemaking. It was one of the most wonderful moments of my life. Look: It was right there! I remember: She parked her car there and we climbed down the cliff to the beach. Let's stop and go down to take a look!"

"I'm sorry, Dietrich," Jules said, "but we're a little pressed for time."

Dietrich pulled his service revolver from his hip holster and pressed it against the back of Jules's head.

"I said, let's stop." His voice was suddenly steely cold.

Jules glanced at Nick and pulled the car over to the edge of the cliff, where he parked.

"Now, all three of you get out," Dietrich ordered.

Jules and Nick climbed out of the front seat as Brook, and the German climbed out of the back, Dietrich holding his gun.

"Climb down the path to the beach. I'll follow you. And don't try any tricks. I have full authority to shoot to kill French people."

Jules started down a steep path, followed by Nick, Brook, and Dietrich. Perhaps fifty feet below them was one of the semicircular bays that dotted the coast, a lovely, empty place with a white beach. A few gulls floated lazily in the air as twilight approached.

"Now, ladies, take your clothes off," Dietrich said, when they reached the beach. "I've wanted to fuck both of you all day, and why not here, where I lost my virginity? Eh? That would be a good joke, wouldn't it? Jules, you stand over there and watch. Maybe you'll learn something about the art of love. You:" He pointed to Nick. "You're first."

"Dietrich," Nick said, stalling for time, "if you want to do this, why don't we wait till we get to Jules's house? It's a bit chilly and a bit public to make love here on the beach."

"There's no one around, and what if there is? They'll see a German screwing a French woman, which is only fair. To the victor belong the spoils, eh? And Germany whipped the shit out of you Frenchies. Go on: strip. I want to see you."

Nick looked at Jules, who shrugged slightly: What else can we do?

"You may," Nick said as he took off his hat, "be in for a surprise."

"What do you mean?"

"You'll see."

He took off his coat, dropping it in the sand. As Dietrich watched with lusty fascination, Nick pulled off his panties then slowly raised his skirt.

Dietrich gaped.

"Why, you're a man!" he gasped. "What the hell—wait a minute: Now I know why you look familiar! You're that American they want in Paris, the one whose posters are all over the city—"

He grunted as Jules smashed a rock down on the back of his head. The German dropped to the beach, unconscious. Quickly, Jules reached down and took the gun from his hand, pressing it against his right temple.

"Now," he said, "you'll see how a Frenchman makes love to a German."

He fired point-blank, killing the German instantly.

"Let's hide the body in that cave," he said as Nick pulled up his pants and put his coat back on. "By the time they find it, it'll be bones. Let me get his wallet and gas coupons first . . ."

He rummaged through his pockets, pulling out the wallet and ID papers. Then Nick picked him up by his shoulders and Jules took his feet. As they carried Deitrich up the beach, Nick said: "Thanks a lot for quick thinking. I thought I was a goner."

"You never know: He might have screwed you anyway."

"That's what I mean."

"It might have been interesting to watch, but I have an idea he meant to kill all of us afterward. We've got to hurry: We have a date with a submarine in a few hours. Have you ever gone down in one?"

"No."

"Are you afraid?"

"After what I've gone through today? Are you kidding?"

The Luftwaffe had taken over the Luxembourg Palace overlooking the magnificent Luxembourg Gardens, and Goering had taken the biggest suite of rooms for himself.

Now he was on the phone.

"Give me the Fort de Vincennes," he said. "The commandant." After a moment, he said: "How is the prisoner de Belleville?"

"Very weak, Herr Reich Marshal. I don't think he can take much more."

"Question him one more time. If he still refuses to talk, shoot him."

And he hung up.

Jules's house on the Chemin de la Messe in Perros-Guirec was a somber, three-story gray stucco building constructed at the turn of the century by either a) an aging countess, or b) an aging stage star, or c) an aging prostitute, according to the locals. No matter that the house was grim: Perched atop a forty-foot hill sloping down to a rocky beach, it had a heart-racing view of the English Channel and *les Sept Isles*, the seven small islands offshore, one of which was a bird sanctuary.

At eleven that evening, Jules led Nick and Brook down a steep incline in front of the house. Nick had changed into an old suit of Jules's that didn't fit him. When the three reached the water, they climbed into a small rowboat, Jules manning the oars. The night was dark except for the twirling light of the lighthouse on the *Ile aux Moines*, the nearest of the seven isles. Jules rowed into the still waters of the Channel, his oars slapping softly. After five minutes, he said: "Here's the buoy."

Jules put the oars inside the boat and reached over to put his hand on a buoy, steadying the boat.

Ten minutes later, slowly and silently a black submarine surfaced near them, looking up close rather like some frightening sea monster. Jules rowed the boat to the sub's hull, where a rope ladder had been thrown over by the crewmen. Brook climbed up first, thanking Jules. Before Nick climbed onto it, he shook Jules's hand.

"Thanks for your help," he said. "And good luck. Someday we'll throw these damned Nazis out of your country. And no one will ever forget your bravery."

"They'll forget," Jules said. "Just as they'll forget the evil of the Nazis. In fifty years, all we've lived through will just be a myth. But it was still worth living through, wasn't it?"

"Absolutely."

Nick climbed aboard the sub.

As Jules rowed back toward the shore, the sub silently slipped beneath the black waters of the English Channel.

33 AT THREE IN THE MORNING, long after the last guests had left Dudley and Gloria's cocktail party at Whitehall, Sebastian got out of bed, put a bathrobe over his pajamas and slippers on his feet, then left his room and went down the spiral staircase to the first floor of the beautiful mansion. Outside, it was raining and an occasional flash of lightning brought distant rumblings of thunder. Sebastian made his way to the kitchen, then opened the back door that led into the four-stall garage. Finding a flashlight on the tool-rack next to the door, he turned it on and played its beam around the big garage. Due to gas rationing, Gloria only used one of her three cars; but Sebastian knew that their gardener kept a five-gallon can of backup fuel for his pickup truck. Going to a corner, he took the handle of the can and brought it back to the kitchen door.

Back inside the kitchen, he unscrewed the cap of the can, then carried it into the dining room, dribbling gas on the floor as he walked. He went through the dining room into the library and drawing room, leaving a trail of gasoline behind him. Then into the entrance hall and halfway up the curving staircase until all the gas was gone.

He carried the empty can back downstairs.

Upstairs in Gloria's bedroom, Dudley bolted upright in the bed.

"Gasoline!" he said, shaking Gloria beside him. "Darling, wake up. The house reeks of gasoline!"

Gloria sat up.

"You're absolutely right," she said.

Dudley jumped out of bed.

"Someone's trying to burn the house down!" he yelled. "Get out of bed!"

He opened the door and ran out into the upstairs hall just as Sebastian, at the foot of the stairs, tossed a burning match into the gasoline. Whoosh! The blue flames raced through the house to the kitchen and up the spiral stair, forcing Dudley and Gloria to back away. "It's that bloody crazy son of yours!" Dudley yelled. "Is there a servants' stair?"

Gloria, verging on panic, took his hand.

"This way."

They ran down the upstairs corridor to a door at the end. But when she opened it, flames billowed up from the kitchen.

"Oh my God, the whole house is going!" she screamed, backing away from the smoke and slamming the door.

Dudley went to a window and threw it open to look out. A large maple tree stood just outside the window.

"We can climb down the tree," he yelled.

"Dudley, I'm afraid—!"

"No other way! Put your arms around me and hang on."

She obeyed. They climbed up onto the sill, Gloria's arms around his waist, Dudley having ducked outside the upper half of the window, hanging on to the wooden eyebrow with one hand as the other reached out to grab a major branch of the tree.

"I've got the tree," he yelled. "Let me get on the branch, then I'll help you over."

"Will it hold us?"

"I think so. It looks strong. You all right?"

"All right? No, I'm terrified!"

"Okay, let go of me. Hang on to the bottom of the window."

She obeyed. Dudley swung onto the branch. By now smoke had filled the upstairs corridor of the house and was curling out the window, causing Gloria to cough.

Dudley held out his arm.

"Take my hand," he yelled, "and hang on to it with all your strength!"

"Dudley, I'm afraid!"

"You'll be fine! Come on."

Leaning out, she grabbed his hand. Holding her in an ironlike grip, Dudley swung her onto the tree.

As Whitehall became a pillar of fire, Dudley and Gloria climbed down the tree to the ground where they saw Sebastian standing on the front lawn, watching the mighty blaze with a look of satisfaction.

"He's gone mad," his mother said, sadly. "Stark, staring mad. Oh Dudley, what can we do with him?"

"What you should have done years ago," he yelled, running across the soggy lawn to Sebastian. He grabbed his arm with one hand and slapped his face with the other, causing the teenager to howl with pain.

"You bloody maniac!" Dudley was yelling. "You could have killed both of us!"

"I wanted to kill you!" Sebastian screamed. "I wanted to! I wanted Momma to be with Mark in Heaven!"

"Where we're going to send you is going to be more like bloody Hell!" Dudley roared, pushing him backward onto the grass.

Gloria ran up to them.

"Don't hit him again," she cried, taking Dudley's hand. Then she looked at her son. "Oh Sebastian," she said, "what demons you must have in you. What horrible demons. Somehow, we'll have to get them out."

The sun beat relentlessly down on the small rubber raft, which was drifting slowly south, five days after the U.S.S. *Jersey City* had been torpedoed. The three men on the raft lay helplessly on their backs: One quick rain squall two days before had enabled them to catch some water by holding their shirts, but that water had by now been drunk, and Joe Washington was so ravenous he thought he might go crazy.

"We gotta get food," he said after a long silence.

Richard, who was lying on his stomach, was watching for a fish to come near the surface. He had almost caught one the day before, and he knew the chances were slim, but he was persistent. He didn't know what else to do.

Joe sat up and stared down at Graydon de Belleville. Graydon knew what he was thinking.

"I'll be gone soon," he whispered. "You have my permission to do what you're thinking."

"You be quiet!" Richard snapped. "You're not gonna die, and there's not gonna be any talk about you know what."

"Who the hell are you to say what I can talk about?" Joe said. "Besides, I didn't say a Goddam word, it's this white man that said it!"

"He's got a name," Richard said. "Just like I got a name and so do you. So use it."

"You didn't answer my question: Who are you to tell me what to say or do? I suppose you're gonna say you're an officer. Well, hey man, look around. I don't see much of an army out here, do you? There's just the three of us, unless I'm crazy. So I can say what I damned please, and if Graydon dies, I sure as hell am not gonna throw his body to the damned fishes! Yes, it's a disgusting idea, but my dying is a helluva lot more disgusting to me. And if you don't like it, that's too damned bad, Lieutenant." The last word was a sneer.

"Okay," Richard said, "you've made your little speech and I know where you stand. Now here's where I stand: If you try to touch this man, dead or alive, you're going to have to kill me first. You got that? You understand?"

Joe Washington stared at him a moment. Then he smiled slightly.

"Yeah, I understand," he said. "And maybe I *will* have to kill you."

He took the leather belt out of the loops on what was left of his pants and stretched it with both hands.

"You gotta sleep some time, Lieutenant," he said.

Richard looked at the taut leather belt.

"You know," he said, "I'm not the enemy. The Nazis are the enemy."

"Fuck the Nazis: They're white men. The enemy out here is death, and I'm not gonna die if I can help it. You got that, Lieutenant?"

Richard shook his head sadly.

"You don't get the point," he said. "The point is somebody's got to have some standards of decency in this world. And if we rationalize ourselves into committing cannibalism, which is about as low as you can get, then we've lost this war."

"Excuse me, guys," Graydon de Belleville said in his weak voice, "but I think there's a ship over there."

Feebly, he pointed his finger at the horizon, where the silhouette of a ship could be seen.

Richard squinted, shading his eyes with his hand. Then he stood up and started waving and yelling, as did Joe Washington, using what was left of his shirt as a flag.

"Goddam, I think they've seen us!" Richard shouted.

In fact, the ship was turning, steaming in their direction. It was a Portuguese freighter, bound from the Canary Islands to neutral Lisbon.

Within ten minutes, the three Americans were taken aboard. Graydon de Belleville was taken to the ship's sick bay, where an English-speaking doctor examined his wounded arm.

"Will you have to cut it off, Doc?" Graydon asked, voicing the fear he had carried for five days.

"I don't think so," the doctor said. "You're a very lucky young man."

"You don't know how lucky," he said.

At two-thirty in the morning, Bernard de Belleville was once again tortured in the Fort de Vincennes. Once again, he refused to answer the torturers' questions. Too weak to walk, he was dragged down the stone steps that led to the execution ditches in the fort's cellars—a room with a number of wooden execution posts behind which a dirt and sand floor rose almost to the stone ceiling to absorb bullets. He was tied to one of the posts, then a firing squad was brought into the room.

Just before he was shot, Bernard cried out:

"Vive la France!"

Two months later, Jean Moulin, the leader of the Resistance, who had returned to France, was captured in Lyon by the Gestapo and tortured to death for refusing to tell what he knew.

Exactly at noon on the hot, sultry day of August 15, 1945, in Studio 8 of the NHK (Japanese Broadcasting Corporation) Building in Tokyo, Japan's most popular newscaster, Chokugen Wada, sat pale and tense at a table behind a microphone and said: "This will be a broadcast of the gravest importance. Will all listeners please rise. His Majesty the Emperor will now read the imperial rescript to the people of Japan."

After the strains of the national anthem, *Kimigayo*, were heard, the reedy, high-pitched voice of Hirohito was heard by millions of Japanese, for the vast majority of whom it was the first time they had heard their god-Emperor.

"To our good and loyal subjects," he began "after pondering deeply the general trends of the world and the actual conditions obtaining in our Empire today, we have decided to effect a settlement of the present situation by resorting to an extraordinary measure . . ."

What the Emperor was saying in his convoluted Court language was that Japan was unconditionally surrendering, ending the war in total defeat. Millions of Japanese listening to the Voice of the Crane, as the Japanese throne was called, burst into tears and lamentations.

One listener, Colonel Sokichi Igitaki, was in the bedroom of his Tokyo home where he was recovering from a war wound, having been sent home from the overcrowded military hospital. The murderer of his brother-in-law, Edgar Morrow, turned off the radio, got out of bed, put on his finest silk robe, and took his father's dagger from the wall. Going into the next room, he seated himself cross-legged on the tatami mat and opened a scroll. Dipping a brush into an inkpot, he wrote a *waka*, or thirty-one syllable poem:

Having received great favors from the Emperor,
I do not have even half a word to leave
In the hour of my death.

He put the brush down, then positioned himself so that he was facing the Imperial Palace.

Removing the dagger from its sheath, he plunged it into his abdomen, then slashed twice to the right and straight up. This was *kappuku*, a form of *seppuku*, or *hara-kiri*, so excruciatingly painful few could force themselves to do it. His blood gushed from his belly, spilling onto the scroll and tatami, which gave the dying man a final sense of satisfaction.

According to the etiquette of *seppuku*, if he stained the mat with his blood it meant he considered himself blameless.

"There's an old saying that when someone saves your life, then that person has to grant you one wish."

The speaker was Lieutenant Graydon de Belleville. He and Captain Richard Shelby were eating dinner in Graydon's suite in the Waldorf-Astoria Hotel in New York.

"I never heard that old saying," Richard said, sipping some of the 1934 Château Lafite-Rothschild Graydon had ordered from the hotel's extensive wine cellar.

"I think I heard it from the Asian part of our family—but I'm not sure," Graydon said, with a grin. "I might have made it up. Anyway, you saved my life on that damned raft, so now you have to grant my wish and my wish is that you come to work for me when you get out of law school."

Richard looked surprised.

"You mean, in Paris?" he said.

"In Paris, and possibly here in New York as well. Now that my father's dead, I'll have to spend some time in Paris looking after our real estate holdings there—which are in not such great shape. My father never really was interested in them, archeology being his passion. I also have to help my mother carry on their work in Palestine."

"What was that?"

"For a number of years, they had been buying land in Palestine for the resettlement of European Jews. Now, after what's happened with the Nazis, that's taken on a new importance. But I also want to get into real estate here in the States as well. I've got a lot of crazy ideas kicking around in my head. I mean, now that this war is about over, I think the world's going to be seeing a lot of changes, and I want to be part of it. I'd like you to be part of it with me. And I'll start you off at thirty thousand a year."

Richard dropped his fork.

"Thirty thousand?" He almost gasped. "Hey, Graydon, how do you know if I'll be any good?"

"I know. I watched you on that raft. I can't tell you how I admired what you said about decency. Hey, I was glad you saved my life, of course, but I was really impressed with you. I want you to be part of my team. I hope you're tempted?"

Richard picked up his fork and knife and cut into his steak.

"Another advantage," Graydon went on, "is that in France we wouldn't have to be eating room service. We could be downstairs in the dining room. They're not prejudiced the way Americans are. I'm not saying the French are angels and don't have some prejudices, but it's a lot better there than it is here."

"Keep talking. You're definitely tempting me."

"Have you had any other job offers?"

"Actually, I have. From Lady Belgrave, who's been so great to me all these years and paid for me to go to college and law school. She sold her plumbing company to American Standard for a fortune because Indianapolis had too many unpleasant memories for her, as it does for me, and moved to England with her new husband so she could put Sebastian in a psychiatric home run by Dr. van Osgold, the London psychiatrist she first took him to. She wants me to be her personal attorney."

"Are you thinking about it?"

"Well, I owe her a lot."

"She's part of our family. I can talk to her and maybe work something out to please everybody. And you have plenty of time to make a decision."

"So tell me some of these crazy ideas you have kicking around in your head."

"Well, in the first place . . ."

"Some pretty picture, isn't it?" said the army corporal who was driving the jeep around Berlin. In the backseat sat Colonel Nick Savage, who had come with the victorious American army and was sight-seeing his way through hell.

"Yes, real pretty," he said, looking at the mounds of bomb-blasted rubble.

"Someone told me you were once ambassador here?"

"That's right."

"It sure must have changed a lot. What was it like before the war?"

"A lot prettier than this. But the politics were a lot uglier. And the politicians."

"Do you think they'll hang them? Those guys in Nuremburg?"

"I think a lot of them will swing. And I certainly hope so."

"Too bad the numero uno got away. I'll bet the Devil's having a good time with old Adolf."

Nick's head was flooded with memories as he drove around the city, which was destroyed almost beyond recognition. The center of the city around the Leipzigerstrasse and the Friedrichstrasse was almost completely wiped out. The major railroad stations—Potsdamerbahnhof, Anhalterbahnhof, Lehrterbahnhof—were empty shells. The Tiergarten, where he had been duped by the actress, looked like a battlefield, its lovely old trees bare stumps. The great square of the Wittenbergplatz had been so thoroughly pummeled by American and British bombs it was impossible to tell where it began or ended. The huge K.D.W. department store was rubble. The Romanisches Café, once the hangout of writers and artists, was rubble. The Eden Hotel, rubble. The Adlon, where Nick had once entertained Fritz Lieber before he was murdered, was rubble. The Pariserplatz by the shrapnel-pocked Brandenberg Gate was obliterated. The once-proud German people, who had so adored their Fuehrer, were now starving, in rags, picking through the rubble looking for scraps of food, clothing—or anything.

"Do you think the Germans will ever climb out of this mess and be something again?" the driver asked.

"Nothing would surprise me," Nick said.

"Well, anyway, the war's over and I'm about out of it. I'll sure be glad to get home."

Nick thought of his family, the survivors and the dead.

"Yes, it'll be good to get home."

On August 23, 1939, the jewel in the crown of France, the *Normandie,* left Le Havre for its one hundred and fortieth transatlantic crossing. It arrived in New York on August 28; four days later, Germany invaded Poland, and the war stopped all passenger service on the Atlantic. The French Government entrusted the ship to the United States. But after Pearl Harbor, the American government seized the huge ship and began converting her into a troopship. The smart black and white hull was painted a dull gray, and such fripperies as eighteen thousand bottles of wine and four hobby horses were taken off as hundreds of Naval and Coast Guard personnel, as well as eight hundred civilian workmen, toiled at a frantic pace to get the ship ready for wartime service.

Among the new equipment brought aboard were 14,130 new kapok life preservers, which were dumped helter-skelter throughout the ship, most of them in the grand salon. On February 9, 1942, as workmen were cutting down the deck-to-deck stanchions that had provided illumination in grander days, sparks from a blowtorch set some of the life preservers on fire. The fire swiftly spread throughout the ship; oddly, it took eleven minutes before the alarm reached the New York City fire station at Twelfth Avenue and Forty-ninth Street. Every available piece of fire equipment rushed to the scene, including fireboats in the ice-clogged Hudson River. An estimated one hundred thousand gallons of water were hosed into the ship before the fire was put out, but by then the *Normandie* had begun to list to its port side. Twelve hours after the fire started, the great ship turned on its port side and settled in forty-three feet of water into the mud of the Hudson.

It took millions of dollars and eighteen months to pump out the ship, but by August, 1943, it was upright again, a miserable ghost of its former glorious self. In 1945 it was auctioned off for $161,680 to a certain Julius Lipsett of 80 Wall Street, who proceeded to have the most beautiful ship ever built cut up for scrap.

"Dudley, darling, I have wonderful news," Gloria, Lady Belgrave said. "Sebastian is cured! Dr. van Osgold is going to let him out of the sanitarium!"

Her husband, Lord Dudley Belgrave, stared at his wife over the dining room table in Belgrave Abbey, his destitute ancestral home that Gloria was planning to rebuild at heavy expense. "You can't be serious," he said.

"No, it's true! Dr. van Osgold says the three years of therapy have finally worked, and Sebastian is normal. And thank God, he doesn't talk to Mark anymore!"

"Gloria, darling, your son is a bloody monster."

"That's not true!"

"He tried to kill both of us! He burned down Whitehall!"

Gloria looked uncomfortable.

"Well, that was then, when he was sick. But now he's cured. Oh, Dudley, it's going to be so wonderful! Sebastian really is a terribly smart and talented boy! I think he could even get into Harrow or Eton. And when we've finished fixing Belgrave Abbey, it's going to be the most beautiful home in England, and he'll be so happy with us! You'll see, darling. You'll see."

"God protect Harrow and Eton," he said.

In his padded cell at the St. Aldwyn Home for the Mentally Disturbed, Sebastian sat on his bunk and smiled.

"I have good news, Mark," he whispered to himself. "Of course, I can't talk to you in front of the doctors, but I can tell you now. They're letting us out."

On New Year's Eve, 1945, eighty-two-year-old Rachel Savage gave a party in her Park Avenue penthouse for what was left of her family.

The war had savaged the Savages, but there were still quite a few left.

There was nineteen-year-old Willow Wang, a slim beauty who was attending school at Radcliffe. Her family had suffered through the war in London, as had everyone else, but had survived, and Lance had been an RAF ace. The Japanese had burned the Nanking hospital that Willow's grandmother, Jasmin, had dedicated her life to, but she and Charlie were rebuilding it. One of Willow's best friends was her cousin, fifteen-year-old Amanda Savage, who was at school in Manhattan. Her six-year-old brother, Justin Savage, was a handsome boy who had inherited his red-gold hair from his mother, Samantha, and perhaps from a more distant gene from his great-grandfather, the legendary Justin, his namesake, who had founded the family dynasty in such a spectacular fashion in the past century.

The Italian branch of the family, who had fled the Fascists to England in the thirties, was represented by twenty-one-year-old Gabriella Vespa, who also was at school in America, England still reeling from the ravages of the war and burdened by all sorts of rationing, even a half year after the war's end. Gabriella's parents, Beatrice and Bruno, were involved in complicated lawsuits trying to get back the family's ancient palazzo on the Corso in Rome that the Fascists had, in essence, stolen from them by extortion.

The French branch of the family was represented by Brook and Graydon de Belleville. Graydon was a particular favorite of his grandmother, Rachel, who thought, as Brook did, that he was showing signs of being an excellent businessman and had thrown himself into his parents' Palestine interests with surprising energy. And to Rachel's great pleasure, he was also hinting he was thinking of converting to Judaism. Graydon had formed a business partnership with young Richard Shelby that had shocked many people: blacks were still considered to be secondary citizens, but Richard was getting in on the ground floor of a social revolution that promised to change the face of America. Graydon and Richard were extremely active in real estate ventures in America and France. Right now, Graydon seemed enormously interested in Gabriella, who was sitting next to him at the dinner table.

But Gabriella's eyes were on an extremely handsome young man with dark black hair sitting next to Rachel. He was wearing a well-cut dinner jacket.

"Isn't he dreamy?" Amanda whispered to Gabriella, sitting beside her.

"Absolutely fabulous," Gabriella whispered back. "And so charming! I was talking to him before dinner, and he's really totally suave. One would never know he was, as someone told me Lady Belgrave calls him, a bit eccentric."

"Oh, I don't think he's eccentric at all. And if he is, then I'm crazy about eccentrics. I think I'm falling in love with him! Is that terrible? I mean, Sebastian is my cousin, after all. Is that sort of awfully incestuous?"

"I'm not sure. Of course, in England my parents hardly talk to his mother. My mother thinks Lady Belgrave is a social-climbing floozie, so I've never really met Sebastian. I've just heard about him. And isn't it strange I meet him in New York, of all places? But he is absolutely fascinating. And Grandmother adores him. They say he looks exactly like his father, Cesare, for whom she had a real soft spot. That's why she brought him over from London for the holidays."

"Yes, I think I am in love." Amanda sighed. "And I think Sebastian is probably terribly wicked."

"That's why he's so attractive."

Finally, there was Nick, who had received a letter of commendation from the new president, Harry Truman, and the Legion of Honor from General de Gaulle for his mission to France.

At midnight, Nick stood up and offered a champagne toast—though his glass was filled with water.

"To all of us," he said, "and to the memory of those who are no longer with us: may the memory of the old year have taught the world something. And may the new year bring us all happiness."

Murmuring "Cheers to that," the Savages welcomed the new year, which promised, for better or worse, to bring in a new world.

Then the matriarch of the clan, Rachel Savage, stood up. She was wearing a silver evening dress that dated from before the war, but still fit her well. Her white hair was beautifully coiffed, and her diamond and ruby necklace and earrings gave her a magnificence that seemed to have vanished, at least for a while, from this shell-shocked, post-war world. She surveyed the room for a moment, then said: "I agree with everything my dear son, Nick, has said, and of course we all hope the future will be better. But at my age, I also look back to the past. I think of my dear husband, Johnny, and his parents, Justin, who founded our family, and his wife, Fiammetta, who gave us all a needed dash of Italian pepper." The family chuckled. Rachel turned to Brook, who looked a bit aged after her ordeal. "And I think of my darling Brook and her husband, Bernard, who died a hero's death defending the France he so dearly loved. Brook will never forget her beloved husband, nor will any of us." She turned to look at the luscious Willow. "I think of our Chinese relatives, who survived a war in many ways as horrible as the war in Europe. That Jasmin and Charlie Wang came out of the war unscathed—not to mention alive—is a testimony to not only their courage, but their ingenuity. And they're rebuilding their hospital in Nanking, which the Japanese so cruelly burned, which gives us all so much hope for the future."

She paused a moment. Then she smiled.

"Well," she said, "we've all come a long way on a very bumpy road, haven't we? But I somehow feel we're all the better for the experience. God bless us all."

The Savage family, in all of its disparate elements, murmured, "God bless us all."